THE GOLDEN BASILISK

The Lost Ancients, Book 5

Printed in the USA.

Interior Format

The Golden Basilisk

THE LOST ANCIENTS: BOOK FIVE

MARIE ANDREAS

Marie Andreas

Books by Marie Andreas

THE LOST ANCIENTS
Book One: The Glass Gargoyle
Book Two: The Obsidian Chimera
Book Three: The Emerald Dragon
Book Four: The Sapphire Manticore
Book Five: The Golden Basilisk
Book Six: The Diamond Sphinx

THE ASARLAÍ WARS
Book One: Warrior Wench
Book Two: Victorious Dead
Book Three: Defiant Ruin

THE ADVENTURES OF SMITH AND JONES
Book One: A Curious Invasion

Acknowledgements

I KEEP SAYING THIS, BUT NONE of these books would have come about without the love and support of all of my family and friends.

I'd like to thank Jessa Slade for editing magic—she keeps the stories on target. For my most awesome team of beta readers/typo hunters who plowed through the entire book and helped tighten it up: Lisa Andreas, Lynne Facer, Patti Huber, Lynne Mayfield, and Sharon Rivest.

Above and beyond thank you to Ilana Schoonover for her amazing editing, typo hunting, and last minute fixing she did under massive pressure—thank you so very much. Any remaining errors are mine alone…or Crusty Bucket's.

My cover artist, Aleta Rafton, creating yet another awesome work of art. And to The Killion Group for formatting of the entire book and print cover.

CHAPTER ONE

"MINKIES! WE'VE GOT ALL THE minkies! Dance minkies!" The high-pitched voice echoed in the narrow confines of the high canyon walls, and I knew I was going to have to squish the speaker once I found her. However, stumbling around in a dark, narrow canyon, while trying to avoid stepping on my companions sleeping around the campfire, wasn't easy.

The faeries had taken off right after dinner—as had been their tendency the last three nights on the road. The first day on the road, Garbage Blossom had taken her vow to protect me seriously. She sat in front of my face and stared at me as we drove away from the formerly hidden elven enclave. The rest of the faeries had flown around the wagon, scouting ahead like it was a game.

Not Garbage.

She watched me until I finally took a nap to avoid her. The scenery on this side of the enclave hadn't been that exciting anyway.

When we'd set up camp that first night, there was the tiny, orange faery, following me everywhere. I woke up the next morning to a maniacal orange face mere inches away from mine.

Luckily, Garbage had gotten bored within a few hours on the second day and forgotten her vows not long after.

For the past three days of travel, the band of faeries: Garbage Blossom, Leaf Grub, Crusty Bucket, and another assorted twenty formerly wild faeries would show up for meals once we'd set camp, then pretty much take off and fly ahead.

Sadly, their singing and obsession with the mythical creatures called minkies had begun again as well.

This time it was during my watch. I only had an hour left so I thought maybe they wouldn't be singing tonight. I was wrong and a tight slot canyon was possibly the worst place for them to start. Faeries were terrifying singers. They'd been known to cause week-long pub brawls simply by completing one of their songs. It was not pretty.

Most of the area we'd covered had been flat and filled with little more than shrubs. But yesterday Padraig had changed direction and led us toward a huge cliff face. The slot canyon he led us through barely allowed the wagon and horses to pass, and only a lot of elven horse whispering from Alric got them to enter it in the first place. Deep rust, orange, and soft rose-colored walls ascended about three times as high as the wagon. They widened out a bit after the first half hour, but hadn't gotten more than a dozen or so feet away from us on either side.

Camping within those lovely, multicolored canyon walls made a perfect acoustic amplifier for the torture that was faery singing.

"Minkies! Why have you been gone so long?" That was Leaf Grub. She didn't often join in for the singing, that appearing to be the twisted domain of Crusty Bucket. But the closer I got to the voice, the more I heard. There was an odd, and unfortunately extremely discordant, humming, as well as snippets of song from both Crusty and Leaf.

"Minkies. Minkies. Minkies." More than three voices for that.

The sound was becoming chant-like and made me move faster. The canyon had a slight bend, so I couldn't see them, but I was getting closer.

A dark buzzing form dove near my head, but stopped

about a foot over me and purred. Bunky, my own personal chimera construct. The chimeras had come from somewhere deep below the ruins in Beccia, left there for whatever reasons by the powerful beings who created them. I'd only known of twenty from that original batch, but during our battle of a few days ago, it was made clear there were far more than that. Close to a thousand was my guess. Since I had been fighting for my life at the time, and they vanished once the battle was over, I wasn't sure. Bunky was no help. I couldn't understand him and while the faeries could, they rarely repeated anything helpful. Even Padraig and Alric, who both were able to understand some of what Bunky said, couldn't get him to discuss the rest of his kind.

Bunky had been captured by the faeries months ago when we were first trying to figure out what the chimeras were. He decided that even though he was thousands of years old and a magical construct made of a metal-like material, he was one of the faeries. He protected the girls and myself and had an odd fondness for trying to head-butt Alric.

Bunky recently found a new friend in the form of a gargoyle construct created by Siabiane, an ageless elf of massive power who lived just outside the elven enclave. The gargoyle was made after the original Ancient relic, the glass gargoyle, that had started this entire disaster. Well, started my inclusion in it—I had a bad feeling these events had been eons in the making. We were currently hunting the mages who'd stolen the relic gargoyle, along with the obsidian chimera, and a very dangerous emerald dragon. I'd ended up with the fourth relic, the sapphire manticore, somehow inside me. A small mark of it was hidden on my cheek.

My night vision was nowhere near as good as pretty much anyone I was traveling with, but a soft gronking sound told me the gargoyle was up there with Bunky. Neither of them sounded concerned so there was no threat in the area. Aside from the assault on my ears.

The three of us rounded the corner and found our miscreants. I thought they'd run out of the ale they'd stolen from Locksead's henchman, Jackal, a few months ago—either I misjudged those tiny magic bags they carried or they'd found another source. Since Padraig and Covey didn't drink, and Alric hadn't brought any on this trip, I had a feeling that there was a pilfered elven bar somewhere back in the enclave.

Twenty-three faeries were all sitting around a small fire, drinking and singing. I'd never seen them start a fire before so I figured one of them stole a twig from our fire. Drunken faeries with flame was not a comforting thought.

"Could you keep it down? The others are trying to sleep." I refrained from adding they were giving me a massive headache.

"Must get minkies," Garbage worked into her chant-song.

"They needed," added Leaf.

"Fighting minkies." The last was Crusty, and sung more than said even though she was sprawled out on her back and her eyes were closed. She was pretty close to needing to go into a bottle to sober up. Unfortunately, the only bottles around belonged to the faeries and I didn't know if I could grab one from them fast enough to shove her into it.

"You want to fight the minkies?" At least my question stopped the chanting. That was something.

"No. Is silly," Leaf said from where she stared into the fire. "Need minkies to fight. Cats too." She looked over to me with sad eyes. "No kittens."

I waved to Bunky as he and the gargoyle hovered over me. "Can you two go watch over the camp? This might take a while." It would be Alric's watch soon, and so far we hadn't run into trouble, but we were chasing two insanely powerful magic users who really wouldn't like being followed. We knew they were heading for the Spheres—huge, carved boulders said to hold the secrets of the Ancients. They wouldn't be happy to find that we were following them.

Bunky bleated, then he and the gargoyle flew off. I dropped down to a crouch to better see the faeries. As annoyed as I had been about their singing, and the fact they obviously stole more ale, seeing them solemn and silent was even more disturbing.

"Girls? What's going on?"

"Is not going. Needs to be going, but not. Is bad," Garbage said.

They were difficult to understand most times, but this was worse. I'd never seen them like this.

"But what—"

All twenty-three faeries cut me off by suddenly jabbering, even the semi-conscious Crusty. It was just random noise for a few seconds, then suddenly changed and they in one voice shouted, "Minkies!"

I was about to tell them to keep quiet but then a number of tiny lights appeared directly in front of us. Most floated up, but one hovered over the fire, then drifted to Crusty. And popped.

A small creature, a few inches bigger than the four-inch faeries, stood there. It was vaguely like a weasel, but had six legs instead of four, and appeared to be very comfortable in a bipedal position. It was covered in short dark fur that changed color as I watched. And those deep black eyes that watched me were scary intelligent.

The fur became blinding white, finally changing to a more medium brown. I only had a quick look before twenty-three faeries, in various stages of inebriation, squealed and piled on top of the creature.

A creature that must be the fabled minkie. After hearing about them for years, I really expected something more…

impressive. It looked like a variation of some of the large plain rodents. But I'd never seen them arrive like it had. I wasn't sure if I was disappointed or relieved.

I tried to get the faeries attention for a few moments, but there was no way I was getting them away from whatever that thing was, minkie or not. I rocked back on my heels and watched as the tiny lights that had appeared when this one did vanished as they drifted higher. Small petals branched out and seemed to be helping them move—they looked like flowers made of light as they slowly made their way up and out of the canyon.

This hadn't answered what the minkies were nor why the faeries wanted their cats along with the minkies. Months ago, I'd caught the faeries betting on cat racing. They'd managed to gather most all of the free roaming felines from the town of Beccia, taken over an abandoned barn, and started racing for money. What these strange lights, the fur-changing creature under the pile of faeries, and cats had to do with fighting, I had no idea. And the middle of the night was definitely not the time to try to figure it out.

I was about to break up the faery-minkie love fest and get some answers, when a clattering of pans—as if every single one we'd had in the wagon suddenly started flying and brought a dozen friends—came from behind me.

I gave the pile of faeries one more look, then got to my feet and ran back down to the wagon. I had no idea what I was expecting, but it certainly wasn't finding Bunky and the gargoyle dive bombing the wagon, and Covey throwing every single pot and pan she could find at them.

I ran closer and realized that the battle wasn't between Covey, Bunky, and gargoyle, but all three of them fighting against some tiny dark purple creatures. They almost looked like the bright lights that had emerged when the minkie appeared except their glow was dark, purplish, and menacing. Even if my friends weren't fighting them off, I would have a bad feeling about them.

The light creatures didn't seem to be fighting, although given their shape I had no idea what they could do *to* fight, but they were actively trying to land on Covey. Then I noticed that both Alric and Padraig were sprawled out awkwardly near the fire. They'd both been asleep when I left to find the faeries, but their current positions indicated they'd gotten up, and then had been knocked unconscious.

By those little purple light things? My heart raced, but I held back from running to Alric. He was still breathing, they both were. They just weren't moving and the positions they were in indicated they had been in motion when they fell.

Covey ran out of things to throw and both Bunky and the gargoyle were overwhelmed as they attacked the purple lights. Three of the lights drifted down and briefly landed on Covey. She dropped like an empty sack of ale bottles.

I screamed and the lights turned toward me.

CHAPTER TWO

THEY DIDN'T MOVE FAST, MORE like they were swimming through the air at a steady pace. I might be able to outrun them but they were coming from all directions, and Bunky and the gargoyle didn't appear able to slow them down.

I didn't have many options. Up until a few months ago, I was a magic sink. Not only could I not do magic, only the strongest spells would work on me. Somehow that drastically changed when I found myself with unexplained magical abilities. My spell casting was limited, and seemed to work much better with dragon bane, a whiskey, but I did have one spell down well. Push.

I mentally dug in deep and pushed those purple lights as hard as I could. Spell casting didn't come as easily for me as for Alric or Padraig. Even my push spell took effort. I had no idea what they were, but they'd taken out three of my friends—three of my exceptionally skilled-at-defending-themselves friends. That two of them were heavy magic users might have stopped me from trying my own spell. If I'd thought about it.

Luckily for me, I was developing a tendency to act without thinking.

The light creatures tumbled in the air but didn't move as far as I'd hoped. I tried again and put all of my effort into them going away, far away. Spell strain usually hit me afterwards when I tried this hard, but not *while* I was spell casting. This time my head felt like it had been struck so hard I reached a hand up expecting to see blood. There was none. I kept focusing on the lights.

Finally they vanished. Literally. One moment they were there, refusing to be moved by my impressive magic—such as it was—the next, they were gone. I wasn't sure if I'd sent them away, destroyed them, or they went to find easier prey.

Bunky and the gargoyle came swooping in, and only then did I realize that I had dropped to a sitting position. It must have happened while I was trying to disperse those things. The world seemed a bit blurrier than it was previously, so I figured staying down might be a good idea.

Bunky hovered nearby but didn't try to touch me. Good thing. Normally I wore thin gloves to be able to touch him without side effects. Those effects being a flood of memories that weren't mine. I seemed to be the only one it happened to and the way I was feeling right now, I would probably pass out.

The gargoyle didn't care and dropped right into my lap. Like Bunky, he was a construct, but I never sensed anything when I touched him.

I petted the gargoyle between his brows and looked at my collapsed friends. All of them were unconscious, breathing, but still not moving and I wasn't sure how long it was going to take before I felt able to stand. I was going to have to call for help.

Since they weren't singing anymore, I couldn't hear the faeries from this distance, but I might be able to get at least my three to come this way. The rest would no doubt follow.

I concentrated my thoughts on my original three faeries: Garbage Blossom, Leaf Grub, and Crusty Bucket. I built a huge pile of full ale bottles in my mind and sent the faeries the image. In the past few months we'd found that I could call the faeries with my mind—sometimes. And only if I gave them an image strong enough to grab their attention. They knew there probably wasn't ale, but that wouldn't stop them from making sure.

A full minute passed, and not a single peep from any faery heading my way. So I started tipping the bottles over and letting them spill out in my mind. That had been a suggestion from Padraig when I couldn't get the faeries to respond a few days ago. Worked well this time too.

"We want," Garbage was the first to get to me, but the mob was right behind her. She hovered in front of me, her tiny hands on her hips and her lower lip stuck out.

"Sorry, no ale. Only what you ladies have," I said. Then I pointed to Alric, Padraig, and Covey. "Some purple lights knocked them out. Lights that looked sort of like the lights that showed up when your friend appeared."

As soon as I said purple lights, Garbage spun and flew to Alric. Without a word the faeries all separated, a third going to each person. They sat on them. Nothing else, no magic, no secret words, just sat.

Bunky flew over all three of my friends but he seemed as confused as me, judging by his movements. The gargoyle stayed on my lap and allowed me to pet him.

Within a minute my friends started moving and all of the faeries flew up into the air.

"We be back sun time," Garbage said as she and the others started to fly off.

"Wait, where is your friend?" I looked around but their small, six-legged companion was nowhere to be seen. "The minkie?"

Garbage spun on me and flew into my face. "When you see minkie? No one see minkie."

The rest of the faeries started swarming around.

"A few minutes ago, you guys chanting, lights, six-legged furry thing showed up?"

Garbage and the others looked confused, but they also looked like they had no idea what I was saying. "No minkies. Gone. Long time." She flew over to Covey as the faeries left the campsite. "She hit head. Not good." Then with another look of concern aimed my direction, she led the rest of her flying gang out of the area.

Bunky flew after them and the gargoyle took off after him. Leaving me on the ground and very confused. Faeries didn't lie, not directly anyway. And I knew Garbage. She wasn't trying to be sneaky; she honestly felt no one had seen a minkie. Even she and the other faeries. Maybe that wasn't a minkie I'd seen, but they'd all called it that.

The world had stopped swaying, so I got to my feet.

"What happened?" Alric was the last to rise and he looked the most out of sorts. Alric was an elven high lord, a being of power and beauty: right now, he looked like someone had woken him out of a nightmare about a bad hairdresser. His white blond hair stuck up like a bunch of drunken faeries had been sleeping in it, his normally bright green eyes were bleary and half-open, and his clothing was skewed. All in all, my normally very good-looking quasi-boyfriend was not meeting that criterion right now.

"I was with the faeries," I said. "I heard pots crashing, so I ran back here. You two were out and Covey was using our cookware as projectile weapons."

Covey shuddered as she dropped one of the battered pans back into its cubbyhole in the wagon. The side folded open when we made camp so I could see how ransacked it was. "Those…things."

The purple light creatures had given me the same reaction—odd since they were actually pretty in a way. Their underside glowed a light pink as they drifted toward you. Rather, as they came in for a landing to knock you out. Who knew what their plan was after that. I echoed Covey's shudder.

"I had just woken up when I saw them. We have stories of light creatures, but they aren't supposed to be evil. I went to wake up Padraig and they came for me." Alric rubbed the side of his head, felt how messed up his hair was, and patted it down. If it had been me, my hair would still be a mess. Elven hair seemed to resort to silky and beautiful without much trouble. One quick shake and it was all in order. Annoying to say the least.

"They take over your body, some sort of transference from the skin—but clothing doesn't slow it down much. I believe I've read about them in one of my books, but I'll warrant we all have red marks showing where they touched us." Padraig rose and went about retrieving scattered cookware. The black hair that fell to his waist shimmered in the firelight as he moved. For a thousand-or-so-year-old elf, he looked pretty damn good. Until he turned and you could see his right side. His wife and three friends had been murdered, and he horribly scarred, when the bastards we were after stole the glass gargoyle from Padraig's study. That one of them had been disguised to look like Alric, one of Padraig's oldest friends, hadn't been good for either of them. Luckily, the truth had been exposed quickly once the real Alric and I came into the elven enclave.

Padraig's scars, like Alric's true elven looks, were masked by a glamour. A deceptively simple, yet powerful, spell that blocked others from seeing the true person. For some reason, I could see through even the strongest glamour now. No one had been able to figure that out, and it got added to the list of 'weird things about Taryn'. The long, and apparently growing, list.

Covey gave another shudder and stalked away from the wagon to help bring in the rest of the cookery. Covey was a trellian academic, which wasn't as much of an oxymoron as would be thought. Although her people had finally escaped from years of savagery and berserker tendencies, most were not huge academic minds. Covey was one of the foremost experts on elven history, lore, and magic—that was until we realized that the elves really were still alive and had been hiding for the last thousand years. She could hold her own with them though. And she had the advantage of being an even fiercer fighter, with or without a dip into berserker rage, than any elf I'd met.

"Could *they* have sent the lights to stop us? Covey dropped really fast once those things touched her and none of you looked good when you were down." I hadn't been stung by the creatures, and I feared what would have happened if I had. Who knew how long it would take the faeries to come back to camp if I hadn't been able to call them?

"I don't know. I would think if they knew we were following them, the reaction would have been a lot bloodier," Alric said.

The two mages, Reginald and inquisitor Nivinal, had escaped almost a day before we'd been able to follow, and as far as we knew they had no idea anyone realized where they were going. We needed to keep it that way.

Alric had been checking the edges of the camp for stragglers, then came back to stand next to me. "Are you okay?" He rubbed my arms then tilted my face up to make it visible in the firelight. "You're bleeding."

I had checked my head for blood earlier, but not my face. A trickle of blood was coming from my nose. Alric handed me a bit of fabric. It stopped flowing after I wiped it away. But that wasn't a good sign. The spell had taken a lot more out of me than it should.

"I used a push spell on the lights; they were really heavy for only looking like bits of glowing fluff. I'm not really sure if I sent them away or they vanished on their own."

Alric frowned and nodded toward the wagon. "It's my turn to stand watch. I know it will be cramped, but all three of you should sleep inside until daybreak. There's no way to know if those things will come back."

Padraig handed Covey the last of the pans, an extremely dented skillet, and darted past her to go further into the wagon. He came back later with a few battered books.

Ones from his arcane magic and Dark collection. Padraig and Alric were both experts on the Dark, a group of elves who'd managed to nearly destroy their entire race in their attempt at conquering it. Myself, and all the people in the surrounding lands, thought the elves had died out a thousand years ago. The elves had thought the Dark had been destroyed in their final battle—also a thousand years ago. We were all wrong.

"I'm staying up as well," Padraig said as he piled the books near the fire. "Day will be here soon enough and I'd like to find out what those creatures were before we come across them again."

Covey looked toward the horizon. Everything looked like the dead of night to me, but she had better eyes than I did. "I'm going to research as well. The sun will be up in a few hours."

I looked at all three of them, and then shook my head. While their eyes might allow for reading obscure books by firelight, mine certainly wouldn't.

"You three have a great time, I'm getting some sleep." I went into the wagon, and pushed enough stuff off the bench in the back to make a bed. Then swore and climbed back out. "Oh, and keep an eye out for the faeries. They have been up to something and I'm not sure it's something we're going to like." At their nods, I went back into my created bed. That last bit went without saying. I had no idea if I'd seen a minkie, nor exactly what they were. But at any given time the faeries were probably into something that was going to bring trouble to someone.

A moment later, Alric stuck his head in. The look of concern on his face destroyed any slightly romantic thoughts I might have entertained at his arrival.

"Are you sure you're okay? You look pale." He sat down on the bed next to me.

"I'm fine. Figure out what those things were and maybe we'll know why they were so hard to move with magic."

He watched me for a few moments, then gave me a quick kiss. It was almost impossible to have any type of romantic development when we were traveling in such close quarters with friends.

"You'd tell me if anything else came up? Was there any reaction from your *friend*?" He briefly touched my left cheek where the tiny sapphire manticore mark was hidden.

I sighed. Alric was smart, talented, and sexy, but he could also be a mother hen. "Nothing. Just like the past few days." The powers from the sapphire manticore had helped us during the fight in the enclave by holding the shield covering it in place a bit longer. It hadn't done anything since then. If it weren't for the fact the mark was still on my cheek—under a glamour of its own—I might think it had somehow left me.

I must have shown my annoyance at the daily inquiries about the internal relic, because he got up and left.

Or it could be the massive yawn I gave.

I heard my three friends muttering softly outside the wagon, but didn't have enough energy to stay awake and try to listen.

CHAPTER THREE

A RAY OF DIFFUSED SUNSHINE POKED me in the eyes until I gave in and rolled away from it. I'd gotten better at short bouts of sleeping in the past few weeks but wasn't a fan. It had started during our trip to the elven enclave when Alric and I were prisoners of the elven guards. The knights who were bringing us in sang every night. Unfortunately, the harmonics in the enclave they lived in were different than the outside world and their singing could have fallen under the definition of torture. Sleep was sporadic under those conditions and I learned to grab whatever I could.

I could dodge the ray of sun, but there was no getting around the amount of noise taking place around me. Covey muttered to herself as she fussed with things two feet away from me. Most likely complaining about the state of her cookware. Never mind that she was the one that created all the dents.

I was about to move again to see if I could block her noises when the unwelcome sound of horses echoing through the canyon hit my ears. I jumped out of my blankets and saw Covey grab the sword she'd become fond of and leap out of the wagon.

Of course, *my* sword was nowhere to be found.

A number of months ago, I'd inherited an odd, elven spirit sword, something that appeared and disappeared at the whim of its owner. At least the ones that Alric and

Padraig had did. Mine seemed to come and go whenever it felt like it. And apparently now was not when it felt like it.

I grabbed my dagger instead and followed Covey out of the wagon.

And tripped over my sword lying in the dirt in front of me. I grabbed the stubborn thing and rolled to my feet, managing not to look too insane as I turned toward the sound. It was coming from behind us, the sound of horses running too fast for a twisty narrow canyon.

My three friends were all off across the camp from me and heavily armed. I would have joined them but the lead horse barreled into our camp right at that moment.

I steadied my stance, holding both blades out but not too far away from me. The horseman was already slowing down but I did move to the right in case he kept coming. The rider was an elven knight, full helmet down so I had no idea if it was one of the good ones, or a follower of the Dark that we'd missed.

Another rider came up behind him, also in full elven armor, after them was a small wagon pulled by a single horse.

The first rider looked down at my weapons, did a quick glance to my friends, then shook his head and removed his helmet. Long blond hair tumbled out.

Flarinen.

He'd been the one responsible for taking Alric and I in to the elven enclave to answer for crimes we didn't commit. We'd never completely seen eye to eye about anything, but had a mild truce going by the time we left a week ago. The elven king and queen had sanctioned this trip, as well as one to the south by my patroness Qianru and another to a hidden group of elves to the north by my friend Harlan, and his newest love interest, Orenda.

So then why was the captain of the knights charging after us as if we'd robbed the throne?

The second knight held back at the entrance of our camp,

but Flarinen slowly walked his horse forward. Padraig and Covey moved to either side of the entrance from where the canyon curved into this area, but Alric walked forward. Like me, he held his sword at the ready.

"Come now, you can't still wonder what side I'm on?" Flarinen didn't move off his horse, but he did wave for the second rider to stay back. The wagon driver had a cloak with the hood pulled down over their face.

"We can and we will," Alric jutted his chin toward the second knight. "Take off your helmet if you please, and tell your wagon driver to come forward."

Flarinen glared at him. Along with being a decent swordsman, the tall elven captain was the master of the glare. "Do what he says, we don't have time to waste." Flarinen hadn't moved toward his sword, but did get off his horse.

The second knight removed his helmet, but stayed on his horse. A young elf with short deep red hair, I didn't recognize him so I couldn't tell if he was a follower of the Dark or not.

The wagon slowly moved forward and stopped.

"Hood off, if you'd please," Padraig said as he and Covey closed in.

The form took off his hood. Lorcan. Rather the body of Lorcan, a powerful, elven mage who'd had his body stolen by his brother Reginald—who happened to be a Dark mage before he'd lost his own body to death centuries before.

I wish I'd had time to grab a bow and arrows. Flarinen had brought one of the Dark mages we were chasing right into our midst.

"All of you, stay where you are," Padraig yelled. He and Alric moved forward slowly. "Tell me why I shouldn't destroy you right now." He was focusing on Reginald in Lorcan's body, but he had his left hand up as if holding an invisible ball—he had a spell armed and ready.

Before anyone could speak, a ruckus mob of singing,

screaming, and giggling faeries tumbled into the area—all of them aimed right at Reginald.

"Wait!" I knew it wouldn't do any good, the girls never listened to me, but I had no idea what Reginald could do to them.

They ignored me, flew right through all of us, past Flarinen, and the red-haired knight and enveloped Reginald.

I ran forward although I wasn't sure what I could do. I stopped running when I saw the faeries were all kissing Reginald.

Although the being looked like Lorcan, a kindly, ancient elven leader, the inside was all his evil brother. So what were the faeries doing, and why would Reginald be laughing about it?

"It's Lorcan," Flarinen said with his usual sneer. At least that hadn't changed. "His brother left his body long enough for him to get it back."

I looked from Flarinen, to Lorcan, to Padraig and Alric. They'd pretty much said that it would be impossible to do that. Yet here were my faeries, smothering this person with kisses. They didn't even do that to me.

"It's true, my child. His spell dropped for a brief time two days ago, and I found myself with a body again." Lorcan gently pushed aside the mass of faeries.

I walked forward. I kept my sword and dagger ready. I could try a spell, but whether it was Reginald or really Lorcan, my magic wouldn't stand a chance. "What happened when we were in your rooms?"

The small, gentle smile that faced me was all Lorcan. "You and your faeries almost died. Well, you did; they're tougher. Someone had poisoned my nectar. You drank it and collapsed, all the while accusing Padraig here of trying to kill you. Your flying friends swam in it, but really didn't have any problems."

I hadn't told anyone about that.

Padraig ran forward and pulled Lorcan off the wagon

and into a huge hug. "Well met! I feared we'd not be seeing you back in your rightful form."

"Is him," Garbage said to no one in particular. She led the rest of the faeries further up into the air but they stayed over the camp.

Lorcan patted Padraig on the back and I came forward to hug him myself. He'd been around since his brother pulled the body snatch, but in ghost-like form. It was good to see him back together.

Covey had only known him as the evil Reginald, or the ghost-like Lorcan, so she stayed back watching us all.

"I don't understand what happened." Alric came forward, his well-behaved sword vanishing immediately at his mental command. "Or why you're here. We can't turn back."

"What happened to me is part of why I had to have Flarinen and young Kelm here escort me to you. I have my body yes, but we're not sure for how long. I need to be there when you stop Reginald to make sure I keep it."

Flarinen shrugged. "There was no way I was going to let anyone else do this duty."

"You've done your duty," Alric said. "Lorcan is safe with us now. Go back home."

Alric and Flarinen had grown up together in the elven enclave. From what I'd gathered they had pretty much hated each other their entire lives.

"We're staying with you." The grin was pure nasty as Flarinen helped Lorcan down from the cart. "Orders of the king and queen. We stay with this group until I resolve the problem of our missing mages and regain the relics they stole. I am to take charge."

"Flarinen, I am still recovering from my ordeal, but I will smack you myself if you don't tone it down." That was the Lorcan I'd come to know. Pale, and thinner than he had been, but the light in his eyes was all him.

Garbage drifted down slowly and hovered directly in

front of Flarinen. She folded her arms, narrowed her eyes, and that familiar lower lip jutted out. "Is lying."

Flarinen's image of a powerful knight of the elven realm was shattered as she darted forward, only stopping an inch in front of his nose. He kept from falling over as he stumbled backwards—but only barely.

"I am not," he said, but winced as Garbage moved into his space again. "Okay, Kelm and I were to escort Lorcan to join you, then stay on as support. Kelm is a new knight and hasn't been involved with or had contact with any of the ones from the Dark. He and I are the only two completely cleared at this point."

From the look on his face you would have thought he was being forced to admit royal secrets.

Lorcan smiled and patted him on the cheek as he walked by. "Good boy."

"So how did this happen? What happened?" I had my sword in my hand, which didn't mean we were still in danger. It meant I had no control over my sword.

Padraig's sword had also vanished.

"The how is what we need to find out," Lorcan said as he walked closer. "All I know is that two days ago I was drifting about, watching the rebuilding of the palace, and I slammed into a wall." His grin was huge as he looked around. "I started swearing before I realized the implications."

Padraig grinned and patted his friend on the back. "It is good to have you back. Between us, we can figure out how to keep you in your body."

A sharp noise tore into the air and the canyon wall across from us cracked. Whatever it was didn't cause any rocks to fall and the hairs on my arm stood on end as a flow of freezing air hit me.

Alric pulled me away and Padraig motioned for the others to do the same.

"That's not natural," Alric said as he lifted his hand. He

normally cast spells without the fancy movements favored by Padriag but he did an elaborate twist with his wrist now.

He pushed us back another step.

Padraig stepped forward. Alric was a tracker, spy, and fighter—and not a weak magic user. But Padraig was by far the stronger. Both of his hands moved so fast I couldn't see his fingers at all. A moment later, the crack slammed shut and the chill drifted away.

"There was a breach in the magic lines there," Padraig said calmly. "Something popped through, but I closed the breach." His voice was calm, but the look he shot both Alric and Lorcan was not. All three of them wiped the concern away quickly, but I knew what I saw.

I didn't even know magic lines could breach, pop, or do anything of the sort. I was going to need to switch my magic training to Lorcan or Padraig it appeared. Not that I didn't enjoy training with Alric, but he was avoiding some subjects. Not to mention if we did get any alone time I'd rather not spend it on magic.

"Bored now." The faeries flew silently over us, and Garbage managed to drop in front of my face before I noticed.

I looked up. It looked like our pack of faeries were there, but Bunky and the gargoyle weren't.

"Where's Bunky?"

"He bored too." Leaf dropped down out of the flock. "He go find another big boom."

Not boom again. They used boom for everything from major world-changing rips in dimensions to falling out of a tree. And they never could explain things more than boom.

"Which boom, sweetie?" I appealed to Leaf as sometimes she was easier to get through to than the others. Garbage was belligerent just because and Crusty often wasn't even sure where she was. I hadn't bonded enough with the rest of the pack to get much information out of most of them.

"That one." She pointed to where the crack had been. That got everyone else's attention.

"You knew about that?" Padraig held out his hand and the five closest faeries landed immediately. Then Garbage landed in the middle and pushed the others off. The smile she gave him was maniacal for any other being, but for her a rare sign of true affection.

"Yes. Big boom. You stop. Is good." She smiled even larger. "Go now?"

Padraig looked over her head to me, but I shrugged.

"I have no idea how they knew. They weren't even here." I studied all of the faeries. "Had they known it was there, they would have been flying through to wherever it went." My watching paid off. Leaf and half of the others all had a flash of guilt across their faces.

"Damn it. Why didn't you tell us it was here?"

Garbage glared down the rest of her pack, then tried to look contrite. I had no idea how many hundreds or thousands of years old the faeries were—it hadn't been long enough for her to get that look down. She ended up looking more deranged than usual.

"Shouldn't be. Needed to see before boom." Crusty piped up from the middle of the pack. "Not right boom. Bad boom. Telling now."

Garbage rolled her eyes but didn't even waste a glare on Crusty. "Only went part way in. Just showed up."

So that crack had recently appeared, but they'd had time to fly through before we even knew it was there.

Alric had been ignoring the faeries and was focusing on the patch of rock where the crack had been. "We need to get moving now. There's a weird magic residue, and I don't think we want to be here if that thing opens again."

CHAPTER FOUR

THE RAIN STARTED THE MOMENT we got moving. Flarinen and Kelm rode a bit ahead, something Alric had been doing since we started this trip but he gave it up without a word once Flarinen claimed it. I knew it wasn't because of any thought of Flarinen leading; it was that Alric was already looking for ways to build distance between them.

Instead he tied his horse to the back of the larger wagon and drove Lorcan's smaller one with Padraig and Lorcan inside. That was a bit of a fight. Lorcan insisted he could drive, even in the chilling rain. Padraig talked him out of it and Alric had to talk Padraig out of driving as well. None of us had any idea how long Lorcan would keep hold of his body. I had to assume his brother wasn't pleased about losing it. Padraig and Lorcan needed to find out how he'd gotten it back and how to keep it. They both needed to spend the time traveling reading spell books.

Which left Covey and I flipping a coin for driving our wagon—as in who would have to. Of course, Covey won. Never play games of chance with a trellian—they always win. I'd never been able to catch her cheating. And that wouldn't go with her personality. But I also never won.

I covered up as best I could against the rain and drove our wagon behind Alric and the others. The ravine we were passing through was widening a bit, now it was wide enough for four wagons to ride side by side, but the scenery hadn't changed.

Watching the slowly moving gait of the horse in front of me gave me plenty of time to reflect. Especially after my first attempt at starting a conversation with Covey in the back lead to a loud snort followed by snoring. Not that I could blame her, all of us were tired.

Growing up, all I wanted to be was a digger. Have a chance to find out what really happened to the elves. Having to bounty hunt during lean times led me to Alric—and pretty much the end of life as I had intended it.

A twinge of guilt hit me about the town that had been my home for fifteen years, and hopefully would be again. Beccia was rough and shabby, but it was home. And, like me, it had taken some hits over the past few months. Some might even say it was because of me and the relics that the town had taken those hits.

My guilt came from not thinking about them recently. The mayor of Kenithworth had shown an unhealthy interest in Beccia. Unfortunately, I was focusing on the rest of the relics, along with a bunch of rakasa, syclarions, and some seriously misguided elves. Sending my friends to go check on Beccia backfired as they turned around and followed after Alric and me anyway.

Which left me in the cold rain and having guilt about my friends.

The rain stopped soon enough—a good thing as a flash flood could wipe us all out—but my guilt continued.

"You're thinking so loud that a body can't even get proper sleep," Covey said from the window behind the wagon driver's seat.

"I'm thinking how I seemed to have managed to doom all of my friends, and I'm not even sure what for." My wallowing was in full force.

Covey's laugh was always startling, usually because it was so rarely heard. "Yes, you forced all of us to follow you on this."

I looked back toward the window. "If I hadn't gotten involved none of you would have. Okay, except Alric. He was already involved. But we'd be back in Beccia, happy as ever."

Her smile faded. "I don't know how long that would last. I've been looking at Padraig's books and they fill in a lot of gaps from the scrolls I've been able to translate in the last few months. This wasn't random. The relics coming back into the world, people knowing about them." She scowled. "This seems to be preordained. Not our participation in it, but the coming back of things from the past. It's almost as if they are on a trajectory to return, but there's no way to really pinpoint the timing."

I knew how much that admission annoyed her. The idea that events were preordained, that we didn't have a say in them at all, wasn't a concept that set well with her. Or me.

"Yeah, but if we'd stayed in Beccia we might have had a few more years of ignorant bliss." I shook my head as the reality of things hit. "It doesn't matter, we're here now. And there's a slim chance we might make a difference."

"I wondered how long it would take you to realize that. Now, try not to think so hard, it disrupts my sleep." Covey gave me a smile, and then dropped the curtain.

She was right, or rather, I was. Any of us could have stopped this hell-bent trip at any time—and none of us did. I did spare a good thought for Foxy and Amara back at the Shimmering Dewdrop in Beccia. Good people and a good pub with good, cheap beer. I sighed.

The canyon we were riding through grew curvier, but fortunately stayed at its wider space. I heard the horses coming toward us long before I saw them.

Alric stopped his wagon at a slightly less curvy section, and we waited for the riders to come to us. My assumption was Kelm and Flarinen, but my assumptions weren't always working out.

That my sword suddenly appeared, in my hand this time,

wasn't a vote of confidence in my assumptions either.

It must have been because of the curves in the canyon, it took forever for the riders to appear. It was Flarinen and Kelm, but they appeared to be chasing Bunky and the gargoyle.

Bunky flew low over my head and dropped down next to me. The gargoyle overshot but swung around wildly, gronked, and landed almost on top of Bunky. The gargoyle was a construct, made of metal to look like a relic made of glass that was fashioned after a gargoyle made of stone. Yet the emotions of panic were clear on his little metal-glass-stone face.

Flarinen and Kelm had to stop at Alric and the wagon, but they didn't seem to really be chasing my friends. The faeries had gone ahead as well and I really hoped the fact they weren't with Bunky meant they'd found their own mayhem to get into.

"Defend! They are upon us!" Flarinen did look impressive with his armor glinting in the bit of sun, his sword raised high above his head. And I was sure had we been a battalion of knights we would have roared back in agreement.

As it was, Lorcan, Padraig, and even Covey came out of the wagons, armed and ready. Alric stayed on his seat, but his sword was out.

Flarinen spun and waited for whatever he thought was following them. Had I not seen how disturbed Bunky and the gargoyle were, I'd think Flarinen had been drinking. He'd reacted as if the enemy was at his heels, but there was only he and Kelm.

I looked down at the two constructs. The way they were watching Flarinen, it might have been he and Kelm who scared them unintentionally while they were running away from whatever they were running away from.

We waited a few more moments. My sword stuck around, so at least something believed Flarinen.

Finally, Alric jumped off the wagon, handed the reins to Padraig and stalked over to Flarinen. "What are we defending against? Or did that rain upset you?"

Flarinen spun back and forth, then shook his head and got off his horse. "I'm not imagining things. There was an entire battalion directly behind us. I saw them and heard them. They changed direction toward us once they spotted us." He took off his helmet and his eyes were looking a little wild. "They were right behind."

Kelm also took off his helmet and nodded. "It's true. I've no reason as to why they aren't here, but I saw them as well. The walls shook with their horses' hooves." He wouldn't look at any one of us for more than a second. He finally settled on Lorcan as the safe person to talk to. It made me wonder what Flarinen had told him about us.

"Then where are they now?" Alric got too far into Flarinen's space. "I know we had one magical crack in the canyon appear, are you saying there was another and it, what, swallowed the entire battalion?"

"No. But I know what I saw." Flarinen took a step closer and the two were almost bumping chests.

This pissing match between these two was already old. I looked down at the constructs, both were settled down now, but neither were resuming their flying. "Did Bunky and his friend take off when you started after them? Or before?"

Flarinen shook his head. "We were not chasing them. They had been ahead of us, but they turned back and flew past us as the battalion came into view."

"I trust Bunky and the gargoyle," I said after watching both for a moment. "They were more disturbed than I'd ever seen them, and I don't think it was because of Flarinen and Kelm." Based on his reactions, I'd gathered a while ago that Bunky understood me, I just couldn't understand him. He demonstrated that by lifting off the wagon seat, followed by the gargoyle, and both flew over to Flarinen and Kelm. They didn't land on them, but they also weren't afraid.

"Where did you first see them?" Lorcan asked, then turned to Padraig, "I think we need to see this area."

Padraig gave a tight nod and looked expectantly to Flarinen.

"About a fifteen-minute fast ride from here. The canyon opens up at that point into a wide valley. Kelm and I were checking the perimeter when they appeared."

Lorcan nodded and he and Padraig got into their wagon.

"I think we all need to be ready for wild magic," Alric said as he climbed back into the driver's seat of their wagon, "we're getting closer to where it's been reported."

I hadn't gotten off my seat during the exchange and was surprised when Covey climbed up next to me.

"There's no way I'm missing this, especially if it's involving wild magic." She had the deranged intense academic on the prowl look that usually only appeared when she was about to dive into a few hours of digging through a bunch of books.

Flarinen turned and he and Kelm lead us down the canyon at a brisk walk.

Alric had started his wagon forward when Covey took the reins out of my hands and clicked to the horse to move.

"I was going to do that, you know."

"Yes, yes, but we can't take a chance that we'll miss it." She was far too excited for this to be good for me. I hadn't heard of the term wild magic unless it was Alric aiming the words at me and my inability to always control my spells.

"Do I want to know what wild magic is?"

"Pockets of magic that get trapped in time. Completely unpredictable and powerful. The scholars of Kherin claim there used to be far more of them and they have dissipated over the centuries. I've never seen one, but if that is what we have, it must be incredibly strong to have survived this long."

I waited for more. When no clearer information was forthcoming, I shook my head. "For simple folks like me? What is it?"

The toothy smile she turned on me with would have made a normal person jump off the wagon.

"Ghosts. We might have magically powerful ghosts. Right here, in the land where the Ancients once lived."

CHAPTER FIVE

"ISN'T THAT WONDERFUL?" SHE ADDED with the same enthusiasm that I would have used if I found a lovely pub with free drinks.

It took me a few moments to come up with a reply that didn't involve me screaming, jumping off the wagon, and running back to Beccia. We'd run into ghosts back in the elven enclave. Covey had only seen them briefly as we fled Qianru's home. I'd seen them far closer than I ever wanted. Ghost elves fighting a long-lost battle, but somehow turning that battle into trying to destroy us. Yes, there were some magical things going on that were probably behind the direct attacks on us, but that wasn't much comfort.

"How can you be excited about more things that might be out to kill us?"

Covey was impatiently jogging our horse to move faster. But unless she was planning on riding over Alric's wagon, we were stuck until the canyon widened out again. There was room for two wagons side by side here, but barely, and there was rock and plant debris along the sides. "Just because they're ghosts doesn't mean they have to try to kill us." She let go of the reins with one hand to give a flippant wave. "Aren't you the least excited that there might be ghosts of the *Ancients*, not only elves or the other races, but the Ancients out here?"

The chill that went through me had nothing to do with my damp clothing. "I'll agree that I obviously am interested in who and what the Ancients were, but I'd rather find out by discovering some new ruins. Intact ones preferably."

There was simply no way ghosts could be good. Judging by the reactions of both elven knights, these weren't warm and friendly beings. Granted, they'd thought what they faced was flesh and blood at the time.

"But think of what we could ask them. What really happened?" The gleam in Covey's eyes was so strong I was afraid she'd not only ride us over Alric's wagon but into the abyss itself for the chance to find out what really happened to the Ancients.

I'd thought that since we found the elves she might settle down and become less academically aggressive. I was wrong. All she did was push her energy onto the long-lost Ancients.

Unlike the elves, who history had originally said had simply vanished, it was pretty well known that something huge, fast, and nasty destroyed the Ancients. They were supposed to be incredibly powerful beings who were wiped out in a single moment.

That moment was over 2,500 years ago. Their supposed power was mostly a thing of myth and legend since little had been left behind, but it made for great stories. Huge, powerful, immortal beings snuffed out in a moment like a cheap tallow candle.

One of the things they did leave behind, or so it was speculated since they were far older than anything elven, were the Spheres that we were currently heading for. Originally seven massive boulders, perfectly round and each made of a single rock. Now six remained, with a pile of dust, rubble, and hand-sized rocks to indicate where the seventh had been.

Maybe the ghosts were guarding the Spheres. Again, that wouldn't be a good thing as we were at least ten days ride out from them. No one knew much about the Spheres; they weren't easy to get to and many an ardent explorer never returned from the journey. The Spheres sat near the center of the Robani desert, an area speculated to have been the hub of the Ancient empire. Rare scrolls, from elven scholars, and a few from the trellians, referred to a great kingdom, glorious and of unmatched beauty, surrounded by a mountain chain. Then they referred to a great desert. Not much was said about how one became the other.

"You're thinking about it, aren't you?" Covey broke into my thoughts. The old Covey rarely sounded this cheerful. I found myself missing the old Covey.

"I'm thinking about how finding ghosts isn't a good thing."

The rest of my complaint was cut off as Alric's wagon came to a stop. I hadn't been paying attention to our surroundings as I contemplated our doom. The canyon walls had been slowly increasing in height as we rode the past few days, and they now loomed high enough above us that the great hawks above us were little more than specks.

Alric jumped from his wagon, stuck his head inside, then he stepped back as Padraig stepped out. Lorcan followed, but he went to take the driver's seat.

Both elves had their swords.

"Hold the reins. I'm going to find out what's going on." Covey jumped off the seat. The silence was heavy, as if it was caused by something not allowing sound to escape rather than people simply not choosing to talk.

The clatter of horse hooves echoed around us, a completely normal and natural sound in an unnaturally quiet moment. I debated jumping down and following Covey. But if I did that, with my luck this horse would take off. The canyon had widened out so I did nudge her forward.

I pulled alongside Lorcan and his wagon. Alric, Padraig, and Covey were stalking forward, and the gargoyle and Bunky flew overhead to join them. A "there is no way that's natural" mist filled the space in front of them. Even

Bunky and the gargoyle wouldn't go forward into it. But considering that they were missing, it looked like Flarinen and Kelm had.

I didn't want to break the silence, but I did look to Lorcan with a shrug. The slow shake of his head, followed by his own shrug and a heavy frown didn't make me feel in the least better.

Alric had said magic could be felt. It was something I'd never been able to do, but my sword had popped off again, and there was nothing else for me to do. Waiting had never been my strong point.

I closed my eyes and mentally tried reaching out to the fog. Maybe I could find out something about it. Images—like the ones that happened whenever I touched Bunky with bare skin—knocked me out of my seat. Literally. My eyes were still shut, jumbled visions racing at me, when I felt myself fly away from the wagon. I fought to free myself amid sudden yelling and horses whinnying and stomping. The images vanished in time for me to see a pair of dancing hooves come for me. I rolled away from them but then a pair of worn, black boots took their place.

Alric stood between me and the panicky horse. I couldn't blame the animal. I'm sure I hung on to the reins as long as I could while I was being pulled off the bench.

"What happened?" Alric was talking to me, but watching the horse. At least I assumed he was talking to me.

I got to my feet slowly. The mist was gone and we were facing Flarinen and Kelm. Both were fully armed and looked surprised to see us. I shook my head and focused on Alric.

"I have no idea. I tried to see if that mist was magic, then a bunch of weird images slammed into me and the horse almost took me out." I looked around. "Where are Bunky and the gargoyle?"

Alric whispered a few soft words into the ear of the horse. She immediately settled down. Then he turned to me. "They took off as soon as the mist collapsed. I saw a few color blurs ahead before the next turn and I think they were following the faeries. Which was exactly the time you went flying out of your seat."

Running hooves ended our conversation. I looked up as Padraig stepped in front of Flarinen as he charged toward us.

Flarinen looked around sharply, as if realizing he had his sword out and no one to attack. He sheathed it quickly. "We'd lost all of you and had ridden all the way back to your camp but found nothing. Rather, we found blood, lots of it, but nothing else."

Covey scowled at him, then looked back the way we came. "Aside from the fact that you are on the wrong side of our wagons to have done that."

Kelm moved forward but kept his horse a length behind Flarinen. "We saw what we say. None of you were here." His voice drifted away and he sheathed his own sword.

Padraig moved past both knights, then stopped a few feet behind them. "Were you riding hard through the gorge to our camp?" He moved his feet in a circle in the dirt, and then dropped down to pick up something in the dirt.

"Yes, we were going as fast as we could. There was nothing," Kelm spoke out before Flarinen did.

Flarinen shot his underling a stern look then got off his horse and silently went to Padraig. "There's nothing here."

Padraig held up a small silver and gold disk. Even where I was I could see a hole in it toward the top. "This doesn't belong to either of you, yet it was on top of the churned dirt you rode over. It's also not dusty or damaged. And the ground is even more churned a few paces back. As if two concerned knights were riding full bore but being held in place."

Covey stalked over, looked at the ground, and then took the disk from Padraig. She pulled back as if it burnt her, but then looked closer. She didn't throw it but she handed it back to Padraig quickly.

Alric moved in as well, but while he gave a cursory glance to the disk, his eyes were on the dirt. "They were here for a while, running in place. So that mist was a spell? To do what? Separate us?"

"I'm not a magic user, but I know artifacts," Covey said. "That charm is part of a linkage of gold and silver coins, it's not real, or at least it was believed to not be real. It belonged to one of the high mages of the Ancients and was what caused the fight that destroyed them."

CHAPTER SIX

THAT QUIETED EVERYONE DOWN. EVEN Lorcan looked at the piece but shook his head. "I am a student of many things. Alas, this aspect of the Ancients was not part of my studies."

Feeling left out, I also moved forward for a closer look at the disk. A feeling of dizziness snuck up on me, so I didn't touch it. It was thicker than it looked from a distance. The silver and gold blended near the middle in a fanciful design. "I thought the relics we're chasing were what destroyed them." The disk didn't look dangerous at all, even if I didn't want to touch it.

I gave the disk another study, taking a step back when Padraig held it up for me to take. "Looks like something from a fancy necklace or bracelet. So you're telling me the great and powerful Ancients were destroyed because of sparkly jewelry?" I was going to be extremely disappointed in them if that was the case.

"It is believed the relics combined into a single weapon was what destroyed them. This piece, or rather it and the rest of the pieces it was attached to, was what reportedly linked them together." Covey was looking at it in Padraig's hand. But she didn't touch it again and kept rubbing her hand on her pants.

"I think I'll keep this in the chest for now." Padraig ripped a small piece of fabric from the inside of his cloak and quickly wrapped it up.

Flarinen had stayed back, but now moved forward to where Alric poked around in the churned-up ground. "So all that I saw and felt was simply…magic?" The level of disgust in his voice on the last word made even Lorcan raise an eyebrow.

"Yes." Alric went past the churned ground. "It was triggered here, but only when you turned around. It didn't catch either of you on the way up. What made you turn around?"

"The screams," Kelm burst out. He dipped his head at Flarinen's look.

Flarinen held his glare on his man a minute longer before turning back to Alric. "We heard a commotion. It sounded like you were under attack."

Padraig joined Alric. "That's unusual, why bring them back? Why not spell them on the way out?"

"And what would have happened had *we* entered that mist with them already trapped in it?" Covey joined the two elves in looking at the ground, but she was more focused on the rock debris near the side. "And why are there so many new rocks?" She pulled back a shrub that was hugging the wall.

I'd take Covey's word that the rocks were new; I wasn't familiar with this area. This type of landscape was similar to the trellian homeland. If she said the rocks were new, they were new.

"I think we need to leave, immediately. Another crack is starting to form." Lorcan had silently moved behind Covey and I but was now backing away. "It's a trap spell, an old and nasty one. I should have recognized it when we saw the first crack."

He didn't run but was inside his wagon before the rest of us moved. Padraig didn't question him but quickly joined him.

Alric turned to us. "Be ready to ride hard if need be." He waited until we went for our wagon, then leapt up on the seat of Lorcan's wagon and readied the reins.

Covey and I ran for the driver's seat.

"You can stay inside if you like. I'll drive," she said as she grabbed the reins.

"I'm fine. I'll stay with you." The heavy silence of earlier was returning. I almost tried to call the faeries to me, but if things did go bad, I'd rather they weren't in it. Not to mention, depending on the badness level we might need them and the constructs to get us out.

Flarinen shook his head but was back on his horse immediately. "Are we going back, or do we try to keep moving forward?"

Alric nodded to something I couldn't hear from inside the smaller wagon. "Forward. There's more of the trap in place behind us. But keep pace with us. They might separate us again."

I had a bad feeling he, Padraig, and Lorcan knew exactly who *they* were. Our quarry had either found us, or figured out they were being trailed. I didn't have a chance to clarify, and wasn't sure I really wanted to, because Flarinen wheeled his horse around and started at a trot.

Kelm stayed a bit behind, but his hand rested on the hilt of his sword. Flarinen was scanning everything as we passed but made sure he stayed near us. He was such a pompous jerk it was easy to forget that he was actually a highly skilled captain of the knights.

No one spoke so the cracking sound coming from behind us was even louder.

I looked back and saw the walls behind us starting to shatter, and smaller pieces come tumbling off.

Flarinen glanced over his shoulder. "I believe we might need to move faster?" he asked, not ordered, which alone might have been enough to cause the world to shake, but he was already increasing his horse's pace.

A sharp crack and a growing roar came from behind and Covey slapped the reins.

"Run!"

Flarinen took off but stayed within range of the first wagon. Kelm kept pace with us. He was close enough to see that even though he was young, and his pale skin and bright red cheeks didn't help that any, he knew what he was doing. The pacing of his horse and the one pulling our wagon was perfect.

The trail ahead widened out even more and for a moment I thought we'd made better time than expected and already hit the Robani desert. We hadn't, and I didn't recall such an area on the maps. The walls rose around us, even higher than before. But we were in a valley of sorts.

And it had only one entrance—the one we were riding through.

Covey noticed it at the same time I did and started to turn our wagon. Just in time for us to see the rock collapse that had followed us swallow the way we came in.

Kelm noticed us spin around and moved to follow us. He didn't yell, or gasp, as I was sure I did. But his light blue eyes grew almost human in their roundness.

Alric did yell and swear when he saw it. Flarinen appeared to be trying to make up new words as he too turned around.

"This can't be right," Alric said, "there's nothing this broad out here, and this trail has been used for centuries."

"Any time recently? Your people have been more or less in hiding for a thousand years." Covey brought our wagon to a halt. "Something might have changed."

"Something that could move the very land?" Flarinen had ridden a bit back toward the way we came, but the dust of the collapse was settling and it was clear that we weren't getting out that way.

"I am not the only scout," Alric said as he drove his wagon next to ours. "While not as heavily traveled as it would have been before we went into hiding, we have had people through here. *I've* been through here." He studied the high cliffs circling around us and finally shook his head. "It's been fifteen or twenty years since I rode through, but there wasn't anything like this."

Lorcan and Padraig had come out from their wagon. Neither looked happy.

Padraig watched the cliffs for a few moments. Then he turned back to us. "This looks familiar, but I can't pin it down."

I wasn't sure how a giant, and extremely empty, dirt bowl could look familiar. The lack of plants was only one of the oddities. There hadn't been much in the way of plant life on the path the past few days, but I figured it was because we were going through some pretty desolate areas. This looked more as if it was planned. Hard-packed dirt as far as I could see.

"You travel through dust bowls often?" I asked more to fill up the empty space that was engulfing the air around us than to find out the answer. It looked like we were standing in a desert floor surrounded by miles of mountains. Even though the sun was hitting us now, the clouds that had brought the rain were long gone, and the air temperature was dropping.

"He's right. There is something familiar about this set up, more so than the actual location," Lorcan said as he looked around with a confused but almost solving it expression on his face. Mimicking Padraig.

"There is something here, something we're not able to see." Alric had gotten down from the wagon and his sword was out.

I jumped when my sword popped from the scabbard and into my hand. That was a new and unwelcome trick.

Covey dropped off the wagon and into a half crouch; her short spiky hair raised like the hackles on a dog. She didn't look berserk—yet.

Flarinen and Kelm stayed on horseback but strategically moved to the edges of our group.

I shook my hand, but the hairs on my arm were up. A low howl worked its way up from the wall furthest away from us. It was soft, and discordant, as if nature itself was trying to escape some horrific confinement.

Bleating broke through the silence, and the welcome sounds of faeries yelling. At least the sounds were welcome until I realized they were war cries.

When we lived in Becca, the faeries kept their things—including their war feathers and war sticks in a small child's toy castle. They carried them in their odd little black pouches now.

Bunky and the gargoyle were leading the charge with his bleats and the gargoyle's honks filling the still air.

"We fight!" Garbage raised her stick above her head. War blades, or staffs, looked like nothing more than small, sharpened twigs. But they acted as a focus for the faeries' magic and had helped us out many times.

Tension filled the air as all of us waited. We'd put the two wagons in the middle, and Alric spelled the nervous horses to keep them calm. At least we had something to keep our backs against in the battle.

CHAPTER SEVEN

AND NOTHING HAPPENED.

The temperature dropped a few more degrees and one of the faeries hiccupped. But nothing else happened.

"Any one of you skilled academics want to take a guess at this?" I wasn't sure what I was supposed to be looking for, but I didn't want to take my eyes off the empty space in front of me to look at my friends.

"No," Lorcan said. "But this feels old, quite old. Those we chase are not behind this."

Alric stepped forward and away from the wagons. I watched him as he crossed in front of me with Flarinen a step behind him. Neither responded when Lorcan called to them, but marched forward as if they saw an enemy.

"Do we go after them?" They were the best fighters we had aside from Covey, so I wasn't sure how much help I could be.

A roar of massive rocks colliding cut Lorcan off. Immediately, an arena rose before us. We were at its entrance, and thin ghostlike images filled the stands. Alric and Flarinen nodded to the far wall where a balcony held a waving figure. I couldn't see any of the ghosts well enough to determine what species they were and if Padraig and Alric could see, they weren't going to tell us. Their eyes were wide open but they moved as if in a trance.

I'd had enough, if this was some twisted ghost battle, they weren't going in alone. Yet as much as I tried, I couldn't move. Like one of those nightmares where you need to run and you can't. I fought down the feeling of terror that rose in my gut. Out of the corner of my eye I saw the others in the same predicament. Even the faeries, Bunky, and the gargoyle were frozen in mid-air.

Two forms became more solid as they marched toward Alric and Flarinen. Two giant syclarions in archaic armor. Neither were in their dragon form, for that I was grateful. But both were armed with huge pikes.

Alric and Flarinen both crouched as the enemy approached. The fight was swift and brutal—but surprisingly not bloody. The swords seemed to go through the syclarions even though they appeared as solid as we did. More importantly, those pikes went right through Alric and Flarinen. But they weren't completely harmless. Each time the syclarions got a blow in, our people stumbled a bit. The more blows, the longer it took them to shake it off.

Finally, the larger syclarion swung his pike up and sent Flarinen out of the circle. There was no damage I could see, but he landed in a crumpled heap and didn't move.

With two now fighting him, Alric succumbed quickly. I screamed as he was flung near my feet but I couldn't move to help him. The ragged way his chest moved told me he was alive, but injured.

Kelm and Covey were freed next. I didn't know if it was a spell, or honor, but neither of them even paused to try to escape.

The same two ancient-looking syclarions faced them—along with a third. Two went against Covey. She fought well, so did Kelm, but this time it was moments before both Kelm and Covey lay at our feet.

I couldn't turn my head, but surely I would be next. Instead, Lorcan, Padraig, and I suddenly stumbled as we were free. But a shield of some kind had gone up instead, unfortunately, and our unconscious friends were on the other side. The faeries and Bunky and the gargoyle couldn't move, but the three of us could. The syclarion fighters and the arena faded but were still visible.

"Do either of you have dragon bane?" I kept my voice low. There was no reason for whoever was doing this to release us.

Padraig had been studying the shield but looked up sharply. "Is this really a time to get drunk?"

"I need to go a little out of control right now."

"If you think it will help, I have some in my wagon. Padraig, could you get it?" Lorcan nodded. "The scrolls mention other uses; the drink is from the time of the Ancients. It was rumored that they controlled great beasts with it. Beasts like the true dragons who were lost when the Ancients were destroyed."

Padraig came out with a small brown bottle. "There's not much, but hopefully it will help."

I took it and smiled. That was one of the many differences between Alric and Padraig. If I asked for something from Padraig, he got it for me. Had I done the same with Alric he would have cross-examined me like crazy to find out why I wanted it.

I uncapped the bottle and started pouring it on myself. Not the best feeling in the world as the smell was nasty. But I made sure I drained the small bottle.

Both elves stared at me with looks ranging from confusion to outright concern.

"Weren't you going to drink it?"

"That helps in one way," I said as I saw Covey rise for another round, then collapse into a heap. "I need the other way."

Lorcan and Padraig were pulled inside the shield without me.

Nothing more than a dull tingling hit me where the dragon bane had splattered and my movements were slowing down, not speeding up. We'd never really understood how or why the dragon bane did what it did, so maybe it had stopped working.

I continued to fight my sluggishness as I watched both Padraig and Lorcan succumb to the syclarions. The faeries, Bunky, and the gargoyle were pulled in next, but they crashed to the ground almost immediately.

The pressure around me dropped and the shield fell. I could run away if I wanted, but there was no way in hell I was abandoning my friends. Not to mention finding a boyfriend who wasn't trying to kill me was rare enough that I wasn't about to leave Alric behind.

My body burst into flame as soon as I crossed the line where the shield had been. At least everywhere that the dragon bane had struck felt on fire. My jaws ached and a haze covered my eyes. I needed to destroy these things.

There were now five of the syclarions, and we came so close in battle I could tell all of their attire was a few centuries old—or older.

My body moved on its own blocking pike thrusts and getting in more than a few strikes. Two of the syclarions had vanished after multiple strikes, and then I was trapped between the remaining three. A burst came from within and I moved faster than I'd ever done. All three took enough hits to vanish.

My body felt stretched and achy, as if there was too much energy to be contained in something so small as myself. A tiny voice said I needed to drag my friends to safety. I moved toward Alric, my hand appearing claw-like as it reached to him, then everything went dark.

Chapter Eight

MY FIRST THOUGHT UPON WAKING up was that I'd been run over by a fleet of armored war chariots. My second thought was wondering how was I having thoughts when clearly my head was shattered. The third thought was that I was going to kill a bunch of yelling faeries, providing I really wasn't dying with a shattered skull.

"Mine! Is mine!" That was Leaf Grub and she was hitting a pitch that rattled the ends of my toes.

I forced open my eyes to see all twenty-three faeries bouncing around on a pile of clothing. Closer inspection, aka I squinted, revealed there was a body under those clothes. "I need you to all shut up."

That got their attention, but it didn't convince them to obey. All of them, with the exception of Leaf, flew over and landed on me with enough force to crush my feeble attempt at rolling up on one elbow.

"You did good!" Garbage yelled as she stood on my chest.

I closed my eyes as the stabbing pain that followed that exceptionally loud pronouncement ran through my head.

After making sure my head wasn't going to shatter anew at the sound, I opened my eyes. "I really need you, all of you, to be quiet. Very quiet."

Crusty tumbled closer to my face and opened her mouth, but Garbage jumped on her and covered her mouth. "We quiet."

That was a couple of firsts. Garbage actually respecting what I asked—the look of admiration that she gave me was almost as terrifying as her singing. And that even Crusty immediately settled down.

The rest of the faeries remained standing on me, but not a peep was heard and they didn't move a muscle.

I wasn't going to try and figure out the weirdness of faeries right now. Bits and pieces of what happened before this started crawling around in my mind.

"Where are we, where are the others, and who was it you were jumping on?" The last one wasn't crucial, but I did want to know. Leaf was still on him and her eyes were almost crossed with the look of adoration on her face.

Crusty started to answer, with what I knew was going to be a loud, rambling response. Garbage shut her down with a glare.

"You save us all. Bring here. Here good." She waved around us and I focused a bit more. We were on a packed dirt floor of a large empty storage room. A pile of moldy potatoes languished in the far corner, along with a few empty and busted crates. There was a short stairway and a heavy wooden door—the kind with metal bars in it. Now that the girls were quiet, I heard the sounds of a street beyond the door.

"Girls? Where is the light coming from?" A closed-up storage room, no windows, yet I could see everything.

"Is him," Leaf finally paid attention to me, and pulled back part of the fabric on the hopefully not dead man she was cuddling. He gave off a soft glow and it echoed around the room.

"How is…Never mind," I said. "Where are the others?"

"Think there," one of the extra faeries said and pointed toward the door to the street. Penqow was a black and white faery and had been with us for a few months, but like most of the newer ones, rarely spoke to me. How much of that was their decision and how much was because of Garbage, I had no idea.

"They're out there somewhere and we're in here? Any ideas how we got in here?"

All of the faeries pointed as one to the pile of rags Leaf was standing on.

"So the man over there brought us here?"

Garbage laughed and the rest giggled. "No, silly. YOU bring here. He bring here." As she said the first *here*, her arms went wide. As she said the second, she pointed to the packed dirt I was lying on.

Somehow I brought us to a town, even though the last thing I recalled was the world fading before my eyes. Then this unconscious man a few feet from me brought me in here, and collapsed.

"Did he bring you all in here too?"

"Is no. We follow you," Crusty said as she wiggled free of Garbage. I didn't even think Garbage remembered she'd been sitting on her.

I struggled to roll up on my elbow again. I immediately felt a bunch of tiny hands at my back pushing. Garbage stood on my shoulder giving commands.

I would have been annoyed, but they actually helped. The body near me was close enough that getting up on my hands and knees could get me to him, so I didn't bother standing up.

There seemed to be more clothing piled on him beyond what he was wearing. I pushed some aside. The breath I drew in was completely involuntary. He was gorgeous.

"Is mine." Leaf rolled off the clothes she'd been standing on as I pulled them away but she stayed on him.

"Okay, he's yours. What is he?"

"He faery. Boys always trouble."

I took a closer look. His features were almost too pretty, as if someone had taken an elf and glammed him up into almost looking like a woman. But enough sharper lines in his face gave indication he was male. His skin was a toasted brown, like the bark of one of the lighter trees at the edge of a forest. His long hair was also brown, but much darker. He looked nothing like any faery I'd ever seen, and he was giving off a soft glow.

"Seriously? I didn't think there were male faeries. How can he be the same as you lot? In case you didn't notice, he's my size." Actually, judging by his legs, he was closer to Alric's height. Regardless, he was definitely not someone who would be related to a four-inch high faery.

He groaned at that moment and all of the faeries flew over to him. Only Leaf stood on him, but the others hovered over him. His glowing faded.

"Burnt out," Crusty said. She flew down and patted him. His glow flared briefly, and then faded again.

"Boys stupid too." Garbage flew to the far side of him and started pushing him. He didn't react at all.

"Yep, is done." A few of the faeries muttered that.

Leaf marched over to his face and peered down. "You no do. Go now." She flapped her wings as his body flared once, then vanished.

Like that damn minkie had. I rubbed my eyes.

"You all saw him, right? He was here, you said he was a boy faery, he glowed, then he disappeared?"

Garbage had been gathering her faery horde around her, but froze and tilted her head. "Yes, was here. Too much, then go poof."

At least she didn't say boom. I had so many questions that I had no idea where to start. At least, unlike the minkie, we all agreed he had been here. That was going to have to hold me until we dealt with a few other things.

Like where we were and how we got here.

I tried questioning the faeries, but got even worse answers than usual. Apparently, we were here, and I brought us here so it must be good.

At least with the vanishing boy faery and our debate of

where we were I'd regained some strength. My muscles all hurt and I had faint bruising where the injuries I'd taken in the fight that I now remembered were. And I had the start of a massive headache. Which was completely unfair since I hadn't used any magic in the fight, just whatever my body did while under the influence of dragon bane. Of course, who knew if magic was used getting us here.

I managed to stumble to my feet and use my memory of the room to slowly make my way to the stairs. When our faery boy night-light went out, so did almost all the light. A small crack from under the door was all that was left.

A thought hit me—if I had somehow transported us, where would I have gone? I'd been thinking of my friends in Beccia before the mess with the vanishing canyons started. I stubbed my toe in my enthusiasm to get to the door, but didn't care.

Pulling open the heavy door made my toe hurt worse. The dingy alley before me would have looked out of place in the meanest of areas in Beccia. And the low slung yet still managing to look horribly unstable building across from us definitely wasn't up to Beccian standards. And that was truly something I never thought I'd say.

"Girls? Think hard, do you know where we are? Where are our friends?" A feeling of panic was rising, but I squished it into a corner for the moment.

Twenty-three faeries all talking at once was almost as bad as their singing. Especially if your brain was trying to crawl out of your ears to go find a peaceful place to hide.

"Just one of you. Garbage? Where and where?"

"Here where you go. Others that way." She pulled free of the pack and pointed down the worse end of the alley. All of it wasn't nice, but toward the left was viler.

There was no way I was going to get where we were out of them. Names were vague and changeable in their view anyway, so even if they found one, it would probably be wrong. First thing then was to find my friends, let those with more functioning brains figure out what the hell happened.

The alley bent sharply as if something catastrophic impaired it from moving in a normal manner. Mostly we were facing the backs of buildings. They formed one continuous line and I could only tell there were multiple buildings because ages ago someone had painted them. The colors were faded and muddy now. The alley itself was poorly paved and covered in mud. Not only fresh mud, but old mud that had been splattered up the walls of the buildings for years and never washed off.

If I actually sent us here I must have been drinking more than Crusty.

A slight drizzle started as I rounded the corner—just what this place needed was more mud. The alley opened up to a street at that point, but it wasn't much of an improvement that I could tell. The buildings were almost as ugly from the front as they had been from behind. The road was a little better paved and rose a bit in the center to help rain and mud slide off. Of course, that meant that while the road was wide enough for two wagons to pass, when both wanted to stay in the center things got a bit close.

There weren't many people out, and those that were had heavy cloaks with hoods pulled tight over their heads. The only thing I knew for certain was that we were not in Beccia. And that wherever we were, I would never have sent us here.

After pointing the direction that I needed to go, the faeries stayed close to me, keeping low, as if the atmosphere of the place was getting to them as well.

They weren't keeping low enough though. The hooded and cloaked citizens of the town were paying attention to me as I walked down the street. Rather, to the bright bits of color flying above me.

"Girls? Where are Bunky and the gargoyle?" I slowed down my pace but didn't stop.

"They hidden. Watching others."

That was good.

"I need all of you to go find them and stay hidden."

Garbage flew down to my eye line and scowled. "No leave you. I promise."

Apparently remembering that she'd promised the elven king and queen to protect me hadn't been needed while in the canyons. I almost shook her off, then nodded.

"I need you to stay with the others and keep them out of trouble. This isn't Beccia, the people here might try to hurt you." She puffed out her chest in pride, but I cut her off before she could mention her fighting prowess. "They could hurt others while trying. I need you to stay out of sight until we're all together and we figure out what's going on." I left out where we were since she seemed to believe I did this on purpose and was proud of it.

"I'll keep Leaf with me," I said. "If I have any problem finding everyone I'll have her get help. Where are the others?"

Garbage nodded and Leaf flew over with Crusty trailing behind. "That way. Take longer two legs, but we wait. You trouble—need two." After she pointed roughly the same direction we were already headed, she and the pack zipped high into the air and vanished.

Leaving me with Leaf and Crusty.

Both seemed alert and focused, at least for them, as they hovered in front of me. I opened my cape and they both flew in and settled in a pocket. "Okay, I need you both to settle in for now. No singing, drinking, anything. You got it?"

Two cheeps were their response. I looked inside the pocket at two artfully innocent faery faces. Not reassuring, but I needed to find my friends.

A few of the locals continued to watch me, but when nothing exciting happened they went upon their way. Everyone kept their heads down and I had a feeling it was more than simply the weather.

I rounded yet another corner and came to a stop. A gallows stood before me, and one that looked permanent judging by the age of the wood and the rust from cheap nails bleeding down. It also had two males hanging from it. They had cloth sacks over their faces, but long hair extended past both. One blond and one black.

CHAPTER NINE

MY HEART FROZE. THERE WAS no way those two were Alric and Padraig. Even Garbage would have noticed them being dead. That logic didn't stop my throat from tightening or my stomach from curling into a tight ball.

"Leaf? I need you to check and make sure those aren't our friends." I was proud that my voice only shook a little.

Leaf climbed out of the pocket, with Crusty right behind. But neither of them flew over.

"Nope. Not them." She started to push Crusty back into the pocket.

"How can you be sure?" She'd barely looked at them before climbing back in.

"Smell wrong."

I was about to insist they fly over anyway when a hooded man bumped into me and grabbed my elbow.

"We've been looking for you for days, where have you been?"

I dashed away a tear before he could see it, but hearing Alric's voice when I thought I might be looking at his body was a justifiable reason for a tear or two.

"I was lying in a storage room...wait, days?" I'd been unconscious when I'd been brought in there, but it didn't feel like it had been days. I hadn't felt stiff enough to have been there for days.

"Four days, but I'd rather wait until we're someplace less

exposed before I tell you everything." He looked down and pushed back my own hood. "You *are* all right?"

I gasped at his face. He had a huge bruise covering his right cheek and a smaller one on his chin. "I'm fine. You're not though."

He laughed. "I'm fine."

As he spoke, he started us walking past the gallows and down another side alley. If possible, this one was even more ill-used than the one I'd found myself in.

Alric pushed back his hood as he studied the area, then knocked on a ragged wooden door three times.

A little orange head popped out of a knothole above the door, peered down at us, and then vanished. A series of clinks and a rustle of chains were heard and the door swung open.

It took a few moments for my eyes to adjust. With the gray lumbering clouds outside it was by no means bright, but the entrance of this building was extremely dark.

I found myself engulfed in a hug that smelled suspiciously like Covey, then led through a cloth wall. The entrance was dark, and kept so by a heavy curtain. But the inside was well lit. We were in an old stable, one that showed signs of my friends' recent habitation, but probably hadn't been used for a hundred years prior.

Not only were Padraig, Covey, Flarinen, Kelm, and Lorcan waiting there, but so were our wagons and our horses.

"Okay, so how did we get here, why wasn't I with you, why was I unconscious for the last few days, and how in the heck did our wagons get here?"

"You were unconscious? Where? How?" Covey had been holding onto me and she now spun me around looking for injuries. Leaf and Crusty took advantage of the manhandling and flew out of my pocket to join the rest of the pack in the rafters. I was pleased to see Bunky and the gargoyle up there as well.

"Not far from here, I have no idea how. But a male faery

brought me there."

Lorcan had been coming around one of the wagons, but his step picked up. "I am quite glad to see you, my dear." He gave me a tight hug. "But male faeries?"

"They is stupid. Unfinished," Garbage yelled down from the faeries' perch.

"I didn't think there was such a thing." Alric helped me remove my cloak, led me to a side table with benches and put a warm cup of tea in my hands. I hadn't realized how chilled I'd gotten outside.

"Dumb."

"Not dumb, was yummy!"

"Still undone."

"But helped."

All of the faeries decided they had to weigh in on the situation. Beyond their first comments, though, all I could hear was a bunch of high-pitched screeching. Bunky and the gargoyle lifted off their perch and came down near us. It was hard to tell, but Bunky looked annoyed.

"Girls!" They were in danger of bringing down the none-too-solid-looking roof with their noise.

Covey let loose a loud and piercing whistle. That shut them up. I wanted to ask one of them to explain the entire male faery situation, but they were too worked up. Leaf had been the most favorable about him, so once they calmed back down again, I'd separate her from the pack and see what I could learn.

"Anyway, when I woke up the girls were with me, there was an unconscious male person lying next to me."

"Not person!" Garbage yelled, but I refused to look up.

"The girls said he brought me in, but not sure from where. Oh, and he glowed. Then he stopped glowing and vanished."

"Not finished. Told you."

I never thought I'd be thinking this, but I really wanted Garbage to go get drunk somewhere. Whatever the guy was, she obviously wasn't a fan. But she was really getting annoying.

"Okay!" There was a flurry of giggling and screaming and all of the faeries flew off to a small loft at the far end of the room. I heard bottles clinking as they were dragged out of the impossibly tiny black bags the faeries all carried.

"I didn't aim that thought at you!" Although it had seemed like a good idea at the time, I was already regretting it. Not to mention the faeries shouldn't be able to pick my thoughts out of my head. Supposedly, I should have to focus on them.

"Have you eaten?" Covey's voice broke into my annoyance with the faeries. This new caring Covey was taking some getting used to.

I shot one more look at the loft with the giggling. "I don't think so. But I also don't feel like I was lying on a dirt floor for four days. So who knows what went on?"

Padraig had now also come up to hug me. Flarinen and Kelm both nodded, but didn't approach. Flarinen also had a few bruises on his face. Considering all of us had been in some serious fighting with whatever those syclarions were, bruises weren't too surprising. Except that only Alric and Flarinen had them, and elves are freakishly fast healers. I'd have to ask someone about their fight later.

"So you have no recollection at all of bringing us here?" Lorcan asked as he joined me at the table.

"The faeries said that too, that I brought us here. I have no idea how that could have happened. The dragon bane worked, eventually, and after you were all taken out by the syclarions, I defeated them. But as I was trying to bring you all to the wagons, the world faded. The next thing I knew, I was waking up beside a glowing faery boy and the girls."

"Still stupid!"

"Go back to drinking, Garbage." I yelled back. If they drank enough they'd pass out and give us a bit of rest.

"This is fascinating," Lorcan edged closer to me with a small book and pen in hand. "Did he have wings? Was he the same size as the girls? What color?"

"No wings, about as tall as Alric, and he was sort of tree colored, darker skin, but his hair was lighter brown."

"There is no precedent for male faeries. Now, granted, we discounted and distorted the tales we had of the faeries over the years. Yet I do recall some scrolls speculating on them before the Fall. Not a lot was known, as the faeries became scarce after the destruction of the Ancients, and they were far more common here than in the elves' ancient homeland before we migrated." Lorcan spoke out loud, but low enough that he appeared to be muttering to himself.

Covey perked up at that. The new softer, gentler Covey was immediately replaced by the hungry academic. "I wondered why the elves didn't overlap the Ancients more. I'd love to hear anything you know." Okay, that was a change. The old Covey would have hounded him until all of his useful information was taken and only an exhausted husk remained.

"I'm sure we'll have time on our trip. Once we figure out where we are in relation to where we need to be. I'm not sure how far we are from the Spheres." Lorcan scowled at some papers at the far end of the table. "Nor from where we started."

I was going to ask but the wonderful smell of stew hit me at that moment. I might not have believed I was out for four days, but my body felt it.

I shoveled in a few huge mouthfuls then looked up to notice everyone was watching me.

"What?" I said around my most recent mouthful.

"You're eating like someone who's been unconscious for a few days, that's all." Alric swung a leg over the bench and sat down next to me. "I was worried." His smile faded and he took my face in his hands. He would have kissed me if my mouth hadn't been full of stew. Still, it was good to see genuine concern in those amazing green eyes.

We stared at each other for a few moments until Covey gave a cough. "Hate to break this up, but Lorcan does have a point. We've no idea where we are."

That wasn't good. These were some seriously smart people. Well, and Flarinen. I wasn't sure about Kelm yet. The rest were the smartest people I knew.

And after four days they had no idea where we were? Where I supposedly dropped us. Great. I ate some more stew.

"Now, to be fair, we haven't been out much. Mostly only to look for you, but there was some pretty horrific weather when we first got here and going out was problematic." Lorcan was looking anywhere but at any of us. Not a good sign. If he'd been doing this avoidance the entire time I was gone, I was surprised that Padraig hadn't called him on it.

A closer look at his face told me that Padraig was avoiding the situation as well. I slurped the last of the stew. Maybe they were right; either this was the best stew I'd ever had, or I hadn't eaten in a few days. I pushed the empty bowl away and turned to Lorcan. "I'm not sure if you just don't want *me* to know, since supposedly the opinion seems to be that somehow I brought us here, or you two don't want any of us to know. But I can tell you have some pretty solid ideas."

I must have developed better people reading skills over the last month, both Covey and Alric looked surprised. First at my observation, then when they watched Padraig and Lorcan. Flarinen had been skulking around the edges, but his scowl showed he'd been listening.

"You two know where we are?" Alric got up from next to me. He respected Lorcan, and Padraig was one of his oldest friends, but that low voice usually meant he was seriously annoyed.

Lorcan held up his hand, both as a calming gesture and to keep Padraig from the response he was about to make. "Now, I wasn't certain until we got Taryn and the faeries back. I had some clues, based on the odd weather, and the sullenness of the populace. It's been mere rumors you know, no one has ever actually been able to confirm or deny the existence of such a place." He gave a shrug and an awkward laugh. "No one has ever made it back, you see."

Alric tipped his head back. "You mean to say you believe we are in the *actual* Null? Not just a town named Null? The neutral ground of good and evil where everyone lives in limbo, never dying, never moving on? It doesn't exist."

Padraig stepped forward. "That is the myth of the place, but I believe we can safely confirm that it is not some deathless limbo."

"I saw two men hung from those gallows and they looked pretty dead to me." I wasn't going to mention that at first I thought it was Alric and Padraig. It still made my stomach clench.

"And we saw a fight three days ago where a woman warrior was run through. They buried her," Covey said. She looked far more interested in the myths than the reality.

"I'm not saying the Null of myth exists," Lorcan said. "But I do think this might be where the travelers who fail to make it to the Spheres end up. There is some very strong magic going on."

"And they stay here? My brief walk through didn't indicate a place we'd want to stay at. How and why would I have brought us here?"

"There could be more to it," Flarinen said. "I noticed that when we first woke up here, I was ready to fight." He gave a shrug and motioned to the bruises on his face. A move Alric echoed. "But in the past few days I've felt my drive weaken. Kelm and I are doing our daily routines, but it is getting harder."

"I should have noticed that," Lorcan said. "I put it down

to my unique body situation."

"So we fell into some sort of trap, designed to keep travelers from finding the Spheres. I won the fight but we got dumped here. And there's a spell around this place to keep people complacent?" I looked around at the supplies. We'd had plenty because of our trip, but if people never left? "And how is everyone out there not starving to death?'

"More spells," Padraig said. There was more admiration on his face than I wanted to see. "The shops have the necessities to survive, yet I've never seen people bringing in supplies. Whoever created this place was a power far beyond any magic user today. They made sure no one would leave."

Covey paced and fingers flexed and relaxed. She might not have noticed the lethargy creeping in, but she was pissed about it now. "I'm not a magic user, but I know enough that we can find a way to break the spell. We need to force ourselves to stay active like Flarinen and Kelm have been. The weather was bad, but not dangerous, yet all of us stayed in here unless we were specifically out looking for Taryn or the faeries."

"All excellent points. But I think we're missing another one," Padraig said. The prior admiration for this long-lost spell caster faded. "If we fell into this trap, we have to assume our prey did as well."

CHAPTER TEN

I HAD BEEN STARTING TO PUSH away from the table, but slid back down to the bench at Padraig's words. Nivinal and Reginald, the two mages we were trying to catch. Realizing they might be here didn't make me feel as good as possibly catching them should have. In fact, the stew didn't seem quite as happy in my stomach as it had been.

"We should have thought of that days ago. We must find them and destroy them, immediately." Flarinen seemed livelier than he had been a moment ago. If we could keep him mad enough he might be able to get us out of here.

I knew I didn't feel like facing the mages down and judging by the looks on the faces around me, no one else did either. Even Flarinen's excitement slowly ebbed from his face.

"This place is even doing that to us," I said. "I don't want to find them. I want to stay here and shuffle along and do nothing. Considering the entire reason we're out here was to get those relics back from those two, not wanting to do that is a problem." I turned to Lorcan. "We have to break this spell or we'll stay here forever."

I hadn't seen or heard much from the faeries since I banished them to get drunk. "Girls? Can any of you fly?"

Half a dozen brightly colored heads popped over the loft railing to look down at us. About half had their flower petal hats on.

"Is good. Where go?" Garbage raised herself up on her

arms, flapped her wings a few times, and tumbled head over ass out of the loft. Good thing she fell near Alric and he had fast reflexes.

She waved at him then climbed over his thumb. "Nope. Was wrong. Boom."

There went the idea of using them to see if they were affected by whatever this spell was. "What about Bunky and the gargoyle? Were they with you the last four days?" They'd both flown over to the loft when the girls started their drinking party.

Padraig looked up toward the loft, but aside from the few faeries near the edge, passed out it looked like, there was nothing to be seen.

"They were, but we told them to stay in here after the first day," Covey said as she peered up as well. "There was some unsavory interest in them."

"Same with the girls when I was trying to find you. That's why I sent them to you all."

Alric nodded. "Which would have been more helpful if they had told us where you were when they got here. All they would say was you brought them here."

"How'd you know to come looking for me?"

"I've learned to fill in the gaps when they speak."

I shook my head, but nothing new rattled out. "It might be the spell speaking, but I have no other ideas."

Garbage was conscious, albeit barely, and rolled around in Alric's hand. "Sing song place, she brought us to the sing song place. Here we stay, here we wait." She briefly opened her eyes and stared intently at Alric. "You need wait back there. No leave. Stay, wait."

Crap. Every once in a while, one of the faeries spouted something that vaguely sounded like prophecy. Not that I really believed in those things, but there was too much weirdness to ignore them completely. And that sounded like a prophecy.

Alric looked down at her and nudged her with his finger. "Hey, sweetie, can you explain what you said?" His voice was soft and melodic, like one would use with a skittish horse.

Garbage pushed herself up but didn't stand. Even from where I stood I could tell she was looking serious—or rather she had on what she believed was her serious face. Then she opened her mouth and let loose a belch that would have made a pub full of miner dwarves proud.

"Dunno. What say?" Then she blinked a few times and collapsed back into the palm of his hand.

"She passed out, didn't she?" They hadn't had enough time to get that drunk. At least I wouldn't have thought they did. Of course, since they carried their ale with them in their secret magic bags, they could have been drinking the entire time they were watching me and the male faery.

Alric had time to nod. Then the wooden door behind us exploded.

Pulling back the curtain revealed it hadn't actually exploded and was standing. But something hard had slammed into it.

Alric and Flarinen both stepped forward and paused. I almost fell over when Flarinen nodded and waved Alric forward. I really needed to find out what had happened between the two of them while I was out cold.

Alric removed the chains they had locking the doors. He kept his right hand near his dagger as he peered outside.

Night had fallen far quicker than I would have thought, although with those heavy clouds from when I'd been out there before, judging the time of day would be iffy at best. There was something tacked to the door. Alric took a step further, looked up and down the alley, then grabbed the note off the door and slammed it shut. He might have added more chains and locks to the prior collection but I wasn't sure.

"Someone knows who we are, or at least what we're after," he said as he stepped back into the room. "But they don't know we have you back." He handed me the badly scribbled note. It demanded the gargoyle, the chimera, the dragon, and the manticore or they would kill the girl. The drawing was really badly done but looked enough like me that it was obvious who they were talking about.

"I don't look that bad, do I?" I handed the note to Covey then patted down my hair.

Covey's laughter died when she read the note. "They are clearly clueless when it comes to where Taryn is, so we can assume they simply knew she was missing based on our inquiries. The fact that they are aware of the relics indicates it's either our mages or someone who has been talking to them." She scowled at the note then looked to Lorcan. "Do you feel any different?"

He took a deep breath, closing his eyes as he did so. "Not at all. I really would have thought that being near my brother might cause a reaction. Since I was afraid it would be something bad, I have to admit I'm grateful to feel nothing."

"Could he have taken another body?" I asked. I had no idea how Lorcan's body got snatched in the first place, but it did seem odd that after hundreds of years as a ghostly spirit, Reginald suddenly found a way to steal his brother's body.

"He could have. I have given some thought to the how and why of his body thieving. I believe Nivinal helped him. Whereas I originally believed it was some connection between he and I as brothers that allowed him to steal my form, I now think he could have taken anyone."

That silenced the room. Reginald was not only trapped in the same tiny town we were, but could body hop?

"Now, now, I don't think it's as bad as you are thinking," Lorcan spoke to all of us, but he was watching me. "The magic they have used is not common, but there were some references to it in one of Padraig's books. At any rate, this spell takes a powerful spell caster. Even someone like Siabiane couldn't do it. He won't be hopping about—we need to figure where he has currently hopped to. As for that letter being from either of them, that's doubtful. It is far too crude. My guess is that my brother, in whatever form he is currently taking, got drunk and spoke of things he shouldn't have. There is no doubt of which one of them is in charge. I have a feeling if Nivinal knew what he was doing; Reginald might find himself turned into a gnat."

That was a little better. I was never going out of this stable if I thought that mad man was floating around in different bodies at will. I never found out if he could release at will that shadow monster he let loose to tear up the elven palace, or whether it was tied to the palace. And I didn't want to know. I had nightmares about the way that thing devoured those guards.

"Which brings us back to trying to break this spell, and avoid anyone who might be looking for us." Padraig said.

"But why would they ask for the rest of the relics if they got their information from Reginald? He has the first three," I asked. I didn't mention where the fourth one was. Flarinen and Kelm didn't know, but the rest did. Not to mention as far as we knew there was no way to get the weird sapphire manticore out of me. I rubbed my cheek where the invisible mark lingered.

"I think we need to do some investigations into this tomorrow. I'm going to suggest we also post guards in shifts inside here," Flarinen said. He was assertive, but not the pompous ass I was used to. I'd like to think he changed, but chances were it was simply part of the dampening spell that was affecting all of us.

Alric looked ready to argue, then shook his head. "The fact I was about to say we don't need to do that tells me we do. Until we break this spell, we all have to fight it."

He'd laid Garbage down on the table after she passed out, and she hadn't moved. She did now. "Fight! We fight! Kittens! Minkies! Fight!" She hadn't opened her eyes, and

I was pretty sure she was asleep, but her yells brought a few straggling cries from the faeries above us.

Lorcan jotted a comment in his book. "I think I will keep notes of what our wee friends have been saying. There's a chance we will find wisdom in their words."

I looked at the passed-out, drunk, orange faery drooling on the table and shook my head. I really hoped we didn't have to rely on her and her kin for wisdom. Ever.

They silently divided the watch. Lorcan and I were both left off the list this time, and even though I'd possibly been asleep for four days, I was too tired to argue.

Padraig had been the last watch and he was sitting near the fire reading when I got up the next morning. Judging by the smell, he was also making eggs and mushrooms.

The others were asleep, and from the snores echoing from the loft, so were the faeries. Garbage was twitching on the table so I picked her up and fit her into the small pocket on my shirt. She curled into a ball and stopped twitching.

"No visitors?" I kept my voice low and took the cup of tea Padraig offered.

"I've just started my shift, but nothing so far and none before." He closed the small spell book he'd had open.

I would have asked about it, but I recognized the symbols on the front—it was one of the Dark collection. I knew those books were important for us to figure out how to stop Reginald and Nivinal, but they disturbed the heck out of me.

He noticed my look. "Nothing on breaking this spell, not yet anyway. I have a feeling the solution might be tied to the myth of Null itself. All we can do for now is force ourselves to be active."

Garbage twitched in my pocket, and the familiar feeling of feet kicking made me reach in and pull her out.

She seemed groggier than usual after drinking herself into a stupor; usually the faeries woke up completely sober.

Right now she seemed like she had a hangover.

"Garbage? How are you feeling?"

"No boom. Bad." Her eyes started to slip closed, then flew open. "Is bad!" She flew out of my hand and up to the loft. I couldn't see what she was doing, but she made enough noise to wake the two dead men hanging from the gallows down the road.

"Up, up, up! No sleep. Bad!"

The rest of the faeries must not have responded fast enough because soon a rainbow of half-awake faeries were being pushed out of the loft.

Some woke up enough to fly before they hit the ground, others not so much. But they shook themselves off regardless. All were groggy and hung over like Garbage.

"No sleep!" Garbage soon had all of the faeries, plus Bunky and the gargoyle, who flew down of their own power, out of the loft and hanging around the wagons.

I looked closer at the two constructs; Bunky looked annoyed, the gargoyle looked confused. Neither looked groggy. I nudged Padraig and pointed to them.

"You're right, the faeries are obviously affected, but those two aren't." He went over and petted both of them. "Makes sense, given their existence. I would have hoped the faeries would be out of range of this spell as well."

"So who was attacking the faeries? And couldn't they have done it quieter?" Covey walked over to us while rubbing her eyes. Garbage was rattling every faery to get them to stay awake. And she wasn't being quiet about it.

"They realized they are affected by the spell, like us, and Garbage is not happy." Padraig finished cooking his pile of breakfast and slid some onto a plate for me, then a second one for Covey.

"Sorry they woke you," I said a moment before I started eating. Yup, whatever had happened, I was starving. Either that or Padraig wasted some magic making these the best eggs ever.

"But why now? Why not while they were guarding you?" Covey poured some tea and sat down to eat. She looked almost as groggy as the faeries, but she obviously was going to stay awake.

That was a good question. If we'd been here for four days, the girls should have been lethargic when I woke up.

"They seemed normal when they arrived here. I assume they were that way when they were with you?" Padraig kept his voice low, all three of us did. But Garbage was still yelling at her faery pack. That it was all in native faery didn't cut down on the noise or annoyance. I was surprised the others were asleep.

"As normal as they ever are. But I was unconscious for most of the time. Maybe they'd been sleeping for most of it?"

Garbage pulled away from the rest of the faeries, hovered in front of my face, then dropped to the table. I was faster than she was and managed to get my plate away from her feet before she landed.

"Is you. No spell, you sleep."

Leaf had been trying to shake off her grogginess but flew over as well. "Was *him*."

"No him! Him stupid." Garbage put her hands on her hips and squared off against Leaf. Leaf mimicked her and stepped forward.

"Need him. He stop this."

Then the two degenerated into a native faery yelling match. I had no idea what they were saying, but it did pull the rest of the faeries over to watch. They all looked far more awake and aware than they had a second ago. I took my tea and plate to the end of the table.

Finally, they stopped yelling, but not before the rest of our people stumbled out of their bedrolls.

"Fine. Is both." Garbage stepped back from Leaf.

"You're saying you weren't affected by the spell at first, because of Taryn and the male faery? Even though both were unconscious?" Alric came forward and took some tea but waved off the food.

I wasn't sure how much Alric had heard since he came out in mid yelling match, but he'd heard enough.

"Yes," Garbage said sullenly.

"Did it have to do with the way he was glowing?" As far as I knew none of my faeries could do that, but I wasn't sure what purpose it would have really served if both he and I were unconscious. It had to have been an automatic reaction from him against something.

"No," Garbage said, then looked over to Leaf. "Yes. Maybe. They not finished."

"You've said that before, but what does it mean?" Lorcan didn't look as groggy as the rest of us, but he did appear to be fighting it.

"Boys here long time. Then boom. They vanish. Now trying come back," Leaf finally answered him when Garbage folded her arms and stayed silent.

"They no be here. Not finished."

I could tell Lorcan was going to try to get them to elaborate, but Garbage was furious. This wasn't the time to question her. I shook my head.

"Girls, why don't you see what you can find out about this town. But don't be seen. I know you can do that." When they wanted to at any rate. "You're right, there is something bad here and I need you to help us."

After being, in her mind anyway, shown up by Leaf, Garbage brightened at being needed. Maybe getting them out and about on a mission would help get answers later.

"We do!" She motioned to the pack, and then they all flew out the smoke hole. Bunky looked ready to follow.

"Not you two, please. We need some protection here too."

He beamed. Well, as much as a thousand-plus-year-old metallic construct could beam. Then he and the gargoyle flew to the rafters above us.

"What kind of spell could hit those faeries?" I looked to my friends. My exceptionally bright friends. That all four of them stared back at me blankly wasn't reassuring.

CHAPTER ELEVEN

LORCAN CLIMBED OUT OF WHATEVER mental hole they'd all fallen into first. "Actually, the fact that they are affected could have great bearing on the type of spell being used."

He sat down and waved Padraig back to the table. "I think if we concentrated on an old balance spell, one that wouldn't need upkeep as long as it stayed in balance, and one that can impact extremely diverse and high operating metabolisms equally, we might be able to narrow things down."

Padraig had been about to sit, then, instead, went to the wagon. "We're going to need all of our books then."

Alric joined him in hauling out every single spell book they had. Lorcan must have brought a lot on his own, because there were way more than I'd seen before.

"Do you want help?" Covey was almost drooling as she lingered around the books. I knew there were some magic books that she wouldn't be able to read, definitely any of the Dark ones. But I recognized some of them more as historical works. Spells would be in them, but they would also have a lot more extraneous information besides.

"By all means, another set of gifted eyes is always welcome," Lorcan said as he deftly shifted some of the more academic works her way.

"That leaves us," Flarinen said.

He and Kelm had stayed off to the sides during the great

faery screech-fest. But they looked ready for something—anything—at this point. Knowing that you'd been slowly squished into inaction due to a spell would piss off anyone. Being a high-ranking elven knight made it more of a personal insult.

"I think the four of us need to get out into town and see what is going on," Alric said. "Looking back over the past few days, we really saw nothing. This spell hit us faster than we thought."

"Agreed." Lorcan looked up from his first book. "We know Reginald was here, and he and Nivinal could be trapped like us. We need to know for sure. If they escaped, we might be able to use the same way."

"But someone should stay and guard." Flarinen gave a pointed glance at Alric and me. Without waiting for a response, he went to put on his armor, then shook his head and put his padded gambeson on under a tunic and cloak instead. He did buckle his sword on. Probably a good idea, a pair of fully armored knights would be extremely noticeable.

"I think all four of you should go," Padraig said. He held up his hand before Flarinen could complain. "You shouldn't go together, two groups would be best. As for protection, I think myself, Covey, Lorcan, and our two friends up there are more than enough to keep things safe." He held his hand out, then frowned at it, narrowed his eyes, and held it out again. His sword appeared, but almost as reluctantly as mine usually did.

Alric had been watching, and then did the same move, with the same results. His sword actually took three tries to appear.

"Is the spell causing that?" Both of their swords looked solid as they put them in their sheaths. But neither elf looked happy.

"Nothing can break a spirit sword unless the owner gives it up voluntarily." Lorcan looked as concerned as Padraig and Alric did. "But something is definitely interfering."

I went back and grabbed a pair of daggers from the wagon. If those two had trouble calling their well-behaved swords, there was no way I was risking calling my spastic one. Best case would be it not showing up in the middle of a fight. There were plenty of cases that I could think of that were worse than that.

"Kelm and I will take the north end of town. We'll circle the outskirts, then come back through the center." Flarinen refrained from any smug comments about failing magic swords. Probably due to the fact that the spirit swords were considered sacred, in a way, by the elves. But the comments were there in his eyes.

"Agreed," Alric said. "Taryn and I can work our way through the south. There are more bars down there and I know you don't feel at home with those class of people." Alric added a few extra daggers and knives. He was always well armed, but he seemed to be piling it on more this time. He was disturbed by the behavior of his sword.

With a nod to the others and a wave to Bunky and the gargoyle who watched from the rafters, we headed out.

Flarinen and Kelm quickly distanced themselves from us, which was fine by me. Even the new and mostly improved Flarinen was a pain in the ass.

"I hate to say it, but for once I'm glad I can't count on my sword," I said as we walked down the opposite way of the alley. This wasn't the direction I'd come in from yesterday, but you couldn't tell any difference in the appearance.

"It is disturbing, but I trust Padraig to figure it out, along with everything else. Actually, I haven't seen Padraig crack a book in two days—that should have let me know something was wrong." He shook his head then stopped as something dropped at his feet.

"I think your friend found you." He stepped back and gestured at the ground.

My sword was there, in its scabbard even. I wasn't sure if

I wanted to pick it up. On a good day it came and went as it pleased. Any day here was not a good day and the spell covering the place was obviously messing with things. I briefly wondered what it would do if I stepped over it.

I shook my head and picked it up, buckling the belt around my waist. With my luck the damn thing would keep plopping in front of me until I tripped over it and broke my neck. "You'd better behave," I said to the impressive looking sword I now wore. "Seriously, popping out once during a fight will get you left with a bunch of drunk faeries armed with tar and feathers." I wasn't certain, but I thought I felt the sword shake. As it should.

I wasn't completely clear as to how spirit swords came about. They supposedly latched on to strong pure elven souls and protected them during their lives. Mine had popped up during a fight and more or less hung around. Alric and Padraig said it was simply because I hadn't trained with it since I was young like both of them. I personally thought I ended up with some fancy trickster sword that was the joke of the spirit sword collective.

Maybe I'd hit on something with the faery threat. I'd have to make sure the faeries had access to at least a little bit of tar and a feather or two next time they were around it. The sword was gorgeous, with detailed markings that even impressed the elves. Therefore, assuming it might be vain enough not to want a bunch of tiny messy drunks crawling on it was a safe bet. Of course, up until a year ago thinking about a sword caring whether it got dirty or not would have had me heading for the Shimmering Dewdrop and a few dozen pints.

"Are you done threatening your sword?" Alric had a half smirk. He was already slipping into the fighter/thief part of his persona, but he obviously thought my reaction to the capricious sword was amusing.

"I think it and I have a better understanding now, so yes." I patted my sword and followed him down the alley.

It dropped us out at a much busier section of town than where I'd come from. The place looked horrific. Run-down storefronts and bars co-mingled with an odd magic wares shop and a land surveyor. That small shop was packed. I peered around the crowd to see the front. The dirty flimsy-looking window was almost covered in signs of all sizes advertising maps to get out of Null. Myth or not, Lorcan was right about where we were.

It was odd to watch the people churning around the window front. The door wasn't open, and a crude wooden sign said 'closed'. But they all pushed forward to see the signs. The weird part was they didn't seem to be motivated. It was as if some small part of their brain knew what was needed and was forcing them to be there—but they weren't quite sure what to do about it.

I shivered and stepped back. There was no way I was going to let myself or my friends become like that. My hand went to my sword.

"Now that was interesting," Alric said. But he looked at me, not the odd crowd behind us. "The look on your face as you turned was of a true warrior. And I think your sword rattled again."

"We can't become like them," I said with more force than I'd intended. The people behind me were more terrifying than the syclarions I'd fought a few days ago.

"I'll make sure we don't." He grinned as he said it, then his face dropped and a scowl appeared. I knew I saw through his and Padraig's glamours, but if I didn't I would have sworn he slipped one on. The laughing, handsome elf of the moment before vanished and a surly looking person of uncertain heritage now walked alongside me.

"That's really disturbing when you do that. Rather, that you can do that." I walked around a drunk blocking our path. At least I hoped it was a drunk, I couldn't tell if he was breathing or not and wasn't going to check.

"Years of training. I can't always use magic." His voice

was his, but rougher and gravellier. Far closer to that of his persona of Carlon than himself.

"So you're being Carlon right now? No glamour?" I had pretty much hated Carlon the moment he kidnapped me, then really hated him when I found out it had been Alric in one of his personas the entire time that I was worried he'd gone missing.

He shrugged. "Some, but not enough to give me away if the magic breaks. And I'm only tapping into some of Carlon's attributes. I might need to be more vicious than he was."

"These personalities are like different people to you, aren't they?" My friend Harlan often went in disguise, or so he called it. But it was always still Harlan. Alric had been roaming the outside world for years, where he couldn't let anyone know he was an elf. He'd gotten good at it.

He was making for the largest pub on the street. While I probably would have picked the smaller one right near us, my reasoning would have been that I could really use an ale right now. Alric was trying to figure out what was going on and how we could get out of here. His reason won.

The doors were made out of thin wood that didn't completely reach the top or the bottom and did nothing to keep out the cold. By the way they were hung I'd guess they weren't originally here when the pub was built.

It was early in the morning, so I was surprised that the place was open and there were so many folks already here. Looking around I realized that they probably never closed, at least not with the doors we walked through. The people here weren't starting their day drinking, they just hadn't finished their night.

A long bar faced the entrance and ran most of the length of the place but the majority of the still-drunks were at tables. No groups, not even a pair, only fifteen solitary drunks of a number of races and both genders.

The bar was bigger than any in Beccia, but thanks to the worn, dingy, wood floors, walls, and ceilings, and the fact that said ceiling appeared ready to collapse on the patrons at any time, it managed to look small and unwelcoming. That a full-blooded male dwoller was behind the bar didn't help at all. Dwollers were mostly insane; they fed on the blood of others and could almost function in society when well fed and under control of someone more powerful than they. Good or bad, this one seemed well fed.

Not a place I would ever have chosen to drink in.

Alric slunk up to the bar and the dwoller behind it. I followed along as I really wasn't about to go try and talk to any of the people at the tables. The unspoken word is that if you are by yourself, and you've been drinking all night long, you deserve to be left alone.

"Black ale for both," he spoke so low I barely heard him and I was right next to him. The dwoller was a few feet away, but with the hyper hearing common to most of their people, he obviously heard. With a nod, he pulled two glasses to the tap.

He said and did nothing untoward as he slid one in front of Alric, but paused and gave me a sickly grin as he put mine down closer to me than it needed to be. "She yours?" Dwollers had elongated canines that made their sss's sound like a bucket of snakes.

I fought the shiver crawling up my arms and tried to glare him down.

"Mine. For now. You want to buy her?" Alric took a long drink and wiped the foam away with his cuff. "I get tired of redheads so easily."

Redhead? Crap, what did he do? I could see myself in the bar mirror—more or less—but enough to see I looked like me. But if he glamoured me I wouldn't see it.

"She's a lively one then?" The dwoller reached out to touch my face, but I had a dagger at his wrist before he got within an inch of it.

"Very." I kept my voice steady but did my best to channel Covey. I couldn't play change the persona like Alric, but I would be damned if anyone saw me as a target here.

A look of surprise flashed across the dwoller's face, but then he resumed his grin and gave a nod. With an equal nod to Alric he went to the far end of the bar.

I put away my dagger and moved closer to Alric. "What do I look like? And why the hell didn't you tell me?"

He didn't answer, but took another long, slow drink. I was about to pour mine over his head when he finally turned to me.

"Just a few modifications. You have long red hair, a scar on your right cheek, a kind of nasty looking one if I say so myself. And are built like a farm hand. I didn't tell you because I wasn't sure it would hold with the way magic seems to be fluctuating around here." He shrugged. "But it did."

I pointed a finger at him, but instead of yelling at him I took a drink of my own ale, then a second one. The tension of the past day shook itself free. "Okay, but next time, warn me. Carlon was always such a bastard."

"But he comes in handy," Alric finished his ale, then leaned against the bar with his back to it and studied the room. Quickly at first, then slower.

Anyone looking at him would have thought he was simply a scraggly guy watching the door, most likely for someone he pissed off. But I knew him better. Well enough to realize he'd seen someone he wanted to talk to. If my guess was right, the person was directly to Alric's right. A young man with gray hair. Some breeds had gray hair naturally, not a part of age. But this didn't appear natural. And unlike the rest of the bunch, he appeared sober even as he was lying on his table trying to look drunk.

"So, what's with your new friend?" I held my glass of ale to my lips and kept my voice low.

"He's recently here, but came through with someone

and is trying to find them. I think whoever he came with might be helpful to us."

That was less than informative. "How can you tell?" I didn't clarify what part I was asking about, I didn't see anything Alric did. I was beginning to feel ridiculous holding the glass, so I took a drink then sat it behind me on the bar.

"His hands have unique calluses, ones from mining equipment. He's too young, regardless of that ridiculous hair, to be the lead miner, so he was working with someone, probably a secret mine, and they ended up here in Null. His master went to find something and left him to wait." Alric flagged down the dwoller and ordered a lighter ale and a plate of stew and bread. The dwoller nodded when Alric said to bring the food to our new friend when it was ready. "And in spite of him trying to look like he's been here all night like these others, he hasn't. Let's go talk to him, shall we?"

Without waiting for my response, he pushed off from the bar stool he was leaning against, took the new ale, and walked over to our guy. I finished my own ale before I got up and followed.

"Hey there, haven't seen you around. New?" Alric flipped the chair across from the boy around, slid into it and put the light ale on the table. "First one is on me."

The guy perked up at Alric, his words, and the ale shoved in his face, but he wasn't as young as he looked. Rather he was younger than he was trying to look but older than I'd expected.

"I've been drinking all night, I don't need another one." He pushed the glass back, but not far. He was trying to do what Alric did, change his voice. But he was as bad at that as he was at lying.

"Look, kid, I know people, it's my job. You're young, no money, no food, no drink. I take care of those things; you answer my questions, and those of my partner, yes?" As he spoke the dwoller came out from behind the bar carrying a greasy plate. Not fancy, but the meat and veg looked reasonably cooked and could be identified. Two aspects I always looked for in food.

The guy had fought taking the ale, but he lost against the food. As soon as the dweller walked away, our new friend shoved food in his face so fast I thought he would choke. With a nod to Alric he also downed his ale.

"Thanks," he said out of the side of his mouth. "We did just get here. Some of our stuff came but not our money. Or it was taken when we were out."

"How long ago did you come here?"

"Woke up yesterday, think I was only out for a day. My master was with me. He got real mad when he figured our stuff was gone, and said he knew who did it. Which would be weird because I don't even know where we are or how we got here. But Mackil seemed to know exactly how to get here and what happened. It was like he planned for us to get taken." He managed to get all of that out and still finish half of his food and ale.

Alric had been watching him, but he turned to me with a scowl. The same one I was sure I had once the guy's words settled in. If no one could get out, then how would this Mackil know how to get in, be trying to get in, and why would he want to, and how would he know that someone took their belongings and they didn't come through with them?

CHAPTER TWELVE

"HOW DID YOU—" ALRIC'S INTERROGATION was cut off as the two flimsy doors slammed open. Actually, the one on the right flew half-way across the bar.

"We've been cut off, boy!" The voice that came through the now gaping doorway sounded like a huge man, I'd guess someone Foxy's size by the reverberations alone.

I was not ready for a four-foot-high dwarf who'd clearly been living on the wrong side of a bar table for a few years.

He was sober right now, and his short white blond hair was almost aquiver with how sober and pissed off he was.

Few dwarves lived in Beccia. I think we were too low-brow for them and they were insulted as a race about all of the restrictions about digging. Dwarves taught their young to mine pretty much as soon as they could crawl, and they didn't take to being told where, when, and how they could dig. Not to mention the idea of having a patron made them choke. Mostly we'd see them march through town once a year or so as they moved from summer to winter digs. Beccia was in-between the two mountain ranges, but not close enough to be more than a walk through.

This one never would have gotten past all of the bars in Beccia long enough to have gotten pissed off about the digging situation.

Unlike most of his kind, he wasn't wide. He was stocky, but he was practically waif-like compared to the troops that marched through town. Most likely it was due to hard times combined with excessive drinking. The serious drunks often forgot to eat.

He didn't acknowledge Alric or me, but whipped out a chair and slammed himself down next to the man we'd fed. "I'm Mackil. Two more of whatever he had," he said then hooked a thumb at us and smiled when he got a good look at Alric. "They're paying."

Alric didn't look fazed in the least—once his brief annoyance at being interrupted vanished at any rate. I swore I saw a smile crack his practiced scowl.

"*Mackil*? Really? That's what you're calling yourself now?" He shook his head. "By the way, this is my...partner, Glanis. Don't piss her off; she's not as warm and fuzzy as I am."

Glanis? I supposed he could have come up with a worse name. I did like the 'don't mess with me' part. I patted my sword to reinforce the image. And said a thank you under my breath to it for being here. As for them knowing each other, or rather the dwarf knowing one of Alric's personas, I wasn't sure how I felt.

"It's close enough to the family name so I can remember it when I'm in jail and the bastards are demanding something to call me by." He nodded to the silent guy we'd fed. "That's Rue. He's a breed but a good worker."

I looked closer at Rue. It wasn't polite, but I seriously doubted that was even a concept in Null.

Mackil caught me looking. "Yup, human/dwarf. Too tall and gangly for one of us, but I took him in as my apprentice anyway." He turned away from both Rue and I and focused back on Alric.

"What are you doing here, Carlon? You working a job too?"

Alric shrugged. "Maybe. If so I can't be talking of it. And you?"

"Oh, I'll talk about it all right. I got robbed. Was a simple job, pick up some items, get picked up and brought here, get paid, and get sent back. The bastards robbed me and have gone into hiding."

I looked to Rue, but he shrugged and gave a small nod.

"What kind of idiot deliberately sets himself up to come to Null?" Alric had ordered more ale, but I noticed he didn't touch his—I did the same.

"You're here, ain't ya? Either you came on purpose, same as me, or ya got caught." The food was put down on the table, both servings in front of Mackil, and he managed to fling it around enough to get some in his mouth.

"I had a sure-fire way out—they gave me a blood swearing."

"You got a blood swearing from someone in here?" I had to jump in. I ignored the glare from Alric. I'd had enough magic training to knowing what a blood swearing was. A spell contract enforced by a blood draw. Nasty things.

"Naw. They wasn't in Null. This was a spell contract." He rolled up one sleeve and showed off his tattoo. A huge red X covered the width of his forearm and a signature, also in red, was scribbled underneath. I couldn't be sure but it looked like it began with R. "They was taking precautions if they got pulled in while heading for the Spheres. The spell warned me a day ago, so I got the stuff they ordered, and Rue and I went to the spot they said."

"The Robani desert?"

"That's where they got snagged, and by your voice, so did you." He patted his arm. "This little baby guaranteed wherever I was, me and anything I was hanging onto would be brought here."

I wanted to ask what they'd made him bring, but didn't want to mess up Alric's game. I'd figure out how we were going to play this when we were back in the stable.

"What did they take?"

"Damn bastards. They took their own box, couldn't use it anyway, was locked in serious spells. That's what happened to Rue's hair—tried to open it and it spelled him.

But they also took my money and my way out. I've been here before, and gotten out every time."

Alric leaned forward, close enough to bite Mackil if he wanted. And right now he looked to be growling. "How in the seven hells of the Navirain province have you gotten out of here? Look around, no one gets out of here unless it's going in the ground."

Mackil snorted and finished his first ale. The bar keep had taken him at his word and given him two of everything we gave Rue. The first plate of food was gone as well.

"Yeah, forgot you'd been missing for a while. There's been some changes out past that town you hung out in, Beccia. A compound with some serious magic shit." He drained half of the second glass then scratched his side for almost a full minute. "Thing is, magic everywhere is becoming stronger. I got paid good hard coin to test a system to get people past magic barricades. The gent behind it said he knew of one that was foolproof-no way out, but gave me enough gold that even if it failed pulling me back, I'd be set for life. Stuck here, yes. But rich is rich. Had to go way out in those damn canyons, got jumped by some syclarions, they took me out and I woke up here." He shook his head. "Got pulled back a few hours later."

Alric rocked back in his seat. "That's not the same as knowing how to get out of here. And where are your magic using friends now?"

I felt the ale rumble around in my stomach. I should have known we wouldn't find a way out that quick.

Mackil snorted again and almost choked on his food. "I'm not misspeaking, you mis-guided son of a two-headed goat. I got sent back three more times, this is over a number of days, mind you, last month. They was checking their ranges, and more than one mage wanted to play. The last time the bastards didn't pull me back. So I found my own way." He shrugged and motioned for the dweller to bring him more ale. As an afterthought he pointed to Rue.

"They'll be buying one more for each of us."

I expected Alric to shake him off. We did need help, but this scum wasn't it. Instead, he nodded to the barkeep.

"So, with my secret way, I made it back. There must be a time veil in there somewhere—time slips around looser than it should. Being as I'd stolen from them mages, including the way to get back, I couldn't go back to working for them. Luckily, Reggie came along."

At least now it was clear why the mages near Beccia didn't bring him back. They knew he robbed them and felt it was safer to leave him stuck. They obviously didn't know that he'd taken the way out of Null. His value had gone up for us by a lot. Hearing him mention Beccia wasn't good, but hopefully when he said outside of it, he meant far outside.

Alric sat back and studied Mackil with a Carlon look. In other words he was scowling so much he was making my face ache.

"What was the name of the main mage?" I really didn't want to know and hadn't planned to ask—it sort of came out. Either it was a name that would make me sick to my stomach or it was someone I didn't know. I had no idea if the mayor of Kenithworth was a mage or not, but I did know he was interested in Beccia.

"Some dwoller freak, Cirocco. Seemed to be the man behind things. Had some little weasel working for him, Grimwold. He was the one who recruited me. I think they were actually looking for Carlon here."

The mayor I'd been expecting, I wasn't too surprised about Reginald being involved, although he and Nivinal shouldn't have passed anywhere near Beccia.

But Cirocco? He was one of the crimelord wizards of Beccia and had been involved with some nasty business when I first met Alric. Actually, he had been part of why I met Alric—they'd put a bounty on him and I'd been forced to bounty hunt to make ends meet.

If they were looking for Alric, they wanted *him* and not Carlon. Considering Grimwold had last been seen on the run in Kenithworth and Cirocco had been in jail, this wasn't a good development.

A movement near the busted doorway caught my attention. Covey strode in growling at anyone who looked her way. While we'd been providing food and drink for Mackil and Rue, the pub had added a good dozen patrons. Like the over-nighters these were all solo drinkers, but unlike the original group, they were far livelier.

They had enough wits about them to know to look away when a pissed-off trellian entered a bar.

"Damn it, where have you been?" She paused to nod to Mackil and Rue, then glared back at Alric and I. "You've been gone for four hours." She pulled back and looked at me, then shook her head and shot a second glare at Alric. She wasn't a fan of magical glamours, and she knew where mine had come from.

Alric nodded to Mackil. "I'll find you later; we have a deal to discuss." He tossed a few coins to the dwoller and we moved away.

"We can't have been here four hours. It's barely been one."

Covey took ahold of both of us and pulled us out the busted door. I wouldn't have called things sunny, but they were brighter than before. A lot brighter. Damn.

"So the time veils aren't anchored," Alric said, but he was mostly muttering to himself. "And they aren't just outside of town. This could making getting out a lot harder."

I'd never heard of a time veil, but seeing this loss in time we had, and the way it was used, it was pretty obvious. What type of place had random time lapses wandering around messing people up?

"Flarinen and Kelm got captured." Covey was to the point. She also didn't let go of either of our arms as she pulled us through the street.

"Captured? I thought the entire point of this place was that no one had the energy to do anything? And just so you know, we had no idea we were in there that long." I felt like I had to defend myself on that score. Covey wasn't a fan of pubs or drinking.

"Padraig and Lorcan are narrowing that down. It appears to be more of a lethargy spell, then after it has established itself, it changes so the victim does not want to leave." She finally decided we were moving along fast enough as she dropped our arms. "Flarinen found a group that had gotten past that and managed to piss them off."

That wasn't too surprising.

We walked past the alley for the stable and past most of the buildings on this end. This area was mostly ramshackle and abandoned houses. At one time Null had claimed a much larger population.

About half of the houses had either no one living in them or no one who wanted to be noticed living in them. This entire town made Beccia look like the capital of the kingdom.

Padraig was standing behind one of the buildings. He had his hood up but turned to give us a nod. His eyes widened slightly when he saw me, but he smiled. No one seemed shocked about Alric's changes to me—except me.

"Any change?" Covey asked as she pulled up her hood as well.

I pulled mine up to join in. Alric had his up the moment we'd left the pub. Apparently hoods were a Null thing. They did fit with the atmosphere.

"Nothing." Padraig went back to watching the house across the way—a collection of houses, really. They might have been single houses put closely together when they were first built, but over the years or decades someone had cobbled them together into a massive and ugly fortress.

"And we received a note," he said and held a piece of battered and abused paper over his shoulder.

I took it, as Alric was busy checking out the building. Knowing him, he'd probably already figured out thirty places he could break in.

Crude writing, but the meaning was clear. They had our warriors and they would be slaughtered if we didn't give them the artifacts.

CHAPTER THIRTEEN

"WE KNOW THEY'RE IN THERE?" Alric studied the building and his hand twitched toward his sword.

"Yes, unfortunately. Covey and I have been here for about two hours now. We left Lorcan guarding the stable and he was to send you on to us when you checked in." He glanced at both of us. "When you didn't show up, Covey went to find you. I've seen Flarinen twice and Kelm once. They move them between the rooms. Both look battered but were walking on their own."

"Any sign of our mage friends?" Not that it would help really, we had no idea whose body Reginald was in, and Nivinal was a master of disguise. I looked at the crude note again. There was no way those two ego-maniacs would be involved with people this dumb.

He shook his head. "Could have been, but I seriously doubt it. Besides, they have the artifacts already. No reason to grab our people even if they knew we were here. They'd be more likely to kill any of us they caught."

Covey threw back her cloak and I noticed she had her sword. I wasn't used to her being armed. She could be a far more dangerous weapon on her own if she allowed herself to go berserk. But I wasn't going to suggest it.

"I'll get them," Alric said. He started to slip away, but Padraig blocked him.

"You're not on your own now. We need to work together

on this."

"I can do it." His voice sounded more like Carlon than Alric.

Padraig stepped closer. "You haven't even asked how many guards there are or the locations of our people."

Alric started to shove him away but stepped back instead. "I'm sorry, you're right. This place is getting to me."

"And you're tapping in a little too well to your Carlon persona." I pushed back his hood. His jaw had been locked, but slowly relaxed.

He let out a breath. "Like I said, it's getting to me." He nodded to Padraig. "I'm assuming you have a plan?"

He gave a sideways grin. "I figured *you* would. There are fifteen guards I've seen and probably two or three more that I haven't. Flarinen caused more trouble, so they have him in that battered room on the third floor, five guards inside, and one making the rounds who should be passing in sight within a few minutes. Kelm was moved down to that room with the window facing us." He pointed out the areas and Alric watched them for a few moments. The guard made his round before vanishing behind the side of the building.

I shook my head. "So they told us where to come to get our people? Didn't they think we might try to fight to get them out?"

"They didn't tell us to come here. Lorcan was able to spell the paper to find them; but they don't know we're here. The drop point is a mile or so out of town."

"I have a plan," Alric said and nodded to Padraig. "For all of us. Padraig, I know you can fight, but you're also our strongest magic user and we'll need someone to stay back. I think we agree that using magic openly wouldn't be the best idea just in case the mages haven't figured out we're in town yet, but it might be our last hope if things go sideways. The three of us will go in, Taryn will distract as many of our guards as possible, Covey grabs Kelm, and

I grab Flarinen."

That was way too simple of a plan for someone sneaky like Alric. But we didn't have a lot of options.

One problem. "How am I going to distract them?"

Alric's grin was all him and kind of scary. "Like this."

I felt nothing, but Covey and Padraig both gasped. I was terrified that I was dressed like a dancing girl, or worse. The inability to be affected by almost all glamours meant I couldn't see it without help.

"Do I want to know what I look like?"

Padraig fished into his cloak, pulled out a scrying mirror the size of his hand, and muttered a spell over it. I reached for it, but he held it up. "It's better to see the full impact."

"What did you do?" I realized I sounded like Garbage and that matched the way I felt. I looked like me, sort of.

I was wearing skimpy armor, not anything any self-respecting knight would wear in a fight. It was designed for sex appeal, not protection. My sword was unglamoured but fit right in with the rest of the garish ensemble. I also had four familiar relics connected to the armor in chains around me.

"Seriously?" I wasn't sure which pissed me off more. Probably the armor but if the sex appeal didn't get their attention, the relics would.

"Now, hear me out, all of you." Alric raised his hand but kept his voice low. "There are rumors going around about the relics, there have been for years and there are more now. Before our unplanned trip to the elven enclave, I'd planned to go back to Beccia and track some of them down. One of the rumors is of a guardian deity from beyond our world." He turned me slightly away from the others. "Notice how her skin shimmers? Otherworldly, yes?"

Padraig laughed but turned his eyes back to the house. "You're creating a myth to cover whatever happens with those relics down the line. And Taryn is at the center."

Covey shook her head and patted my shoulder. "Better you than me. But you do look…interesting."

"Taryn isn't really the center, but she'll be the figurehead for now. When we get back to civilization we can create the rest of the myth. Right now, this will work. Taryn walks slowly into their camp, taunting the guards. I've placed a low-level shield on her so they can't hurt her. It won't last long, but it should work for this. Then Covey and I get the knights back."

"And I use a spell to disguise it all after it's done." Padraig shook his head. "I know, no obvious magic, but we now have a cover for it. When you get out, Taryn will wave her hand, and a small concussion spell will take them down. We're building a myth, might as well make it good."

I bit my tongue before saying that I could do the spell. Pretty much finesse wasn't my strong point with spells and now that I knew what Alric was up to, I agreed this needed a lighter hand.

I was still annoyed about the skimpy outfit though.

A few more final touches to my persona, and to give time for Covey and Alric to go around the long way, and I started slowly walking out. The relics were all chained to my person, so I had nothing in my hands. It felt like some all-powerful and sexy deity really should have something to wave about, so I took out my sword.

"Who dares call me forth?" Okay, Alric thought that looking like I did would be enough, but if they wanted a deity of some sort, I would give them one. "I have been summoned."

That did it. The guards hadn't noticed me, to be honest not many were in the front, and the ones that were had been playing some sort of card game on top of a barrel.

My yelling got their attention though.

There were eight that I saw, which meant too many were still unseen.

"What are you doing here? Your people are at the drop

point." A burly minotaur shoved his way forward. His size was impressive until I realized how much larger his gut was and that his mismatched armor only covered part of his torso.

I wasn't a huge fan of minotaurs, mostly a war-like and often dim race. But if he was their leader then he was who I'd deal with.

"I know where the protectors are hidden; you can't hide them from the guardian." I figured this was a new myth and I could add to it as needed.

By the time I finished speaking, the first two guards were upon me. The minotaur had pushed his way forward, but let his people do the fighting.

The first person to reach me was a tall woman, almost as broad as the minotaur. She swung, but her eyes were on the relics, so her blow wasn't as good as it should've been. Alric said he had a shield on me, but that blade was coming in regardless.

I deflected the blade and swung around to strike a second guard coming up from the back. Both strikes were stopped by my sword, but if Alric's shield had worked, I wouldn't have had to fight back. I was glad I had some defensive sword training.

Then I realized that all of the attackers were slowing down. I had more than enough time to strike back at five of them before the rest got much closer. Handy, if that's what Alric's spell was supposed to do. It would definitely help build the myth. Still disconcerting, since I was going to be surrounded by fifteen to twenty fighters eventually and there was no shield. Slow was good, but not getting through at all was better.

I drew my dagger and worked on keeping as many of them away as possible. The minotaur had a huge two-handed sword, but was still holding back and didn't seemed concerned about helping his crew.

Not that I blamed him. I wouldn't take someone who

looked like me seriously either. Especially at fifteen to one odds. I really hoped Covey and Alric got out soon with our people. I heard fighting and yelling in the house, and two of my attackers paused to look back at their leader. He nodded and they ran back, still in slow time. I noticed their speed picked up the further they got away from me.

Except then two of the remaining attackers, the woman and a short, one-eyed trellian, both moved in faster than before. Alric's spell was losing ground and I hadn't seen a signal of any sort that Flarinen and Kelm had been freed.

I swung around and barely ducked in time to save my head. That was it. The yelling from the house was continuing, so obviously my friends were fighting. Alric's slow-down spell was failing quickly and I was about to face a dozen trained fighters in normal time.

I gave a final charge forward, going for the woman as the strongest aggressor, and trying to get all of them to fall back. Alric and Padraig would probably be pissed at what I was about to do, but I was out of options. I was not going to be killed wearing this horrible armor.

The second I'd pushed the attackers back, I dropped to one knee and hit the ground with my sword. Then I let loose my ever-erratic push spell.

This was about the only spell I had down well enough to do any damage. That still left a large margin for error. The first time I did it in a moment of panic; I'd flung a vile satyr out of a forest. He'd started it by trying to kill me and I'd reacted automatically. Since then Alric had helped work on my control. In theory.

I meant to push them back enough to get some fighting room. Instead, they all went directly into the ground up to their necks.

I honestly didn't know who was more surprised, them or me. A few months ago, I'd buried an extremely unlamented ex-boyfriend-turned-hideous-monster while using this spell. But I'd been high on a cliff above him when I cast the spell. That the attackers before me went in the ground instead of away from me when we were only a few feet apart was definitely weird.

Nevertheless, effective. None of them could move. Judging by the yelling and twisting about they were still alive. The minotaur and the woman fighter both looked like they wanted nothing more than to rip my head off.

Behind the house I saw Covey and Alric leading Kelm and Flarinen toward the far alley.

I raised my hand as if I was casting a spell but instead of a wave to knock them out coming from Padraig, a flood of black smoke covered the area. It was only knee high but considering so were all of their heads, it was effective.

I bumped a head or two on the way out of the circle; but they all had bigger issues to deal with.

Padraig was waiting for me, and the look on his face wasn't good. "My spell shouldn't have done that." The stunned look told me he wasn't used to his spells not working.

"Mine shouldn't have either, and Alric's shield spell turned into a slowdown spell before it disappeared completely." I looked at his side. "And your sword is gone." It had been in his scabbard before I went in, but it hung empty now.

He swore as he looked down. An intense look of concentration filled his face, but the sword didn't come back. Mine was in my hand though.

I held the sword close to my face. "You sticking around?" I shrugged and put it away then faced Padraig. "Can you un-glamour me? They weren't knocked out and the yells seem to be getting more aggressive." I didn't want to be roaming around looking like this, especially if there was a gang of pissed-off fighters looking for this persona.

Padraig clearly wanted to try again to get his sword back, but was also wise enough to know we didn't have the time.

His spell casting was far more dramatic than Alric's. It

had always been fluid; words and hand gestures flowed together into a spell. Not this time. He shook his head a few times as if there was a bee near it. Then tried again. A trail of sweat trickled down the left side of his face but finally he let out a breath.

"Done," he said then turned to lead us down a different direction than Covey had brought us. He changed alleys three times and I wasn't certain but it felt like we were going backwards once or twice. Finally I recognized the alley the stable was in.

Padraig knocked, and Leaf peered down from the knot hole in the door, then popped back in. At least the girls were back.

The chains came off and Alric stuck his head out first, then pulled me in. Padraig scanned the alley then ducked in behind us.

"We all made it, right?" The silence of our trip back was now catching up with me. My magic often misbehaved, but people like Alric and Padraig, two long-lived elves who'd grown up using it, should never have things go wrong. Alric had his sword, but he didn't look happy.

"Yes, but Flarinen and Kelm both were tortured." Lorcan and Covey were bandaging a nasty cut on Flarinen's sword arm.

"I can fight." Being rescued, even worse, by a common thief, as he thought of Alric, was probably upsetting him more than the damage they'd done.

Alric was examining Kelm's wounds but they looked mostly to be bruising. He didn't say anything but at least he looked grateful and smiled at all of us briefly.

"Anyone have a guess as to what happened out there? Alric's protection spell downgraded to a slowing down spell, and I had to use a push spell. They ended up chin deep in the ground instead of going away, and Padraig's spell turned into smoke." I turned to him. "Unless you changed your plan of attack?"

The scowl he wore even moved the scarred side of his face.

"Not at all. Lorcan, my spell went sideways, and my sword vanished." As he spoke I noticed it had come back, but I knew it hadn't when we were at the door. "This area is messing with more than just the will to leave."

Lorcan patted Flarinen's shoulder and pulled down his sleeve over the new bandages. "I was afraid of that when you both had trouble calling the swords. But nothing can break your connection to them. It's simply impossible." He turned to me. "I see yours is in place?"

I patted the metal troublemaker and shrugged. "I have no idea why, but it's sticking around."

"They are looking for you," Kelm said quietly. Those bright blue eyes were focused directly on me. "The people who took us. They described Lady Taryn well."

"Just Taryn please." I smiled. This was the first time since joining us that he'd spoken to me. "They mentioned me by name?" There was no way that was going to be good.

I'd looked at Kelm too long, he turned red and looked down. "No. But they described you well enough that it was clear. They didn't say why they wanted you though."

"I think we need to hear what happened to Flarinen and Kelm," Alric said. "Then Taryn and I have some interesting news about a way out."

Everyone else spoke at once, but he held up his hand. "It will wait, and it's only a possible, and unreliable lead." He tilted his head to Flarinen.

I noticed both knights had their weapons, they must have found them on the way out of the compound they'd been held in. Flarinen was seated and wouldn't take his hand off the hilt of his sword. He was trying to be the cocky bastard we all knew and hated, but there was a concern in his eyes that hadn't been there before.

"I have to admit that I am ashamed they were able to take us, and it was completely my fault. Kelm acted within his training and did the knights proud."

The entire stable went silent. I'd heard the faeries giggling and snorting in the rafters when we first came in—even they were quiet now.

"But, Captain—" Kelm stared to talk but a raised fist cut him off.

"No. I am the one who failed. We followed a rumor that the power behind this place lived near the edge of town. We went, they trapped us, and we were overwhelmed." A flash of anger stomped out his self-loathing for a moment and looked far more natural. "They were idiots and undisciplined. The only leader I saw was a former caravan guard gone to seed."

He went back to self-loathing but waved to Kelm to go on.

"They first tried to rob us, but aside from our weapons, they found nothing. Then a runner came and there was a flurry of interest in who Captain Flarinen was. Then they started beating us up to find out where the relics and Taryn were."

Alric frowned. "How do so many people here know about these things?"

I was about to ask Flarinen some questions, something I never thought I'd ever do, when a chill passed through me. Literally. I screamed as a ghostly form wafted through me and came out about chest level. The shape solidified a bit as it pulled free of me but was hard to make out. Slowly short white hair came into view, then the rest of a familiar looking, annoyed dwarf. Mackil.

"Damn, boy, you have some fine companions!" He looked me up and down and waggled his eyebrows. "And a trellian too! And sorry, me buckos, I don't go for males, but I'm sure you're all fine examples." He sloshed to one side. Interesting that a being who wasn't standing on the ground, was not corporeal in the least, was managing to tip over because he was drunk.

"What happened to you?" Alric walked completely around his drunken, ghostly friend. "We only left you a few hours ago."

Mackil chuckled and blew himself over. "Hours? More like weeks." He leaned closer to Alric. "You may be prettier than ya was the last I saw ya, and you dumped that scary redhead, but you aren't any brighter."

Alric and I shared a look. First Covey said we'd been missing for hours when we thought we hadn't and now Mackil said it had been weeks since we saw him and Rue at the pub. Time waves in the desert on the way to escape were scary, but with maps hopefully could be avoided. But having them drifting around town was terrifying.

"I think you're missing an important issue," Lorcan said. He came up to Mackil and ran his hand through him. "I doubt your friend was in this state when you saw him?" When both of us shook our heads he peered closer at Mackil's face. "Yes, I can see it. So when did my brother steal your body?"

CHAPTER FOURTEEN

ALRIC STARTED SWEARING UNDER HIS breath but the words were too low for me to make out which ones he was using. Not to mention they sounded to be in elvish. "Damn it, when did he get you?"

Mackil had been focusing on Lorcan as he waved his hands over, around, and through him. The movements meant something to Lorcan, but Mackil acted like it was a game and kept spinning around to follow the hands.

"Your brother did this to me, eh? He's a right bastard is what he is." He drifted over to Alric with Lorcan trailing behind. "He got me a few weeks ago. Hey, it was right after you and that mean-looking redhead took off with the warrior trellian lady." He smiled and wiggled his fingers at Covey. "Yup, my bastard contact shows up, gets me and Rue drunk, then bam. I wake up like this and he's got my body."

"If he can't drink, is he staying drunk because he was when he…was removed from his body?" I didn't want to say died. He was happy so far, but Mackil was an ass and I didn't want to deal with that after the day I'd already had. At least time had stayed more or less in order on our end and it was late afternoon.

"That is a good question and one I'd say is an affirmative." Lorcan grabbed one of his never-ending supply of small blank books and started scribbling in it. I'd have thought it would be odd to see another person go through the same horror that you just got out of. But, like Covey, it appeared that scientific inquiry won out over bad memories. Even if those memories were of being mostly dead.

"Reginald was your contact? The one who betrayed you when you brought him his supplies?" Alric asked.

"Hmmm?" Mackil had been watching his hand go in and out of Lorcan's head but he tried to focus on Alric. "Yes, that blustery blowhard...that's why you look familiar!" He tried to push Lorcan but instead shoved his entire arm through Lorcan's chest. "You look like your brother! Or how I remember he looked. Haven't seen him in a while. You two twins?"

Padraig had been off to the side, swearing at something he was trying to create in his hand. Finally he came over with a simple glow. "This will help you focus." He let it drift up to the height of Mackil's eyes.

"That's nice." Mackil sounded both more focused yet more drifty at the same time. At least his energy was staying focused on the small ball of light.

"Isn't it? Now when did you first meet Reginald?"

I pulled myself out of the conversation at that point. Alric and I had already heard the story.

"If he knew him when he looked like Lorcan, but Lorcan got his body back, whose body was he in when he stole Mackil's form?" I'd kept my voice down as I asked Alric, but Mackil still looked up.

"Ah, he was that damn dwoller bartender. Still could tell it was Reggie though. Never did trust dwollers, like them even less now. He friended me up after you left, got both Rue and I drunk, then this."

That wasn't good. I was extremely glad that Alric had gone behind my back and put a glamour on me. Hopefully, Reginald hadn't recognized Alric either. Considering who we were, I'd think if he had noticed he would have chosen to body swap Alric instead of Mackil.

"That's interesting," Lorcan said. "More information

I've found in the books indicates body grabbing is not easy, needs a lot more magic behind it than my brother ever had, and there needs to be a connection of some sort between the two individuals."

I thought of the nasty bartender; he was awful even without knowing he was actually Reginald. "What connection did he and the dwoller have?" A number of scenarios came to mind, all of which were going to give me nightmares.

"Needed energy," Mackil said. "Reggie broke up with his partner, stole something from him. He needed energy so he let the dwoller bite him, then turned the tables and bit him back."

"So they're not together anymore?" Alric asked.

"No, I knew that when he took over my body. Now that was a weird feeling let me tell you." Alric, Padraig, and Lorcan played question the drunken ghost for a few minutes more, but he'd only gotten a tiny slice of what was foremost on Reginald's mind as the transfer took place. Or at least that was all he could recall now.

The two mages having a falling out was good in that it weakened their collective powers.

"Where's Rue?" I knew trying to figure out what had happened to our possible source for getting out of here was more important, but I felt bad about the kid.

"I don't know. He'd passed out before the dwoller sucked the life out of me and made me like this. When I woke up he was gone and weeks had passed." He started to frown but Padraig waved the glow again and he went back to watching it.

"How do you know weeks went by?"

"Well, because…I don't know."

"How long until nightfall?" Alric looked to Lorcan.

"About two hours if it stays on schedule. It's not a good idea to be out there when night hits," Lorcan said.

"I need to borrow your trick glow, Padraig," Alric said. "I'm going to take Mackil back to the pub and see about the time lapse. We might not be able to get out of here if there are time waves running rampant."

"I'm going with you," I said without even realizing the words had come out of my mouth. Yes, Alric was the love of my life, but I knew he didn't need me to protect him on this. But I needed to be there.

"Us too!" Garbage yelled as she, Leaf, and Crusty swooped down from the rafters. The rest of the faeries nodded solemnly but didn't try to join in. Bunky and the gargoyle rose a foot in the air, buzzed, then settled in next to the remaining faeries. They were going to stay and guard.

I had no idea why these three felt the need to go. I'd say it was the chance for a pub trip, but if that had been the case all of them would have gone. And Garbage had a determined look on her face.

I pulled my hood low as we left the stable. I peered down the alley as the door chains were put in place behind us. Null was a weird little place, and the spell pressing on us made it even odder. Yet, aside from our people being taken, and Reginald stealing Mackil's body, it didn't seem dangerous. Depressing yes, but not scary. But the feeling of eyes on me was disturbing.

Alric was quietly talking with Mackil, trying to keep him focused on the spelled glow and get more information out of him.

I waved the faeries down to me. They'd automatically flown out of the stable when we left but the feeling of being watched was heavier now. "How about you three ride with me? It's warmer." I held open my cloak and they all dove into the pocket. "What did you three see when you were out? Any trouble?" Yes, my version of trouble and their version were totally different things but some information might be useful.

The other two finished climbing deeper in the pocket they shared, but Garbage stayed out.

"We no stay here. Sing land gone bad." Then she scowled

at me as if it was my fault and climbed in to join her friends in the pocket. A moment later, she pushed her way back out, shot me another evil look and hopped to Alric. She wormed her way into his shirt.

Great. I'd gone from briefly being great because I'd brought us all here, something I was now sure I hadn't done, to being bad because this place wasn't what it was supposed to be. I was about to drag Garbage back out and find out more of what she'd meant, but Alric and Mackil stopped in their tracks. Okay, Alric did, Mackil drifted around a bit.

A thin column of smoke, not noticeable at first because it matched the heavy gray sky, rose from a few streets over. Alric started jogging that way and I noticed his sword was back. When we'd left the stable he'd only been armed with his throwing blades and a dagger. I was sure he had more but that was what was visible. But now he had one hand down on his scabbard as he ran.

Mine was sticking around as well, and I quickly found why he had one hand down as he ran; swords bouncing while running wasn't fun. I did the same, then skidded to a halt as Alric stopped in front of me. We'd come out on the main street, near where we were earlier in the day. But now the assayer's office was in flames. The people who'd been trying to get in this morning were now standing around and watching it burn. Soon the entire row of buildings, including the pub we were going to, were engulfed.

"Aren't they going to stop it?"

Alric's face was screwed up and his right hand came up like Padraig's did when casting a spell. Finally he shook his head. "I can't stop it with a spell."

"But why—" My words were cut off by an explosion as the pub's alcohol supplies caught fire. Both of us were knocked off our feet and Mackil tumbled backwards a few buildings.

I shook my head. There had been a wave of pressure that

came at the same time as the explosion, but didn't seem to be from the explosion.

"Get out of the way! Daft idiots!" Both Alric and I scrambled clear of a donkey cart that was about to run us over. The driver had plenty of room, the road was wide enough and his cart was small. He just didn't like us laying in the road. Neither did I.

I was off to the side, dusting myself off when I realized I was standing next to the assayers shop. And it was intact. Nothing was on fire, nor did it look like it ever had been.

"Alric?" I couldn't even finish my sentence. That had been real—the heat was strong enough to reach us in the road—but the smoke, the ash, all of it was gone now.

"I saw it too." He held up the spelled glow and Mackil drifted over. "You've been here longer. What the hell happened?"

The ghost seemed thinner than before, only his outline remained. Then he shuddered and came back into view.

"That would be the time waves. You have to be careful crossing the land to get out—they'll get you every time."

"Mackil, we're not in the desert, we're in town. What are they doing in town?"

"Oh! That I don't know. They only stay in the desert."

"Is right. They no be here." Garbage was out of the pocket and glaring at the air above us. It could have been my imagination but I swore I felt the air pressure vanish. "Is not good." She slid back into my pocket again and there were enough people roaming around that I didn't want to dig her out.

"Let's keep going to the pub," Alric pulled his hood up, reached over and fixed mine as well, then held the glow up to Mackil.

There were far more people inside than there had been this morning, or afternoon, depending upon which time section you went with.

Rue was at the table we'd left him at. He was working

on dinner, and smiled when he saw Alric. "Mackil's friend. Good to see you again."

Alric hadn't had time to put a glamour on me before the ghost Mackil found us in the stable. And I was thinking he didn't really want to show his magic in front of him. But if I kept my hood up, and my hair pulled forward, it should help anyone who actually knew me from spotting me.

I'd keep telling myself that.

"This is my friend, Leesa," Alric said. Then he held up the glow and Mackil drifted closer.

But Rue didn't even appear to notice. I could see Mackil, Alric obviously could as well. But no one in the pub even looked over our way. A few people even stumbled through him.

"Where's Mackil?" Alric had noticed the lack of anyone seeing him as well. Mackil floated in place, transfixed by the glow.

"He took off." Rue shook his head. "After you and your lady friends all left, the barkeep brought us more drinks." He turned red. "I passed out, and Mackil was gone when I woke up. I thought about looking for him, but decided to stay here instead."

"Today?" Alric looked as surprised as I felt. Mackil might be a ghost now but he'd appeared certain that it had been weeks since we saw him.

Rue took a slow drink of his ale. "Aye?" He looked around the pub, but no one was close by. "Is this another test?" He waggled his finger between Alric and I. "Are you two with that other fella? The one with the magic? He seemed a lot scarier than you, no offense. And I had nothing to tell him, not cause I didn't want to but there's nothing to tell. So, yes, *today*."

"Other fella?" I leaned forward so I could keep my voice down and still be heard. I also kept my hood low. "Was he tall with a sinister look?" Yes, Nivinal could change his appearance, but I think the last one we saw him in was his permanent one. He was vain enough to want to have his best face forward at his time of triumph. And he'd definitely thought the battle in the palace was going to be his moment.

Rue leaned forward as well. "That would be the one. He wanted to know where the dwoller bartender was, kept asking everyone. Managed to clear this place out for a bit, folks were so frightened by him. Then he got to me and I told him the barkeep vanished when my master did. He asked who my master was, got really mad when I told him. He blasted a hole over there, and walked out. Guess he didn't like doorways."

Crap, so clearly Nivinal knew that Reginald had been in the dwoller's body, and now he knew he was in Mackil's. There was always the chance that if Nivinal was mad enough at his former partner, he might destroy him. The hole in the side of the pub was huge and there was no doubt that he walked out that way. But we needed Mackil back in his own body if we were going to be able to use him to get out of here. His mental connection with his former self was nowhere as strong as Lorcan's had been. As he currently was, he couldn't help us with anything.

Alric was quiet for a few moments. "We're not like that other man, and yes, you'd do best to stay away from him. I'd recommend avoiding your master also, at least for now. He got hit by the wrong end of a spell and might be behaving dangerously. You don't want to get between him and the guy looking for him." He clapped Rue on the shoulder and we walked to the back where the hole was.

Mackil, still watching the glow and unseen by any except us, drifted along behind. He definitely appeared to be fading.

"That was good of you to warn him to stay away from them both. But what are we going to do? If Mackil was the one with the way out of here, and our Mackil is fading, how will we get out?"

"We'll figure out something." He paused as we approached the hole in the wall, held out his empty hand toward the shattered edges, and closed his eyes briefly. The tilt of his head was almost as if he were listening to something.

"Damn it, I was hoping I could get some residue, but I can't. We know who did it, but aside from being an ass, *why* do it? This isn't just a hole, he created something."

I was a second behind him as he stepped through the other side. I screamed as he vanished before my eyes.

CHAPTER FIFTEEN

A WHIRLING GRAY CIRCLE HAD SWALLOWED Alric. My heart was pounding so hard I knew everyone heard it. I glanced back, but while a few people in the pub looked my way, no one even came over. Not at the vortex, not at my scream. What I should do was go back and get Covey, Padraig, Lorcan—heck, even Flarinen. *Someone* to help.

But I couldn't leave Alric trapped wherever this led. I waved to Mackil who had managed not to follow the glow after Alric. "This is urgent; I'll pay you your weight in gold if you go back to the stable and tell them where we are." I had no gold, but he didn't weigh anything. I was hoping there was enough of the original greedy Mackil to get him motivated enough to focus on the task.

He tilted his head, then smiled. "Agreed." With that, he vanished.

It might be my eyes, but the whirling circle appeared to be shrinking. I couldn't take a chance it closed before the others got here. I held onto my scabbard and jumped into the swirling mass.

Intense cold tore through my body and I heard a lot of faery swearing. I'd forgotten Leaf and Crusty were in my pocket; Garbage had vanished with Alric. I put my hand over the pocket inside my cloak, trapping them there. The vortex was spinning and whipping by. I didn't want to take a chance I'd lose those two, too.

They started kicking as well as yelling louder. I tried yelling back but the winds tore away my voice.

Suddenly we tumbled out of the winds and cold and I landed on all fours. On a green patch of grass…in a forest? Null was in a desert.

Since I'd put my hands out to brace myself, the faeries kicked their way out of my pocket. Leaf looked concerned as she buzzed out of my pocket and Crusty looked like she always did—confused.

"What you do?!" Leaf waved her hands in the air, doing her best Garbage impersonation, pointing out trees, rocks, the ground, everything. "No be here."

"That thing took Alric, I couldn't stand by and let him vanish."

She narrowed her eyes, crossed her arms, and flew closer. Finally she nodded and tilted her head. "Is okay. We fix. Garbage know."

"Taryn?" That was definitely Alric's voice, but faint. We must have come out at different areas, as I'd only been a minute or so behind him.

"Here!" I couldn't tell exactly what direction his voice came from so I stayed in place. He was the tracker, let him find me.

He must have been further away than I thought; I was about to call out again, when he came through the trees to the right.

I ran to him but stopped before I touched him. I didn't make it a habit of memorizing my boyfriend's clothing, but with Alric it was simple. Unless he was in disguise, he wore variations of black on black. Sometimes with an added layer of black for contrast.

He stood before me in a flamboyant green cape, a lighter green, embroidered tunic, and dark brown boots wrapped around matching leggings.

"How did you…you just left." I waved a hand at his finery.

Garbage flew down from above and joined the other two. All three chattered loudly in native faery.

"I fell through that vortex two weeks ago. Garbage made me keep returning to this area though." Alric stepped forward and kissed me. "You shouldn't be here, but I really thought I'd never see you again."

I returned the kiss, but was confused as hell.

"So what was it, why did you get here two weeks before me even though I was right behind you, and why are you dressed like that?"

"It was a trap, one I should have expected and might regret the rest of my life that I didn't. It sent us into a time wave, one that had been manipulated and made into a weapon. The time between our arrivals was most likely due to the spell breaking down. Nivinal might not have been expecting to trap us in it, but he knew anyone with magic would be drawn in."

He brushed back my hair then held me close again. "You shouldn't have come."

I pushed back so I could see his face. There was affection there, but also a lot of sorrow. "What aren't you telling me? Where are we?"

"The where hasn't changed. We are where Null *will* be. It's the when. There's not much in the way of civilization out here, but as near as I can guess, from a brief trip to a local village, we're about a thousand years in the past."

Garbage buzzed low again. "See? Told you was bad."

"How can we be in the past? If this is a time wave shouldn't it go away eventually? The one in the bar somehow vanished, leaving Mackil thinking it had been weeks, but Rue believing it had only been hours." I fluttered my hand in the air as a shudder took me. A thousand years in the past didn't feel good right now.

A wave of cold, different from the one that had engulfed me in the vortex of the time wave, hit me and I dropped to the ground. This wasn't right. I couldn't be here. Nothing but that thought filled my brain. I felt Alric's hands on my arms as he held me, I vaguely heard words, but couldn't tell what they were. I couldn't be here. It felt like all of nature was trying to push me out of this place—or rather this time.

"Snap out!" A pair of tiny hands started hitting my right cheek. A moment later another tiny pair went after the left cheek, and someone started biting the tip of my nose. The cold, dead feeling fled, and my eyes flew open to see a blue blur trying to chew on my nose. I shook my head and sent all three faeries flying off.

Garbage and Leaf held back, but Crusty tried to fly back to my nose. I grabbed her and held her away from me. "What are you doing?" I understood the other two, in their weird way they were trying to get me back to this place from wherever I was fading off to.

"They took rest of face." Crusty smiled and patted my thumb where it crossed in front of her. "You good now, no bite."

I wanted to explain to Crusty that biting really was never a good option, but I knew it wouldn't stay in that little blue head longer than it took me to say it. I let her go and she flew up a few feet overhead with the other two.

Alric had rocked back on his heels until the faery fest was over but moved closer now. "Your color looks better, that's good. What happened?" He rose to his feet then held out a hand to help me up. With him in his finery, I felt like a slob being helped up by a prince.

"I don't know, just an overwhelming feeling that I shouldn't be here." I shuddered as a residue of that empty space echoed through me.

"Understandable. I felt it too when I first landed here. We shouldn't be here; neither of us were born this far back. Our bodies have to adjust."

I dusted some grass off my cloak and watched the faeries cavorting around. "That explains them not having problems I guess, since according to them they've been around for thousands of years."

The girls had been discussing something among themselves, but Garbage broke it off and flew down to face me. "Is longer, much longer. We go find things. Stay here." She scowled, then turned to hit Alric. "Both. Here."

Before I could object, not that it would have done any good, all three took off like tiny delinquent streaks of color.

"I guess we wait?" I looked around but there really was nothing out here. Not that Null was impressive, but at least it had a pub. "Where have you been living for the last two weeks?" Alric was fine living in the wild, but I couldn't reconcile that idea with how he looked right now. If I'd ever had any books as a kid that had elven princes in them, Alric would have fit right in.

"I have a small place a bit back in the woods from here. An abandoned woodcutter's croft. But if the faeries said wait here, I'll take them at their word. Garbage knew you would be coming, even though she didn't tell me. Just kept pushing me back here."

I blinked at him a few times then shook my head. "You're not real, are you? I fell somewhere back in Null and am dying." First his garb, then we're supposedly a thousand years in the past, and he was deferring to the faeries? There was no way this was reality.

Alric's laugh hadn't been common since we'd left the elven enclave, but it was a welcome sound now. "I assure you that this is sadly real. I'm listening to the faeries because they have an advantage here over us, or they will if their memories of this time come back."

That was one problem we'd encountered in the past few months. We discovered that the faeries had been around a long time, but they had almost no memories of what happened during the past.

"That doesn't explain the clothing." I glanced down at my sad traveling clothes, hoping that maybe coming here had changed the clothes to the time. Not at all.

"I might have liberated some clothing from a vendor in town. Rather village. A small village a few days walk that direction. I couldn't pay for it since my coin is a bit out of date here."

Crap, I hadn't thought of that. Our coins were all stamped with the kingdom of Lindor, a kingdom that had only been around about five hundred years. I pulled out a gold piece and flipped it around. The king and queen, the kingdom, and its worth—nothing else. "Actually, if we were from some far distant land, our money would look odd. But gold spends the same wherever it's from."

Alric nodded. "I was planning on taking some money from a few upper class folks and getting by that way. But your way would be more subtle—until we run out of coins."

"See? Not being a thief can sometimes be a good thing."

"Fine, but it's hard to change after—" He cut himself off. A few moments later I heard what had stopped him. Wagons, wheels, and hooves. Running hard. And a lot more horses than a pair to pull a wagon.

Alric grabbed my hand and we ran behind a large clump of tall shrubs. The road was well hidden and only a few dozen feet from us. A lathered pair of horses pulling an ornate carriage came tearing through the woods. Half a dozen riders fanned out behind them and judging by the frantic look on the carriage driver's face, they weren't friends.

The carriage had gotten past us when the front right wheel exploded. At least that was what it looked like from where I was hiding. In my time carriages were not made to lose a wheel at high speeds—they weren't any better in this time.

The driver yelled something to the horses as he was flung from his seat. Instead of both animals running on and probably killing themselves by dragging the broken wagon, both slowed down. Eventually they stopped and rested with sides heaving and heads down.

They'd gotten far enough past us that the riders passed us as well. Six riders all dressed in browns and yellows on white horses. The garb would probably blend in well in the forest, but the horses certainly wouldn't. They also looked too fancy for common thieves. Thieves who also wore masks made of fabric and beads that covered their lower face and ears.

Alric started to move and I thought maybe he figured they were far enough past us that we could run the other way. The faeries had told us to stay here, but things had changed. They'd find us when they came back.

Instead of leading us away, Alric pulled me behind a heavy clump of shrubs closer to the broken wagon and the attackers.

I couldn't ask anything; even my softest voice would give us away, especially now that we were moving closer to the problem instead of further away.

The attackers reached the driver lying on the ground. He was moving, but his groans were clear. He wasn't able to get up, let alone fight.

Two of the horsemen rode around him, taunting him it sounded like, but it wasn't a language I knew. He'd been trying to roll to his feet, but flopped backwards. One of the attackers walked his horse forward, and the driver held up his right hand, shouted a few magic sounding words, the attacker was blown off his horse and vanished into a puff of smoke.

The second attacker yelled and the other four came closer. The driver tried his spell again, but his voice was weak. The leader of the attackers yelled out and all of the riders rode over the driver. It happened so quickly, no one could have stopped it. Weak or not, the scream that came from him was something that would haunt me forever.

I looked away and tried to keep the contents of my

stomach from coming out. Alric said nothing, but gave my hand a squeeze.

The attackers ran him over again, though it was clear, even from where we were, that the driver died on the first pass. They then turned to the carriage.

It was on its side, the spelled horses calm even though the one who cast the spell had died. No one had come out of the carriage that I could tell.

"Both of you get out and you won't meet the same fate as your driver." The voice was heavily accented and low. If I hadn't seen at least part of his face, I would think it came from a syclarion.

There was no movement from the wagon, but a branch fell from one of the trees behind us and the attacker closest to us quickly turned our way. When another branch fell further away he shook his head and turned back toward their leader.

"We want the gold, jewels, and the lady. She'll fetch a fine price in the market. She might not live long after that, but someone will have fun with her." The man laughed and eventually his men did as well, although not as heartily.

The door to the tipped carriage pushed open, but no one came out. I couldn't imagine getting up and out of a wagon that way would be easy.

I pulled on Alric's hand, then mouthed 'we have to help them'. Yes, there were more of them than us, and they were heavily armed and ruthless, but I'd be damned if I was letting some woman be sold into slavery. Not to mention I was mad about the driver.

He smiled and kissed the top of my hand. 'Already on it,' he mouthed back.

An elaborately beaded arm came out of the wagon, followed by a blonde head and the rest of the elaborately beaded dress and the dress wearer. She had her back to us, and her movements were slow and measured. She must have been terrified.

"Where's your man? We'll deal with him before we deal with you."

The woman had climbed out of the carriage, but on the far side and all I could see was the top of her head.

"You killed him," her voice was oddly accented and familiar. "Galfin was my escort and my friend. And you murdered him. There is no one else in the wagon."

She came around the edge of the carriage, but I couldn't see her face; she wore a light drape of lace, colored to match her dress, across it. But a gash on her forehead explained why she hadn't gotten out of the mangled carriage sooner. Her hair was pulled up high to show off the jewels rimming her delicately pointed ears. I now knew who she was—those eyes belonged to only one elf I knew.

Siabiane.

CHAPTER SIXTEEN

"KILLING HIM WAS A FOOLISH way to spend your last moments. I only regret I couldn't stop you in time. You will be regretting that as well." Siabiane flipped her right hand up and four of the remaining attackers rose in the air and burst into flame. She then sent the leader up in the air, and flew him around a bit as he screamed. He passed far too close to us for my comfort and his hands reached for us. I bit down a yell as a familiar looking tattoo flashed by. The image worn by those elven knights who had followed the Dark.

Siabiane flew him close to her and she placed her free hand on the side of his head. "Ah, you are naught but a minion, but your masters are linked to you. Let them feel this." She let him go and waved him higher and higher. Then she burst him into flame. There wasn't enough left of him to even drift down to hit us.

She stayed looking at her dead friend, then slightly turned our direction. "I know you are there but I don't know who you are, nor if you intend harm. As you have seen, I am not someone to be trifled with. Please come out slowly. I am working through a lot of anger right now and I don't want to take it out on someone innocent by accident." As she spoke, she gently waved her hand over the mangled body of her friend. He vanished.

Alric rose slowly, both hands held in front of him to show he had no weapons. I followed his lead.

It was odd seeing someone you knew, who you realized wouldn't know who you were for a thousand years or so. Siabiane, like most elves, aged very slowly. Yet she looked younger now. Maybe a thousand years did age even one like her, and she appeared to have a lot less care in her eyes than she did when we met her.

She removed the lace from across her face and stepped forward. "An elven lord and a human—and something else? And whatever is it that you're wearing, my child?"

I dusted off my cloak but it was pointless. I fit right in with the citizens of Null—meaning my clothing was dusty and drab. And probably not anything anyone of this era would wear unless they were begging for scraps.

I also hadn't thought about the being human aspect. Even though I was part dryad on my mother's side, I looked human. A species that wasn't common in this area during this time. I smiled but turned to Alric to get us out of this.

"I am Alric, this is my companion Taryn. We have journeyed far to get here, but all of our belongings were lost. Taryn had to borrow clothing from a washer woman a few days ago."

Siabiane tilted her head and studied both of us. Then, finally, as if whatever she was looking for remained out of reach, she shook her head and dropped the hand she'd been using for her spells.

"There is something familiar…I can't touch it right at this moment, but I shall soon." She moved a step closer to me. "But there is something wrong about you, beyond you being a human, which is fascinating by the way, I will have many questions of your people. But there is something beyond that." She peered closer at me. "You're not supposed to be here."

The words echoed what I'd felt when I collapsed when I first got here. The Siabiane of our time was wise and had vast knowledge. I knew we were a bit early in her lifespan, although she apparently was even older than Lorcan, but I had a feeling there was more knowledge in her head right now than in the entire elven enclave of the future. That she knew I was out of place was not good. But then why didn't she know Alric was out of place as well?

"I have been lost as of late," I said quickly.

She nodded slowly. Then her smile dropped. "Hopefully, your attackers were not of the same ilk as these. They were not common footpads, even though they were trying to appear as such. There is something brewing in the kingdom, a darkness that could destroy all. That was why Galfin and I rode to the capital. The queen must be warned."

I could practically see Alric's thoughts churning before he spoke. We'd arrived here before the battle of the Dark, before the elves even knew what they had lurking in their midst. That was going to make any time we spent here that much worse.

"I have heard little of the troubles, but I come from the kingdom of Lathing. We are small and not a land to draw enemies."

I hadn't heard of Lathing, but Siabiane's nod showed she had. It must not only have been small, but far from here.

"You have come far indeed. I will share with you what I know if you will allow me to provide a ride for the two of you to Glaisdale." She held out her hand to me. "But first, let us get your friend into something more fitting." She tilted her head, looking me up and down. "And only a slight glamour to make you appear elvish. Humans are too uncommon in this kingdom, and we don't want unwelcome attention."

I was about to ask how we were going to ride anywhere when the wagon slowly rose upright, a new wheel appeared and the horses rustled from their spelled stupor. Siabiane led me around to the door of the carriage, then dropped my hand and went inside. A few muffled swear words later, she stuck her head out.

"You are shorter than I but I think I can make this work.

Come in." The wagon was far larger than it had looked from the outside, but it seemed a bit cramped due to all of her cases being tossed about.

"You're moving to the enclave? I mean to Glaisdale?" I was going to have to watch what I said. There had been a huge and powerful city before the battle with the Dark reduced it to a bunch of sheltered enclaves. I remember Lorcan saying that Siabiane had helped establish the royal enclave after the battle, but I didn't know how long before that she'd come to the area.

"Is that a human term, enclave? Sounds so charming and cozy." She pulled more clothing out of the cases as she spoke. "Alas, Glaisdale is not charming or cozy. Well, it is charming, but the type of charm exhibited by someone who knows how charming they are. I am not moving there, but one of my long-time correspondents, Lord Lorcan, has asked for a consultation. I will stay a few months, then travel on."

I kept the dress between us; I didn't want her to see my face. How could we stay with her and Lorcan and the others and not let them know what was coming? That the entire elven kingdom was going to almost be destroyed and the survivors would stay hidden for a thousand years?

Or could we tell them? Maybe being back here at this time could change everything—stop the battle with the Dark. Save the thousands of elves who had died. I felt her eyes on me and shoved those thoughts far away. I needed to talk to Alric first before we said anything. The same thoughts had to have been running through his mind, yet he'd stayed hiding in the woods for two weeks.

"This is lovely," I said as I held up the green and silver gown. "Are you sure you don't mind me borrowing it?" It was of a similar style to hers, old fashioned by my standards but classic enough that it could hold its own regardless of the time. The sleeves were long and beaded; the gown flowed elegantly.

"No. I'm not lending it to you, you will have to keep it. You and your man Alric will arrive with me as my entourage. Consider the gown and other clothes your first payment." She motioned to some clean undergarments that looked disturbingly my size and that I swore hadn't been there a moment ago. "I can tell there is something odd about both of you, but I know you're not evil. I will help you where I can." With that she left the carriage and shut the door.

I would have preferred a nice bath before putting on such fine clothing, borrowed or given. But that would be asking a bit much.

The gown seemed too big as I slipped it over my head, but then it shrank to my size. That was a spell I'd have to get Alric to teach me when we got back. I avoided the part of my brain that kept wanting to add *if* to that sentence.

There were also a pair of delicate, but sturdy, slippers. I hated giving up my comfortable boots, but they really wouldn't have fit in with this dress—or with my two companions. I set them aside along with the rest of my original clothing, then stepped out of the carriage door.

Alric and Siabiane had been in low conversation as I opened the door, but Alric stopped mid-sentence when he saw me. Siabiane had her back to me, but turned with a smile.

"Yes, the gown fits you perfectly. And we definitely need to spell your eyes and ears to look elven. A human who is obviously a beloved companion to an elven lord would be scandalous. I, of course, love it. But I am not at all a person like the stodgy individuals in Glaisdale."

I felt my face go red, but it was more from Alric's stare than from Siabiane's observations. He even came forward and held out his hand for me to descend the carriage steps. Maybe all the finery around him was making him revert to his younger days in court. Alric never talked about his family much, but his father had been a high-ranking official in the palace at some point.

"Crap." I bit my tongue. I'd just realized that while Alric wasn't born yet, his parents would be and if he looked like either of them it could cause problems. I glanced at Siabiane...I couldn't bring that up to her.

I was saved when a trio of colors arrowed in on us.

"Told you stay." Garbage flew right in front of my face, not paying attention to Siabiane or the carriage. "What that?" She did notice the dress. "And who...is YOU!" She turned around and saw Siabiane watching her with almost rounded eyes.

"A truth bringer? Three of them? I thought they were long vanished in the mists of time like the Ancients themselves." She held out a hand that suddenly had a bit of sugar in it.

Crusty and Leaf flew forward immediately, but Garbage held back.

"Why you here?" She flew forward and sniffed Siabiane. "You right place. Them not right." She then pushed the other two faeries aside and dove into the apparently growing pile of sugar.

"They are yours? What magical land do you hail from that you have three mythical truth bringers?" Siabiane watched all three as they pushed and shoved to get to the sugar.

"I'd not say they're mine, really. I'm responsible for them, I guess, and they travel with me. We're family." I'd never thought of it that way, but it was true. They drove me crazy, but those three were the closest I had to a family.

"They are wondrous. But they need to stay hidden." She held up her hand and spoke to all three. "My wee ladies, I have to ask a boon of thee." When they all stopped gorging and looked up, she smiled gently. "My people loved your kind in days of old, but we haven't seen you for a long time and seeing you now might cause my people pain. Can you stay hidden, eyes not see, spells not sense?"

Leaf and Crusty nodded slowly, but both looked to Garbage. Garbage puffed up her chest and pulled out her war stick from her tiny bag. She held it up solemnly. "We do."

I'm sure I made a fine sight—fancy dress, shoes, etc., and my jaw hanging down to my chest. We'd been together for over fifteen years and I had never been able to get them to agree to even a simple request so easily.

"Thank you, my ladies. I have one more request and I think it's been asked of you already. Can you promise to protect Lady Taryn?" She looked up at me and her eyes suddenly held a sadness I'd not seen before. "I fear she will need your protection greatly in the times to come. Never leave her."

All three flew about a foot into the air, bowed to Siabiane, then landed on me. Even Crusty seemed sober.

"We do." All three spoke at once and a chill went down my spine. Siabiane knew something or felt something. And she had enough power to get my flying drunkards to promise something, and hold that promise. This was even worse than when they promised to do that before the elven king and queen.

"Now that we have that settled," Siabiane said as she reached into the carriage and pulled out a cloak that matched my dress. She put it around my shoulders and closed the clasp. "We should get moving. And if you'll note, all of your new clothing, including this cloak, has secret pockets for our tiny friends."

I held open the cloak and all three faeries zipped inside and made themselves at home.

Siabiane moved back into the carriage and had everything back where it belonged in less than a minute.

I shot Alric a look. He was always pointing out that magic shouldn't be used for trivial things. He dodged the look and instead went forward to check the reins and the horses' gear.

Siabiane motioned for me to come in the carriage. Once

I sat down she shook her head. "I personally believe you are quite lovely as you are, as your young friend does. But we really can't cause too much attention, so hold still." I felt a coolness flow over me. I never felt anything when Alric glamoured me—it would have been less annoying if I had.

Siabiane squinted at me closely. "Do you have a spell blocker of some sort? My spell seems to have run into a… no, I was wrong. It's fine now."

I'd felt a final little burst of coldness and realized it was concentrated in one spot—the place where the sapphire manticore was hidden. At least that glamour had stayed in place even if the damn relic itself apparently tried to fight back against the newest glamour. Explaining to her what had decided to take root in me and what it really was would have been even more disturbing than telling her we were from the future.

Alric stuck his head in. "Are we ready? My distance in this land may be a bit off, but I'm thinking this will go directly through to Glaisdale?"

"Yes, we have quite a ways to go, but we should be able to make good time." A sadness crossed her face. "I have ways to make our travel far faster than normal. My good man Galfin wanted to run for a bit at normal speed. He loved the land here—that was where they caught us and I couldn't save him." Her eyes grew clouded for a moment, then she shook her head.

"They will not catch us again."

"Agreed," Alric said. "I have some small magics and will help if I can."

"And a bearer of a spirit sword no less. And Lady Taryn as well. Appearantly, you have some strong magics that I didn't notice either of them until now." Siabiane looked at the sword and scabbard I'd put beside me. "That will not go with your clothing, and you really can't have one. Can you make it vanish?"

I looked at my sword. I'd wanted it to stick around so much that chasing it off seemed a bit off putting. But I tried anyway.

Siabiane stared at the still present sword. "Well, sword? Your being here will endanger your carrier. Is that your purpose?"

My sword vanished immediately.

She nodded to Alric. "As for yours, it might be better if it didn't let anyone know it is a spirit sword. The council has been getting quite worked up about these blades, and since you're not from Glaisdale they might take you as a thief. Can you disguise its essence?"

I had no idea what she meant. But he nodded and passed his hand over it. His sword looked the same to me but Siabiane smiled.

"Small magics indeed," she said. "Like your fair lady friend, there is far more to you than appearances indicate."

Alric gave a deep bow and shut the carriage door. I felt the carriage rock as he took over the driver's seat.

We started moving and I found myself wondering what to talk to her about. Anything I said ran the chance of giving us away and until I had a better idea of what would occur if we went around changing things, I didn't want that to happen.

"I don't suppose you'd feel comfortable telling me where you two really came from?"

I gave a weak smile and tried to think of what I could say. Part of me was excited that we might be able to stop the elves from their horrific battle and subsequent hiding. But I couldn't bring that up.

Something about the way Siabiane had spoken to the faeries before brought an image and a name to mind. The witch who'd rescued me and placed the faeries in my care. She'd spelled me when I left and I'd never been able to recall her name. I could now. "Mathilda. You wouldn't happen to know anyone named Mathilda?"

"What is that, dear? Is that a friend of yours? An old-fashioned name, but I can't say I know anyone with it." She snapped her fingers. "Perhaps Mathildaringa? What do you know of her?"

I nodded. That name sounded right, but not one the witch had used much. "There's not much to say, not much I can recall. It happened fifteen years ago, she found me and saved me. I'd been attacked and left for dead. I honestly didn't recall the name until I was speaking to you."

Siabiane laughed. "Something about me reminded you of her?"

That couldn't be it. Mathilda was short and wrinkled. Kindly, but old and more than a little odd. I shook my head.

"She was in disguise again, was she? Honestly, she has taken this witch thing too far. She's my sister. My younger sister."

CHAPTER SEVENTEEN

NOW THAT I WAS STARTING to recall more of that odd woman who dumped the faeries on me, I really had a difficult time believing that. Disguise or no.

Judging by Siabiane's laugh my reaction was clear on my face. "She really is, and if she would stop disguising herself and lurking around in forests in that walking house of hers, it would be more noticeable." She leaned forward. "We're not like other elves. A few more offshoots in our family tree, but I don't point that out to any of them."

I told her what I recalled of her sister, but it wasn't much and I had to be sketchy with my timelines—I was talking about something that happened fifteen years ago to me, but wouldn't be happening for almost a thousand years for Siabiane and Mathilda. I had no idea where that crazy old witch was at this point in her life.

"A walking house explains a lot though." I said it more to myself than her after I finished my short tale. She caught it anyway.

"What was that, dear?"

I shook my head. "It never moved when I was recovering, but right after she made me the guardian of the faeries, she sent us off to pick berries. I turned back a few minutes later but she and the house were gone. I never saw her again."

"She's always been a wild child, not proper like me." The wink in her eye told me this earlier Siabiane was as much a free spirit as her sister, only less blatant.

"You look weary, my child; you can rest for a bit. While it won't take as long traveling my way as it would the normal way, it will be a while before we arrive." She rose and moved to the other bench. "I believe you could even stretch out of you'd like."

I was about to decline when a fierce yawn forced its way out. It had been a long day and that wasn't even counting the time waves. Who knew how long I'd actually been awake? I nodded my thanks around a second yawn then slipped off my shoes and folded the cloak for a pillow—after tumbling out some dozing faeries. All three left me without a second look and cuddled in Siabiane's lap like a trio of tiny, brightly colored kittens.

I must have been more tired than I thought, because the next thing I knew Alric was calling the horses to slow and Siabiane was waking me.

"We aren't there yet, but Alric saw something of import."

We'd come to a complete halt by the time I'd gotten my shoes and cloak on. I felt self-conscious in the fancy dress and the cloak helped me feel less noticeable.

Siabiane was already outside and Alric was down from the driver's seat. Once they saw me get out, they both motioned for me to stay put.

"I saw a rider-less horse, just back in the woods a bit. I can go see what there is alone." Alric had his sword out and was already starting to walk off the road.

Siabiane was right behind him. "I've no doubt you are far fiercer than your dandy looks imply, my boy, but I need to see as well. There is much I already need to report to the queen; signs of more aggression must be noted."

I didn't even argue as the two walked off. If it was another dead body, I'd seen enough. And all this talk of Siabiane warning the queen made my stomach hurt. Whether she was warned or not, it didn't work. The elves still fell.

Alric and Siabiane both came back less than five minutes

later. Alric was leading the horse he'd seen, but there was no one else with them.

"Just the horse?" I was hopeful. Maybe it was a simple case of a thrown rider and an escaped horse.

"Unfortunately, no." Siabiane held up a torn satchel with an emblem I didn't recognize on it. "It appeared to be the remains of the syclarion ambassador's second-in-command. Most likely dead at least two days. The syclarions are our fast allies; this death will not be easy to process for the queen."

She had been looking down at the satchel, so I hoped I'd schooled my face well enough by the time she looked up. Syclarions? Allies? Granted up until a few months ago I didn't realize how bad they were, but they were never great friends of anyone in Beccia. They were accepted nuisances that mostly kept to themselves and sometimes brought in good money for the digs. I shuddered as I recalled the fate of a digger in a syclarion site almost a year ago. I'd been trying to find out why the digs were closed only to find that a syclarion and his people were running their own dig and obviously had enough money to shut down everything else for a few days. The syclarion leader had decided one of his men was not working fast enough and murdered him without a thought.

I'd been hiding in the bushes, so I didn't see it. But I heard all of it and it wasn't something I'd soon forget.

Since then, my run-ins with syclarions were definitely not friendly.

I looked to Alric but he gave a quick shrug. A lot of information was lost when the battle against the Dark ended—being friends with a race of killers was part of it.

"I released his body to the elements. We can bring his horse and the news back to our queen." Siabiane was so somber that I wanted to comfort her, but considering how many times a syclarion had tried to kill me in the past year, I wasn't very sympathetic.

Alric gave a slight shake of his head, reminding me not to say anything, then held the door for Siabiane and I to get back in the carriage. I stayed awake this time, with the faeries in my cloak and my shoes on.

I was almost more nervous about the next stop than I'd been about meeting elves the first time. I heard the city before I saw it. And that was with my face pressed up against the carriage window. Even the faeries were peering about, but they stayed close to me and my cloak now. They were taking their promise to stay out of sight to Siabiane seriously. I knew if they held still and focused they could become invisible, and cloak whomever they were sitting on as well. But that could be tricky and only worked if no movement was involved. Better to have the more secure way of not having them out and about.

The city of elves was far louder than I expected and sounded more like what I would imagine Beccia would on market day if it was about twenty times larger.

The noise was simply a giant mass at first, but as we drew closer, sounds sorted themselves out. I closed my eyes. I had grown up wanting to know what happened to the elves. So I became a digger. Then I found out there were still some elves alive in the world and I met them in the royal enclave.

I was now going to see the original elves, a kingdom at the height of their power. Right before they imploded and almost destroyed themselves.

There were a lot of mixed feelings to say the least. I was excited—all of my childhood dreams of the wondrous elves were going to come true. I was also so sad and sick at what was about to happen to them—and that we couldn't stop it—that I wanted to run screaming the other direction.

There was some directed shouting that sounded to be aimed at us, or rather at Alric since he was driving the carriage. Since he was born long after the war, he'd never have seen the city except as I had—digging through the ruins.

Siabiane tapped the roof of the carriage and Alric brought the horses to a halt. They'd been at a slow walk since we were within earshot of the city. She waved at an elven knight. He looked so much like Flarinen in profile that I almost said something.

"I say, it has been a long time since myself or my companions have been here, is the palace entrance for carriages still to the left?" The guard had been looking ahead and turned at the carriage, then Siabiane. His lip had automatically been curling into a snarl—must be an ancestor of Flarinen—but dropped to a bow when he saw Siabiane.

"Lady Siabiane, it has been far too long since we have been graced with your beauty. I can ride escort if you would prefer."

There was no way those words could have ever come out of Flarinen's mouth. Maybe the similarity in looks was a coincidence. Then I saw the look he shot Alric. Or not.

"Thank you, Captain Jarlt, I believe we will manage just fine. I will mention your courtesy to the queen." Siabiane nodded and shut the carriage door.

"Are all of the knights like that? He was a different person when he first turned to us." I was back to guessing he might be Flarinen's father or even grandfather.

"Sadly, many are. I dislike using my position as one of the queen's advisors like that, but I really hate dealing with them."

Alric had turned to the left and we worked our way through a series of increasingly nicer buildings. I was trying to place the ruins I used to dig through into what we rode through—but I couldn't. There was no similarity. Not to mention no full map of the ruins had ever been made and the parts that were outside of Beccia were mostly the edges of the city. It was heartbreaking to know that within a few short years these beautiful structures would be abandoned and swallowed up by the massive gapen trees incorporated into the landscaping everywhere I looked. The trees were controlled now—that obviously changed when the elves fled.

"I thought you said there were dangers afoot? Everything looks peaceful." Okay, that wasn't the best word. There were plenty of folks hustling around, at least until we started getting to the larger homes sitting behind gated walls. The main thing was it looked normal and not that far off from one of the larger cities like Kenithworth. Just populated with elves.

A sadness filled Siabiane's eyes and she watched the houses go by. "It does, doesn't it? But there has been a change in the air since the king died. They claimed it was a hunting accident, but I knew better. Accidents do not happen to hunters as skilled as he was. Had I been here I could have followed the truth. Which was why it happened when I was far in the southern lands." She shook her head, then turned to me. "But don't mention that suspicion to anyone, especially to anyone in the palace. It has been three years now, and Queen Heliane has come to terms with it. Her daughter is too young to need those rumors circling her father's death."

I nodded. After all, I was a walking pile of secrets I couldn't tell anyone in this time. What was one more? I didn't know if the current queen survived the war, or perished later. But I'd bet her daughter's name was Jelinath.

"State your name,"The guard was on the other side from my window, and judging by the tone I really didn't want to see him.

"Lord Alric from the kingdom of Lathing, my companions are the Lady Siabiane and my wife, Lady Taryn, also from Lathing."

Siabiane and I shared a look. I'd become a wife without ever saying I do. Siabiane nodded slowly and kept her voice down. "That actually is bright of him. Even though by coming from one of the heathen lands to the south, your lord and lady titles won't have much weight, it is better you are linked through matrimony—even if fictitious."

"You are not Lady Siabiane's driver." The guard went from bored to aggressive immediately.

"He was murdered by rogues that shouldn't have had access to the royal road. I saw no knights in attendance; they were allowed to slaughter him in front of the Lady. Do you wish I bring her out to recount the tale to you?"

I hadn't heard that tone from Alric in a long time. He'd been raised a noble, and although he rebelled later on, he could channel that attitude better than some of the best thespians on a stage.

"I apologize," the knight said. "I meant no disrespect and this news is grievous. Most of our knights were called away to the north and we're too thinly spread. Please proceed to the front and we will have the carriage taken around to the back."

Alric had already moved the horses forward when I heard him say thank you. The timing was enough to act as a dismissal.

"What's going on to the north?" I asked Siabiane.

She shook her head. "Nothing that I have been privy to, and Lord Lorcan and I communicate almost every day. It is not good that guards were withdrawn and the senior royal advisor was left unaware."

The horses came to a halt and the clanking of fully armored knights coming down stairs could be heard. It said a lot about how my situation had changed over the past year. I'd never seen knights in armor up until a few months ago, yet, now I could recognize that unique sound sight unseen.

The door to the carriage opened and a double row of knights, six on each side, lined the way. The Siabiane of my time was respected and feared, but unknown to most as she'd locked herself away not long after the enclave had been created. Clearly, the one of this time was far better known. At least by anyone involved with the palace.

The closest knight held out his hand for Siabiane and once she'd descended, the next one did the same with me. The look on his face said he had no idea who I was, but being with Lady Siabiane weighed enough to not take chances.

Alric stepped in beside me, smoothly taking over from the knight. "I shall escort my wife." There was no question, simply an assertion. The knight tipped his head and followed behind.

The palace steps were enough like the façade of the palace in the enclave that they could have been the same structure. Except that this one was twice as big and was far older and richer.

I allowed Alric to pull me up the stairs, but the grandeur hit me hard. More important, the fact that this building, all of these buildings, or rather what was left of them, were buried under the outskirts of Beccia got me. Actually, considering the size of the city, they were under Beccia itself as well.

The massive doors swung open and a short man dressed in white robes came running down. He smiled to Siabiane, but turned to me and wrapped me in a hug.

"You are finally here!"

CHAPTER EIGHTEEN

THE HUG HAD TAKEN ME by surprise—no one should be hugging me in this time unless it was Alric. I peered down at the hugger in question once he finally released me. He didn't look like an elf, more like a child of a dwarf and an elf, and possibly something else that liked to live in trees.

The faeries kicked around a few times, but, luckily, after he had let go. Trying to explain to a total stranger why part of my body was flailing about wouldn't have been fun. Even less so on the palace steps.

"Nasif? I don't believe you've been introduced to Lady Taryn or her husband, Lord Alric. They are from the south, and are dear companions of mine," she raised her voice a bit at that, "who have never been to Glaisdale."

"That doesn't matter—I knew she'd be coming. Yes, I did." He leaned in closer and winked at my chest. "And the wee ones as well."

I looked over his head to Siabiane, but she quickly took his arm and led him into the palace. Alric and I followed.

"That was more than a little odd. Do you recognize him from the enclave growing up?" Elves had freakishly good hearing so I'd pitched my voice in a breathy whisper.

Alric smiled and kissed my hand as we ascended the last stairs. "No, but even though the enclave was not as big as this, there were many in the palace I didn't know. I trust Siabiane's acceptance of him."

We were at the doors by then and a new set of guards. The rest of the discussion would have to wait.

The entrance to the palace in the enclave had been a massive hall, with multiple stairwells leading to floors above and beyond.

This was the same concept, but even grander. Only this time Alric's grandmother wasn't here to lock him up. Damn. I'd been worried about his father being in this time, but his grandmother was even more likely to be in the palace at this time. That woman could scare an army of syclarions and rakasa.

"Ah, Lady Siabiane, gracious greetings, my old friend." The voice came from behind us but I felt my back stiffen; it was Lorcan. I knew logically that there was no way he'd know who we were. He wouldn't meet us for a thousand years. But the voice sounded so happy and welcoming I wanted to turn around and fling myself into his arms and tell him everything. Give him and his people a chance to save themselves. To save himself from almost dying in the first battle of the war. Lorcan had a long scar on his neck, one he usually kept glamoured. He'd been attacked when the fighting began and should have died. But someone saved him. That, along with having to rebuild his culture, and then being made into a ghost by his own brother were things I wanted to protect him from.

Alric turned us around slowly to give me time to brace myself.

Siabiane wrapped Lorcan in a warm hug, then she stepped back and motioned to us. "I want you to meet two dear companions, Lord Alric and Lady Taryn. They rescued me when Galfin was murdered on the royal road and I trust them with my life." Her voice was pitched just loud enough for any court hangers on to hear. She'd just given us security in the palace.

Lorcan came forward, looking so much like the Lorcan I knew, yet at the same time, so different. He took my hand first and kissed it like a courtier. Then he took Alric's and shook it well. "You have saved one of my best companions; I too am indebted to you." He turned back to Siabiane. "We have much to discuss. I can arrange for guest chambers for your friends."

She smiled but shook her head. "We do need to talk, but I would feel better with them nearby. There is more than enough room in my suites for all of us. They can have the blue rooms." She turned to us. "All of your belongings will be brought to the suite. The guards will take you up there now and I will join you for dinner soon."

I couldn't help but stiffen as a guard came to lead us to our rooms. Yes, this wasn't the enclave's palace and the chances of me being locked in a tower room jail were exceedingly slim. But the similarities were too close for my comfort. There had been internal intrigue going on in the enclave when I was locked up. There was no way anyone could tell me there wasn't a hell of a lot of intrigue going on here right now. I wasn't sure how far away from the first attack we were, but Siabiane's concerns about the death of the king and the attack on a supposedly safe road both said bad things were happening.

I hoped that Alric and I could find a way back to our time before it happened. Seeing the elves before their destruction was bittersweet—having to live through it—or try to—wasn't something I wanted to experience.

But my worries were unfounded. For now at any rate. The guard led us to a pair of massive doors that appeared to be over half of the floor we were on. At least if the lack of any other doors short of a matching pair across the hall was an indication.

With a bow, the palace guard opened the doors. "Your chambers are to the left. Your bags will be up shortly and if you require anything pull on the red velvet cord in the corner." He waited until we got into the foyer, then shut the doors behind us.

I couldn't help it; I automatically took a few steps back and listened at the door for any locking mechanisms.

"What are you doing?" Alric had also taken a step, but toward the rooms on the left.

I gave them one more second to trap us, then finally turned to Alric. "Sorry, flashbacks to the enclave."

"I would say you're being paranoid, but this is not a good time to be here. I now wish I'd paid more attention in primary classes as a boy. I'm afraid even knowing the exact date wouldn't help me guess how close we are to the start of the war."

I followed him into the set of doors to the left. The main doors had opened into an elaborate foyer, with two more pairs of doors at each end.

I was right behind him when he pushed open the doors and I stood there in the doorway for a good while after he'd gone further in. I'd expected maybe a nice bedroom, something fancy with hopefully an attached bathroom, but that was it.

Before me was a living area larger than my entire house in Beccia. Including the front yard. Three high-end sofas surrounded a massive fireplace with a nice sized fire already crackling. Five smaller chairs were sat around the rest of the room with a pair overlooking the largest window I'd seen in my life.

I wandered around the living area, touching things, testing out each sofa and chair, when Alric stuck his head back into the room.

"You'll want to see the rest." He ducked back down the hall before I even got out of my chair.

There was a short hall that lead to a single door, which, if anything, was fancier than the other two pairs combined.

The door was open so I went inside. Alric was looking out a window, but that wasn't what made me gasp. The bedroom was huge. It also had a fireplace, also already set with a nice fire. The bed looked amazing, and after far too many nights of sleeping on the ground I couldn't be blamed for running to it and jumping on. Not easy with the long fancy dress I'd forgotten I was wearing, but I managed.

Alric turned around laughing. "That actually wasn't the main thing I thought you'd go for, but I agree on your choice. You might want to look in there though." He stayed near the window and pointed to the partially closed door across from the bed.

I managed to roll myself off the huge bed and pushed open the door.

Not only was the bathroom in our suite, there was a massive bathtub inside of it. I hadn't had a bath since I'd had to leave Beccia. Showers were becoming the rage, and far cheaper to install. Not to mention on the road you got what you could find.

"Oh, how lovely," I said. Then pulled myself away. I was going to get a bath in that tub, probably many. But I had no idea how long Alric and I would be alone and we needed to make plans. It said a lot about how messed up my life was right now that I was alone with the man who was probably the love of my life and I wanted to talk.

"What can we do to get back to our time and is there any way we can warn them or stop the war before we do?"

Alric moved away from the window and rubbed my arms. It might have even turned a bit romantic until the faeries all started kicking me in the chest. I opened the pocket and took off the cloak. They flew out and tumbled in the air around the room.

"You can explore all you want on our side. Don't go into the next set of rooms unless Siabiane invites you and if there is anyone other than her or us, you go invisible or hide, got it?"

Crusty didn't even look up from where she was skimming the carpet and diving under the bed. Leaf nodded, and Garbage just waved at me. At least the rooms should keep them out of trouble for a little while.

Alric turned and held out one of the overstuffed chairs near the fire for me, and took the one next to it. He looked tired.

"I don't know. Once I realized when I'd been brought, and that it clearly wasn't one of the temporary time waves, I started looking at my options in case I couldn't figure out how to get back. Garbage wasn't helpful beyond admonishing me to stay near where we came through—she somehow knew you and her friends would be coming, but didn't tell me that. But that was before you got here." He rubbed my hand. "We have to get back to our time."

That had kind of been my idea since I'd landed. I narrowed my eyes. "So you would have stayed here?"

"Not willingly, but I really have no idea how to get out. You are another thing entirely."

For a brief moment I thought he was being extra sweet. Alric really wasn't the demonstrative sort. Then he put his hand on my cheek. Right where the sapphire manticore was hidden.

"Whatever has led the relics to come back has got to be stopped. That can only be done with all of them."

He removed his hand and I felt an echoing coldness. It could have been the lack of warmth from his skin, but it had a more familiar feel. The manticore froze things—lots of things, but fortunately not me. It worked through me since it had decided to move in.

"That actually makes no sense. If they need it all together as well, wouldn't having a piece lost a thousand years in the past make it impossible to get it?" This time stuff was already messing with my head.

"Or they wait for you to die and take it from your bones. At any time."

I put my head in my hands. When had my life as a digger turned into this? The answer sat next to me.

"I should hate you, you know," I said as I took a deep

sigh. "None of this would have happened if I hadn't been hired to bring you in."

Alric pulled me over to his lap and traced my face with his fingertip. "Is it all bad though?" The kiss he gave me and my enthusiastic response answered itself.

We finally broke apart when noises came from the outer room. "Well, *husband*, do you want to go check? It's probably our bags." Not that they were really our bags—neither he nor I had anything that wasn't created by Siabiane. It would have looked odd to arrive without anything though.

He gave me another kiss, just a quick one this time, then went out the door. A moment later I heard a crash and Alric carefully called out, "Taryn? Can you come out here slowly?"

I knew he would never ask me to come out if there was something dangerous, even at the risk of his own life. But there was a strain in his voice I'd rarely heard.

I went down the short hall to the front room. The center sofa was knocked over and Alric was partially pinned under it. A short hooded form was keeping him down. At first I thought he was holding a knife. I moved closer, the person hadn't turned around, then I realized it was a pen, not a knife.

"I really need to talk to her...to you...and her...and them." The cloaked arm pointed to where the three faeries sat on the mantel of the fireplace. So much for them staying invisible around strangers. I glared at them, but they smiled and went back to watching Alric and his captor.

"Oh, for crying out loud, what is going on? Get off my *husband*."

His speech was far more rambling than it had been when he first ambushed us, or rather me, but I finally realized who it was. Siabiane's friend Nasif.

Nasif threw back the hood of his cloak and bounded off the sofa. Alric winced but then slid out from underneath.

"It IS you. I thought it was before, but I wasn't certain.

Now, I am certain," he said, then waved at the girls who were showing no signs of going invisible. "Hello, ladies!" He even went so far as to hold out a hand that was now suddenly filled with sugar. If there were few, if any, faeries around during this time, how did so many people know about their addiction to sugar?

And be able to win them over so fast. "It's Padraig all over again." I'd muttered it to myself, but whatever crossbreed Nasif was he had acute hearing.

"You've heard of our valiant Padraig? You couldn't have known him before what happened actually happened since you weren't here then. So he must turn out okay? I so worry about him. It wasn't fair."

Having robbed him of all of his sugar, the faeries flew back to the mantel.

I looked over the small rambling man's head to Alric. We must be close to the start of the war. I assumed Nasif was talking about when Padraig had been attacked and left in a deep sleep for a few hundred years.

"We've heard rumors of him," Alric said as he dusted himself off and fixed the sofa. "It was horrible for one such as him to be brought so low."

Nasif looked between the two of us for a moment, then ran over and jumped onto the sofa facing us. "I know, you know. Well, I know many things that you don't know and will never know. I know all there is to know of the Ancients and their wee friends." He nodded to the faeries. "I also know about those relics," he pointed to my cheek, "and about the time shifts. You five got caught in a wave that had been weaponized."

I stood with my hands on the back of the closest sofa. I opened my mouth a few times, looked to the faeries who shrugged and dangled their feet, then finally went around and sat down on the sofa I'd been leaning on. Heavily. Most of what he said was still smacking itself in to my skull as I tried to process it. "The faeries were close friends of the Ancients?" That was the only thing that connected enough for me to comment on.

CHAPTER NINETEEN

EVEN ALRIC'S BROWS WERE LOWERED in thought as he processed what Nasif said.

"Yes. They were fast friends, long ago. But those memories were lost. When the Ancients were destroyed, much of what they held dear was lost or changed. The wee folks were lost in the dark times after the Ancients vanished. The land they knew had changed, and crude, throwback syclarions were roaming the land. Queen Mungoosey took her remaining faeries and fled."

"Hail Queen Mungoosey!" All three faeries shouted at once. "High Queen Princess Buttercup Turtledove Rat-BatZee Growltigerious Mungoosey, Empress of all." I waved them off before they launched into a second round of her full name. I never had figured out how a small flying faery cat had such a long name. Nor why she was the only faery cat I'd ever seen.

"So how do you know about us?" Alric had come around and sat next to me, but he looked as confused as I felt.

"I study time waves; no one else here even believes they exist. Siabiane humors me, but even she has her doubts. Don't tell anyone but I have been working with the time waves to try and travel to the past." His arms flailed around as he got excited. "If I could go back far enough, I could be there when whatever destroyed the Ancients happened. I would finally know the truth."

I looked to Alric. We'd been flung back a thousand years.

If he could go back fifteen hundred years from here, he would see what happened to them. I admitted to myself that sounded intriguing. Only if we could make our way back, that was.

"Of course time waves only seem to work in one direction, so if I made it I wouldn't be able to come back and tell people." He looked so earnest that it was hard not to share his enthusiasm.

Then his words hit and my stomach dropped. "There's no way back?" The feeling that I couldn't be here was slowly crawling back. Like a dull headache that faded but wouldn't go away.

"Not that I can tell, however there are changes all the time, about time. What time are you all from? I know you're not from our time; your signatures are completely skewed." He waved one hand to encompass all five of us.

"As near as I can guess, about a thousand years." Alric looked worried, but even he, with all of his years of adventuring, spying, and thieving, had never come across something like this.

Nasif let out a long whistle. "That is truly amazing is what that is. A thousand years. What is the world like? How big has this city gotten? It's already far too big in my opinion. If it weren't for my research needing to be here, I'd go live elsewhere like Lady Siabiane." He stopped and cocked his head. "I don't want to know, do I? And you can't tell me, you can't tell any of us. If you change whatever happens, and from the sorrow on your faces it is not good at all, you will cease to exist. That means this time would become a loop, never moving forward." He then broke down and started muttering formulas, drawing them in the air in front of him. "No. You can't tell us. Even Siabiane."

A knock came from our suite door, followed by the woman herself. "I'm sorry to intrude, but they've brought up your bags and I took the liberty of ordering the cooks to bring up dinner. It should be here shortly. I hate to impose on your first night here, but there is a small ball tonight to honor the queen. I would be most grateful if you could join us for a short while." She came in and nodded to Nasif with a sigh. "I had a feeling you would be here." She turned to me. "He gets odd fixations sometimes, spouts a lot of nonsense, and will talk forever. He does seem to be fixated on you, my dear."

The faeries flew off the mantel and swarmed Siabiane. "And us! He likes us!"

Siabiane raised one delicate eyebrow at the faeries being visible.

I shrugged, still trying to process the words *ball* and *going to*. Maybe I could figure a way out later—I'd never been a dancer and doubted that was going to start now. "I know, but he already knew about them, so I guess they felt it was okay."

I looked to Alric and crazy Nasif, then back to Siabiane. We couldn't save the elves from what was going to happen. We didn't even know when it would happen, but things seemed to be going bad quickly. We needed to get back to our time and stop any new disasters that would befall if Nivinal figured out how to use the relic weapon. I had a feeling we needed Siabiane on board as well—both now and in the future.

Nasif stopped his mad scribbling in the air, looked at all of us, and then nodded. "Yes, you should tell her. She'd most likely figure it out eventually. Brightest of us all, she is. But it might be too late." With that he went back to shaking his head at the invisible numbers and words he was writing in the air. He even went so far as to wipe out one he didn't like.

I wasn't exactly sure how to bring it up, but Alric took that job.

"We're more than simply waylaid travelers from the south. We are actually from the spot you found us, only a few years later."

Siabiane looked to Nasif, but he was calculating something, so she studied both of us for a moment. Then she held out her hand and Garbage flew over. "It's not that I doubt you, and Nasif has been claiming this can, and does, happen for years. But there are also serious spells out there, ones that can make people believe the most unusual things about themselves." She held Garbage up to eye level.

I'd never seen my little orange miscreant be so focused.

"Truth bringer, what say ye? Are you from a different time, along with your companions?"

Garbage didn't speak at first, then she nodded. "Yup. No here, here bad. He go, she follow, we go. Needs go back."

Siabiane smiled and held her hand up to indicate Garbage could go back to her friends.

"I hate to say this, Nasif, my old friend. But deep in my heart I believed you were wrong. Time needed to be pure and linear." She gave a sad smile. "It was the only thing that was. We shall deal with this as we deal with all complications. I do think between Nasif and I we can find a way to send you back to the time you came from."

"A thousand years in the future, more or less." I filled in since no one else was going to. I figured longer time jumps would be harder, but since we were the only ones who managed to do it, maybe that wasn't the case.

Siabiane did pale a bit at my words. "Oh dear. I so do wish I could find out what the world is like so far from now. But that cannot come about. No one beyond us must know, and you *cannot* tell us anything."

Nasif finished his calculations and nodded. "I warned them as well—nothing can be said. Nothing changed. That goes for the wee ones as well."

The three faeries had stopped paying attention to us and were focused on their tiny black bags. All looked up at once and nodded. I heard a clinking sound—a familiar one.

"If you're going to drink, at least go into the next room. And remember, you cannot leave these rooms unless one of us say."

The faeries all nodded and flew to the bedroom.

"What was that noise?" Siabiane watched them go.

"Those little bags of theirs hold a lot of things—including probably a pub's worth of ale. I will warn you, you might have heard rumors of the faeries from long ago, but I doubt they ever warned about their singing. Especially their drunken singing."

"Faeries were never said to drink, well, anything beyond flower petal water."

Alric let out a snort as he tried not to laugh. "That's one rumor that was horribly wrong. Those faeries drink more than a troop of thieves after a successful haul. It wasn't in the books I read about them either."

Nasif got up and sat down at least five times, each time in a slightly different spot on the same couch. "Yes, things change. Wee ones change. Queen Mungoosey most likely didn't like the change."

"Not at all. I think there's been a falling out among them. There might have also been an issue because Garbage led the faeries—even Queen Mungoosey—to help save me, Alric, and a bunch of other important people and things that I can't mention." I caught myself before I said glass gargoyle. The less said about specific events in the future, even if they probably wouldn't impact this timeline, the better.

"They could have changed over the years," Siabiane said. "Or my sister changed them. That was probably the case. Mathildaringa always sticks her nose in where it's not needed. But she usually has a good reason for it." She stopped and her eyes grew round. "I realized that when you said she'd helped you, you meant a long time from now."

"And we shouldn't be talking of that," Nasif said with a

smile.

A knock came and soon the front room was filled with platters of food and all talk stopped.

After we all ate our fill, including the faeries who tumbled out of the bedroom to grab some food, Nasif left.

"You will have an hour or so before the ball. I took the liberty of creating appropriate garb for both of you."

"Are you certain we should go?" Alric asked. "The more exposure to everyone, the more chance we will let something slip."

I knew Alric never let anything slip by accident—unless he was seriously injured. He wanted to avoid the ball as much as I did.

Siabiane looked at both of us, then smiled and tilted her head. "I think the universe is safe. I also believe you two need to go, see the queen, see how the elves live now. When we get you back to your time, you will know who we were." She didn't mention the impending tragedy, as Nasif had. But it was clear she'd read enough on our faces to know something happened to change all of this. She'd come to the city because of bad changes, but she hadn't known how bad they were going to become.

Alric gave a flourished bow. "I would be honored to escort Lady Siabiane and Lady Taryn to the ball."

I really wasn't sure how I felt. Terror was one aspect. I'd never been to a dance let alone a ball. Or if I had when I was younger I didn't recall it. But excitement was there as well. A real elven ball, with my real elven boyfriend. I'd be lying to myself if I didn't say I was excited. The little girl I once was would have been happy to die right after this ball.

"Excellent. I shall be back in an hour or so." Siabiane's smile was relaxed. That was another reason for going; her life, like all of the elves, was about to catastrophically change.

CHAPTER TWENTY

THE FAERIES WERE STILL DRINKING and rolling on the side table. "Girls? Change of plans. How about you three stay in the front room, drink, sing, whatever you want. Just stay out there tonight and guard the place? Alric and I have a meeting to go to, and I know you three can keep everything safe here."

The faeries hated meetings. A ball they might have fought over, but not a meeting.

"We stay!" Leaf yelled.

"We guard!" Garbage added.

"We drunk!" Crusty warbled.

I assumed she meant drink, but she was already well on her way to drunk, so that might have been what she intended.

All three gathered their bottles and clanked their way back to the front room.

"Are you going to be okay with this?" Alric came in after the girls left. "You looked terrified when she first mentioned the ball."

Problem with being involved with a highly skilled elven tracker was that he was extremely aware of everything.

I sighed. "Yes, no, I don't know. I would love to see a real elven ball, even a small one. But I've never danced in my life. Does one have to dance? Can I watch from the sidelines? Maybe I can limp and we can say I hurt myself."

He laughed and came closer, then lifted up my chin

to kiss me. "You can do whatever you want. However, I would love to dance with you. Never fear, I had enough dance lessons as a child for both of us." He nodded to the closet. "Siabiane magicked some clothing in here for us. I have no idea what she had in those bags of hers."

Looking into those amazing leaf green eyes there was no way I could say no. I bit my lip, then nodded.

"Okay, but since you're my husband, you'd better make sure I look good out on the floor. Now, about the clothing."

I pushed open the closet and almost fell over. The dress I was currently wearing was fancier than anything I'd ever worn, but the fluffy deep green and blue concoction in front of me was more dress than I'd ever seen before. I was by no means a fashion girl, but this dress could make me one.

Long tapering sleeves would reach well past my fingertips but looked like they were supposed to. Tiny jewels in the fabric sparkled as I took it out of the closet. It was fitted in the bodice, then flared out softly past the waist. The way the colors blended made them look like petals on a flower.

I had no idea how long I stood there holding it before Alric gently took it from me and laid it on the bed.

"Are you sure you're okay?"

"That's pretty," I said stupidly. My brain had pushed aside all of the horrific things of the past year, our current situation, everything except this gown. Covey would have probably slapped me at this point. I shook my head. "I'm fine. How are your clothes?"

Alric turned away from the closet holding up a distinguished looking tunic, leggings, and cape combo. It was all black with green and blue trim finely worked on the edges. "If you want a bath before we go, you should probably do it now."

I broke away from my gown and trotted off for a quick

bath. Alric took one after me, and by the time he came out I was dressed and waiting with Siabiane in the front room.

Seeing his outfit and seeing him in his outfit were two different things. He was stunning. I admitted that I looked good, but he looked amazing. Black might not normally be a color of the current nobility, but after this ball, that might change.

Siabiane smiled. "You two will be the stars of the ball. And no one will know who you really are. Sometimes the best place to hide is in public."

We went to the hallway outside and Alric held out both arms, one for each of us.

The palace was huge, but fortunately, or unfortunately, the ballroom was near where we came down the stairs. I would have liked to see more of the palace, but would satisfy my curiosity with the ballroom.

Alric paused inside the entrance so they could announce us, but it was also my chance to take it all in without tripping over my feet. The delicate shoes that I had on under the gown weren't anything like my digger boots. The terror and fear of the past few months fell by the wayside as the magic of who the elves were, and who I was at this moment, took over. The room was glorious and magical.

I followed Siabiane in a simplified curtsy toward the raised dais ahead of us. I was certain she kept it simple so I could copy her, and I was grateful.

The queen was lovely, regal, and sad. She had more black in her entire gown than any other attendee aside from Alric. She nodded to us, and they announced the next guests.

The digger part of my brain couldn't help but try to classify the statues and art that filled the place as we moved forward. I was certain Qianru owned parts of a few of the statues. The floor itself was a work of art, a deep marbled gray worked with delicate designs.

Siabiane's version of small and my version of small were

two different things. There were easily two hundred people in the ballroom by the time they stopped announcing names. There were a number of curious looks thrown our way, but Siabiane tossed them back with a smile. She might not live in the city, but she was well known enough that her stay-away looks were respected.

I know Alric was afraid of us giving something away and messing with the future. I was more afraid of making a fool of myself.

The musicians in the corner started at a nod and wave from the queen. A soft waltz filled the room.

"Might I have this dance?" Alric gave another of his bows and held out his hand.

My heart was pounding so hard it felt like a tribe of rakasa were chasing me. I forced a smile and put my hand in his.

He pulled me close. "You trust me, right?"

I nodded.

"Then relax."

I took a deep breath and he whirled us onto the dance floor.

I'd never seen this part of Alric. When I'd met him he was a wanted thief with a nice bounty on his head. Then I found out he was an elf, and a noble born one at that. I'd never seen that side of him until now. Alric was good at adapting new personas, and this was probably another one for him. But it was amazing to see the change from a closed-off, serious tracker and fighter, to a gracious and charming elf noble. If I wasn't already in love with him, this night would have done it.

I was so busy thinking of the change in him I didn't even notice how he was guiding us around the floor for the first few minutes. My feet were following his lead, and while we weren't doing any of the fancier steps that some of the others were, we were still upright and moving through the floor, which was better than I'd feared.

The dance ended and I found myself wanting to go back to the dance floor. The next number was an elaborate group dance that looked to involve groups of three. Alric most likely could handle it, but I knew I couldn't.

Siabiane came over to us. "You both dance beautifully, and you made many of the palace hens mutter about the two beautiful strangers. Thank you for that. I would like to introduce you both to the queen—actually you caught her eye as well and she requested you be presented."

My heart started doing the rakasa rumble again. There wasn't a logical reason. Aside from thinking they might try to lock me up for the rest of my life, I had been fine meeting the royals of my time in the enclave. But this was the king's mother. A woman who had ruled at the highest time of the elven empire and lived through its lowest. Knowing what she was about to go through leant a serious turn to meeting her.

Even seated on her throne, it was clear she was at least as tall as Siabiane, if not taller than her. Her long dark hair was piled severely atop her head and looked to be designed strictly to hold the simple, gold crown in place.

We bowed and curtsied as Siabiane presented us.

"I am pleased to meet the people who helped save my friend." She gave a genuine smile in Siabiane's direction. "I know she is most formidable on her own, but there are times we all need assistance." She paused and peered closer at Alric. "I was told neither of you are from here? Yet you show a remarkable resemblance to Lady Marlisa's little daughter. Not so much to the parents, but very much to the girl. Sadly, she was ill so they did not attend tonight."

I'd been glancing between Alric and the queen. We knew there was a chance that family of his would be here. I didn't know his great-grandmother's name, but I'd be willing to bet it was Marlisa. The sick little girl was most likely Alric's powerful grandmother. She'd scared me the only time that I'd met her—it would have been interesting to see her as a child.

"Thank you, your majesty. I believe our family does have some distant relatives in the capital, but we've been in Lathing for a long while."

The queen nodded, then a lady in waiting caught her attention with another guest.

"Thank you both again for your help, and enjoy the rest of the evening."

Siabiane nodded to us as well and went to go chat up a few stuffy looking men in the far corner.

Alric and I were turning away when a soft voice called to us.

"I can see who you are, my lord." The speaker was a tiny, bird-like woman sitting alone at a small table for three. She was also the oldest elf I'd ever seen. Her face was lined and wrinkled, but her grin was fierce and her bright blue eyes were intelligent. "I am Nuthaina, and I have been watching both of you." She patted the chairs next to her. "Please sit, it's hard for me to make the rounds these days."

Alric bowed and held out one of the seats for me, then took the other. He looked extremely uncomfortable, almost as if he was afraid of her.

"I am Taryn, and this is my husband, Alric." I was surprised at Alric's failure to introduce us. He'd sat at her request but was looking wild around the eyes.

"No, he's not," Nuthaina leaned close to me, "but I promise not to tell anyone you're not married. I also won't tell them you're human." She looked at my ears so pointedly I reached up automatically.

"No one can see but me. I see all." She tilted her head and narrowed her eyes at me, then finally shook her head. "Except for you. Human you are, and not his bride, but the rest is blank."

A sharp turn to Alric made him jump back a bit. "Now you, on the other hand…why do you fear me?"

"I don't. It's been a long and trying day. I believe we

should be getting back to our rooms." He wasn't rude, Alric could channel rude if the need called for it. But he was so rattled by Nuthaina that he was ready to run out of the ballroom.

"For someone who has lied most of his life, you are suddenly very bad at it. You have heard of old Nuthaina, haven't you? Maybe a family member long ago had his fortune told and life exposed."

She didn't give Alric a chance to respond, just grabbed his right hand almost faster than I could see, and flipped it over to look at his palm.

"So much pain, fear, worry." She traced different areas of his hand.

I expected him to pull his hand away, he was easily much stronger than she was, but he simply drew his body as far away from her as he could.

"You have been through much, and most you hide under this." She patted his cheek. "But you need a purpose, one that is yours and yours alone. You have one, buried in your mark, but it has been forgotten." She covered his wrist completely with one hand and placed the other where I knew his high elf mark was on his cheek. "This is who you are meant to be, it was passed to you through the noble blood you carry."

A quick flash took place under both of her hands and then she allowed Alric to pull free. The mark on his face remained hidden, but on his wrist was a new mark. It was the same color as his high elf marks, but smaller, and vaguely horse shaped. He blocked my view of it by rubbing it.

"What have you done?"

"Only what should have been done long ago. There is a heavy heritage you carry in that mark of yours. Did your father die young?"

He shook his head.

"Then he failed to tell you the full meaning of your

family mark. Your line is an old and powerful one. A family around since the time of our lost Ancients. Your family pledged to kill the person or persons who led to the destruction of the Ancients." She beamed and rubbed his wrist. "It was a geas, one upon your family. It faded with time, but I have reactivated it and given it power again. You don't have to worry about doing the right thing in this—you won't have a choice." The way she was smiling, she seriously thought this was a wonderful situation.

Alric looked terrified and I couldn't blame him. Everyone wondered if what they were doing in life was right, but that didn't mean they wanted to be locked into a path. Not to mention that magic spells and things like geas weren't always as straight-forward as expected.

"Whoever destroyed the Ancients is long gone by now; there is no need for this." He held out his wrist.

She patted it and rose to her feet. "Time is more fluid than thought by anyone. You might find yourself facing their destroyer. You *will* kill them." Her eyes held his for a few moments and the ballroom felt like it had suddenly gone cold. Then she pulled back and smiled.

"Have a special evening, you two. You both look so lovely." She trotted off before Alric recovered enough to respond.

"What was that, and who was she?"

The worry on his face was replaced by a scowl. "Soothsayer. I recognize the name, but she wasn't around in my time." His eyes looked haunted as he glanced around the ballroom. "Would you mind if we called it a night? It has been a long day, and I suddenly don't feel like being here anymore."

He had my chair pulled halfway out before I nodded.

CHAPTER TWENTY ONE

I AWOKE THE NEXT MORNING RELISHING the soft bed. It really had been far too long since I'd been lying in one. Then I realized I was alone.

Siabiane had been thorough in creating clothing for me. I even had a nightdress and robe. I tied the robe on and went out to the front room. Alric was gone. Even more disturbing, so were the faeries.

I went to the window, but it wasn't that late in the morning, so it wasn't like I'd overslept. Alric must have woken and decided he needed to skulk around somewhere. In our current situation that wasn't a bad idea. But I did already miss the charming and gallant man of the previous night. At least the man who had been with me before Nuthaina put a curse on him.

Alric had briefly explained that it wasn't a curse per se, but something he would have to do. To me, that was a curse. I agreed that whoever destroyed the Ancients should be punished—if they weren't already long dead—but being forced to do anything was horrible.

Looking at the city before me was both awe inspiring as well as heartbreaking. The enclave had been gorgeous, but this city was breathtaking. The view I'd had from the carriage coming in was nothing compared to what I could see from this window. I might not be in the highest building, but I was very close. An entire quarter of the city was spread out before me like an upturned jewelry box. I turned to look out another window, and a familiar shape came into view in the corner. A silvery dome.

I dropped the curtain as the reality of what was going to happen here slammed into my gut. It might not even be the same building, but that rounded dome reminded me of the room that Locksead had used in Beccia as his hideout. It had been almost intact when it had been swallowed by the gapen trees.

I went and threw myself on the sofa.

"We help!" Crusty and Leaf popped out from nowhere and landed on my stomach. It was amazing how much impact two four-inch faeries could make when they landed

"Where were you two?"

"You say stay invisible so we do."

"I meant when there were strangers."

Leaf nodded enthusiastically. "Was stranger. He come, look at you, start to go in, then Crusty bite. Gone now."

I sat up immediately and looked for anything I could use as a weapon. "How long ago? Where did he go?" I looked down at Crusty and gave her a rub between her wings. "That was good to do, brave, but too risky. He could have seen you."

My heart started pounding. Alric was gone and some stranger had been in our rooms? I knew there was no way Alric would have left the doors unlocked. Unless he hadn't left voluntarily.

I went to the door, but it didn't look broken and the locking mechanism seemed to be working fine.

I started to ask Leaf how long ago the man came in, or any distinguishing markings about him, but I gave up before I opened my mouth. The girls were not good with descriptions, nor, for that matter, time.

"I want you to both watch the door and if anyone comes in, and I mean anyone, I want you to sing as loud as you can." That would get my attention and possibly scare the hell out of whoever was trying to come in.

I checked the lock once more then went to find something more suitable to wear.

The clothes Siabiane had found for me—more likely magically created—were all my size. They looked to be new and lovely variations of the beat-up tunic and pants that I'd come in wearing.

I grabbed a tunic and pants set then looked around for my old boots. They were worn but fit perfectly and I'd made sure they came with us out of the carriage. They were tucked in behind another newer pair.

Dressed, I gathered the faeries, tucked them inside my tunic, and stuck my head out into the hall. The hallway was empty but since this was the one inside Siabiane's suites that wasn't surprising. I went down to her door and knocked softly. It was early, judging by the sun, but I had a feeling she was one of those up-early-and-loving-it type of people.

I waited a few seconds and knocked again. Still nothing.

Checking the main hallway, again not terribly surprised it was empty since I was sure there was only one other set of suites on this floor, I went to the stairwell. Up until that moment I'd been worried about some evil folks waiting outside of the locked doors to grab me. So I hadn't really thought about where I should go next.

I followed the stairs down to the ground floor. While not as impressive as the main entrance hall, it was far more glamorous than anything I'd ever seen. There were few people up and about and most seemed bent on errands and moving quickly. I wandered around, looking at the art that covered the walls. Small statues set inside alcoves again made me think of Qianru—it was possible she even had some of these in her collection. I'd have to take a better look next time I had the chance and we weren't all racing about to try and stop the end of the world.

"Hello, you're one of our guests, aren't you?" A soft voice came up behind me and I almost jumped a foot in the air.

A tall, thin elf, all in white, but with the royal crest on his left shoulder stood behind me. "They are having a breakfast down that hallway. Take the second set of doors and you'll find them." He didn't even wait for my answer, just gave a small smile, nodded, and went on his way.

I felt stupid gaping after him, but he was moving too fast for me to politely follow. I was sure I wasn't one of the guests he thought I was. But I was *a* guest, and maybe Alric had gone down to get food. And taken Garbage with him? Unlikely.

Having no better direction to go, and feeling hungry, I followed the elf's instructions. I could grab food to go and eat as I tried to figure out even where to start looking for Alric.

The doors were large, but not as grand as the one leading into Siabiane's suites. The room was a soothing lemon yellow color, with huge windows at the far end. And what looked like enough food to feed an army.

I was about to go see if I should sit first, or go get food, then sit. I almost screamed when I was grabbed and pulled back behind a rack of fresh bread.

"Didn't you get my note?" Alric looked frazzled—something I rarely saw on him. He kept looking around the side of the rack, then pulling me back out of sight of the diners. "There is something bad going on: someone has taken Siabiane."

That got my attention. "Who has taken her? And what note? And yeah considering what is coming, there is probably a lot of bad going on." He wasn't acting or looking like himself. I felt a kick from one of the faeries. "Where's Garbage?"

"Why do you care about the trash? I need you to come with me to the edge of town; we need to get Siabiane back."

He pulled on my arm but I pulled back. We were mostly hidden by the rack so I tapped on my tunic. "Leaf, come out and tell me who this is."

Leaf came out and even looked around to make sure it was safe. She started to smile at Alric, then shook her head and growled. "Bad man come in room."

Alric, or the person pretending to be him, jumped when Leaf showed herself. He tried to get past me, but I wasn't going to let that happen. I grabbed his arm as he tried to get by and pushed it high up against his back. A few things popped in it. I leaned in close. "I don't know who you are, what in the hell you were doing in our rooms, nor why you look like Alric. But I will break your arm in three places in two seconds if you don't drop the glamour right now."

Leaf stayed where she was but she kept her eyes narrowed and still had that low growl going on.

Recently I'd started seeing through glamours. Yet this one had worked on me. Maybe it was because of the trip back in time, but I didn't like knowing that the ability to see through them wasn't as consistent as we thought. Since none of us knew why it had started, there was no way to know what might change it. The glare I gave the person before me went up a few notches.

I knew a glamour was simply surface, there were no real changes to the person. But I almost dropped the man's arm as the skin rolled under my hand. The handsome face before me changed and went longer—like as in a syclarion snout longer. He also went a bit taller, but shorter than most syclarions.

I really hated syclarions and this one was not changing my feelings about them. "Where the hell is Alric?" I asked and pushed his arm higher. It wasn't easy when he was Alric's height—a few more inches made it even less so. I managed to keep it up there.

"I don't know. Stop it! I don't!" He twisted as I pushed his arm higher. "Please. I was told to come here and get you to come with me. Your husband was gone, but then I was attacked in your rooms. I saw you come in here so I tried again."

We'd been behind the rack for too long, eventually someone was going to come around the corner. I needed to get him out of sight.

"You will change back into Alric and we are going to walk back to our rooms. Smile and nod at people, but say nothing."

He had been looking concerned but now looked confident again.

"And if you do anything to annoy me, or endanger anyone, I will have Leaf give you the bite of death. It's a slow and painful way to die."

Leaf played it up and leaned forward and bared her teeth. The syclarion almost broke his neck pulling back, but nodded and changed into Alric.

Well, sort of Alric. I might have scared him too much as his attention to detail from before was seriously lacking. This Alric was pale, awkward, and had stooped shoulders. Anyone who knew him wouldn't be fooled for a moment. Luckily, I was really the only one who knew him in this time.

I lowered his arm but hung on to it tightly. We almost made it to the stairs when I heard someone calling my name. Nasif. I nudged the fake Alric to move faster, but Nasif was fast when he was determined.

"Taryn! And…Alric?" His greeting ended in a glare as he got close enough to really see the person next to me.

Okay, so this copy was now so bad you didn't have to know Alric well, just have seen him once or twice.

"Nasif, we have a situation, and I need to get him back to our rooms. Immediately. And he might not want to go."

Nasif nodded for a bit. I was afraid he was going to start drawing calculations in the air. The fake Alric was getting twitchy and I didn't know if I could hang onto him if he made a run for it.

Finally Nasif grabbed the fake Alric's other arm and turned to face the people below us who were now starting to look up. "I believe you are correct, he doesn't look well at all. Come along, let's get you back to your chambers."

Nasif wasn't much taller than me, but he was wider than any elf I'd met and the bull-dogged way he strong-armed the fake Alric up the stairs told me I was probably right about his mixed elf/dwarf heritage.

We got up to the suites and Nasif nodded to the main door. "Siabiane would have keyed this to you both. Place your hand on that part next to the handle."

I did and the door popped open. The same worked for the door to our suite.

"But then how did this one get in? Leaf and Crusty said he broke into our rooms after Alric had gone."

"Wouldn't be the glamour spell," Nasif said as he shoved our prisoner into a chair. "You had a door breaker spell too, didn't you?" He sniffed the fake Alric carefully. "And it wasn't yours. Neither was the glamour you had. This one wouldn't fool anyone."

"Show him what you really look like," I said.

The syclarion dropped his sad excuse for a glamour and Nasif jumped back.

"A syclarion? But you are friends of the elves, why would you spy on one of our guests?"

I refrained from saying what I thought of that friendship but did set Leaf on the arm of the chair. She must have been taking lessons from Garbage, her scowl was almost as fierce. The growling was all her though. Until she did it earlier, I'd never heard any faery growl. Maybe they'd spent too much time with their kitties.

"Where is the real Alric?"

"I don't know...I was hired to do this. Well, convinced to do this, as I don't think there will be any payment really. And I don't believe in their cause." He turned to Nasif. "We are friends, our peoples, right? Why would we need to change that? What happened long ago shouldn't matter now."

I looked over his head to Nasif. He wasn't making a lot of sense but what he said didn't sound good. A cause? I hadn't known that the syclarions and the elves were friends. But that they were not going to be possibly in the future couldn't be a good thing. No elf had mentioned the syclarions as an instrument of their downfall. It was the Dark, the threat from within the fabric of the elven empire, that almost destroyed them.

Nasif kept watching him, but worry was slowly growing on his face.

"Leaf, is he telling the truth?" I asked.

She was already right next to him but she moved closer and touched his arm. That was new.

She sat back on the arm of the chair after a few moments. "Yes. Is ungood, but bigger bads around."

The syclarion was ungood, not bad. I knew the faeries didn't communicate as clearly as would be helpful, but there was usually a reason for the distinction. Most likely, the one before us wasn't evil, but his friends were. Great.

"What happened long ago?" Even if he wasn't out to destroy the world, I knew for a fact many of his people were—definitely in my time, and possibly in this one as well.

"Our people were destroyed by the Ancients. They say the elves and other races stood by and let it happen." He shrugged. "It's an old story, one not believed by most of my people."

"The Ancients are gone, wiped out completely by *someone.* But your people remain. How can you say they were destroyed if the other side is gone?" A thought hit me. "Were your people the reason the Ancients were lost?" I'd never heard anything even close to that until now, but of course the Ancients were all destroyed and most of this area was a wasteland. There weren't a lot of people in the area at the time. There would have been no one to tell the truth.

A chill went down my spine.

"The myth says the Ancients ruined our people in the final battle. And that they destroyed themselves as well. Our people used to be far stronger and bigger. They caused a sickness to weaken us. We lost most of our race." He held up a hand. "But even if true, there is no reason to blame the elves. You're our friends."

This was all new theory to me, and all I had was a confused and scared syclarion—interesting, I'd never seen either reaction in any syclarions I'd met. Nor had I heard of this myth and I knew if there was even a whisper of it in our time, Covey would have been aware of it. As thought provoking as this was, I needed to find out his plan, and if it involved Alric. I wasn't beyond thinking that Alric and Siabiane might have gone somewhere and they didn't want to disturb me. I would hold that thought close until it was ripped from me.

"Who has Alric?" I'd have to hope once we found Alric we could get more information out of our friend here.

"I don't know. They told me he was gone, and for me to get you outside. That was all."

"Who is behind this?" Nasif had been silent, but now broke in. He was almost such a clownish character that to see him serious was like seeing a totally new person. "There is someone, here in the palace, who put you up to this. Who is it?"

The syclarion looked to me but I folded my arms.

"I don't know."

I waved for Leaf to go touch him again, and he fluttered his hands at her. "I can't tell. They will kill me."

Nasif leaned close into the syclarion's face. "*We* will kill you if you don't. That faery looks sweet, but could kill you in such a way you'd take days dying. Tell us who was behind this."

The syclarion looked ready to cry—again another first in my interaction with this race.

"The ambassador," he said it so low that I could barely hear him. Nasif had far sharper hearing though.

"Ghilonious? My friend? I have breakfast with him twice a week. He doesn't have any hidden agenda against elves. Who are you really working for?"

The syclarion started shaking. "I tell the truth. I live on a farm five days ride from here. I was told to come here and wait until needed." He looked panicked now, like he couldn't get his words out in time to stop us from hurting him. "They didn't plan on this, what I did today, but I was waiting for them to call me to infiltrate something, not sure what. Yesterday there was a lot of concern, and I got called in, and spelled, you're right they weren't my spells, to come get the lady when she was alone. They weren't going to hurt you, just talk to you."

I'm sure my face went pale. The syclarions in my time were hunting for me, at least the ones working with the Mayor of Kenithworth. But how could ones a thousand years in the past know of me?

CHAPTER TWENTY TWO

"I NEED TO SPEAK TO GHILONIOUS," Nasif said as he jumped to his feet. "This has to be a mistake."

"And if it isn't? Do you think he's going to come out and say it? Alric and I are trusting you because Siabiane and Lorcan both trust you—and we trust them. You can't risk it."

Nasif stopped at the door, but then shook his head. "I'm not going to ask him anything about *this*, but I need to see him. I will not give anything away."

He was almost out the door, but turned back. "You, what is your name?"

"Dueble."

"Excellent, Dueble. You will stay here and obey Lady Taryn in anything she says until I come back, is that understood?" The flighty elf-breed of before was replaced with a shorter and rounder Lorcan in terms of personality.

Dueble nodded slowly. If he hadn't been a syclarion, I'd feel sorry for him. He really did appear to have fallen in with people way over his level.

Nasif shut the door and Dueble and I stared at each other for a few minutes.

"Are you…crying?" I asked. He had his face partially turned away from me, but there looked to be a wetness on his cheek.

"No," he said with a quavering voice. He also wiped at his face quickly. "Maybe. I was trying to make a name, and maybe some money. There's a girl back on the farm next to ours. But she says I'm not ambitious enough." He looked down at himself. "And I'm too small. I can't do anything about my size, but I thought I could change my fortunes. I wouldn't have wanted anyone to hurt you though."

"I'm glad to hear that." Alric's voice was a welcome sound, but he always disturbed me when he snuck in like that. "I would have hated to explain to Siabiane why there was blood in her lovely suite."

I turned and wasn't too surprised by what I saw. Alric stood next to the wall, his sword out, and Garbage was on his shoulder…in war feathers.

Leaf immediately flew to Garbage. Crusty must have had some special sense. She'd been asleep inside my tunic this entire time but kicked her way out and joined her friends.

"Who we war with?" Leaf asked with a little too much enthusiasm.

"Him, you watching him."

Leaf turned and looked at Dueble then lifted her shoulders in a shrug. "He ungood, but not bad. Scared." To demonstrate, she made a fierce face and lunged back at Dueble.

Even though she was five feet away from him he flinched enough to rock back the chair he was sitting in.

Alric put away his sword. "So where did he come from then?"

"He was pretending to be you, we had a discussion, and Nasif and I brought him here."

Leaf puffed out her chest. "And me!"

"Yes, and Leaf. He also broke into our rooms after you left. You could have left a note, you know."

Alric had been moving closer to Dueble, but more out of curiosity than anger. That changed when I told him what Dueble had been doing.

"I did leave a note. Siabiane wanted to show me some… things. You were exhausted so I left the note." He looked down at Dueble. "Hand it over."

"I...okay." Dueble reached into his tunic pocket and handed it to Alric. Who handed it to me.

"Going with Siabiane, back soon. Taking Garbage with me." I read aloud. "That wouldn't have helped much even if your copy hadn't picked it up."

I wanted to know what Alric and Siabiane had gone to go see. But Dueble already knew about the faeries, he didn't need to learn any more secrets.

A light knocking came from the front door. I got to my feet and motioned for Alric to stay. "You keep an eye on him."

I opened the door and found Siabiane and a fuming Nasif. His heavy brows were so drawn in on themselves I could barely see his eyes.

"I believe there is a confused syclarion here?" Siabiane walked into the room. Nasif stalked behind her.

"Lady Siabiane! I have...I mean I didn't...I don't know what I was doing!" Dueble completely broke into tears, gasping and sobbing like a four-year-old who lost their stuffed dragon. "Don't do anything to me."

Had he seen the look on Nasif's face, Dueble might have realized there was a larger threat close by. I wasn't sure what kind of magic user Nasif was, but I knew Siabiane was insanely powerful. She wasn't the one looking like he was going to explode.

"Now, Dueble, is it? Yes, I have heard about you. Our problem is that there is something going on and some high-ranking syclarions are missing. The ambassador's entire entourage for one thing."

Dueble's eyes went huge, which for a syclarion wasn't easy. They had long narrow eyes that weren't prone to roundness. He managed though. Then he threw himself on the carpet and started sobbing harder and rolling on the ground.

Seriously, this was the most un-syclarion syclarion I had

even seen. Siabiane was trying to talk to him, Alric was making sure he didn't try to roll away, and Nasif looked ready to chew a hole through someone.

I called the faeries over. "Can you go snap him out of this? The way you did me?"

Had Dueble seen the grins on their faces he would have snapped out of it himself.

They swarmed over to him, Leaf on the right cheek, Garbage on the left, and Crusty on his snout. I was going to call Crusty off, but they moved too fast. A few strikes later and he'd stopped wailing and fought to sit up on the carpet.

"Girls, he's done." I had to call them back, they were having a bit too much fun. They reluctantly flew back to me. Garbage peeled her war feathers off her overalls and shoved them in her tiny bag.

"I don't know anything." He sat there sniffling and looking at the carpet. "The ambassador and his people are part of the warrior caste and they do what they want."

The faeries had gone back to the mantle, but Garbage got to her feet. "I'll talk him."

I wasn't sure if she was going to make him talk, or talk at him until he surrendered in terror. But Siabiane stopped her.

"Thank you, my dear. But I think Dueble, Nasif, and I need to have a private talk." She got to her feet and Nasif came forward to help Dueble to his. "We'll be in my suites." She gave Alric a small nod, and they left the room.

I waited until the door shut before finding out what was going on.

"Okay, now what was so important that you took off on me like that?" I didn't add that after last night I had hoped some of his sneaking about would stop.

Alric's sword had vanished again. At least both of the swords were behaving better in this time than they had been back in Null. Mine had popped back up in the closet with all of the clothing and it was still there when I got dressed.

He ran his fingers through his hair, and flopped down on a sofa. "She showed me Padraig. He collapsed a few weeks ago and Lorcan and Siabiane were able to create an enclosed protection spell. Otherwise the spell that hit him would have destroyed him. They have no idea what caused it or where it came from. Which was pretty much what we knew in my time."

I knew seeing his friend like that must have torn him up. In our timeline, Padraig was brought out of his sleep right when Alric was a young boy, but seeing his best friend like that must have been horrifying.

He closed his eyes. "It's so hard knowing what they will be facing. And that we can't warn them even if we get stuck here."

"We stop it." Garbage and the girls had been sitting on the mantle swinging their legs. They were bored since their toy Dueble had been taken away.

Which might have been one of the reasons he was taken away.

The idea of the girls trying to stop what was happening was almost as scary as what was about to happen. "No, I think they don't need us, or you, stopping things. Besides, Queen Mungoosey wasn't happy about your interference in Beccia, what would she think of this?

Garbage stuck out her lower lip and sat back down. "You right. She not like." Her face perked up. "We go drink."

All three flew into the bedroom without waiting for us to say anything.

"I don't know what we can do. If we get trapped here, we'll need to stay out of the way. Live far away from everyone. If we survive."

He was echoing some of my darker thoughts from this morning, but it seemed worse coming from him. Or maybe just worse being said out loud.

"There must be a way back. That time wave was triggered to send whoever went through it way out of time. We need to find a way to turn that around." I had no idea how it worked, but paths couldn't be one-way only.

Both Alric and I looked up and spoke at the same time. "Nasif."

Then Alric shook his head. "We have no idea how far he's come with his theories—there's no mention of him or them when I was growing up. And no, I didn't know everyone in the enclave, but he would have stood out if he survived."

A knock from the front door broke that sobering thought, but it was quickly followed by Siabiane. "I'm sorry for interrupting, but I think you should both come over to my suites." She looked around. "Where are the faeries? Will they stay in this room if you ask? They are giving Dueble a nervous breakdown."

A high-ranking official of his people had set him to have me kidnapped—or worse—then left him holding the bag. And the faeries upset him? I had a feeling there were other things going on. Although fear was all about perception, and those faeries could be extremely disturbing.

Alric got off the sofa and his sword appeared immediately.

"And those spirit swords of yours need to stay here too, please."

With a shrug Alric banished his sword. I walked into the bedroom and checked in on the faeries. Sure enough they'd set up camp on a night table and had three open ales. I didn't recognize the label, so I had no idea where they got them.

"Girls? I have an important job for you, we need this room guarded. You can't let anyone in except us, and you need to watch all the windows."

Garbage and Leaf looked up and nodded; those two hadn't had enough ale to fog their brains yet. Crusty dove into her bottle as I watched. That was fine actually; I didn't care what they did as long as they stayed here.

Alric and Siabiane were softly talking and both stopped as soon as I stepped into the room.

"Do I want to know?"

Alric shook his head, but Siabiane nodded. "She has the right to know. You aren't part of our future, but Alric is. If you both are stuck here he will have to die before his younger self is born. A thousand years is a decent run of life, but it's hard when one is immortal. Elf children are rare; we don't breed as fast as other races. He will have to kill himself at least a year before his birth to make certain he is born. It's complicated."

Alric didn't look that upset, but I knew in part it was because his mind was working on a way back. I nodded. If we were stuck here, I would be dead of old age long before he had to kill himself.

Siabiane shook her head. "It is not something of worry right now, just something I needed to point out to him. However, I believe Dueble is actually going to be valuable to our cause to get you back to your own time." She turned and left the room.

Alric and I followed.

Siabiane's private suites were a mirror image of the rooms we had, but larger. The front room had not only a living area, but also a huge dining table.

Dueble seemed to have recovered as he and Nasif were in two chairs in a larger grouping and discussing something animatedly. That they both used similar wild hand gestures almost made me laugh.

"Gentlemen," Siabiane pitched her voice loud enough to get through whatever they were talking about. "We have much to discuss." She turned back to Alric and me with a concerned look. "I know we agreed that no one else should know. In fact I am extremely aware that with each new person learning about you we risk changes that could cause immeasurable harm. But I want you to hear Dueble's story. Then if you agree, we will move forward."

I nodded. I was deferring to her, Alric, and Nasif on this already. Time travel, time waves, or flinging your enemies into the past were not things I'd ever encountered as a digger.

Alric watched Dueble for a few moments, then nodded. "Agreed."

We took the rest of the chairs in the grouping and Siabiane nodded to Dueble.

He looked nervous, but the signs of his rampaging crying were gone. "I want you to know, I wouldn't have let them hurt you. You believe me, yes?"

He was so earnest and concerned I might have to rethink my entire worldview of syclarions.

"Yes." I forced a smile. "You were as much a victim as me." I wasn't sure I completely believed it, but it did seem he'd been taken advantage of.

"You will see how much as we speak. I was brought in, yes, but it was well known that there was something odd about the ambassador and his people. All of them were larger than the rest of us, not as big as we supposedly were before whatever happened with the Ancients, but much bigger than our people are now. Bulkier. Meaner." He held up his hand to Nasif. "I know he was your friend, but his people were different than the rest of my kind. That was probably why he became a leader so fast."

I nodded. The syclarions of my time weren't like Dueble, but sounded like they might be like this ambassador. "So the syclarions were once big, massive beings of power, they lost a fight with the Ancients, which somehow cost the Ancients their lives. They are now smaller and weaker, except for a select group that while not as big as your people were historically, are much larger and more powerful than the general population."

Dueble beamed. "That is the dilemma that I never

thought of until Nasif and I were talking. The ambassador's group, about thirty individuals I believe, travelled here a little over three years ago. Being stronger, larger, and far more magically powerful than all of us, they quickly took positions of power." He leaned forward and dropped his voice. "What if they didn't come from around here. Or around this *time*." His eyes tried to do that going round thing again, still with not great results, and he pointed to the ground excitedly. "*This* might not be their time."

I looked to Alric who was carefully keeping his face blank. Nasif wasn't.

"Isn't that amazing? What if this group did come back, or forward, we have no idea at what point the syclarion form began to change. Why would they have come here and where did they go to? I was shocked when I went to Ghilonious's offices and not he nor any of his people were around. It appeared that they had been hastily packing, so I presumed he'd run out and left some of his things. But what if they didn't leave of their own accord? What if they infiltrated the palace for a reason, and were carrying it out, when something or someone pulled them all away? Out of all of his people, only his second in command had been here since the prior ambassador."

He got up and marched around, then looked at me. "They were very interested in you, my dear. Oh yes. When I looked closer at what was left behind I realized no one would leave this information behind willingly. It was too damning. They knew when you came from."

It took a second for the when instead of where to settle in my brain. Nasif winced as the words left his mouth, Siabiane gave Nasif a shake of her head, and Dueble's eyes extended again. And all the focus was on me.

"You're a time traveler?" He turned to Nasif. "Maybe that's why they wanted her." And back to me. "Did you know Ghilonious? Is he an enemy of your people when you come from?"

I had no idea what to do. He was way too ready to believe in time travel and no doubt even a short time with Nasif had fueled that fire. They'd gone from Nasif distrusting him to appearing to be best friends in under half an hour. And Nasif was obsessed with time travel.

"I think we've run out of options," Alric said. "Not to mention I don't think Dueble would tell anyone, would he?" Alric hadn't called in his sword, but he did give Dueble one of his more dangerous looks.

"Never. I can't tell anyone about anything that's gone on here. My people, my real people, are simple farmers. We live well with our neighbors. Time travel and spying isn't for us."

He anxiously looked between all of us. His people might be farmers, but he definitely had an urge for excitement.

I looked around to see who was going to fill him in, then realized everyone was looking at me. Fine. "Alric and I were sent here by an evil mage from our time. We're from about a thousand years in the future and no, we can't tell you anything that will or will not happen, and we need to get back home or our being here could destroy the timeline. Oh, and the faeries are from our time too."

"That is why he wanted you," Nasif said. He was standing behind the chair and looked almost as excited as Dueble. "I might have liberated a few of the more interesting documents. He knew someone was coming back to this time—he didn't know who or when until you arrived."

He went over to the dining table and spread out the pages. Everyone else got up to look, so I trailed along. But my head was starting to hurt, and that odd gnawing feeling of not being able to be here was growing again.

I tried to read the lines on the pages, but either whatever was going on in my head was interfering or Ghilonious had incredibly horrific writing. I couldn't read a word.

"See here?" Nasif pointed to a bolder line. "Here's where he first mentions travelers out of time. It's dated a week ago but it looks like he's known about it for a while. Then when Siabiane brought in her two friends yesterday, he starts getting worried." Nasif tapped another page. "Alric disturbs him, but Taryn terrifies him. There are three different handwritings. I think they were refraining from talking out loud about what they needed to do in case of palace spies. But Taryn was not supposed to be here. They were going to have you killed." He looked up at that. He'd not really been paying attention to what he was saying, lost in reading the gibberish on the pages. That stopped him.

"Ghilonious was going to kill her?" Dueble managed to demonstrate that syclarions could go pale.

Nasif gave me a wincing smile then turned back to the pages. "No, he and his people were too worried to go near her. Alric wasn't a problem, but something about Taryn disturbed them. He was going to have an assassin do it after you brought her there. Actually, Dueble was going to die with her, they were going to make it look like he died trying to save her."

Yup, syclarions could go extremely pale. At least this type of one.

"What was going to happen to Alric?" I wasn't happy about being one incompetent kidnapper away from being murdered but I was also worried about Alric.

"They needed him for something—well, they needed whoever they were waiting for." Nasif pulled back a bit, and moved closer to Siabiane. "They were waiting for a powerful magic user from the future to come and lead them, it says so here." He tapped one of the pages. "They knew it couldn't be Taryn, unfortunately, it doesn't say why. Just that there was something wrong with her being here. And although I've not seen him use it, any magic user worth his or her salt can feel the power rolling off of Alric."

Both Nasif and Dueble watched Alric as if he'd grown an extra head. Siabiane watched him too but more with curiosity than concern.

"He might not be of our time, but he is of noble blood. And blood bleeds true." She muttered a few words and the mark on Alric's cheek flared into being.

It was funny that while I could see through glamours now, whether I wanted to or not, his high lord mark had remained hidden. The mark looked as it had before, a stylized horse shape. I knew that a larger, more ornate version was under his tunic covering part of his chest as well.

Alric looked embarrassed at first; he'd grown up hating being an elven high lord. It was a rank of birth and he felt it had no value. Finally, when all three kept staring he put his hand over it. "Are you done? Yes, I was born with this."

"And it serves you well. I think we can agree that, like Taryn, Alric was not who Ghilonious was waiting for. Which does indicate your both being sent here was an accident."

I wanted to point out that trusting people because of their noble blood was partially how the Dark came to almost destroy them. But I knew I couldn't.

I also couldn't stay upright anymore.

"I can't be here." I was aware of getting those words out, then the carpet ran up to smack me in the face.

CHAPTER TWENTY THREE

I HEARD VOICES AROUND ME. THE people in the room at first, then more. Far more. Old, young, dying, living. Too many of them and all rushing by me. No, they were rushing through me. Tearing at me as they were lost. I couldn't be here. I was already here.

"Stop!" I yelled and sat up.

I probably scared myself with my yell as much as the others around me. Except Dueble. I scared him enough to cause him to fall over.

Everyone had crouched around me when I'd taken a dive onto the carpet, but Dueble's balance must have been bad. The fall might have been an accident, but when he pulled himself up he looked to be quite a bit further from me than he had been.

The voices faded away. At least the ones that weren't in the room. The rushing feeling also stopped.

Alric pulled me over to his lap and kept brushing back my hair. "Just stay here for a bit, you look awful." He grinned. "Well, you look sick."

Siabiane leaned forward and put one hand on my face and closed her eyes. Everyone was silent. For my part I was afraid if I spoke, it might throw off any magic she was doing. I felt nothing, but a full range of emotions showed on her face. Concern moved into anger, then fear, then sadness. Finally she released my cheek, and a minute later she opened her eyes.

"How old are you?" There was a sadness there that didn't match the question.

"About thirty-five?" I shrugged. "I don't know for certain. My parents died in an accident, and I fled my hometown for Beccia. I have lived in Beccia for fifteen years."

"How does someone not know how old they are?" Nasif wasn't at all disturbed by anything I was doing, and leaned closer.

"I was in the accident that took my parents, a boating accident. A lot of my memories were lost—including my birthdate." It's funny that until this moment, I never really thought about it. The faeries didn't have birthdates, or if they did they certainly didn't know them. So me not knowing mine hadn't stood out.

"I think you might be older than you believe. Obviously, older than you look." With a wave she dropped the glamour that made me look like an elf. Nasif and Dueble both looked startled. Considering I hadn't seen any humans since I'd been here I wasn't surprised at their reaction. My people were probably living in caves somewhere—or the dryad side were still in trees.

"This is another thing you two cannot share with anyone. Our Taryn is not an elf." When Siabiane got nods of agreement from both of them, she turned back to me. "You said your lineage was human and dryad? Nothing else?" Her eyes narrowed as if she was trying to see inside my head.

"Again—lots of memories were lost. But I remember my mother, she had dryad on her side." I snapped my fingers as another thought came to me. "Your sister, Mathilda, she also said I was human and dryad. Kept repeating it while I was recovering."

"Recovering?" Nasif asked.

It was easier to sum up everything that happened after the accident quickly for Nasif and Dueble. Alric and Siabiane already knew.

"You say it was Siabiane's sister who rescued you?" Nasif rubbed his beard. The movement was common to dwarves, but their beards were usually a foot long at least. That Nasif had a beard was impressive for any elf, but it was less than a half inch from his skin. "Is she still running that witch con job up in Kenithworth?"

Siabiane laughed. "Probably, but we're not going to hunt her down to see. Not to mention we really can't risk damage to our timeline by more people knowing. I am surprised she said that. There is distinctly something else in your lineage, but when I try to get close enough to see what it is, it vanishes. It's something very far back."

"I doubt Mathilda has changed even given a thousand years. She was probably on a binge when she saved you. Good heart, but has a serious drinking problem." Nasif got off the carpet and went back to his pages on the table.

Dueble followed him and stuck close by, looking at different comments on the scraps of paper.

The drinking habits of their former caregiver did explain a lot about the faeries. Judging by the way the rest of the faeries didn't drink, and their queen seriously viewed mine as delinquents, it wasn't natural behavior for their kind.

I was laying on the carpet, with Alric mindlessly brushing back my hair. I thought about what Siabiane had said about my heritage. I'd tried, when I was first recovering at Mathilda's cabin, to recall my past. But she kept assuring me it would come back eventually. What eventually happened was that I recovered, got the faeries, and we were all kicked out when Mathilda decided to walk her house elsewhere.

I quickly forgot most of what had happened during my time with her, including her name. Having her name didn't help me as much as I had hoped in terms of gaining back some of those memories. Maybe I could get back to the Siabiane of my time and ask her help in finding her sister.

After we got back to our time, and stopped whatever bad thing was going to happen if Nivinal carried out his plan. I'd assumed he'd hooked up with Reginald for a reason—people like him usually did. So, them not being together should slow him down a bit. But we needed to get back.

"You look annoyed," Siabiane said as she gracefully rose to her feet.

I patted Alric's hand and ungracefully rose to my feet. "I reminded myself that as interesting as my heritage might be, we need to get back to our time. Soon. Oh, and I will be asking for your help in a thousand years to find your sister."

Alric rose as well. "Are there any hints at all as to time travel in those notes? Maybe if the syclarions were taken back against their will, the same might happen to us?"

"Except we have no idea where or when they went to," Dueble said without looking up from the documents.

Nasif nodded. "Very good point, my lad. Time travel is a new study. I'm the only one in the palace who takes it seriously and I don't know much at all. I can use some magic to trace time signatures, but that's in theory. I wish I'd known Ghilonious and his people were from a different time. The studies I could have done." His sigh was loud and heartfelt.

I kept my laugh to myself. Nasif wouldn't have liked it, and explaining would have taken too long. But having travelled with Covey, Padraig, and even Lorcan for a few days had brought me a good understanding of the aggressively academic.

"Would anyone else in the palace have seen them go? Or know what they'd been doing, aside from packing, before they were taken?" Alric ran his hand through his hair. "Assuming they were taken and didn't panic and leave. Yes, these pages wouldn't have been left behind by any rational sort. At least not one who was planning on coming back."

Nasif nodded. "Good point. I was basing my hypothesis

on the assumption they would want to come back. But maybe they knew they couldn't and just had to flee."

"How long ago did they come here?" I asked.

"A little bit over three years ago," Siabiane said, but she too was now trying to find answers in the left-behind pages.

"When did the king die?" I kept my voice low.

Siabiane paused and looked up. She frowned. "About two months after that."

"No, that was an accident, nothing more." Nasif's automatic response died even as he said it. "If it wasn't an accident, do you think Ghilonious could have been behind it?"

"If they came back to our time for a reason, it would need to be a big one wouldn't it? Dueble asked. "And look at this list." He waved the paper around so much that no one could have looked at it. "The ambassador's syclarions were mating with all of the local syclarion women. He had a list of who was supposed to go with whom. I recognize all of these names...they are all with child, or have recently given birth."

Okay, that added an ewww factor to whatever else they had been up to. Along with possibly causing the death of the elven monarch, they were trying to breed themselves into the local time?

"But why? What would that do?"

"Change the genetic make-up of the syclarions in our time, at least the local hatches," Dueble said. "Our country is far from here, so any changes here wouldn't affect them."

Damn it, this could be the syclarions helping the Dark as well as trying to increase their breed to survive the upcoming battles. Except that kids and babies being genetically stronger wouldn't help in a fight.

Which meant they had no idea exactly when the attack from the Dark was going to happen. This entire time thing was really messing with my mind.

Siabiane shook her head at me. I hadn't spoken out loud, but my face gave me away. "Leave the what and the why our syclarion friends were back here to us. We need to get you both out of here. I fear the changes impacted on this timeline by the syclarions might have already caused problems in this time period."

Nasif had gone back to the sheets, but he was looking for something specific. "Give me some time, I can figure this out." He looked to Dueble. "That is if you don't mind spending the afternoon here helping me?"

Dueble looked up with a happy nod. His people might be simple farmers, but he wasn't.

"What should we do?" Alric asked.

"First, can you re-glamour me? If those syclarions were disturbed by me even when I was glamoured, I don't want to take a chance on being seen as a human."

Siabiane smiled and touched my face. "I do think you are quite lovely without the elf disguise, but I agree that we can't have people noticing you."

I was about to say thank you when three blurs of color came tearing into the room. Through the wall. They'd re-discovered that trick of theirs a few weeks ago, but it seemed to only work sometimes. Apparently, this was one of the times.

"Bad, bad, bad!" Garbage got the words out first but the other two were saying them as well. All three had their war feathers on and were waving their war blades.

"What? What's happened?"

I heard a thunk behind me and looked back to see Nasif standing over Dueble. "I believe he passed out at their unique arrival." Nasif's voice was calm, and he didn't look ready to collapse at all. He did look concerned.

Not that I blamed him when it came to the faeries—I felt he was concerned about the wrong thing.

"We no do, things are wrong." Garbage looked so frightened she was scaring me.

I waved her over and held out my hand. "Okay, slowly. What happened?"

She took a deep breath to tell me when an explosion of sound engulfed us. My bones felt like they were being rattled apart. It stopped for a brief moment, but slammed back into action less than a minute later.

I turned to Siabiane but she looked almost as scared as the faeries. Then she shook it off and raised her hand. The sound wasn't blocked completely, but enough to keep my brain from turning to goo.

"What was that?" I knew my voice was probably too loud but my ears were ringing so badly I couldn't tell.

"That was the royal alarm, wasn't it?" Alric had picked up the same look the others had. Dueble and I were the only ones more confused and in pain than terrified.

"Yes it was." Siabiane turned to me. "The queen or the children have been attacked. I must go to them." She grabbed my shoulders. "You must stay here." She looked up and faced Alric and the faeries. "You are outsiders, and an attack that triggered that alarm means fatal or serious." She nodded to Dueble. "You need to stay here as well, particularly if your ambassador or his people were behind this."

He opened his mouth, most likely to defend his people, but a quick nod from Nasif had him close it.

I could tell Alric wanted to be there, fighting to destroy whoever had done this. His sword hand twitched even though the weapon hadn't reappeared.

"We will stay here," I said. "All of us." I watched the faeries, their little popping through walls trick wasn't making them trustworthy. "The girls know they could endanger others if they went out."

"We fight—is bad." Garbage had flown back to the other two, but her words were fiercer than her face. That reaction was more telling to me than the alarms. Finally she nodded. "We stay. Protect."

Siabiane turned to Dueble and gently touched his cheek. He collapsed. "I'm sorry my friend, but I believe you had plans to go out and fight."

I looked from the pile of Dueble to Siabiane. "You read his mind?" That was more than a little disturbing.

"No, my dear." She smiled. "But he is more honorable than many of his people—it was clear on his face."

Siabiane and Nasif both left after that. When the doors opened I heard the full force of the alarms going, but once they shut the sound was muffled again. It took a powerful mage to keep multiple spells running without being around them.

Alric started pacing and rubbing his forehead.

"This didn't happen…before. Did it?"

"No. When Siabiane said the king was killed, I wasn't sure. There was so much lost in the fighting and afterwards that not all of the history of right before the war made it to us. But I knew somehow he didn't make it to the founding of the enclave. The queen did. She was the one who led the rebuilding—her name was on many structures. She died before I was born, but she was there."

"And the children?"

"Queen Jelinath and her sister, Bethise. Jelinath made it to the enclave, obviously. Her sister didn't, but she was alive when the fighting started. Damn it, this isn't how it was supposed to happen. Padraig's collapse was off as well. Granted, Lorcan was the source of my information and we can't really ask him in this time. But the timing seems wrong."

Someone, or something, pounded on the main door with enough force to rattle glasses in here. Then we heard an explosion as the main door to Siabiane's pair of suites blew open.

I pointed to Dueble lying defenseless on the carpet and yelled to the faeries, "Hide!"

No arguments, although Garbage clearly wanted to fight.

All three landed on him, and he and they became invisible.

Alric's sword was in his hand immediately. Mine took a few seconds longer, but I could have kissed it when the willful thing appeared in my hand. I might have been imagining things, but it felt like the sword really wanted to fight. At least that was one of us.

We stood ready as more pounding came from the door before us. There was nowhere for us to go to, and we were far too high to jump out the window.

Like the outer doors before it, the inner door exploded in a rain of splinters. Two battered and bruised syclarions looking far more like the ones from my time than Dueble, jumped through the shattered wood.

In fact, they looked enough like the ones from my time that I was glad for Siabiane's elf glamour. I didn't recognize them, I'd really rather they didn't recognize me.

They both looked around the room, more like we weren't who was expected than assessing for any other combatants. That took an entire handful of seconds, then they charged us.

Alric had moved forward so he took the first one and even tried to partially block the second one from getting to me. Sweet, but it didn't slow him down much.

My sword hand went up to block a blow that could have taken off my head. Then I pushed the attacker's overextended arm back. My sword dipped and got a strike in, not a fatal one but gut wounds always hurt.

It felt like the sword and I were moving as one—unfortunately it seemed to be leading me. The good thing was that it was a better fighter than I was.

My sword training was enough to get the job done, but not gracefully. Now the sword and I were moving with more ease. A few more strikes by the syclarion and I was actually turning to attack instead of only defense.

Alric and his attacker tumbled over the back of one of the sofas, and my syclarion glanced over for a split second.

The sword and I darted forward and embedded it in his chest.

The syclarion had tried to defend too late but he still got in a slice on my arm. His eyes went wide as his brain told him he was dead.

A second later he and my sword vanished.

I screamed. I finally come to terms with my crazy weapon and it gets taken away? Not to mention people shouldn't vanish in front of you.

Alric had his syclarion trapped and disarmed. He held his sword to his throat. "Tell us what is going on. When are your people from?"

The syclarion had a few wounds, none life threatening if he got help soon. He watched both of us. Then he started yelling and trying to force a way out through the wall behind him. "No, it's you. You've ruined everything, you bitch. Everything." The moment he decided that since escape wasn't going to happen behind him, maybe he could rush us, was clear in his muddy eyes. Or maybe not.

I wasn't in direct line with the door, but the syclarion was aiming right for me. Even with his wounds he had no trouble covering the short distance from the wall to my throat.

I had no weapons, there was no way Alric would get to me before the syclarion. The reflex was automatic as the push spell came out. I was afraid I'd be causing a syclarion-shaped hole in Siabiane's wall.

That didn't happen.

Nothing happened at first, the syclarion froze in mid-leap with Alric almost on him. A second later, he vanished. No explosion. No hole. Just gone.

Alric's momentum was too much for him to stop but he turned so he only partially tackled me to the carpet.

"What just happened?" he asked as he rolled to his feet and helped me up.

"I was going to ask you that!" I looked around, hoping

against hope there would be two dead or dying syclarions lying there and they hadn't just vanished into thin air.

"Yours vanished as well? What did you do?"

"The one who charged me had it coming. I know we need to watch our magic usage here, but I didn't have a choice. I used the push spell on him. As for the first, I don't know, but he took my sword with him when he... vanished." I felt something drop on my feet and was glad to see my sword back. It didn't even have any blood on it anymore.

The faeries flew over to us, sniffed at the sword, scowled, then flew around the areas the two syclarions had vanished from. Finally all three stopped in the air in front of me.

"You did boom." Garbage looked like she was confused, mad, and sad all at once. A look I'd never seen before. I'd also never been accused of boom. Overall, I wasn't sure how I felt about it.

"What boom, sweetie? There was no boom." In fact, it was an anti-boom. Had the spell worked as I'd planned it, there would have been an actual boom.

"You boom. Change things."

Leaf shook her head. "Things changed. She put back."

"No, change."

"Is good."

"Is bad!"

The two were going chest to chest in the air. Crusty hung behind them looking vaguely amused.

"Do they always fight like that?"

I'd forgotten about Dueble until his groggy voice came from behind us.

"What happened to me? He got to his feet slowly, but his eyes were on the shattered door the entire time. "More concerning, what did I miss?"

I looked to Alric and tipped my head toward where our rooms were. I needed to find out what the faeries were jabbering about, as it might actually be important. If

I was understanding them, Garbage thought I'd caused a big problem because I sent the syclarions somewhere. Leaf also thought their vanishing was my fault but felt it was a good thing.

"Dueble, why don't you come with me?" Alric asked. "We were attacked and I want to make sure the attackers really left."

Dueble looked groggy but he followed after Alric. "Who are we looking for?"

"A pair of the ambassador's cronies, I'd guess."

Dueble paused, then moved faster. It was good to see him stepping up but hopefully that wouldn't come back to haunt us.

I waited until I heard the door on our suite close, then grabbed Garbage and Leaf and walked over to one of the remaining intact and upright sofas and sat down. Crusty spun a few circles around us, then sat down next to me.

Leaf and Garbage had stopped their argument, but both were still mad. I held on to them. "Girls, this is important. There is some bad stuff going on, some more boom. I need to know what you two are fighting about."

Both started chittering in native faery, talking so fast obviously the only purpose was to get more words out than the other faery.

"Stop. Now. STOP." All three faeries looked at me like I'd said I hated ale. "One of you. Tell me. Not in faery. What is going on?" When both took deep breaths to start their rant again, I looked over to Crusty. "Never mind. Crusty, I want you to tell me. I know you can." Crusty wasn't the brightest of the faeries, and she drank way more than any of them. But she also had no ego, and right now both of the faeries before me were running on way too much of that.

The other two shut up, in part because I still had them in my hands and I closed my pinkie fingers around their mouths. But also, neither were used to Crusty being asked to do anything.

Crusty looked around the room, her blue head swiveling around as she checked to make sure there wasn't another Crusty around that I could be talking to. Finally she moved closer and sat crossed legged on my thigh.

"You is time. Bad men don't want you here, mess up their time. But they no be here. Not their real time."

I smiled at Crusty and rubbed the space between her wings. That was the most coherent I've ever heard her. Now I had to figure out what it meant.

"So the bad men, the ones that broke in here," I waited for her to nod, "they were from another time?" Again a slow nod. "Were they from our time? Our time before we came back here?" I'd seen her eyes start to cross but she relaxed when I clarified.

"No our time, no." She gave a tiny pleased smile.

"But they knew Alric and I were from a different time?"

A happy nod.

"So they were trying to kill Alric and I because we were from the future?"

A stab to my right pinkie finger reminded me who I still held. I let go of Garbage and then a moment later, Leaf. They both flew up then settled down next to Crusty. Very well behaved considering what I'd done to both of them. Garbage glared at me of course.

"Kill you. Not him."

There went that illusion. This reinforced what Nasif had found.

"Me, why me? How am I time?"

Garbage stomped over and sat on Crusty to make her shut up. "Is always time. But now you time here, is bad. She say is good," she pointed to Leaf, "because bad men no be here." She shook her head. "But you no be here either. Need go now. But not go wrong time."

There was pure worry on her tiny orange face. I'd only seen her look like that once, when Leaf and Crusty had been kidnapped and she couldn't sense them.

"Do you know what the right time is, or the wrong time?"

"Need go *now*."

Even though they'd been muffled, I'd heard the alarms in the background. They stopped.

The girls noticed it too. Garbage grabbed my finger and pulled toward the door. The other two did as well.

"Leave now."

"Girls, we have no idea how to get back."

"We take, she magic, you go." Leaf was almost as concerned as Garbage and she pointed behind me.

Siabiane looked anything but her usual pristine self. Even during the battle in the enclave—some thousand years from now—I'd never seen her so disheveled.

Her gown had tears all along the bottom third and there was blood on her sleeves. The small dagger on her hip also looked to have blood on it.

"Is the queen…?" I didn't want to say the words.

"She is alive for now. The attacker was a syclarion, and he hurt her badly, but I have stopped the bleeding." She looked like all of her years had crashed down on her in that moment. "The faeries are right. I can't say how I know, but the attack on the queen should never have happened. We need to get you out of here immediately."

CHAPTER TWENTY FOUR

"YOU CAN'T THINK I HAD anything to do with that?"

"Not directly, no. I'm nowhere near an expert on time, yet I know any change can cause ripples. The syclarions were a long ripple but it's hard to say how much damage they did in three years. Alric is a short ripple—his impact has been slight, but it is there."

"Taryn is a massive ripple. And I agree with everyone—we need you back home *now*." Nasif had come in almost as silently as Siabiane. He looked battered as well and I had a feeling either there had been more than one syclarion, or the Dark had started to show themselves.

I wanted to ask how I could be a bigger ripple than Alric, or as it sounded, the syclarions, when they had all been here longer than me. But I didn't think either of them knew. Any more than I knew why my gut and head were screaming that I didn't belong here.

"Which brings us back to how do we do that?" I asked.

The faeries had been quiet while Siabiane and Nasif spoke, but they riled back up in the gap of conversation.

"We take," Garbage started.

"She magic," Leaf added.

"Go, go, go!" Crusty sang.

Siabiane held up one hand and the girls shut up immediately. "It won't be that easy, ladies. With Nasif's guidance I might be able to send you all back, but I can't be certain of making the exact time. If we are off by more than a few minutes, it could cause more problems than we already are seeing."

"Is easy. *I* listen, I guide," Garbage said.

Leaf pushed in next to Garbage. "I listen too."

Crusty smiled and shrugged.

"Listen to what, sweeties?" This was too important for them to be doing their usual obtuse communications.

"I feel my friends." Garbage pointed to Leaf and Crusty. "I feel rest of my friends too."

"You can feel the other faeries from our time? The ones with the rest of our people?" I'd caught myself right before I said any names. Things were messed up enough, mentioning Lorcan and Padraig probably would cause something even worse to happen.

"Is yes."

"That might work. What do you think?" Siabiane asked Nasif.

"Your power, my calculations, and their homing skills." He shrugged. "It's all we have, so yes, it might work."

I watched the girls, but they were sincere; they could feel their long-ahead-of-us friends. "We need Alric back; he and Dueble are in our rooms."

We all trooped into the second set of suites to find Dueble and Alric packing our things. Well, Dueble was packing and Alric was pacing. They were also engaged in some deep sounding debate.

"I'm telling you, your time might be missing out on something. The dwarven ale from the Youlk mountain range is the best around," Dueble said as he placed my extra pair of boots in the small satchel he was filling.

Ale. The world was falling around us, we needed to leap forward a thousand years and make sure we hit the right one, and they were packing and discussing ales. I couldn't really find fault with that.

"We have to go, now. Siabiane, Nasif, and the faeries have

a plan," I said to Alric. When he turned I saw that his sword was in its scabbard and a pair of knives had joined him. I was holding my sword as it hadn't taken off again after its run in with the syclarion, so he handed me its scabbard.

"You really think we can get back?" Alric said. "I know things can mess up the timeline, but you might need two extra fighters here and now. You don't—"

"And we can't." Siabiane cut him off with a sad smile. "I'm sorry my boy, you want to save everyone, that is deep in your heart. But whatever is supposed to happen, will happen. Without you five here. Even the faeries being here now are causing ripples. They are already alive in this timeline."

I looked at the three of them. She was right, there was another set of these three somewhere in this world right now. I couldn't stop the shiver that went down my back.

Alric actually blushed and looked away. Apparently, being told you care about saving others wasn't something a fierce tracker-hunter-thief-spy should do. At least in his book. It wasn't a surprise to me, or, I was sure, to any of our friends.

"We first need to get to where you came into this time, that will be the best place to open the time wave," Nasif said. "We'll need Siabiane's carriage brought around. Then get everyone on board without others seeing—we have no idea what the syclarion ambassador said about you two before he vanished." He went over and gently closed up the satchel Dueble was filling.

"They have enough clothes, thank you. You should stay here in these rooms. Once night falls, go back to your village and get your people far from here. We disguised that it was a syclarion who attacked the queen as best we could, but the spell will unravel completely by this time tomorrow."

Dueble allowed Nasif to close and take the satchel. I had a feeling he was packing more out of nerves than thinking Alric and I might not have enough clothing in the future. Not that I was going to complain about the extra clothes—the ones I did have back in Null had been on the road for a few months. Replacing them would be nice.

"I'm going with you though," Dueble said. He kept twisting his clawed hands over each other. He didn't want to go. "I have to go. I…I believe in providence. People are where they are supposed to be for a reason. My real purpose here wasn't to try and hurt Taryn. I think I was brought here to help send them back, even though those who brought me didn't know it. I can help with the calculations."

I could never argue with the devotedly religious. Their opinions were based on faith and you can't argue with that. It might or might not be part of his religious beliefs, but Dueble had faith in his path. He didn't *want* to go with us, he *needed* to go with us.

Siabiane looked ready to argue, then slowly nodded. "One more might help. I am going to slip a light glamour on you. Your people were not involved in the attack, but people here will not know that." She lifted one hand. Alric and Nasif nodded, but Dueble looked the same to me. Apparently, my on-and-off-again ability to see through glamours was back on again. It was disturbing that I obviously couldn't count on it though.

"What does he look like?" I whispered to Alric.

"An elf," he whispered back.

Siabiane nodded, then went on. "We will be tight in my carriage though. I'd ask Alric to drive again since he is familiar with my way of transport." Which meant she was going to have us all in the carriage, just like the way here—only we'd be moving at magically accelerated speeds.

"I can ride with Alric out front." Nasif started for the door. "Give more room in the carriage for the rest of you, and if we come across anyone who would question an unknown face, mine should soothe their worries. I have someone I can trust to get the carriage brought around without question, but you should all be near the front when it gets there. I'll meet you there." He looked both ways down the hall, then left.

"Lorcan has a chamber directly next to the main entrance. I know he wouldn't mind if we waited there." Siabiane turned to Alric and I. "I knew by the looks on your faces, that you both know Lorcan in the future—but he can't know who you are now, nor when you're from."

Alric and I nodded and I opened my cloak for the faeries to fly into. "You three need to stay hidden until we are far out of the city. No talking, singing, or gibbering. Understood?" The seriousness of getting me out of this timeline was on their faces as they nodded and flew in. Well, on Leaf's and Garbage's faces anyway. Crusty was the last one in. She hovered in front of my face for a second, then flew up and kissed me on the cheek. "It be good." Then she flew in to join her friends.

I don't think I'd ever fully understand the faeries even if I did live to be a thousand years old.

That settled, we all made our way down the stairway. This morning it hadn't been crowded, but there were still people running about doing things that needed to be done in a palace this size. It was deathly quiet now. There were palace guards, in pairs, on each floor as we went down. All of them bowed when they saw Siabiane. I saw them also take in the damage to her gown. A reminder of what she'd just done. The bows went a bit deeper at that point.

The chamber we were heading to was so well blended into the ornate walls, that at first I didn't see it. As we moved closer I could tell the door was open a bit. Siabiane saw it as well.

"Wait. He either has the door completely open or completely shut. Something is wrong."

These last few months had made me a bit paranoid, but even for me a cracked door wouldn't necessarily mean something horrible was going on. Of course, she knew

Lorcan much better than I did.

We continued moving at Siabiane's slower pace, and she held a hand up when Alric moved to go through first.

"No," she said softly. She only nudged open the door enough for her to see in so the rest of us were trapped behind her.

I was closest to her and saw her back stiffen. She didn't scream but moved forward in a rush. The rest of us tumbled in after.

"Shut the door." She kept her voice down but she ran to the back of the chamber. Two men were fighting. One drew a knife and cut the other man's throat. Lorcan slid to the ground dying.

Reginald looked at all of us with a feral grin. "I told you I was more powerful than him, Siabiane." We were standing against the only exit so he ran to the far corner.

Siabiane put one hand down to Lorcan, then turned and blasted Reginald with the other. A blaze of fire flew from her fingers, scorching the wall around him. His mouth opened in a silent scream as he died. "Not that easy." Siabiane said a few words of a nasty sounding spell. "You will be a ghost, one of the tortured beings. And you will forget." The spell was so powerful that Siabiane dropped to her knees as it was cast.

Alric, Dueble, and I ran to Lorcan. He wasn't dead, but he only had seconds left.

Siabiane crawled to us. "I am so sorry, my love."

"Can we save him?" Alric almost grabbed the weeping Siabiane.

"No." Siabiane got out between sobs.

"Yes we can." I heard the words come out of my mouth. My spells were crazy and uncontained. But everyone kept saying I was powerful.

"Girls, I need you."

The faeries came out and immediately flew to Lorcan.

"We have to save him. Have to." I focused on the faeries

instead of the dying elf before me. They were all slowly landing on him. They looked to me and Garbage nodded.

I grabbed the only healing spell I knew. A basic cantrap that would close a minor wound. I put all of my power behind it. Every bit of magic I ever had or would have came through that spell. The faeries focused it. The gash on Lorcan's throat closed.

He gasped and coughed. Then grabbed his throat and looked at me in wonder.

Siabiane laid one hand on his head. "Forget, my love, and sleep."

Lorcan's eyes closed, but he was resting, not dying.

I dropped to the ground as every bone in my body had turned to goo.

"How did you do that?" Alric was trying to pick me up but I kept flopping all over.

The faeries came over and a familiar slapping began. I managed to recover enough to raise my hand before my nose got bit. This was becoming a new, and unwelcome, habit with them.

"It wasn't just me, it was them too." I kept flopping one hand about to keep the faeries away from my face. Yet I knew without whatever they did, I couldn't have saved Lorcan.

"Us." Garbage flew a lap around the room. "We go. Be good." She landed on Lorcan and kissed his cheek, then all three faeries flew back to me and worked their way into my cloak. I could move a little but things like finger control weren't happening.

Siabiane touched Lorcan's face once more then faced me. "I will be forever in your debt, although I may not remember who you are if we meet again." She nodded to Dueble. "None of us can remember you, any of you. Not until we meet again. Before we came down here, I set a spell that will wipe out everything it can about you all. It will go off once you have left this time."

A slight rapping came from the door. Dueble slowly opened it, then pulled back as Nasif came in and shut the door behind him.

"What happened? Lorcan?" Nasif ran toward his friend.

"He will be fine. He was betrayed, but Taryn and her faeries saved him. She and I will need help getting to the carriage." Siabiane waved for him to help her to her feet.

Nasif pulled on his short beard—the questions he wasn't asking were clear in his eyes. But he nodded and got her to the door. "We need to move fast. Lord Jovan is calling for reinforcements and ordering the city walls to be locked."

Alric had been getting me to my feet, but at that name I almost dragged him out of the room with me. Jovan had been a high-ranking member of the royal elven court. He'd also been one of the forces behind the Dark and came far too close to killing Alric in our time.

"We have to go, now." Alric didn't say more than that, but I knew it was killing him to stay silent. It was tearing me up as well.

We got into the main hall and there were even fewer people out than before. A distant clanking of metal boots marching in step on marble floors came echoing from the far side. Alric lifted me up and almost ran to the main doors with me in his arms. Nasif did the same with Siabiane, and Dueble held the doors open.

"The ladies were hurt in the attack. Lady Siabiane has a private healer," Nasif said to the stableman holding the carriage horses.

Dueble climbed into the carriage first and helped Siabiane and I get settled. His hand started shaking as shouting came closer.

I understood why once I could make out the words.

"Have you seen any of the syclarions? The ambassador and his people have fled."

"Were they behind the attack?"

"No one knows, but Jovan said to watch for any and

bring them in."

The voices went out of distance, but Dueble's eyes were wide. "I need to warn my people." He was torn between helping us, and his village.

Nasif patted him on the shoulder. "I already sent a warning, one they can't refuse. You might have a difficult time finding them when we get back from this."

Dueble smiled and clasped Nasif's wrist. "Thank you."

Nasif shut the door, and Alric got the horses moving.

I wasn't sure how we were going to pull this off. Siabiane had sped up our trip down here by using her magic. She covered a week or longer trip in a matter of hours. After what she did to Reginald, I doubted she had much left. I opened my cloak and called out the faeries. I'd never tried to have them help with a spell before. It had been sheer desperation at watching Lorcan dying in front of me that got me to even try back in the palace. But they'd been rediscovering a lot of old tricks in the last few months, this must be one of them.

"Girls, I think Siabiane might need some help like you gave me before. We need to get back to where we came in quickly. Can you help her?"

Garbage flew over alone at first, squinted at Siabiane, and tilted her head. Finally she nodded. "Not same, but can."

Siabiane looked down as all three faeries came and sat on her.

"You spell, we help." Leaf patted her hand.

"We'd better start moving faster soon," Alric called back from the driver's seat. "They are shutting the main gates."

"I will try, but I don't have much left." Siabiane closed her eyes, and this time she was uttering words. I couldn't hear them, but her mouth was moving. Strain showed on her face but we didn't seem to be moving faster. Of course it had been hard to tell before, but a peek out the curtained window told me we were moving at normal speed.

I heard an odd humming and was surprised to see that

the faeries had closed their eyes and were humming. In tune. That was more shocking than the fact I felt the carriage pick up speed. I had believed the faeries couldn't find a tune if it was dropped on their heads.

When I snuck another peek out, we were clear of the city and moving fast enough to make my head spin. I was closing the curtain when I saw a rider in the distance. Only for a second, then we'd moved too fast for him.

"I saw a rider back there, we're being followed."

Dueble had been watching Siabiane and the faeries but he immediately looked out the window.

"They dropped back, or we outpaced them." I fought off the chill that Jovan was involved. I knew there was no way he could know who Alric and I were—he wouldn't even meet us for another thousand years. But the ambassador shouldn't have known who we were either. If Jovan was behind us for whatever reason, we were not getting out of here. I knew he was magically stronger than Alric and I had a bad feeling he might be stronger than Siabiane.

Dueble was looking out the window. He swore, then lowered the glass to be heard better by Alric. "There are riders behind us."

CHAPTER TWENTY FIVE

I WASN'T SURE IF ALRIC OR Nasif heard him. I peeked again, and we were definitely moving faster and behind us was naught but a blur.

A trickle of sweat went down from Siabiane's temple. She was muttering, but the faeries' humming was so low now I could barely hear it.

"They are trying to catch up," Alric yelled.

At this speed that only meant a very powerful magic user, or users, were after us. I seriously doubted Jovan would pull himself away from the palace—he had a war to start. But he would have had some cronies. As much as he liked to imply that he had been the one to take down the elven empire, I knew there had been a group of them.

Siabiane slumped forward. Dueble grabbed her; she nodded but kept muttering.

My head spun as we increased speed again.

Silence chased us as no one said a thing for a good twenty minutes. I was afraid to talk and disrupt the magic that was happening between the faeries and Siabiane. None of them looked good though and Dueble had braced himself against the side of the carriage to keep Siabiane upright.

Finally she pushed against him weakly. The carriage slowed down.

"We're slowing. I can't see anyone behind us, but Alric is going off the main road." Nasif yelled back and the bumps announced that we'd taken a side road. Leaving the main road was probably a good idea, but I couldn't blame Alric for not doing it earlier. I could only imagine what it had been like driving horses at that speed—even a clear road would be hard.

The carriage continued to slow. The faeries got up from sitting on Siabiane and stumbled over to me. They looked like they needed to sleep for a week.

"Come on, girls, into the cloak you go." I held all three of them up to the pocket inside my cloak and they tumbled inside. I heard heavy snoring a minute later.

"They are truly magical creatures. I am sorry that we don't have them around here now, and that our myths are little more than tales to scare children." Siabiane appeared to be regaining her strength. Two heavy spells in less than an hour and she merely looked like she'd stayed up too late the night before.

I did one heavy spell and I felt like I'd been dropped off the top of the palace a few dozen times. The gnawing beginning of a magic backlash headache was starting as well.

The horses came to a stop a few minutes later.

I couldn't hear anything, and didn't want to yell to find out why we had stopped. My sword stayed with me but if I had to fight in the carriage it would be far too big. I pulled out my dagger instead. Dueble had a pair of knives out and Siabiane had her fingers curved in a spell—she must have been the one who taught Padraig that.

I heard crunching of boots, not fast, and not a lot—maybe three people. Too close to sneak a peek out the window.

"Hail and well met," Nasif yelled out. "We've gotten off track I'm afraid. But the lady wanted some mushrooms to pick."

"You're not going to find any up this way," The garrulous voice didn't sound like a guard.

"I'll pass that along to the lady." Nasif kept his voice

light but Siabiane looked grim. She heard something that I didn't.

"I'm afraid it's my fault we got off-track. Might you be able to point us back? We're in route to Glaisdale. Can we go back that way?" Alric spoke, but he was disguising his voice. I'm sure he was probably crouched down on the bench and had probably found a hat or a full wardrobe to change into.

"Aye, that would be the right of it. Go down to the left, the trail will get smaller, but this carriage should fit. Good travels."

I heard the steps move off behind us.

Alric waited a full two seconds, then yelled to the horses and shook the reins. A thunk and yell from behind the carriage indicated our friendly forest dwellers weren't so friendly.

Thuds that most likely came from arrows at the edge of their range reinforced that. They were bouncing off the carriage instead of going into it. We all hung on as Alric took us to the right and an uneven road.

We ran a few more minutes, then Alric slowed down again and spun the carriage around partially, then stopped.

Nasif pulled open the door. "I hope you all can fight. We lost them, but they'll probably tell the ones from the palace where we went."

He held up a hand to help Siabiane out, then the same for me.

A long gully spread out behind the carriage. Until recently it had a bridge. A nice heavy wooden bridge that was now nothing but a pile of newly cut timber.

"So, the other direction was worse?" I asked.

Alric jumped down from the driver's seat and unhooked the horses. "Most likely the rest of their people were to the left and we'd have run right into them." He came closer and dipped his head close to mine. "I saw a familiar mark on the underside of the speaker's wrist when he pointed."

If the others were curious as to what he said, they didn't ask. Not only were the Dark behind us, they were in the forest with us.

"How close to where I found you did you come through?" Siabiane asked. Like the rest of us, she kept her eyes on the woods around us.

"Very close, I'd say less than a hundred yards." Alric held the reins to both horses and pointed down to the carriage. "They got in a strike on the right back wheel and cracked it. Even if we hadn't hit this bridge we wouldn't have gone far. I can set the horses free, or you can share to ride back."

Siabiane walked up to both animals and stroked their faces. Then she smiled. "Let them go. They will come if they can when we call. If not, let them find new homes." Her eyes met mine and a sadness crossed them. "I have a feeling no one will want to be in Glaisdale soon."

I tried to keep from nodding, but I'm sure she read my reaction.

The horses took off, away from the main road and deeper into the forest.

"Take everything you want to keep," Siabiane said. "We're going to be hiking."

Dueble grabbed the satchel that had Alric's and my clothing. "I can carry this for you." He had put his knives back into their sheaths. He wanted to be helpful, but I had a feeling violence wasn't the way for him. "I've been calculating the numbers you mentioned, Nasif. I think we should be able to get them back."

"Impressive, my boy, we might make a scholar of time travel out of you sooner than I thought."

I felt a kicking inside my cloak. "I hear!" Garbage's warble indicated she wasn't recovered from assisting with Siabiane's spell, but that she could hear her friends and would be able to help regardless.

Alric led us down the embankment. There was more yelling behind us, but no one seemed to be coming this way.

"Not that I'm complaining, but isn't it obvious which way we went?"

"I laid a confusion spell as we passed. No matter how well they know these woods our followers will find themselves going every way except this one." Alric frowned and climbed up the other side. "It won't last long though and will grow weaker the further away we get."

Siabiane moved to the front with Alric and took his arm to change directions. "The bushes you came out of were not far from here. I can sense the trees that lead to it. We need to go this way."

I was impressed. Dryads were usually the only ones with that kind of connection to plants. Siabiane had been being chased, watched a dear friend almost die, and yet she was connected enough to the trees that she was able to recall enough of the place to lead us back.

The way was definitely not a trail. Nor a hunting path. It was more like no one on two legs had ever been down there before.

After a few false paths, mostly because Alric thought he should go one way and Siabiane went another direction, we saw the road in the distance. The bushes we'd hidden behind seemed much larger than they'd seemed at the time, but they were in the right place compared to the road.

Siabiane wanted to go closer to the road, but Alric pulled her back. A troop of riders, wearing the palace green, rode by. Slow enough that they were looking for something—or someone. They slowly passed our hiding spot.

"It's further back anyway," Alric said a few minutes after they'd left the area. "We both came through at the same spot, but two weeks apart."

Nasif was behind us, talking with Dueble, but he caught that part. "Two weeks on this end or that end?"

I turned back. "This end. When he went through I followed after him by less than a minute—he'd been here for two weeks when I arrived though."

Both Nasif and Dueble looked worried.

"Halt! In the name of the queen, stop!" The shouting wasn't near us, and I couldn't see anyone. But the arrow that thudded into the ground about ten feet behind us told me someone could see us. Our green garbed friends had either doubled back or had companions nearby.

"Run! I can recalculate the path. We need a faery though." Nasif ran past me to right behind Alric and Siabiane.

A tree limb exploded overhead.

"That was no arrow—they are using magic," Siabiane said as she slowed down. "I will delay them, you need to keep running. Nasif, we have to get them back at *any cost*. I can see rips in the timeline now. Their being here now is trying to destroy the future." She hugged me and patted Alric on the shoulder. "You have to get back on the first try or the world as we know it will unravel. Now run!"

I wanted to argue about her staying behind, she might have recovered better than me, but she wasn't at full strength. I didn't have a chance as Dueble and Nasif both lifted me up and got me running.

"The best way to help her is to get back home. Faery?" Nasif held out his free hand. I started running on my own so they both let go. Garbage climbed out of my cloak and jumped to Nasif's open hand.

"I hear." She pointed to my cloak. "They hear too, but need rest."

Dueble, Nasif, and Garbage were talking to each other as they ran. No more spells or arrows came our way but the sudden sound of tree limbs breaking and screaming told me Siabiane had met the enemy and was keeping them busy.

"Is this the clearing?" Nasif asked as the trees opened up in front of us.

I had no idea.

Luckily, Alric did. "Yes, over there toward that group of

trees."

Nasif stopped and held up both hands for a spell. Garbage started her odd humming, but it sounded more like she was calling someone this time. Dueble pushed forward, dragging Alric and I along.

"He is going to open the time veil directly ahead. We don't know what the difference in your arrival times might be since you came through separately."

Nasif started running toward us. "Another group is coming. We'll hold them back. I've set up the spell to get you through. When it opens—go!" He threw Garbage toward us and she managed to land on me. I tucked her back in my cloak but she was still humming softly.

A troop of the woodsmen, most likely the ones who stopped the carriage before, came out of the woods to the side where the road was. Nasif and Dueble ran that direction.

I saw Dueble take a hit as an arrow got him in the leg, but he had his knives out and kept running. Nasif flung spells at the attackers.

A glowing silver vortex, twice as tall as we were, opened to our left and Alric pulled me to it.

We were entering the vortex when the woods around us exploded in a fireball and everything went black.

CHAPTER TWENTY SIX

THE FIRST TIME I'D GONE through, all I thought about was finding Alric. I had no idea both of us were traveling through time. But I also didn't feel or see anything aside from cold and wind.

After the initial darkness broke away, this time I felt and saw everything.

Lights, colors, sounds, pain, and sorrow. Everything—all bursting inside my head. As suddenly as it started, it all went back to nothing. The overwhelming lights, colors, and emotions had been scary, but the darkness and silence that replaced them was terrifying. Had the explosion killed our friends? Us? What would happen to a time wave if the vortex for it was destroyed? The idea of floating here in the dark and cold, with no sense of direction or awareness if Alric was with me or scattered to pieces made me sick. But I wasn't even sure if I had a stomach or mouth at that point.

I couldn't feel anything. No arms, no legs, nothing. Maybe I had exploded with the forest and the vortex.

Just as I was about to lose my mind, brightness slammed me in the face.

The noise, lights, smells right out of the abyss hit me, and for a moment I wanted to crawl back into the void. I shut my eyes tightly and tried to cover my ears. Then I heard Alric's voice.

"There you are. Not as long of a lag behind me, only

about a half hour. But you've been unconscious for twice that."

I cracked open one eye to make sure he looked normal. The sounds and colors died down to regular. We looked to be in a desert somewhere; could be the land right outside of Null. And a familiar looking satchel was near me.

"I think Dueble threw it in right before the time wave vortex closed," Alric said.

That final fireball. "Do you think they made it?" I might have just known them a short while, but they'd become friends.

He reached forward and pulled me and the satchel up. There was black dust on everything around us. Part of the explosion had followed us.

He shrugged, but his eyes didn't match the casualness of the movement. "We may never know. Maybe ask Lorcan or Siabiane if we come across her again. But that explosion was huge."

I'd only known both of them a few days. Dueble could have turned me over to killers without knowing it and was a syclarion. I wiped away the tears. I'd always hated his people, but maybe I'd been wrong. In the end, I'd definitely been wrong about him.

"Hey, we can find out, if it will help. Just don't get your hopes up."

I shook my head. "None of this would have happened, we wouldn't have been sent back, who knows what our being back there screwed up, if that bastard hadn't set that time wave up."

"I promise, when we catch him, you can have the first strike." He kissed the top of my head, then took my hand and we walked toward a group of buildings.

Alric's sleeve had pulled up when he grabbed the satchel and a soft glow came from his wrist. I pulled on his other hand and pointed to it.

"You've got a problem." It was already fading, but I figured he wouldn't want anyone to see it.

He looked down and swore. I let go of his hand so he could fix the sleeve. "We need to keep this from our friends for now. I don't want to deal with it on top of everything else."

I frowned. I had found that not telling the smarter folks things wasn't a great idea. Not that it stopped me from doing it from time to time. "She sounded serious about that thing. What if it makes you do something against your will? Maybe Lorcan or Padraig could break it?" I knew next to nothing about geas, but anything that could control your actions wasn't a good thing in my book.

He started to shake me off, then pulled back the sleeve and looked at it. "You could be right. If anyone could break her geas, it would be those two. But not in front of the knights."

I nodded and focused on the town.

It looked a bit different than Null had before, but then again, I'd not seen it from outside of the town.

As we got closer I realized it wasn't not having ever actually traveled to Null that made it look odd. It did look odd. We'd landed in the desert, but Nasif's calculations should have put us behind the pub. At first I thought he'd been off, then I realized we had probably landed close to where we left from—Null had moved.

The town was closer to the mountains than it had been, and the deep gullies that made escape problematic were no longer visible on this side.

And a breeze was blowing. Not a horrific cold clump of clouds and rain, but a nice, gentle breeze.

"I think we did change something, regardless of all of Siabiane's cautions," I said as we moved closer. The buildings were still not in the best shape, old and run down seemed to be standard. But it was more like Beccia, not like some level of the abyss.

It was late in the day, just one more hour and dusk would

have completely fallen. There were people in the streets, but the storefronts were normal—shops and vendors selling shoes, clothes, food. No one was wearing gray, and I saw no hoods pulled up.

People looked me in the face and gave quick nods.

"Are we still in Null?" I whispered after the fifth alarmingly normal looking person nodded as they passed us.

He silently pointed to a sign. "Welcome to Null, come stay awhile." It was outside what looked to be a produce shop of some kind.

"Seriously, what did we screw up?" I was happy that the evil place we'd left wasn't quite so evil, but a change a thousand years ago, that made this kind of impact, couldn't be small. We'd messed up something big.

"I don't know, but I think we need to find the others. The pub is still there." He pointed down the street. From the outside it looked the same. Except the doors were intact. "Hopefully the stable and our friends are where we left them."

We made our way down the main road. I paused. Something was missing. "The gallows are gone."

Alric hadn't even slowed down, but looked around when I mentioned it. "Well, maybe things aren't as violent as they were."

I pointed out past the buildings. A well-used cemetery could be seen. "Or they still are, but no one is punishing them for it."

"We'll find out when we find our people." Alric led us down the side alley. There were businesses there, but no abandoned stable.

My stomach fell. Something about me being in the past had caused those time traveling syclarions to vanish. My spell hadn't done it. I couldn't speak to the entire group of the ambassador's, but I knew the two who attacked us did. What if me being back there had caused a ripple to remove our friends? Maybe they existed, but they never knew us?

Alric was muttering a few swear words and walking slowly down the alley.

Finally three tiny and well-rested heads popped out of my cloak.

"Is back how is supposed to be. Is good." Garbage said with a smugness that indicated she herself had fixed everything.

"Sweetie? This isn't how we left it."

"How *supposed* to be. Was wrong before," Leaf added.

"I fix," Garbage said.

"Alric? You have any idea what they are talking about?" I held up my hand for the faeries. They'd looked like they were having trouble flying before we went through the time wave, but all three flew out.

"Stay low for now, you can't be seen." I tried to grab them but they were extremely well recovered and quickly flew out of reach.

"Is okay now," Crusty said and she flew high above us.

"Maybe they did change something that needed to be changed?" Alric said, but his face looked as doubtful as I felt.

"So the timeline we were originally in was wrong, because we hadn't gone back in time and changed things yet. Even though Siabiane tried to mitigate our impact—we changed things. And this is how it was supposed to be?" My head already hurt from the magic backlash headache that had managed to follow me a thousand years in the future. Talk of time issues was making it worse.

"Yes!" All three faeries shouted at once. Luckily, the alley, while now having businesses, was not busy. There were plenty of areas that weren't used to having faeries roaming around.

"That's too much to think about right now." Alric was watching the businesses carefully, but kept his hand off his sword. "Can you find your friends? Our friends?"

Dusk was falling faster than I'd expected, and while I did see some mage lights flicker to life, I didn't think we wanted to be roaming around after dark. At least not until we figured out what had been changed.

"This way." Garbage took off, but Leaf and Crusty spaced themselves so we could follow.

They flew back out of the alley, and toward the outskirts of town. Right where the compound of buildings had been where Flarinen and Kelm had been held. Only it was the original house, no weird add-ons. And the houses nearby, while small, looked to be in good condition and not overrun by evil people.

I called Leaf back as Garbage was too far ahead. "You're sure this is right? This is where we are supposed to be, where all of us are supposed to be?" There were so many changes.

Before Leaf could answer, the door of the house flew open and Covey came running out. She looked normal. And she grabbed me in a hug which was part of her new normal.

Padraig was right behind her, followed by Lorcan. Padraig clasped Alric and Lorcan waited until one of us was free, then he hugged each of us.

Looking closer at the house, I saw Flarinen, in armor no less, standing guard on the top floor. This timeline might be better, at least for Null, than when we left, but obviously it wasn't completely safe.

"The other faeries told us what happened after you vanished," Lorcan said. "It took quite a while to get the full story, but as soon as I understood, I locked us in a spell bubble. I don't recall seeing either of you in my past, but judging by the changes to Null, something happened,"

I looked to Alric. At least we knew Siabiane's forget spell had worked on him.

Padraig kept smiling. "I wondered if we'd ever see any of you again. Time can be far too tricky to be playing around with. Lorcan's spell bubble kept our original memories intact, but judging by the changes to Null, some things are different."

"A spell was set to erase our visit after we left the past, but yes, obviously it wasn't completely effective." Alric turned and nodded to the city behind them.

Garbage had been swarming with the rest of her faeries, but zoomed back to us. "Did what supposed to. Is right."

"The faeries say whatever changed was putting things back the way they should be, and that things were wrong before," I said.

Lorcan nodded. "The ones that stayed with us were saying the same. Bunky and the gargoyle stayed near the faeries the entire time you were gone."

I felt relief at hearing that. My friends out here all looked the same. I'd feel awful if anything changed about the two constructs.

I turned to Lorcan as we walked to the house. "Did you ever know a man named Nasif? Or Dueble?"

Lorcan smiled. "Nasif, that's a name I've not heard in a long time. A very long time. He was brilliant, absolutely brilliant. Crazy as well." His smiled dropped. "He vanished right as the battle against the Dark began. Some of the survivors said he was one of the Dark, but I knew better. I can't say I've heard of an elf named Dueble though—that's a non-elvish name."

My heart broke. They must not have made it out of the explosion when we left. I knew there was a chance of that—Alric didn't know Nasif from growing up in the enclave—but it was still sad.

"Dueble wasn't an elf, he was a syclarion," I said. "A gentle syclarion. He might have died making sure Alric and I made it back to this time."

Lorcan nodded and patted my shoulder.

We'd reached the doorway to the house and the door swung open as we approached. Kelm wasn't wearing his armor, but his sword was at his side. He looked to Padraig and at his nod, stepped aside for us to enter.

"You aren't just on guard against the locals, are you?" Alric kept his eyes on Kelm.

Padraig answered, "No. We weren't sure who would be coming back—if you came back. You've been gone over two months, not a few days. We had to go out and get supplies, with Lorcan and I alternating, one with the house, the other with whoever went out, to keep the bubble in place. We saw the changes, but you never came back."

I had been about to sit down on one of the comfortable looking sofas—it might have been a thousand years and a few months, but my body was pretty sure it hadn't slept since waking up in Siabiane's guest rooms with Alric missing. Parts hurt that I didn't even know I had. Still, Padraig's words stopped me mid-sit.

"Two months?" Alric shook his head. "I understand there could be some slippage. When we went back there was a difference between us in arrival. But once Taryn arrived, we were only there a few days, and I had only been there for two weeks before her." Alric nodded to me and sat down, at which point, I finished sitting down. "I really wish Nasif and Dueble had survived and were around. I have no idea how or why we're that far off, or if it even matters."

Lorcan smiled. "So Nasif was right with his time theories? He was always trying to explain them to me—could be deadly focused when he wanted to be—but flighty as one of the faeries other times. He could also throw a mean fireball spell. Once took out a secondary kitchen when he got too excited about showing it off."

A burst of high-pitched giggling came from behind us. I looked over to the large table near the kitchen. As soon as we came in all three faeries darted to their winged friends and were all hugging and talking at once. Bunky and the gargoyle watched the reunion like pleased parents.

"His talent was a fireball?" I pulled myself back to the conversation. "That was the last thing we saw before we went through the time wave. Dueble was directing us through, Nasif was holding back attackers. Then everything exploded."

Lorcan nodded. "That would be Nasif. As attached as you are to your push spell, he was to his fireball. And that could have thrown off your timing. The force of the fireball could have pushed you forward."

Everyone had sat by then except Kelm, who stayed by the door, and Flarinen who hadn't come down from his lookout. They might have been on guard against people pretending to be us, but there was more to their vigilance than that. Null might have changed, but it still wasn't a warm and cuddly place.

"I think we need to hear about your trip, especially the time leading up to the trip back. Maybe we can figure out where the impact occurred. Things did change here, as I'm sure you saw, but we have no idea how far the change goes," Lorcan said.

"Is right now," Garbage said, as she fluttered over and sat on Lorcan's leg. "Was wrong before. Right now."

"According to her, the way it was before wasn't how it was supposed to be."

"They messed it up, we fix." She smiled, patted Lorcan on the cheek, and flew back to her friends.

"They messed it up? Who?" I asked, but Garbage had given us what she felt like giving. She was now climbing into an ale bottle.

"The syclarions?" Alric asked. "We don't know from where in the timeline they originally came from."

Padraig held up his hand. "I think Lorcan is right, it might have been a short time, but obviously a lot went on. We can't even guess at the wider changes in this time unless we know what happened in the past."

Alric and I filled them in, alternating, as we each saw different points. Alric didn't mention seeing the fallen Padraig, and neither of us mentioned Lorcan almost dying. At first Covey kept asking for descriptions of the rooms, the palace, and the city. Quickly however, the intrigue of the time jumping syclarions and their theory about the Ancients causing massive harm to the syclarion race, grabbed her attention.

Lorcan held off from asking questions, but his face darkened as first Siabiane, then Nasif fell behind to get us through the time wave.

"Siabiane made it back to the city before the true fighting started, but she couldn't really explain where she'd been. She'd been essential in saving the queen, but then vanished. She returned a few hours later, on foot, looking bloody and with little memory."

"She cast a forget spell to try and cover our being there. It was supposed to target her as well." Alric ran his fingers through his hair. "Nasif and Dueble definitely didn't survive the fireball then, even if Nasif cast it. Siabiane wouldn't have left without them." He leaned forward. "I know it wasn't my time, but had there always been an attack on the queen *before* the battle?"

"Yes. But it hadn't been as serious as you describe and I'm not sure why I don't recall it better."

I had a feeling I knew why. He'd been recovering from almost dying and Siabiane's direct spell on him. He might have even ended up with a double hit of the forget spell.

"What have been the changes? It appears Null is farther over from where it was, the gorges are no longer there, or at least not like they were. And the people seem less..." Alric waved his hand as he searched for the right word. They weren't cheery now, nor, judging by the large cemetery, were they a lot less violent. But they were more normal now. More like a seedy little town that ended up catching the debris from normal society. But no longer psychotic.

"Those have been most of them," Padraig said. "And I agree, it's hard to explain, but the people are less depressed. Still a bit bloodthirsty."

"And the spell? Maybe it's because we've only been back a short time, but I don't feel like I can't leave here."

Lorcan had got up to get some tea for everyone, but turned at that. "Spell? There wasn't a spell here."

CHAPTER TWENTY SEVEN

ALRIC AND I SHARED A look which Padraig noticed and nodded to Lorcan.

"I'd say even with your spell bubble in place and all of our precautions, something changed for us as well. I certainly don't recall a spell on the town."

That wasn't good. I'd hoped that Lorcan's spell had protected my friends from all changes, but it looked like something slipped through. "The spell was insidious, and you all knew about it. Just a lack of motivation to do much of anything. Even the faeries felt it." I got up and went to the table where the faery party was happening. They'd brought out five ale bottles from their magic pockets and were taking turns diving into them.

"Leaf? Honey, do you remember the spell that was here before?" Garbage would have been my go to and she had been the most vocal about saying the time before had been wrong. But she was doing a good job of staying in her bottle.

Leaf had been cheering her on, but turned at my question. "Spell? Is always spells, lots of spells. *You* spell." She tried to poke me but since she was a good foot away she ended up spinning and landing on her face.

"No, the spell that was *here*. The one that made all of you want to sleep. Remember when Garbage threw you all out of the loft in the stable?"

"You are spell! Spell fell in the dell." Leaf stayed lying

on the table and rolled around laughing at her own joke. Which started all of the faeries not currently in a bottle laughing hysterically.

A soft gronk came next to me. The gargoyle bumped my hand for a pet, and Bunky seemed to be bobbing his head. As far as I'd been able to tell at the time, neither construct had been affected by the spell.

Alric came to the table and spoke to Bunky. "You remember it, don't you?" Bunky gave a series of gronks that Alric nodded at and the faeries laughed even harder.

"He says he recalls it and so does the gargoyle."

It annoyed me that a number of my friends, and all of the faeries, could understand Bunky—yet I couldn't. I pulled my shirt to cover my hand and petted him. I'd been knocked on my ass enough lately that I didn't want to risk the flash of disturbing images I'd be deluged with if I touched him barehanded.

"That is worrisome." Lorcan loaded a tray with teacups and a pot and brought it over from the small kitchen. "I have no recollection, and I assume none of you did either?" All of them, even Kelm standing near the door shook their heads. "We must believe we were impacted by the changes, just not at the same level, hopefully, that we would have been. It is truly too bad that Nasif didn't survive. He was a good man, and had he been able to advance his studies of time travel, maybe we'd understand better what happened." A brief shadow of sadness passed his face at the loss of his friend. It might have occurred a thousand years ago, but the reminder of the loss was fresh.

Padraig poured tea. "As for the changes that happened here, that we know of, you mentioned most of them. People come and go, something that didn't seem to happen before from what you're saying."

"If people can come and go, then how did we get here?" Not that the two were connected, but I was now going to see what other changes I could find. Locating them now was better than at a point where they could become crucial.

"We were tracking Nivinal and Reginald through the desert to get to the Spheres and fell into a trap. You defeated the syclarions, but we ended up here." Covey said.

"Are Nivinal and Reginald still here?" I asked.

"Yes, annoyingly. We haven't been able to find them, but we think Reginald is in the body of the dwarf. Your dwarf ghost friend is around, but he's getting fainter. He doesn't have magic so hanging on is going to be harder."

"And the relics?" Alric was looking into his tea, but I knew what he was doing. If that spell blocking anyone from wanting to leave wasn't remembered, there was no way we knew for certain what else had been changed.

"Still looking for them," Padraig said with a smile. "The gargoyle, chimera, and dragon are missing, and our theory is that Nivinal doesn't have them at this point anymore. At least not all of them, which might have led to the falling out between the two of them. And also explains why he's staying here, since the spell against leaving is gone. The manticore is right there." He nodded to me and I felt a coldness hit my cheek. He must have triggered it, as I hadn't noticed any reaction from it for a while.

"It's showing, I assume?" I put my hand on the cold spot and got a jolt.

"Yes, but I didn't do it. Your glamour should be hiding it." Padraig moved closer and touched my cheek. He pulled back quickly as he got the same jolt I had.

"Did we figure out what this one did?" I wasn't sure that panicking was going to help, but I was leaning that way. The coldness in my face was increasing—slowly, but enough to notice. There was no way that was going to be good.

"Not completely. It's the shield from what I can tell, but the scrolls we have really didn't help much." Covey moved to where the pile of scrolls and books from our wagon were collected.

"We do know what the final two pieces are: a basilisk made of gold and a sphinx made from of a giant diamond—but we don't know what they do. The gargoyle balances time and dimension, the chimera acts as a magic amplifier, the dragon seems to increase greed—I'm not sure how that was part of a weapon. But the manticore seems to shield and protect." Padraig rocked back a bit as he looked at me. "And it's growing."

The entire right side of my face had gone numb and I felt something building inside of me. "I think there is something wrong with it. I feel like I need to release something." The other two times this had happened we were under attack from Nivinal as it turned out. "I think Nivinal might have found us." My mouth was dry.

Flarinen yelled from the roof and the walls shook under an impact.

"Stay here," Kelm yelled, then darted outside.

Alric and Covey were fighters, and Padraig could definitely hold his own. Staying here wasn't an option.

Alric and Padraig had their swords out and Covey grabbed hers from the table. Mine was with me, so I figured I might as well join in.

Then the chill from the manticore sent a cold force down my right arm. My hand shook and I was ready to drop my sword, when the weapon turned blue. "Please tell me this isn't bad?" I held my sword up to Lorcan.

His eyes widened, which didn't match the reassuring look he tried to give me. "No…okay, I'm not sure." He tried to touch my arm, but pulled back immediately and shook his hand. "Can you move it?"

The coldness engulfed my side, but a tendril of warmth started out from where Lorcan had almost touched me.

"I think I can," I said as I tentatively moved the sword. Blue was an odd color for a weapon, but it felt lighter than it had before. Spirit sword and a weird Ancient artifact—

who knew what was normal for these two things?

Yelling came from outside and another rattle shook the walls.

"I need to go outside with the others." I ran for the door.

I wasn't sure what I was expecting, but the yelling increased and didn't sound like our people. The area in front of our house was now a battle zone. Our people were fighting off a bunch of short figures who were yelling some sort of chant. My heart went as cold as my arm. Rakasa. We'd done our best to eradicate the small, toothy monsters during the final battle in the enclave, but obviously some had survived. Or they were a larger population than we thought.

Covey let loose a blood-curdling yell as her sword got stuck in the chest of a rakasa. She couldn't get it out but ran forward and ripped the creature's head off.

Trellians had a history of going berserk. It had been a dark part of their history and they'd thought it had been repressed. A year ago Covey found out she could tap into that. She'd saved many of us, including me, but had gone into solitary meditation to resolve that within herself. Regardless of our battles since then, she'd not gone berserker.

That changed before my eyes. The first time she'd changed she'd fought it. Kept herself hidden as much as she could and the change took a while to progress.

This time she seemed to welcome it.

She howled as her fingers grew longer and her fingernails became claw-like. She jumped to a pair of rakasa trying to make it to Lorcan and I and smashed their heads together, then threw them into the distance. The arms she had grabbed them by didn't quite make the trip and she threw them as well.

"Has she done that before?" Lorcan asked. He seemed more academically curious than terrified, which had been my first response to seeing my best friend turn into a killing machine.

"Once that I know of. But not that easily." Further discussion was cut off as a pair of rakasa tried to run through us. They were attacking all of my friends, but it seemed more like they were trying to get through to the house itself.

I ran toward the two trying to clear the gap between Covey and Lorcan and I. My sword glowed an even brighter blue, which almost caused me to pull back. But my sword had a different idea and dragged me along behind it. A burst of blue hit the lead rakasa a moment before my sword did.

The rakasa shattered.

My momentum allowed me to swing through and strike the second one. He too shattered but not as cleanly. Bits of partially frozen and bloody rakasa flew through the air.

The rest of the rakasa around us froze. I wish literally, but they weren't blue. Someone was commanding them. The ones that my friends had been fighting didn't even move as they were run through.

"Well done." A cloaked shape seemed to come out of thin air toward the back of the rakasa pack. "I will take that now." He—even though we couldn't see him, there was no doubt it was Nivinal—reached out an arm toward me and the coldness started to fade.

"Oh, like hell that's going to happen." I raised my sword and focused energy on the manticore staying right where it was. Since it had chosen to be there, it helped me with that.

Nivinal didn't come any closer, and didn't even release the spell on his rakasa troops as my friends slaughtered them. He did raise his hand and I found myself floating about a foot in the air.

Lorcan grabbed my arm as I lifted off the ground and cast a spell back at Nivinal.

I stopped moving but wasn't on the ground. Since my

best spell, push, wouldn't really work in this situation, I tried using one Alric had been trying to teach me on the road. It was simply a spell stopper. It could slow down or end a spell attacking me.

I aimed the still blue sword toward the cloaked figure and sent my spell through it. I tumbled to the ground, and the cloaked figure blew up. Well, it vanished.

Flarinen had been standing the closest to the figure and he looked around quickly but shook his head. Obviously, I hadn't blown Nivinal up. Bunky and the gargoyle had flown out there as well, and both flew higher over the area to search.

Maybe Nivinal had been scared off? Highly unlikely.

The rakasa were also released and while there weren't many left, they were pissed. They also were trying to get to the house. Usually rakasa killed people for no reason—or rather they might have reasons, but they didn't really need them. In this case they were fighting to get through to the house, not just to kill people. Which made them easier to fight in a way, as their usual bloodthirsty tendencies clearly weren't in play.

I rolled to my feet and swung at one of the rakasa, but missed. The coldness from my face and arm as well as the blue in the sword were fading. Still no excuse for a bad strike though. The rakasa didn't even slow down. It leapt over my blade and kept running for the house.

I had no idea what could be in there that was making them so obsessed. As far as I knew the rakasa weren't about physical things.

Except the emerald dragon.

That Ancient relic had been something of importance to the rakasa and they'd been trying to find it when we first encountered them.

"They want something in the house." I ran to catch up with them. I didn't want to yell about any of the relics, and I would have thought my friends would have mentioned if they now had one.

Rakasa were short, only about three feet high maximum, but when motivated, they could really run.

I mentally tried calling for the faeries. They were all drunk like crazy by now, but that was a risk I was willing to take.

I sent images of needing them, adding more ale until a multi colored swarm filled the doorway. The lead rakasa was almost upon them.

"They want to take your ale!" My friends were closing in behind me, but I needed the rakasa to stay out of our house.

The faeries had been bumping around the doorway until I yelled. At my words, Garbage rose up above the others and yelled, "No take prisoners!"

I hadn't really heard of the faeries ever taking prisoners. The only time they stole people was when they relocated some syclarions during a fight. Unfortunately, Orenda had helped them with that and she was probably a few hundred miles away by now.

There were about twenty rakasa, all racing to get in the door, and twenty-three faeries all trying to get in their way.

Garbage and her first wave lifted their war blades high and swarmed over the first three rakasa. They stopped in place, wavering back and forth. The faeries made a second pass, this time I was close enough to see the blades stabbing the rakasa, and the rakasa that were attacked sat down.

When a larger group of faeries had done something similar to a sceanra anam it had exploded. These rakasa didn't explode. But they stopped.

My friends and I caught the back of the rakasa group and killed them. The ones in front of them didn't even turn to defend themselves they were so obsessed with getting in the house. They ran over the three rakasa the faeries had stopped.

We got all of them but one, smaller than the others and faster. He made it into the house.

CHAPTER TWENTY EIGHT

THE FAERIES HAD BECOME DISTRACTED by the three rakasa they'd originally stopped, who were probably never getting up again.

"It's after your ale." I couldn't look back to see if they heard, as I was the closest to the door. I ran in, and felt a gush of wind as the faeries flew over me. The rakasa stopped in the middle of the front room and grinned. Then he flung one clawed hand up in an imitation of a spell user.

And my friends behind me all slammed into an invisible block on the door. Bunky and the gargoyle were trapped outside as well. It was the faeries and I against the rakasa.

I lowered my sword and took a few breaths to try and slow down the pounding in my chest. I told myself it was from fighting and running, not fear.

The rakasa seemed unafraid of the faeries or me. Cocky of it, considering what those faeries had done to three of his kind. Even I had taken out a few of his people.

He didn't speak, for which I was grateful, but tilted his head and flung one finger toward the swarming faeries.

They all immediately dropped from the air.

Garbage had been closest to me so I grabbed her as she tumbled past. She was breathing, but her eyes were shut and she was limp.

A sleep spell? Those types of magics didn't work on faeries. It was one of the first things I'd asked Alric. Life would be so much easier if I could knock the girls out when they needed it.

And if he could knock them out with a finger flick, why didn't he do that to me? My answer came in a massive cold wave that engulfed me as the rakasa raised his hand my direction. Apparently, it wasn't only Nivinal that the sapphire manticore didn't like.

The spell the rakasa sent at me slammed back to him and his left arm collapsed. I assumed it was just numb but I didn't really care. I came forward and raised my sword.

There really wasn't room for a fight here. But I didn't think that the rakasa ran past me and up the stairs because he was afraid of damaging furniture.

I swore and went after him. I was extremely grateful for the spell and shield assist from the manticore, but the shield around me was unwieldy and it took a few moments to get up the stairs.

I hadn't even had a chance to see the upstairs before, but they had bedrooms crammed in every bit of space. I heard a sound like the clanging of pots being thrown about and followed it to a room with two small cots. It wasn't pots being thrown about, but Kelm's armor.

The rakasa ignored me and kept tossing the knights' belongs around. Finally, he pulled out a fabric wrapped bundle. He wanted their clothes?

There was only one thing a rakasa would fight this hard to get, but there was no way that was what I thought it was. How could Flarinen or Kelm come across the emerald dragon? And why wouldn't they have told anyone?

A mental flash hit me of how I'd felt when I'd first found it in Kenithworth. I'd wanted to keep it hidden and run away from all of my friends. The remembered feeling was reinforced by the rakasa ripping off the shirts that were wrapped around it. The coldness surrounding me surged and the feeling of extreme greed for the object slowed down. It was there, but more like a dull bruise rather than an overwhelming need.

The rakasa had no such protection. While it was obviously one of the spell casters for its people, and supposedly knew what the relic did, the madness that filled its eyes told me he hadn't expected this.

The emerald was the size of the rakasa's head and as gorgeous as it had been when I dug it out of the ground. The detail of the dragon was so delicate and elaborate, it forced you to want to move forward to get a better look.

The rakasa growled at me and jumped on the cot behind him. I charged him, intending to tackle him and get that damn cursed dragon back. Then have a long talk with Kelm and Flarinen.

Didn't quite go as planned. I leapt forward at the same moment the rakasa pushed open the window behind him to jump out. We both went out together.

My sword was out but it was pressed between us. It had stayed blue and the rakasa screamed as the cold ate into him. Then we landed.

I was on top of him. While I was not a huge woman, I was still bigger than him. The shield from the manticore and the rakasa's body kept me from hitting the ground.

The rakasa was screaming, the shield was pushing into him and my sword was along his side. He was agile though. He wouldn't let go of the dragon but managed to wiggle out from under me. He looked like he had multiple broken bones and the side where my sword had touched him was frozen and turning black.

He ran away.

My friends came running around the back of the house, but he already had a lead on them. How in the hell he was moving, let alone running, in the shape he was in, I had no idea. Maybe that was the relic's power—greed kept you moving no matter what.

Alric and Covey ran to me, Kelm and Flarinen ran after the rakasa, and Lorcan and Padraig stood at the corner to keep an eye on the front of the house.

"What happened?" Alric reached to help me up. I tried to shake him off before he touched me, but the shield had vanished.

My sword was also losing its blue color. And my face no longer felt like pieces of it were going to flake off like ice chips. This was a good thing.

I dusted myself off and sheathed my sword. "A lot. That rakasa had magic and not only did he lock you all out, he knocked out the faeries. In a second." That was freaking me out almost as much as the whole 'either Kelm or Flarinen had been hiding a dangerous relic in the house' situation. Stopping the faeries like that should have been impossible.

"And he tried to do the same, or worse, to me but the manticore went full shield and stopped him." I dropped my voice. Alric and Covey were the only ones here who'd been around when I found the emerald dragon. "It was after something in Flarinen and Kelm's room. An *artifact*."

Both looked around, but the two knights had finally stopped running down the street and were slowly walking back.

"One, or both, of them was hiding the emerald dragon in a pile of clothes."

"I'll kill him," Alric said, as he went to draw his sword. "I will kill him."

I put my hand on his and pushed it down. "We're not sure which one had it, but considering how strong that thing is for creating greed, I doubt the shirts would have diluted the effect. At least not for long."

I'd filled Alric and Covey in on the effect the dragon had on me when I found it. Alric had carried it for a bit, unbeknownst to me, but inside one of the faeries' bags. He said he hadn't felt anything from it. If we got it back, I was stealing one of those bags.

"What was that thing after and why was it moving so oddly?" Satisfied that there were not any more living rakasa around, Padraig came closer to us.

"It's better we discuss this inside, and the odd movement is because I think Taryn crushed some of its bones when she landed on it." Covey glared at both knights as they walked toward us, but she moved to go to the front.

I started to follow her around the house. "It wasn't just me, the manticore made a shield." I looked where we landed and saw an indentation. That rakasa better have good doctors or it wasn't living long enough to enjoy that relic. I'd seen them eat their own kind—I wasn't holding out for their having anything like a doctor.

No one had come out of the neighboring houses. Considering the amount of noise that had been going on, it reinforced the whole 'Null is not a nice place' situation. The rakasa bodies lying around were something we were going to have to deal with though, even if no one came out.

Lorcan waved his hand and muttered under his breath, and the bodies vanished. At least now the neighbors wouldn't complain—if they'd noticed.

We waited, but it seemed like Flarinen and Kelm were taking far longer to get back to the house than they should.

The faeries were all unconscious. Once they could come back in the house, both Bunky and the gargoyle flew around them bleating.

"They'll be okay," I said as much to myself as them. I picked the girls up gently, all twenty-three were breathing, but all still out cold. I gathered them together and laid them out on the table. "I need you two to watch them. Tell me the moment any of them stir."

Both nodded and sat down as close to the faeries as they could without actually sitting on them. Bunky did look like he was wondering if that might be a good idea though.

Lorcan went to the table and looked at them. "I think they will recover just fine." He smiled at me. "You might want to check on Flarinen and Kelm," he said to Alric.

He nodded and darted out the door. There was a sound of a struggle, and Alric reappeared at the door. At first I thought he was dragging Kelm along, then I realized both of them were pulling in a struggling Flarinen.

Padraig and Covey went to help them. Flarinen was only partially fighting by that point and seemed more distraught and embarrassed than violent.

"We know what the rakasa were after." Lorcan motioned to a solid chair for them to put Flarinen in. I thought he was going to spell Flarinen in place, but he pulled out some rope.

"I am sorry for this. I know there are circumstances that can't always be explained. Alas, we do need some information." He handed the rope to Alric and Padraig and motioned for Kelm to sit in another chair. "I won't have you tied at this time, but you were exposed to the relic whether you knew it or not. Please stay seated and do not get up unless we say you can."

Kelm nodded but kept his head down. He was a new knight and probably looked up to his captain, Flarinen. That his leader had fallen so low was tearing him up inside and it showed on his face.

Alric and Flarinen were not, by any stretch of the imagination, friends. But there was a compassion to the way in which Alric tied him up.

Once he was secured to the chair, Padraig and Alric moved away. Covey moved right across from him.

"I don't have any sympathy for what you are going through. You took a relic, kept it to yourself, and risked all of our lives by your actions. If you even think of trying to leave, I will show you a berserker trellian close up." Most of her features had returned to normal after her short berserker demonstration during the fighting, but she flexed her right hand and immediately the fingers elongated.

Flarinen nodded and watched that hand carefully.

Had that been a timeline change? In my time Covey

wasn't so embracing of her lost heritage. I was glad she was accepting it, but not if it indicated yet another timeline change.

"I deserve it," Flarinen said so softly it was as if someone else was throwing their voice to sound like it came from him. "I found the relic—alone, the others weren't with it, I swear—the day after Alric and Taryn dropped back in time. Kelm and I had split up, looking for evidence of our mage friends. I found two corpses out on the edge of town, partially down one of the gullies that used to be there. They were locked around an item." He shrugged but his shoulders didn't move much.

"So, for over two months you had that thing in your rooms and no one, not even Kelm, knew about it or was affected by it?" I'd felt what that thing could do. For all his annoying ways, Flarinen was a trained captain of the elven knights, but I doubted any of that training taught him how to avoid the powers of concentrated greed.

"No. I kept it up top in the lookout in a lead chest. I tried to always move it if anyone other than me was up there. I recalled where Alric had it hidden when we came to get you, so I took one of the faeries' bags and kept the relic in it most of the time. I only took it to the room last night." His words were emotionless, and his face stayed down.

The use of the bag probably helped him hold off some of the effects for so long. I was ready to abandon my friends, the faeries, and even Alric after just a few hours with that thing.

Everyone sat and looked at each other.

"I understand," I said softly, then raised my voice. "That thing had me completely twisted within an hour of finding it. Had we not been attacked and betrayed, I am not sure what I would have done."

Alric smiled, but there was some guilt in the smile. "I knew you found it. I didn't realize what it was doing to you for the first day. I stole it and a bag as soon as I did. Even if we hadn't been attacked—twice—you wouldn't have seen that thing again."

"I should be mad, and I might be, I haven't sorted things out yet." I shot him a glare just to be sure I was covered later. "How could both of you use the faery bags? I've tried and they wouldn't work for me." Alric probably used some magic on them, but Flarinen refused to use magic on principle.

"I got them drunk and asked them for one and they made it usable for me," Flarinen spoke before Alric did. "They are agreeable for a price. What happened to them?" That was the first inflection in his voice since he'd come in. He was leaning toward the table where the faeries lay.

"I did the same, more or less," Alric said.

"How could I have not thought of that?" I looked to the table where Bunky and the gargoyle were standing watch. "The last rakasa, the one who somehow knew where the relic was, cast a spell on them."

Flarinen shook his head. "I am so sorry. I will leave you all and wander until I have found absolution."

"No," Alric said. "I was wondering if this was going down that path. You do not get to be the failed knight who wanders the land. We already have tales of those. You fell prey to a vicious relic. That's all. I know you knights don't believe it, but you are only elven." He got up and went to the kitchen and came back with a pair of ales. He handed one to me, and sat back down with the second. "You're tied up because we're afraid you'd do something dramatic and overwrought. Not because we were going to hurt you."

"Well. Some of us wanted to hurt you," Covey said as she flexed her fingers again. "But I've always disliked you, so this isn't new."

Kelm had stayed silent, but watching.

"What of Kelm? You can't seriously believe he can continue his training and this task with a fallen knight as his leader?" Now Flarinen was showing some emotions.

"You aren't fallen," Kelm said softly. "No one could have fought that relic. I felt the pull last night, and while you were on guard, I took it out and held it. I would have tried to steal it tonight."

Flarinen's emotions were reengaged and he went from shock to concern to anger in the time of a single faery wing beat. I cut him off before the words reached his mouth.

"There we have it. The dragon relic is strong, it took down two of our most dedicated people. Can we now move on? The rest of the relics are possibly in town and not with Nivinal. Not to mention a missing and hopefully dying rakasa."

Kelm recovered faster than Flarinen. "That creature vanished in front of our eyes. It was slowing down. You did it grievous injury, Lady Taryn," he nodded to me, "but before we could catch it, the being was gone. It was less than five feet ahead of us, there was no way we could have missed it."

Crap. "Was there a hole?" The rakasa were ground dwellers and could create tunnels under the ground.

"No," Flarinen said. "The ground was solid."

"The ground here is probably too rocky for them." Padraig said.

"Then we have to presume Nivinal grabbed the relic and the rakasa," Lorcan said.

CHAPTER TWENTY NINE

"GREAT, SO HE GOT THE relic back, but we don't even know how he lost it in the first place, or if the other two relics are roaming around?" I noticed Bunky nudging one of the faeries so I walked over. The others started debating where, when, and how the relics got separated.

Garbage had flung one arm across her face and was moaning.

This was only the second time I'd seen any of the faeries act as if they had a hangover. "Honey? Are you okay?" I'd kept my voice low, but the twenty-two other faeries all cringed and covered their heads.

"Bad man." Garbage tried to roll to her feet without actually removing her arm from her face. "Took ale."

There were five partially full ale bottles sitting on the table where they'd left them. "They're right there." I didn't think diving back in after being spelled so hard that they passed out was a good idea, but if they thought it would help I was willing to go along with it.

"No. Ale *out* us." She was rolling around and I finally picked her up and put her on her feet.

"Did he take your bags?" I was at a loss and everyone else was debating the relics. Even Flarinen seemed to forget he was tied to a chair and engaged in the conversation.

"No, no, no. Ale. Not us now." She finally removed her arm from her face. I'd seen that look before but never on a faery. She was seriously hung over.

"He made you sober?" Being sober shouldn't cause the look on her face, nor the slow creeping around on the table by the other faeries. Maybe if it was done suddenly though? Forced sobriety as a spell? Faeries' metabolism was unlike that of any other creature.

"Is. very. bad. thing." Leaf staggered to her feet and looked around bleary eyed.

"What will make you better?" At the way they all looked I was willing to drop them into as many ale bottles as needed.

"Uncle Harlan," Crusty said as she rolled to her feet. She made it much easier than the others, but then again she spent most of her time unbalanced whether she was sober or not.

"Uncle Harlan is far from here, honey. Remember? He had to go see the other elves."

"No, is needing," she opened her mouth and pointed inside.

"Sugar?"

"No, num yum."

I hung my head. "Chocolate?" At their nods I waved around the house. "Where are we going to get that here? Not to mention, that stuff knocks you all out, not perks you up." Tea actually perked them up—maybe I could try that. Unfortunately, it perked them up too much and after everything I'd been through, I wasn't up to dealing with speeding-out-of-control faeries.

"We go out, come back right." Crusty even pantomimed passing out then bouncing to her feet.

All of the faeries were up now, and from the looks of them, they all wanted chocolate.

I took a step back into the main part of the room. "Does anyone have chocolate? We need to reset the faeries."

The others had not settled on anything about the rest of the relics, at least not that I could tell. But my call cut through the discussion.

Lorcan perked up. "You know, I actually do. I was hoping to run some experiments on the effect of it on the faeries at different doses, but this is more important." He went into a small room off of the kitchen and came back with some wrapped packages, some paper and a writing quill. He handed the packages to me.

"It might be best if you gave it to them. I would like to observe. Once we have sorted out this relic and mad mages issue, I intend to write a comprehensive work on faeries."

I smiled. Academics. Whether trellian or elven, give them something to work on and even the potential end of the world seemed trivial.

The faeries were stumbling around, but the moment I tore the wrapper on the first piece they all perked up.

I quickly unwrapped the chocolate, piled it around the table, and stepped back. Bunky and the gargoyle looked interested at first, then quickly backed away as the faeries realized what they had.

My dear friend Harlan had found their weakness for it a few months ago. It mostly put them into a stupor, but since when they were actually drunk, they kept drinking until they passed out, maybe this would take care of whatever side effects the forced sobriety caused. I doubted that was the actual spell the rakasa used, but a forced sobriety wouldn't have made the faeries happy at any point.

Or they just wanted chocolate.

The feeding frenzy was scary to behold as twenty-three tiny faeries swarmed the chocolate. Within a few moments it was all gone. Including the wrappers.

The faeries were covered in chocolate as they stumbled around the table. Bunky and the gargoyle took to the air to avoid them. I didn't know if it was the bad reaction to the spell, or the chocolate covering their wings, but while the faeries reached for Bunky as he lifted off, they didn't leave the table.

Garbage staggered over to where I stood while trying to keep chocolate free. "You is good. No matter what did before." She gave me a huge smile, shook a finger at me, then went face down on the table. As if that was the cue, all the rest collapsed as well.

That was cryptic. What did I do before? I wanted to wake her up and ask, but I also didn't really want to touch her. And I was certain she'd have no idea what she meant even if I could get her to wake up.

"Could your two flyers do a recon for us?" Kelm seemed far surer of himself than he had since he'd joined us. Perhaps seeing the pompous and self-righteous Flarinen fail so spectacularly was good for the kid's spirit.

"Kelm thinks the other two relics are still in town and Nivinal doesn't have them." Alric went behind Flarinen and untied him. Their debate must have convinced him Flarinen wasn't going to go out and mope for the rest of his life.

"What makes you think that?" I went back to my seat and my bottle of ale.

Kelm seemed embarrassed now and I realized it might not be all of us that rattled him but just me. There have been men who had a thing for me before, but that wasn't what this felt like. I think he was afraid of me.

I smiled and did my best to look non-threatening.

"Strategy." Kelm looked toward the others. "We know Reginald betrayed Nivinal at some point. Alric told me about his friend Mackil and that he'd been sold out by someone who hired him. What if Reginald brought in Mackil, with the plan of stealing the relics and trapping Nivinal here? He lost Lorcan's body, but also stole and lost the relics." He got up and waved his hands as he worked his way through his thoughts. As long as he didn't look at me, he seemed to be doing fine. "Mackil became his most recent body-snatching victim because he thought taking him over would give him the knowledge he needed to get out. Nivinal set a trap that you two fell into that sent you back in time and changed Null." He'd been speaking so fast no one said anything as it took a bit for our brains to catch up. He looked a bit embarrassed when he stopped. "Or I could be wrong."

"He has some good points," Padraig said. "We're not any closer to figuring out how Lorcan got his body back, so if Reginald and Nivinal fought, a spell could have loosened Reginald's hold on the body."

"Nivinal obviously has control of the rakasa, although I do wonder if the one Taryn fought off was going back to join him originally or trying to keep the dragon himself." Covey had retracted all of her external berserker appearance, but she looked more aggressive than usual. I'd have to ask her about it later. "The rakasa's sudden vanishing indicates he went back whether he wanted to or not."

A yawn took me over and again I was reminded that Alric and I had been up for a long time. Maybe not the full thousand years that we'd travelled, but it felt close to it right now.

"I hate to say this, but if there's nothing we need to fight off right now, I need to sleep." I looked at the faeries, they weren't going anywhere for a while.

"Agreed. Your body's sense of time is going to take a while to get used to the changes." Lorcan made more notes. "At least that's what Nasif would have said. I believe I'll work on an exploration of time travel after all of this is wrapped up as well." He frowned. "I do wish I could do some traveling myself."

"Since we are fairly sure Nivinal used the time waves to focus his spell, and they're all gone now, I don't know that even your friend could have made it possible to travel back again." Padraig had pulled out one of his books and had been reading it while debating the location of the relics. He didn't even look up as he spoke.

"They are all gone? Then nothing from this side helped

us return? It was all Nasif?" Alric asked. He seemed more interested than I was. They, like the spell around the town, were what kept us here. Kept everyone here. At least in the old Null…or if Garbage was to be believed, the false Null.

"Taryn is about to fall over." Covey came and pushed me up the stairs then nodded to Alric. "And you should be too. We can plan for whatever it is we're going to do tomorrow, but she's done."

I opened my mouth to say I was okay, but a yawn came out instead. "I'm agreeing with this on the advice of my body."

Covey led me down the narrow hall and to a small room. I'd gathered that all the rooms up here were small as the space between the doors wasn't much and there were a lot of doors.

She gave me a look, one that was far more old abrupt academic Covey than new hugging and berserker Covey. "Now, how are you really?"

"How am I? You just went berserk without a thought. What happened to meditating the family secret away?"

There were two small beds in the room, one had Covey's belongings all over, the second had my belongings neatly stacked on the end of the bed.

"And how did you guys move from the stable which doesn't exist now to here?" I lifted some of the items; my clothes looked even more worn than I recalled. I'd have to find the satchel we brought back.

"The location changes occurred slowly." She sat down on the end of her cot. "When you two went missing, Lorcan and Padraig tracked down what happened with some help from Alric's ghost friend, Mackil. Once they realized you'd gone back in time, they set us up in a bubble. As soon as the stable began to fade—a disturbing occurrence, let me tell you—he moved us here. Which had also changed by then."

I took off my boots and flopped back on the cot. Either I

was more tired than I thought, or for a cheap looking place, they had really good beds. "Everyone saw it change?" That couldn't have been good, nor mentally healthy.

"No. Lorcan's bubble spell changed our perception. But it's unnerving. Particularly now that we know something did slip through, such as the non-leaving spell."

"And?" I stayed lying down.

"And what? You came back."

"The berserker bit?" I did prop myself up on one elbow at that point. Hopefully this wasn't something that had changed. That would have been far deeper than a spell on a town we'd just arrived in.

"Padraig helped with that while you were gone." She gave an embarrassed shrug—something I couldn't ever recall seeing her do before. "We really didn't have much to do in here while you two were off muddling the past. Anyway, he pointed out that it was a gift, and the more I used it, the more in control of it I'd be."

"Interesting," I said. "So you and Padraig have become close?" I tried to smile but a yawn attacked instead.

"Not that way. I just want him for his mind." She got up quickly. "Now go to sleep." Before I could say another word, she left and shut the door.

I didn't know if it was a side effect from the time traveling, or just the impact of the last few weeks, but I woke up after a horrific dream.

Before venturing on this journey, I rarely dreamed. Now it seemed to happen often. Most of the time I ignored the dreams, good or bad. But this one had me bolting up in my bed and sweating. I might have screamed, but I wasn't sure if that was real or part of the nightmare. A quick glance to the other side of the room told me if I had actually done it, Covey slept through it.

I forced my fingers to let go of my blanket, somehow I'd

grabbed it so tightly they were cramping up, and tried to slow down my heart. The worst thing was, the dream, or nightmare, wasn't even tangible. There were no people or things that I could recall. I had a weird feeling they weren't even there in the dream. Just an overwhelming feeling of terror. I closed my eyes and tried to push past the emotions. Fear didn't just come from nowhere—something caused this.

Slowly images that I hadn't seen before formed in my head. Thaddeus, my patron and attempted ruler of the world. Zirtha, the landlady who really wanted to suck out my soul. Glorinal as he ran his mentor Jovan through with his sword. The mayor of Kenithworth, but with a face that wasn't his. Nivinal as he looked when he'd tried to get to me through the elven shield. The purple floating creatures who had tried to take over my friends. The syclarions I'd fought in the trap in the desert.

All of these were bad, very bad. But they weren't new. Nothing about them should be causing this feeling. Then another emotion slammed into my gut. Guilt. It was fleeting but devastating and somehow tied to all of the monsters that had flashed through my head. Guilt because this was my fault. All my fault.

CHAPTER THIRTY

THE WORLD SHOOK AROUND ME and I realized I had been asleep, but now was being woken up.

"Taryn, you're screaming." Covey's eyes peered into mine and she called a glow to life. There was not even a glimmer of daylight showing through the thin curtains, so it was probably late.

"How long?" I meant to ask how long I'd been asleep, but my tongue wasn't working.

"At least five minutes. I had just fallen asleep when you started. And who in the hell is Whilthanious? You wanted him to die badly."

I shook my head slowly. That name didn't sound familiar in the least and I'd think someone I wanted to die would be memorable. "No idea. What time is it?"

Before Covey could answer a soft knocking came from the door. "Is everyone okay?" Alric didn't wait for a response before he opened the door. Glows in the hall behind him illuminated the rest of our bunch. Minus a pair of knights.

"I woke everyone?"

"You were yelling extremely loudly, my dear." Lorcan pushed past Alric and came closer. "You're still feeling the vision."

It wasn't a question, but a statement. I nodded anyway.

"Can you write down everything you remember?" He handed me the paper and quill he'd had before.

"For a nightmare?" Covey stepped back when Lorcan came in the room.

"This wasn't a nightmare. Padraig? You're a sensitive, what do you feel?" He sat down on the edge of the bed doing his best grandfatherly smile. His eyes were a different story and disturbed me almost more than the nightmare. He looked sad and worried at the same time.

Alric stepped back to let Padraig enter the room. Covey didn't leave, but sat on her cot to clear floor space for Padraig to stand. I had no idea what Lorcan meant by calling Padraig a sensitive, but both Alric and Covey appeared to know.

Padraig's smile as he looked down at me was smaller than Lorcan's but also felt more genuine. He was also better at hiding any concern he did have from his eyes.

"Stay still, this won't hurt at all," he said as he held both hands over me.

I felt nothing, but after a few moments he pulled back. "There is a spell at play here. Something very old and strong, it's been blocked, but it's peeking through the cracks. It's trying to shatter whatever is blocking it." His words seemed to make more sense to Lorcan, who nodded. Alric and Covey looked as confused as I felt.

"So someone put a spell on me to have a nightmare?" Granted it was a nasty one, and I wasn't sure how well I was going to convey that in Lorcan's notes, but a bit over the top for someone to waste a spell on.

"No. But this isn't the time to discuss it." Padraig smiled as he saw the look on my face. "I will explain it, I promise. But right now you should write down what you can and go back to sleep."

The three elves filed out and Covey stayed on her cot.

"So?" She gave a pointed scowl at Lorcan's paper and quill. "Are you going to write that down or not? I'd like to get some sleep tonight if I can."

The glare I shot her felt good, even if it really wasn't

aimed at her. How could someone have cast a spell on me that was old enough to be called old by a pair of very old elves? And so I would have a nightmare? I wondered if the time travel had triggered it. Maybe I'd picked up something on the trip back. It had felt a bit like I was drifting about in there.

I wrote down what I could. Something triggered me thinking back to the people who had been against me, us, since this entire thing began. The feeling of overwhelming guilt had vanished once I'd woken up completely. I tried to capture it as best I could anyway.

I looked down at the brief paragraph and sighed. Not much for Lorcan to go on, but it was something. Covey waited until I dropped the quill and paper next to my cot, and commanded the glow to turn off.

I didn't have any dreams after that.

The next morning came bright and sunny. Obviously another change from the formerly gray and dismal Null of the past. This one had far more appropriate weather. Deserts meant sun and lots of it. We weren't in summer, so it wasn't as hot as it could be.

Covey had already gotten up, made her cot, and left by the time I awoke. I would have liked to sleep longer, but the thin curtains made that a useless thought. This house was probably a boarding house in another life, or a cheap inn. Either way the owners didn't want people lounging around in bed.

I looked through my sad clothes, then noticed the satchel was near the door. Dueble had been right to pack the clothes. I grabbed my clothes, looked down the hall toward the washroom, and scurried over. I did miss Siabiane's chambers. Thinking about where they were now, buried under the jungles of Beccia, made me even sadder. I quickly took a shower, changed, threw everything else back into our shared room, and went downstairs.

I passed the table on my way to the kitchen. It was nicely set with a lovely breakfast, but there was no sign of a bunch of passed-out, chocolate-covered faeries on it.

"Where did the faeries go? And is one of these plates for me?" There were two that had hot food on them.

Lorcan nodded as he came out with a pot of tea. "They seemed recovered, so they went to fly about and see what they can tell about our missing mages. They took the two constructs with them. And yes, you and Alric were the last two up."

That was shocking. Alric rarely seemed to need sleep. Of course, I had no idea what time he'd left the suite when he and Siabiane went to look at Padraig, which was the last time either of us slept. I glanced over to where Padraig, Covey, and Kelm were in animated discussion. It was odd seeing the Lorcan and Siabiane who existed before the battles. It would have been difficult to see Padraig, unscarred, but also destined to remain unconscious for a few hundred years while his beloved culture crumbled.

I was glad I hadn't seen him.

I'd gotten halfway through my eggs and toast, and most of the tea, when Alric stumbled downstairs. He flopped into the seat behind the only other full plate of food. I poured him some tea and slid it over to him.

"Are you okay?" I kept my voice down, but didn't need to. The others were all busy debating the best way to get the relics and get out of here.

He rubbed the side of his face. "Not really. Nothing big, but I had a horrible nightmare last night." He finished his tea almost in a single gulp and Lorcan came by with a fresh pot.

"A nightmare, you say?" Lorcan had been involved in the other debate as well, but the word nightmare caught his attention. "Can you recall what it was?"

"No." Alric concentrated on his toast and eggs.

That was far too abrupt to be the truth and Lorcan looked like he realized it as well. "If it comes to you, please tell me. The fact that both of you had such a night tells me that time travel was most likely the cause. Or at least the trigger." He nodded then went back to the living area where the others were.

"What do you think?"

He finished his toast slowly. "I think there could be some truth to it. Your screams from last night were echoed in my dream." He started to say more then went back to his food.

"Me screaming? Or just screams?" He was starting to really worry me.

"You," he dropped his voice so low I almost couldn't hear him, and I had a feeling he wasn't going to repeat it if I asked. "You were screaming. You were dying and so was everyone around you. I couldn't save you. I couldn't stop what was happening." He finally looked up and his green eyes were rimmed in red. "I watched you die."

I set down my fork and cup before I dropped them.

"How did I die?" This was not a conversation I wanted to have first thing in the morning. Actually, I never wanted to have this conversation. No one I knew was into seeing the future or prophecies. But the look in Alric's eyes made me think there might be some truth involved.

"I don't know." He pushed aside his half-eaten plate and rubbed his eyes with his knuckles. "I couldn't see anything. It was something I felt…" He shrugged.

Like I'd felt terror but overwhelming guilt. "Nothing tangible. Only emotion."

"Yes, that's it exactly." He pulled back his sleeve to show me the geas mark was still glowing faintly. "I hadn't slept well to begin with. I showed this to Lorcan and Padraig right before I went to bed. They can't break it. Even though I didn't age with our trip back through time, it did. They don't know anyone who can break a thousand-year-old geas."

He rolled his sleeve back down and clearly didn't want to discuss it, or both of our dreams, anymore. The food I'd eaten was a lump in my stomach as we both sat silently.

"We have a plan," Covey called from the sofa area. "Now that you two have finished with timeline games, we can move about without a bubble. Lorcan has a good idea where Reginald would be."

Alric and I both pushed away from the table and went back to join them. "Is that who we really want?" Alric asked. "If he'd had the relics I would think he would have taken off. Not to mention, should Lorcan be around his brother?"

"Reginald is currently in Mackil's body and will be easier to find," Lorcan said. "I agree he most likely got caught trying to betray Nivinal and lost my body and the relics for his troubles. Nivinal showed up here looking for the relics, so he probably doesn't have them back. And from the brief information we've been able to find on this body-swapping spell, I'd guess that Reginald's hopped around so much he must not have much ability to jump left. The spell is hard to create, and weakens with each use. Scholars speculated a limit of just a few jumps."

I couldn't help it, the image of Lorcan bleeding out on the floor of his chamber and Siabiane's response hit me. I know she made Reginald a ghost to make him suffer more, but it would have been better for all if she had killed him and left him dead.

"Not to mention Nivinal is going to be a lot harder to find," Padraig said. "I checked out the area he vanished from, there was nothing. He wasn't even there in person, he sent his damn image to hunt us."

I shook my head. "He cast a spell on me. I was lifting off and felt the pull to come to him." The force of it unnerved me. If Lorcan hadn't held me down I'd be with Nivinal. I had no idea how he was going to get that manticore out of me—but I was sure I didn't want to find out. The shield spell had worked, but it hadn't stopped his spell from pulling me.

"He's that strong," Padraig said. "He was the most powerful of us all, except for Siabiane. I know she needed to stay back in the enclave, but I would love for her to be here now."

"On that cheery note, we have a plan for finding Reginald. Rather, a plan to get him to come to us." The look on Covey's face, and the fact it was directed at me, didn't bode well.

"I'm bait," I said with less annoyance than I would have expected. It made sense really, and the shield from yesterday made me feel a bit more secure. As long as Nivinal wasn't there. "How do we know a trap won't get Nivinal? We know he wants the manticore."

"I think I have that covered," Flarinen said from the door. I hadn't even seen him come in, but I pulled back in surprise at his appearance. For the first time that I'd ever seen, he was not in a form of armor. He looked to be wearing one of Alric's older outfits, his usual black on black. His sword was in a beat-up scabbard and his hair dirty and pulled back in a ragged tail.

"He knew who had the dragon, I know he did. I felt someone watching me every time I looked at it, searching for me. I believe he sent the rakasa to us, knowing they'd get the dragon back; his personal plan of action was for you. I'm going to get extremely drunk, make lots of noise, then ride out of town. Lorcan has created a magical dummy that will react like an artifact. It won't hold up long once he catches me. But it should distract him."

"And I've set up a spell around Flarinen, Nivinal won't be able to project to catch him easily. It will take a lot of focus." Padraig said.

"So this plan is, get me out there as bait, and hope that Reginald falls for it. And that Nivinal is distracted enough by Flarinen to not notice what we're doing?" This was way too sketchy to work. But I didn't know what else we had going. We could now leave Null, but we couldn't go without those relics.

"They came here for a reason. We are guessing that Reginald planned to use Makil to escape with the relics and leave Nivinal behind. But they both came here deliberately."

Lorcan's comments ended any belief that Nivinal and Reginald had ended up here by chance. They'd planned on ending up here. "The basilisk and sphinx."

Alric nodded. "At least one of those would be connected to here for them to come to Null in the first place. They had the other three. The mythology around all of the relics is scattered, and even more so on these two."

"I don't see how this is going to work. And if we get Reginald, what then? If you're right and he's lost the relics, what good is grabbing him?" This felt like we were grasping at straws. Null wasn't a large town, but we needed something to go on to find the relics. I wasn't sure Reginald was going to be it.

"That is true—he did lose them," Lorcan said. "But I believe that I can dig deep enough into his mind that I can find out when he lost them and to whom."

Great. The man whose brother almost killed him, but he didn't know did it, and who had his body stolen by said brother, was going to try and dive into his head. I looked to Alric. This could go bad and only the two of us knew why.

Alric was looking better than he had when he first came downstairs, but there was a haunted look in his eyes. Mostly when he was facing me. I didn't like that at all.

"I think that's going to be a problem. We really don't know that much about how Reginald became a ghost, nor what could trigger a body jump," he sounded so reasonable even I almost believed him. "We can try the plan since we don't have much else, but I think Padraig needs to be the one who pries into Reginald's head. Since he already took Lorcan once, the risk would be greater."

"I have to agree with Alric. Even after two months of research, we have no information about Reginald's original change. If we had that we might be able to stop his body hopping and send him where he belongs." Padraig had one of his books out and patted it for emphasis.

Crap. I was sure that both Alric and I had the same look. If the others weren't caught up in their own issues they would have noticed. "Wouldn't you need the actual spell caster who did it to change anything?" I asked. After all, Siabiane wasn't anywhere near here. Maybe we wouldn't have to tell Lorcan the truth.

"I don't think so. I've found documentation, very very old, from hundreds of years before the battle with the Dark. It won't work with most spells, but the strain this type of spell leaves on both the caster and the victim is such that it could be possible to unravel it. Providing the spell caster is known to the person trying to take it apart. You need to know how that person thinks, and you couldn't do that with a stranger."

"And you two know something," Covey said. She'd been debating small points with Kelm, but had been paying more attention to the rest of us than I thought,

Alric and I both started to speak at the same time, but I stopped and nodded for him to talk. "We have to tell them. I have no idea what it will do to the spell, but they need to know before we go after the bastard. I can tell them if you want," he said.

I took a deep breath. I'd been the one who fought to save Lorcan. That wasn't essential to getting to the spell that created Reginald as a ghost, but it was going to have to be part of the tale. "I'll do it." I briefly told them of the attack on the queen, and us needing to leave the palace immediately. There were no questions when I got to finding Lorcan. "Reginald waited until Siabiane was in the room, then slit Lorcan's throat." Just saying it made me want to throw up.

Lorcan went white, but he wasn't as shocked as I'd thought he'd be.

"Siabiane thought you were dead—she was in shock and not thinking right. She blasted Reginald apart, but instead of letting it go, she put a spell on his spirit to stay." I knew Siabiane wouldn't be happy about me telling him, but I had no choice.

"So she saved me afterwards?" Lorcan rubbed the glamoured mark on his neck absently.

"No. The faeries and I did that." I shrugged. "I have no idea how or what they did, but they focused my spell of healing and saved your life."

Lorcan nodded silently then got up and hugged me. "Thank you. It wasn't only them, it was also you. That explains, in part, why I felt so comfortable around you and the faeries when you arrived. I assume Siabiane put a forget spell on me?"

"And Reginald. Plus one over the city once we'd crossed into this time, so she would have forgotten as well," Alric said.

Lorcan let me go and nodded. "I would never have guessed it was him, and no one seemed to know who attacked me or saved me. I was found a few hours later, and moved to a safe place. But the attack from the Dark had begun and the city was beginning to slide into chaos."

"Does this information help? We know who cast the spell, and the main reason we didn't want Lorcan digging in Reginald's head is out in the open now." I really hoped it helped. Even though Lorcan hadn't looked as surprised as I'd expected, there was a tightness around his eyes that hadn't been there before.

"Yes and no." Padraig had been silent during all of this, and was sober now. "Knowing Siabiane was behind it helps, but she's so strong that undoing it will be difficult.

And the news you gave us means that we will be emotionally compromised when we attempt to change the spell. Emotions and spells aren't a good combination and she was obviously not in a good emotional state when she cast the spell."

Someone threw a bunch of rocks at the front door at that moment. Or that's what it sounded like to me. Flarinen in his Alric-wanna-be outfit was closest to the door. He held up one hand for silence, then drew his sword and slowly opened the door.

I shook my head. Rocks? But Flarinen took everything seriously, and since his fall from grace that hadn't changed.

He'd only gotten the door open a tiny bit when a mass of faeries hit the door almost hard enough to knock him on his ass. He recovered before that happened, but it was close.

The original three were not in the bunch, and a few others were missing as well. Most noticeably Bunky and the gargoyle. I spotted two of Garbage's sidekicks, Penqow and Dingle Bottom, and waved them to me.

"Where are the others, what's wrong?" None of the faeries looked injured but they also looked confused and rarely ran around without their leader.

Penqow came forward. "Is with man. He grab them. Send here."

"Someone grabbed the others? A bad man?" Had Nivinal decided to grab the girls hoping to get me?

Dingle Bottom shook her head. "Is got wrong. Man. Took. Them. We come here." She was so proud of herself as she spun in a little circle I didn't have the heart to say she made no sense. Well, almost.

"Do any of you know where the rest of the faeries, Bunky, and the gargoyle are?" I raised my voice as the faeries were now chittering to themselves as they flew around the room.

"This way." Penqow motioned to all of them, and they

all swarmed me and lifted me up.

There were only about fifteen or sixteen of them, and they shouldn't be able to do this.

"Watch out for the ceiling!" I yelled too late and they bounced me off of it, before hastily lowering me.

"Told you not show now." Dingle Bottom rubbed the top of my head.

"Need there now," Penqow said. "No choice."

The other faeries all chattered in agreement and started flying me out the door.

The idea of flying was lovely. If you were one of those odd poets who stayed on hilltops and thought about birds and things. In reality, if flying was fifteen faeries lifting you up and through a door—flying was not lovely.

My friends had been laughing at first, less so when I smacked my head on the ceiling, and not at all when my right shoulder got smacked into the doorframe.

Flarinen's shocked face was the last I saw as we finally made it out the door.

"Come back here!" Covey was the fastest runner of the bunch, even putting the elves to shame, but even she was starting to fade as the faeries picked up speed.

"Seriously, I don't think Garbage wanted you to pick me up." I shut my eyes; the speed they were going wasn't normal and was making me have second thoughts about my breakfast.

None of the faeries answered aside from some laughter, but before I'd shut my eyes, they'd all seemed focused and determined.

Great, so Nivinal, or maybe Reginald, caught the other faeries and these were what, going to trade me for them?

I popped my eyes open as we started to slow down and dropped into one of the few gorges left after the change when we went back in time. It looked suspiciously like the canyons we'd come through before we were spelled into Null, but I knew the faeries couldn't have flown that far that quickly.

I shut my eyes again as they flew down a hole, no bumping this time, but the hairs on my arms were standing up and felt how close we were to the rock sides.

A wave of cooler air hit me, and I was dumped in a pile of fabric and leaves.

"Very good, ladies. You did far better than I could have hoped. Come get your treats."

The voice was low and gravely, and I had a bad feeling I knew the species.

I opened my eyes to find an old syclarion peering right into mine.

CHAPTER THIRTY ONE

THE KNIFE HE HELD BETWEEN us didn't lessen my bad feelings.

"Where are the rest of my faeries?" I assumed he'd captured Bunky and the gargoyle as well, but I couldn't figure out how he'd gotten this group to help him. Unless this really was a trade situation.

The area that I could see, past the scary syclarion and his knife, was far more forest than desert. The sound of running water was also odd. Maybe an oasis? I knew Covey had long ago speculated that there were entire peoples living in the vast desert, surviving in oasies. The fact that I was about to die in one didn't offset the fact she was right.

"What did Dueble pack in your satchel?"

I looked closer into his eyes. He wasn't as old as I thought, and there appeared to be stage make-up adding to his aged appearance. I knew those eyes.

"Dueble?" I almost hugged him, but that knife was in my face.

"What was in the pack?"

"Clothing. You packed our clothing." I pulled at the tunic I wore. "This and more. The red tunic and the leather armor. You packed that." I couldn't recall any of the other specific things, but that one stood out.

He grinned and lowered the blade. "I am sorry for the mode of your arrival and doubting it was you. But it has been over a thousand years since we last met, and Nasif was worried that someone might pretend to be you. We have to be very cautious you know. There are people who would love to find us."

"You both survived?"

He reached out a hand to help me to my feet. I was dizzy from my inelegant mode of transportation so I needed it. The area we were in was an oasis, of sorts. Smaller gapen trees, huge by normal tree standards, small by their own, surrounded us. A gurgling river, looking robust for being in the middle of the desert, ran through the area, and lush plant life covered everything. "Is this place real?"

"Yes, and yes. Nasif will be sorry he missed your arrival, but he had his own important things to attend to. Some of your faeries went with him, some stayed here, and some retrieved you." Dueble beamed and I saw the young, and mostly confused, syclarion I'd met a thousand years ago. Although to me it had been less than two days.

I hugged him. And was immediately surrounded by faeries and two gronking constructs.

"Is good!" Garbage seemed particularly pleased with herself. I knew that in her wee brain, she'd done this all herself.

"Yes, sweetie, it's good." I looked around some more. A pair of houses to the side were at first hidden by the trees. Both simple, but looked sturdy and made mostly of stone. The one on the left had a tendril of smoke from its chimney. It was quite a bit cooler here in this oasis, or whatever it was, than in Null.

"Where are my manners? We never have guests anymore. Please, come inside," Dueble said and nodded to the faeries and constructs, "all of you. I'll get some tea and snacks in you, then we'll catch up."

I started following him. "No tea for the faeries please. Unless you want them to destroy this lovely place."

He opened the door. "Actually, I found that out the hard way." Inside the beautiful stone cabin was a tiny cage and a bouncy Crusty Bucket. "She got into it before Nasif could warn me. The bars are of the hardest metal known. Even then, at first I feared it wouldn't hold her."

I bent down to look at my tiny blue faery. She smiled and talked at me, but she spoke so fast I had no idea what she was saying. "How long ago did she have it?" I nodded to Crusty, but that made her talk faster.

"A few hours ago, when they first came here." He looked down at the cage sadly then turned toward the small sitting room and motioned to an overstuffed chair.

"How did Nasif know about the tea? We only discovered that a few months ago." Speaking of tea, Dueble had a steaming cup of the substance in my hand almost the moment I sat. He also had a tray of biscuits.

"Siabiane told him some tips for dealing with the faeries. Nasif and I arrived in the enclave the day after you left. He was planning on tracking you down, but she explained that none of you had met us yet and that we needed to wait. It was also decided to glamour me until things settled down."

A look of sadness crossed his long face. He really was so different from the rest of his people in this timeline.

The stone cottage was immaculate, but also looked established. Like hundreds of years established. "How long have you been here? What happened to you both during the fireball?"

He smiled. "The whole of it is a long tale, for Nasif and I have been in this area for almost the full thousand years since you left us. The fireball was impressive, was it not? He's only gotten better since then. Of course, we've had to stay low-key, and not cause notice—at least that's what Nasif's research found."

I sipped some tea hoping that the confusion his words brought on would be fixed. I took another sip, and a third. Nope—still confused.

"Oh dear, I did it again. As I said, we don't entertain much. Nasif and I were caught in the fireball, but we didn't die. The time spell grabbed us. We were trapped in a limbo pocket for one hundred and three years. When we dropped out of it, our attackers were obviously gone. However, so was Siabiane and the entire city. The battle with the Dark was long over and it looked like no one won. The palace was in ruins and the other races were moving in. Nasif searched but never found signs of his people, so we believed the stories that they had all died, like the Ancients before them."

He refilled my tea, but his eyes were far from this stone cottage.

"We roamed. My people had all fled, and the syclarions back in my homeland were war-like and violent. We traveled and researched. Null was of great interest. It's not natural, you know. Well, the way it *was* wasn't natural. The faeries are right; you and Alric did change it back."

More tea wasn't helping me understand time travel implications. I put my cup down and went for a biscuit. Maybe that would help. "If we changed it back to what it was, then who changed it in the first place? The town looked like it had been that way for a long time."

"We have debated that for quite a while. This glen is a pocket, sort of like the bubble spell Lorcan put on your friends when you and Alric were in my time. Because of the pocket nature we saw things change differently. But the time waves that seemed to have been a major contributor to the wrongness were around even when we got here. Something long ago caused the time waves to gather, and caused Null."

"Did they also cause the weird spell that sent us to Null?" I hadn't had enough time between when we arrived in Null and going back a thousand years to ask Lorcan, but it hadn't seemed like he or Padraig had any idea what caused us to be sucked into the spell that ended with a one-way, at the time, trip to Null.

"That is a good question and one we've been trying to

resolve. The spell is old, even older than we are. Yet neither Nasif nor I recall it being in our time, but we know it must have been. It could be that the spell exists out of time. Time is far more fluid than one would think, you know."

I smiled and had another biscuit. Like the tea, they weren't helping, but they tasted good and if my mouth was full I couldn't ask stupid questions like, 'what?'

"You are doing it again, aren't you, my boy?" The voice coming from the door was a little rougher, but it was one I knew.

Garbage got to him first. "They get! Told you." I turned to find her pointing at me. Her smug grin grew as Nasif, his beard much longer now, handed over some lumps of sugar.

"You were right, wee one! They did it without you or your two lieutenants."

As he spoke Leaf came buzzing from behind his pack. "I help too!" She led three of the other faeries into the sitting area where they started jumping and jabbering with the rest.

I got up and ran to hug him. Then stepped back and looked at him and Dueble. "You both have been running about for a thousand years. Your beard is longer but neither of you are showing any age—ignoring Dueble's stage make-up. I know elves are long lived but even Lorcan and Siabiane look older now than they did then."

"Plus, I am not a full elf, and Dueble is a syclarion—a species whose life span is about two hundred years, give or take. Good observations." He patted Crusty's cage, but her chatter was almost out of hearing range so he took a cup of tea and sat down in the seating area.

"The blast of that last fireball did knock us out of time for a while, as I'm sure Dueble told you. It also changed both of us. Near as I can tell, and in conferring with Siabiane, she seems to agree, we're both immortal now. Something that caused the time waves in Null pulled into us back then. It changed our make up at the most basic level."

"So..." I shook my head and gave up. There was no way I could sum up what he said.

"I think both of us have been away from people for too long," Dueble said. "I am not the only one confusing her."

"No, it makes sense...really." I quickly drank some more tea.

"Once we explain it to Lorcan and Padraig it will make more sense." Nasif looked around as if just noticing there was only Dueble and I in the stone cottage. "Where are the rest?"

Dueble gave him a raised eyebrow. "It was hard enough getting the faeries to carry her in. Do you really think they could bring in the rest?"

"We probably want to do something though. We were making plans to go after the relics and Reginald. They are going to be a bit upset about me being carted off like that."

Nasif had started stroking his beard as I spoke, but choked when I said Reginald.

"Siabiane told me what happened to Lorcan. I never saw him while we were there, but it was a short trip. So the Lorcan with you is a ghost? Or is really Reginald?" It took him a few minutes to untangle his fingers from his beard.

"It's Lorcan. Reginald dropped control of Lorcan's body and Lorcan's ghost took it back. Reginald is now in the body of a dwarf, Mackil, but it's believed that he's not able to hop anymore." I looked at both of them. It was wonderful to see them, especially when we all assumed they'd died in the fireball. "If you knew we were here, why didn't you go into town? Dueble said you were afraid of a copy of me?"

Nasif looked embarrassed. "I have a fear of changelings. We ran afoul of them a few dozen years past and I've never fully gotten over it." He covered his feelings by pulling on his beard. It seemed to be his go to reaction and it did work much better with the full beard he now had.

"We had a problem with some of them a few months back, so I understand. But we probably need to go back into town and tell everyone I'm okay."

Both of them looked uncomfortable.

Nasif finally answered. "The truth is neither of us go into Null anymore. It might have to do with our unique condition and the nuances of the place itself. But both of us become physically ill if we go there."

That would complicate things, although they might not have tried since the changes happened. "How far away from Null are we? It felt like we were flying for a while." A long distance would also complicate things. I knew a number of people would be extremely happy at seeing these two, but we also needed to stay in Null until we got the relics back. My thinking was that even one of the relics would work for now; it would stop them from assembling the thing. Preferably the gargoyle or the chimera, the dragon could stay where it was forever in my book. Nivinal couldn't put the weapon together without all of them. I didn't want the one inside me to be the only one he didn't have. The more we could get back from him the safer I would feel.

"That was the faeries doing, although I did ask them to take a longer route," Dueble said. "This oasis is hidden not a few minutes from the outskirts of Null. We're in a canyon that is protected by Nasif's spells. No one can see it unless we allow them." He was so proud about the spell. It was as if it was his spell and not Nasif's.

I was happy these two survived, and even more so that they seemed to have become extremely close over the centuries. Being immortal and thinking you were cut off from all of your people would be extremely difficult—having someone else who knew exactly what you were going through had to be the only thing keeping them both sane.

"Then can I go lead the rest back here? How will I find my way back if it's hidden?" I finished my last biscuit and tea.

"I'll go with you, but only to the edge of Null." Nasif also finished his tea.

"I fear the reputation of my people—both during the battle with the Dark and in current times, makes my appearance awkward. We were using glamours but I became immune to them a few decades ago." Dueble pointed to his make-up. "This can only do so much."

"You can become immune to a spell?" That was news to me.

"It is possible, but it takes an extremely long time for it to happen." Nasif squinted his eyes and looked at Dueble. "Although, if anyone could modify the spell to work on Dueble again, Padraig would be the one."

I went over to the table. The faeries had gathered on the desk and at some point Bunky and the gargoyle had joined them. The two constructs were silently sitting next to Crusty's cage listening to her jabbering. She did appear to be slowing down. Cage or not, I was bringing her with us. I trusted these two with my life a thousand years ago. Those feelings hadn't changed. But I wanted to keep everyone together at this point.

"Crusty? How are you feeling?"

She finished her current jabber, which didn't appear to be directed at anyone, and then spun toward me. "Good. Is good. No zoom."

"She say that Bunky told her." Leaf had been engaged in some odd little game nearby, but came over. "Bunky saw no zoom, no cage."

I lifted an eyebrow in Bunky's direction. "Is that true? You're telling her how to get out? You know that if we let her out and she's hopped up on tea she's going to be impossible to keep track of." I didn't understand Bunky, but I knew he understood me.

He gronked and bobbed his head.

"He say he watch," Leaf said, then went back to her game.

"You'll take care of her if I let her out?" I didn't really

have a choice; the cage was heavier than I'd originally thought.

Again a gronk and what I was going to take as an affirmative nod. I peered down closer to Crusty. Her movements had slowed down, and she was no longer jabbering like a broken wind-up toy, but her wings were flapping a bit much.

"Can you settle down? Bunky will keep an eye on you. No ale for a month if you go tearing off." I wasn't sure she had much control over her speed if she was reacting to the tea. I also wasn't sure she even knew what a month was. But a solemn look crossed her face as she nodded. It didn't stay long enough for me to respond, but at least it had been there.

I unlocked the cage.

Crusty slowly walked out onto the table and headed for her friends. Then spun around and took off for the door. That it was shut only slowed her a little. The going through solid objects stunt the faeries seemed to be able to do sometimes, but not always, was disturbing to watch. It was like the back half of her slowly disappeared into the wood.

I ran to the door and flung it open. She hadn't gone far but was zipping around too fast for normal. "Okay, Bunky. She's all yours. You two need to get her and yourselves back to the house in Null. Understand?"

He gronked, bobbed, and tore out after the blue streak bouncing from tree to tree.

Dueble, Nasif, and the rest of the faeries came out as well.

"Go get?" Garbage had a particularly aggressive look in her eye as she pointed to Crusty and the trees.

"No, she's fine. I need you to make sure we're safe going back." It might have only taken fifteen years but I had finally figured out that making Garbage an important member of any event went a long way in getting her to do something. When it worked, anyway.

"Is good, we lead," she said then pointed to Nasif. "You follow."

I started to point out that I didn't know how to get out of this place when twenty-two faeries all grabbed me. "No! This isn't the way. Nasif! Tell them to put me down!" Of course by then I was at a height I really didn't want them to put me down from.

"I'll wait for all of you at the edge of Null!" Nasif yelled as we quickly flew out of sight.

Having more faeries this round did allow them to go higher. I had no idea how they were carrying me though. Unfortunately, mid-flight they had an argument about which way to go and almost dropped me.

Once they'd all regained ahold of me, I looked around for landmarks. "Go right! I see the house, right."

I swear the faeries never had a problem with right and left until now. My right leg went one way, and my left the other. We were all dropping for a few seconds, until Garbage whistled.

"Is THAT right, not other right!"

My limbs untwisted and we descended at a rapid speed toward the house.

I'd only been gone an hour or so, but it was enough for Flarinen and Kelm to put on their armor, and the rest of our merry bunch to load up on weapons and all gather in the front yard.

I was glad to see them, but yelling hello wasn't an option. If I opened my mouth the only thing coming out would be a scream.

We were dropping in height but not in speed.

Covey was more of a hunter than the others and noticed the flock of faeries, and their passenger, first.

I tried mentally yelling at the faeries to slow down, but they were either ignoring me, or it didn't go through.

Covey yelled and pointed so everyone turned around.

Which was a good thing because at that moment the faeries hit an invisible shield of some sort and we all fell from the sky.

Chapter Thirty Two

I'D REALLY THOUGHT WE HAD dropped more in height than we apparently did, as it felt like a long way to fall. Unfortunately, it also went far too quick and the ground was going to smack me in a second. A small part of my mind screamed to use a spell, but the rest of my brain wouldn't stop jabbering long enough to form a word of one in my head.

Alric ran to where I was about to hit the ground and shouted a spell. I immediately stopped and hung in the air about three feet above him. The faeries kept falling and bounced off the ground a few times. They were far more bounceable than I was and I wasn't worried about their rough landing.

Alric slowly lowered me until I landed in his arms. It would have been romantic if all of our friends weren't crowding around us.

"What happened?" I couldn't see a shield but I'd felt it when it knocked us out of the sky.

"The faeries stole you so we thought maybe they were working for the other side." Kelm's words started fast then died down as twenty-two faeries started pulling themselves out of the ground and glaring at him.

"Now, now." Lorcan stepped forward, holding his hands out in front of the faeries. "Kelm isn't a magic user. There was no way he could have dropped you out of the sky. Padraig and I made the shield to stop all flyers. We do apologize and will provide full recompense. However, you must agree that picking up Taryn and flying off against her will was rather rude."

As much as I enjoyed being in Alric's arms, I felt a bit odd with everyone around us, so I scrambled down. "It wasn't their fault. They'd been ordered to grab me and bring me back. Not that they obey my orders that well, but apparently for some people they do." I looked around at the houses around us. People might have ignored a full attack by a projected image of a mage and a pack of rakasa. They were not, however, ignoring a pack of faeries and a person falling from the sky. Windows had faces and a few were even open.

"How about we all go back inside? There are things to tell that don't need extra ears listening."

Everyone nodded and we trooped inside. Except Flarinen. He stopped at the door. "I don't believe we are safe, I shall wait out here."

He'd gone from mopey to snotty in a lot less time than I'd expected.

The faeries also declined to join us and sat in a half circle facing the door—and Flarinen. They didn't look happy and even though Flarinen hadn't dropped them from their flight, they looked like they were finding ways to blame him for it.

There wasn't going to be an easy way to say what needed to be said, so I didn't even try.

"Nasif and Dueble survived the explosion and ended up being flung a little over a hundred years into the future from when we left them. The elves who survived the battle with the Dark had all gone into hiding, and the people who moved into the areas past the ruins said they'd all died. So the two traveled around. They found out when the shield dropped on the enclave that there were elves alive." I looked around and poured myself some water. I'd been talking fast and flying seemed to make me thirsty.

Lorcan's eyes had lit up at his friend's name. "Where are they? How do you know all this?"

I held up one finger and finished my water. "They are right outside of Null, they sent the faeries to get me, and they seem to be time challenged of a sort and can't come into Null without getting physically sick."

Padraig must have known Nasif before he was attacked as well, he smiled when I said they were alive, but it dropped into a frown. "Time challenged?"

"They were out of time, if that's what you'd call it, for over a hundred years. Both of them are now sensitive to time fluctuating areas—like Null. The faeries were right; Alric and I seemed to have fixed part of what was wrong with Null by going back in time. But it's an odd time area." I shrugged. Talking more about time travel weirdness wasn't making it any clearer to me. "Oh, and they think they are both immortal now."

"What? I really must talk to them. Well, Nasif at least. I am afraid I never knew your syclarion friend, but if you, Alric, and Nasif all vouch for him, he must be a fine person indeed." Lorcan got to his feet and went for the door.

"Shouldn't we be armed?" Kelm asked, and the way he was looking toward the closed front door I was sure Flarinen would be saying the same thing. Only with more attitude.

"Nasif is my friend and I don't believe a thousand years would have changed that. However, if there is something amiss with this situation, I am as armed as I need to be." Lorcan flexed his fingers.

That was true. I'd never seen him fight with anything but his formidable magic. I did note that even though they were also skilled mages, both Alric and Padraig were donning their spirit swords. I looked around for mine and realized that I'd left it up in the room I shared with Covey. I turned to go upstairs, then felt it in my hand.

I dropped it, but managed to catch the hilt before it

struck the ground.

"You have to stop sneaking up on me like that." I slipped it into the sheath, which had also appeared.

"I don't know that it can hear you," Padraig said as he walked by me toward the door.

"It can't hurt, can it? Can you imagine if it starts playing games during a fight?" I thought I felt a slight twinge come from the sword. I didn't care what anyone else thought—this thing understood me.

Once everyone was armed, we went outside to an interesting tableau. The faeries and Flarinen were playing a game. I actually did a double take and rubbed my eyes to make sure it wasn't an elaborate trick by the faeries.

Nope. They were playing a game. They'd found a few nuts, rounded with age and being on the ground. The faery with the nut would kick it to Flarinen who would catch it and flick it back over their heads. Without flying, a number of faeries would launch themselves into the air, fight over control of it, then crash to the ground. The winner would then kick it to Flarinen.

"I taught them a game." He flicked the nut back into the air as he spoke.

I looked from the faeries to Flarinen and back again.

"A game," Alric said without a question.

Flarinen shrugged then flung the nut out again. "Yeah. It seemed like the thing to do, they just kept staring at me. Plus the other two flyers, and one crazy blue thing, are probably distracting anyone around us from what is going on here."

I looked up. Sure enough Bunky and the gargoyle were half-heartedly chasing around a slowly descending Crusty. "You dropped the shield spell I assume?" I asked Lorcan, but it looked to me like Crusty and her escorts were definitely flying over the area that the rest of the faeries and I had fallen from.

"Yes, once we realized the faeries weren't doing anything wrong," Padraig said.

"Where are Nasif and Dueble staying?" Alric had added a few smaller blades to his collection.

"Out a little past the city limits, they have a secret spot, but Nasif will be waiting outside of it to let us in."

"I don't know that all of us should go." Flarinen had finished his game with the faeries and rose to his feet. "Kelm and I should stay behind to guard our possessions." He nodded to Padraig, Alric, and Covey. "You have enough fighters."

Alric looked ready to argue, but then nodded. "Agreed. But, I think some of the faeries should stay here as well." He turned to where the girls were flying around. "You all know how to get to this secret place, right?" At their odd assorted chorus of affirmatives, he waved Garbage over. "Can you select five of the most dedicated faeries to stay here? Their job will be to come find us if anything goes wrong. Flarinen and Kelm will stay here, but they'd come find us if that changes in any way. Obviously, if someone attacked them."

His choice of words was subtle, and I would have thought too subtle for faeries. He clearly wanted them to come find us if Flarinen or Kelm left the house—as well as if they were attacked.

Garbage narrowed her eyes and glanced at the two knights. She slowly nodded her head then winked. "We watch. I stay." She pointed out four other faeries, leaving Leaf and Crusty to lead the rest of us.

This was a day of wonders. Flying by faery—twice, Flarinen playing a game, and now Garbage understanding something subtle. This might not be because of the trip Alric and I took, but this was definitely becoming a different world than we left.

With the faeries divided up, and Bunky and the gargoyle opting to stay with Garbage and her crew, we made our way to the edge of town. Unfortunately, flying at a high speed and with faeries who didn't know which way they were going didn't leave much time for noticing landmarks. Plus, outside of town there were few landmarks to notice. Lots of sand, rocks, and odd-looking plants. A small grove of woods up ahead was a welcome sight.

The faeries weren't paying attention, instead they were dive-bombing the few birds we saw along the way. Lorcan had taken the lead, but he slowed down as we got a short distance into the thin clump of scraggly trees.

"Okay, now where?" He put his hands on his hips and surveyed the area.

"Girls…GIRLS!" I had to yell, but Leaf finally recalled she was in command on this and brought the other faeries over. "Which way do we go?

Leaf tore off to the left. Then doubled back, confusing the pack of faeries who were following her, and went to the right.

"Ladies." Alric stood in the middle of the flight path and held out a closed fist. "I have sugar, good, solid, rock sugar. But I can only give it to you when you take us to Nasif." He cracked open his fist enough to let the faeries see what he had, then closed it up tight.

I must have looked surprised because he winked at me. "Harlan gave me some tips before he left."

The faeries all huddled together in the air. One or two would turn to look at Alric, then back to their huddle.

Finally Leaf came up to me. "Only work with you."

I had a bad feeling I knew what she meant.

"You want me to lead?" Maybe deliberately misunderstanding would help.

"We need pick up. Only way." Leaf nodded her head and darted forward to grab a hold of my arm.

Alric grabbed my other arm. "You need to find your way without picking up Taryn. Or anyone else."

Obviously they could do it; they'd found Nasif and Dueble before they'd carried me in. Leaf was being more obtuse than usual. And she probably liked flinging me through the air. She was becoming more like Garbage every day.

"Is no can—"

"Taryn! Alric! Lorcan!" Nasif suddenly appeared from behind a bush and ran forward. He hugged me so fast he was little more than a blur. Then on to Alric and Lorcan. He actually lifted Lorcan in the air. A nice feat since Lorcan was quite a bit taller than him.

"Might I introduce my friend Covey? And I think you know Padraig?" I interjected after the two old friends finished hugging and patting each other on the back. I had a feeling we might want to leave Lorcan with Nasif when we went back. Those two had a thousand years to catch up on.

"Of course. A trellian, pleased to meet you, my lady." Nasif bowed low and Covey actually blushed a bit.

"And Sir Padraig! I am happy to see you! I didn't know you well before your attack, but I followed your work heavily." He looked around. "Weren't there more of you?"

Alric nodded. "Yes, two elven knights, but they stayed to guard our residence. You wouldn't know them; both were born after the battle."

Nasif nodded and looked at the sun. It was late in the day, but the sun wasn't going to set for a few hours. A frown crossed his face. "I would like to meet them at some point, but things come out around here at dark. Unhealthy things that stay away from Null proper. We'd best get to our glen."

Lorcan kept staring at him. "I can't believe you are here and you don't look like you've aged a day. How did Siabiane respond?" They started walking and I noticed the path was straight, not either direction Leaf had tried going.

Nasif chuckled. "I know, and you were always the young one. But it is so good to see you at whatever age. As for your fair lady, Siabiane wasn't as surprised to see us as I would have thought. I do wonder how much of the rest of the world she sees. That was true back in our day, and even more so now." His face was turned as we walked and since I was right behind them, I saw when the smile dropped. "She's far more closed off than she was before… everything."

"A thousand years of helping to hide our people can do that to a person." Lorcan said softly, but he nodded in agreement.

We came to a pair of desert trees, little more than sparse, straggly shrubs. If shrubs could be said to grow six feet high. Nasif held up his left hand and we all stopped, even the faeries who had been arguing among themselves. He chanted a few words too rapidly to understand, and then raised his right hand in a flamboyant gesture.

In between the two trees a space began to grow, golden at first, then finally clear. It was more than a little disturbing to see a patch of deep green between two shrubs in a desert.

"Come on in. Dueble's probably got an early supper on for us." Nasif went through the portal, but stayed right inside and motioned for us all to come through. Might have been the power of suggestion, or the fact that breakfast was a while ago, but I swore I smelled chicken and potatoes.

The glen—a much more fitting name than oasis—looked as it had when I left, except the two stone houses had merged into one. I shook my head, but they were now one giant building.

"Ah, yes, impressive isn't it?" Nasif came up behind me after the others had cleared the portal. "We don't often do it, but with more people coming in, we thought a larger space would be handy. It's more technology from Dueble than magic from me, however."

We moved closer to the house and Dueble came out in an apron. Anyone who had bad feelings about syclarions, even me, would have a hard time with his bright and happy face and a flour-coated apron.

"Welcome! I'm Dueble," he said as he shook Lorcan's hand vigorously before moving on to Padraig and Covey. Covey looked startled; her people were not great friends with the syclarions. But since that had happened after Dueble's time, he wasn't aware of it. If her handshake had been a bit stiffer than the others had he gave no sign.

"And Alric!" Dueble didn't give Alric a handshake, but picked him up off his feet. "It is so good to see you again." He beamed to everyone then waved toward the house. "Please come in."

The two houses had merged into one inside as well. I went and touched one of the new stone walls. It felt solid. Looking down I could see lines in the stone floor. Faint ones, but lines none-the-less.

"Surprising, isn't it? It took years of calculations, but I did it." Dueble wiped his hands on his apron.

"Do you two get that many visitors out here?" My friends were looking around the house but they had no idea what it had looked like before. I agreed the tiny houses I'd seen earlier would have been problematic for a group, but considering Nasif and Dueble were pretty much hiding from anyone in Null, a larger place didn't make much sense.

"Not really…okay, not at all. Nasif has felt we need to keep a low profile in this area because of the Event. But our glen can get cold in the winter, so we share our houses so we don't have to go back and forth."

"The Event?" Part of me felt I didn't need to or want to know what anything called The Event was. There were a lot of events going on around us and I wasn't fond of how most of them were turning out. But as usual, curiosity won.

Dueble bobbed his head. "Oh yes, the end of the world. Very exciting stuff!"

CHAPTER THIRTY THREE

MY FRIENDS HAD BEEN WALKING around the house as Nasif showed them little touches. The faeries had taken over the table and I knew they'd be getting out some ale soon. And Dueble was calmly and happily telling me about the end of the world.

"Excuse me?" I couldn't think of anything more intelligent than that. The silence of the people around me said they'd heard Dueble as well.

"Now, it's not what you think," Nasif said. "It is quite exciting, however."

Alric looked from one to the other. "The end of the world would be exciting? How?"

"No, no, no. The event we are studying is the end of the Ancients' world. And we are getting closer to finding out the truth of what happened." Dueble added on the last bit with a gleam usually only found in the eyes of relic treasure hunters upon finding a huge haul.

"The relics might not have been from a weapon against the Ancients after all." Dueble's eyes got huge and he shrugged to Nasif. "I am sorry, I know your theory wasn't ready, but these are our friends and I got carried away."

Nasif shook his head. "It's fine. They are our friends and I have a feeling they are far more in the thick of events than we are." He turned to us. "Although we have a low profile here near Null, both Dueble and I have become well known academic scholars. It is other academics that we wish to hold back the information from."

Covey tilted her head and squinted her eyes. "You wouldn't be writing articles under the name Doublenasier would you?"

"You know us!"

I would have thought that almost a thousand years might have slowed some of Dueble's enthusiasm. That didn't appear to be the case. He practically bounced with excitement.

Nasif nodded and went to the closest kitchen, since there were now two, and started bringing out ales. "You have heard of us? We try to keep our identities unknown to anyone even in the academic community. But these findings must be shared."

Covey laughed. "That explains why your papers were so spot on for the elven history components. Although, you really didn't do much for the study of elven linguistics."

"True, we had a slight advantage over the rest of the world on anything elven. But I thought my people were gone for certain. I didn't want to submit too many works that would get people asking about where my information came from. I could speculate from findings from others in the field. But not enough work had been done on the language for me to work on those in public."

Covey looked truly excited, something I'd not seen in a while. "I do wish I was in my office. I have many of your articles and would love to discuss them."

"Not that I don't appreciate academia, because I do." Alric's tone said anything except that. "But have you found any way to get the rest of the relics? What makes you think they didn't cause the destruction of the Ancients? They seem to cause a lot of trouble even now."

"Oh, we believe the item created by those relics getting together caused the end of the Ancients; we are simply stating it might not have been intended as a weapon against them." Nasif beamed and bounced his look from person to person, but no one seemed to share it.

"How can it have caused their destruction, but not have been a weapon?" Covey had her predatory academic face on now so I wasn't going to get in her way. No one who valued their limbs would get in her way when she looked like that.

"That is what's so interesting," Nasif said as he scuttled over to a pile of scrolls. "These make reference to the Wathin period. The time of great affluence before the Ancients were lost. It appears that they had been doing many studies on the elements and how to contain them." He leaned forward. "It is here believed that during this time the syclarions found out what they were doing."

"I'm afraid my people at the time were extremely warlike and greedy. They would have wanted what the Ancients had," Dueble said. The fact that he chose to stay with Nasif instead of going to find his people said a lot about how he felt about most of his people.

"So the idea that the Ancients somehow genetically damaged the syclarion race could be true?" Now Alric was getting the academic fever. Although I knew that for him it was all about what was going to happen when those relics got together and how to stop it. He'd never elaborated on the other dimension he was flung into while destroying the glass gargoyle—before we realized that it could come back. But the few things he had said definitely made me not want to visit. If there was any chance of that reality invading ours, I was all for stopping it.

If the gargoyle could do that, who knew what the entire thing put together was capable of.

"What? When did that come about?"

"Who said that?"

Lorcan and Covey spoke almost at the same time. Padraig hadn't said anything but his face showed he was thinking it.

"It was what the syclarions believed before the battle

with the Dark—or at least some of them." Nasif looked fondly at his friend. "Until Dueble told us about it, before the time of the Dark, I'd never heard of it. I'm thinking that after we vanished getting Alric and Taryn home, you didn't have many syclarions around. And the ones that were, wouldn't have been inclined to discuss it."

Lorcan shook his head. "None at all. I recovered not too long before Siabiane came back, but neither of us recalled what happened beyond the queen being attacked and some sort of attack on the city. Many people fled at that point, mostly everyone but the elves." His eyes became hooded. "Within a week the battle with the Dark began."

Covey started pacing—one advantage of the combined stone cabins; she had more room to stomp. "So, these relics combined into something, but not necessarily a weapon. The Ancients genetically damaged the syclarions, but then either the syclarions or some other people destroyed the Ancients."

Nasif nodded. "That is our theory. It is weak and I was hoping you'd have one of the relics, at least, for us to study."

I was about to tell him we did have one, just not an accessible one, when a war cry came from outside. The faeries all fled from their bottles and flew to the door, but, unlike before, this time they waited for me to open it. Like them, I knew that war cry.

The faeries inside the house flew past me to mingle with Garbage, Bunky, the gargoyle, and the remaining four faeries. That Garbage and the other four were in war feathers wasn't surprising given their yells upon arrival. The rest of the faeries flew back into the house and I knew they'd be back out in full war feathers, which I was sure they kept in those mysterious black bags of theirs.

"Garbage, what happened?" Had Nivinal come back to get me and managed to overpower Flarinen and Kelm instead?

"Them gone. Bad men," Garbage said. "We tell you, then

go get." She waved her war stick in the air, a move echoed by the rest of the faeries as they came out of the house.

"Who took them?" Alric was right behind me with everyone else standing around the doorway and out of the faeries' way. Not that I blamed them—the girls all got excited when they had the chance to wear their war feathers.

"No take, they *go*." Garbage growled the last word and I realized Kelm and Flarinen had managed to ditch the faeries.

"What did they do?"

"New game, nice drink. Who drink more? We won, they left."

I looked to Bunky and the gargoyle. The girls might have fallen prey to a trick from Flarinen, but the constructs were immune. "How did they get away from you two?"

Both of them dropped lower and while it was hard to tell on their impassive faces, both seemed annoyed.

"He lock them up. I wake up, get them out. Bad men gone." Garbage was as pissed as I'd ever seen her. I'd feel sorry for the two knights except I was pissed too. Alric kept fingering the hilt of his sword and I had a feeling that images of slicing through Flarinen were running through his head.

"Okay, now you don't know they left. They could have been taken against their will." I couldn't believe that I was defending Flarinen. Not to mention the odds really didn't look like they were overwhelmed. He'd locked up the constructs and drugged the faeries. He'd even won their favor by inventing a game before we left. "Never mind. That wouldn't have happened." I answered myself before anyone else could.

"Where would they have gone?" Padraig asked.

"Where else? To get the relics." Alric adjusted two of his knives and then added two more that Nasif brought out. "They weren't only here to help, and I should have seen it from the start. They are trying to get the relics. For who is a damn good question. Could be trying to save face with the king and queen, or it could be worse."

"Now, I know you two boys have never gotten along," Lorcan said. "But I don't believe Flarinen and Kelm have ill intent."

"I hate to say this, but you also didn't realize your own brother had ill intent until he almost killed you." Covey put her hand on Lorcan's shoulder. "There could be some truth to this. We don't even know if they are working with Nivinal or Reginald."

Lorcan looked ready to argue, then shook his head. "You might be right. Nasif, you are lucky you didn't go through aging all of these years. Old age makes one question the world around you, and your own judgement. But they both were affected by the emerald dragon—there is a chance it is a continuation of that."

"My friend, you are as sharp as ever, and you trust the people around you. And that's not a bad thing." Nasif looked to us all. "I will say that Siabiane trusts your two knights; she told me when we were there. Either the dragon is pulling harder on both of them than we expected, or the captain is trying to regain honor with the royals."

Everyone adjusted or re-attached their weapons as the girls flew around our heads yelling.

"Stop!" I finally yelled at the faeries. "We know you're mad, so are we. But yelling war cries isn't going to help anything. If you want to yell them around our missing knights when we find them, be my guest. Repeatedly. And loudly. But not at us, and not now. Got it?"

The faeries kept zipping across the glen and waving their war sticks, but they kept their cries to a lower volume. That was fine by me. Especially if they saved that noise for Flarinen.

"I don't understand how the dragon could be pulling them from a distance though." As much as I wanted to think Flarinen was a nasty bastard, there was also a scary thought—could the emerald dragon work from a distance?

Nasif and Lorcan both nodded in unison.

"You have been studying the relics as well now?" Nasif asked. "You were all about the power behind magic when I knew you."

"And you were about time travel." Lorcan smiled at his friend. "Padraig became one of the foremost researchers on the relics. He and I have been examining every text we can about them."

Padraig had been discussing something with Bunky, but turned at his name. "As for the emerald dragon, if Nivinal got back, or never lost, the obsidian chimera, he could use it to boost the dragon's power." He frowned. "Particularly for those who had recently held it. He might not have been able to reach Taryn since she handled it too long ago. Alric had kept it in a protected bag when he had it. We'd wondered what a relic that was only meant to elicit greed would be as part of the item—it calls people to it. Whatever the weapon or thing was these relics combined to build, it was designed to call someone, or ones, closer to it."

"So then, Nivinal didn't lose the relics?" I was missing something, but to be fair I was distracted by the faeries and the flight show.

"Or he did lose them then got them back." Alric had finished re-arming himself. "He might have even gone so far as to plant the dead bodies and the emerald dragon where Flarinen would find it. Get it in with us, all of us touch it, and he could have easily called us to him."

"Would that have been bad? We do want to find him and these relics." Covey adjusted her sword.

Nasif had also armed himself. "Not in this way. The dragon renders common sense invalid. You would have been under Nivinal's control had you physically touched it as I assume both of your knights did. Which does bring into question, who is Nivinal? Not the old inquisitor who worked with Jovan?"

"Yes, or as far as we can tell," Lorcan said. "I have my doubts that he was ever who we thought he was, but it appears to be the former inquisitor. There were changes in him during our battle when the shield fell, and Taryn noticed some odd things during an altercation with him at the shield before that. And whoever he is, he is good at projecting himself."

"Jovan turned out to be one of the Dark—but stayed hidden for the thousand years the enclave was under the shield," Alric said. "He'd made it to the south, with a group we think were the surviving Dark, after the battle. He was finally destroyed by his own protégé." He was already heading for the far end of the glen and the way out.

The rest of us followed but there still wasn't a plan.

"I always disliked that bastard, too prissy for my tastes. Glad he got his comeuppance. Is his protégé alive?" Nasif turned and held his hands out toward the joined houses. They faded a bit.

Alric shot me a grin. "I seriously doubt it. In fact, I know he isn't."

"I sort of exploded him." I gave a shrug. I wasn't up to explaining everything that had been involved with Glorinal.

Covey watched the houses fade as Dueble, also loaded with weapons, joined us. "I thought you two couldn't go into Null?"

"It's not a good idea," Dueble said, as he gave a wistful look at the fading homes. "But we can be there for a while. Not to mention, it does appear some things changed when Taryn and Alric came back. We won't be comfortable, but we can be there."

"This is a crux moment." Nasif raised one hand as he walked. "Both Dueble and I seem to sense these odd moments in time. This is one. I've protected the glen as well as I can but we won't be back here for a while. Mark my words, something big is coming and we're going to be a part of it. Most likely whether we want to or not, so my vote is we be prepared."

"Aren't we back where we were? Nivinal now has Flarinen and Kelm, and possibly the other three relics. I know we tossed around me as bait," I rubbed the cheek where the manticore was hidden, "but I don't think that's the best idea. And not only because I don't want to be caught by Nivinal."

Padraig had been silent but he'd taken out a sheath of papers from his pack. "We need to stop by the house and get things ready to leave quickly. One way or another we're not going to want to stay here after this. But I think I have an idea where the golden basilisk is." He scowled at the top page in his hands. "It's not going to be easy to get even once we find it—according to this, it's a construct and does act as a basilisk."

Covey stopped walking and started swearing. "Seriously? Who in their right mind would create something like that and then make it able to move around killing people?" We'd kept walking, albeit slowly, so she caught up. "By acting like a basilisk, you mean the myth, right? Reptile thing that kills people with a look? Is it the spitting fire kind or not? Mythology has both."

Padraig shrugged. "It doesn't break down which mythology was used to create it, nor why it would be a construct and the others not. But I think we should be prepared for both possibilities."

Covey was muttering under her breath. "Not only did the creator of this weapon succeed in destroying the Ancients, they've managed to piss me off. Maybe after all of this is resolved we'll figure out a way for me to go back in time and have a talk with our insane creator."

Nasif laughed, but there wasn't a lot of humor in it. "I don't know that I'd want to meet that person. Insane they might or might not have been, but they were far more powerful than any magic user I've ever heard of. The skill to make these relics—and whatever it is when they are combined—is far beyond any skills known to any surviving race. They would make someone even as powerful as Siabiane look like a magic sink."

Alric had led us to the entrance of the glen, a much farther distance from the house than had seemed when we came in. I started to ask Nasif, but he beat me to it.

"Yes, another defensive trick. The distances are changeable. I have been stretching it as we've gone. Anyone managing to get in here would have a long winding trip to find our homes."

"No talk. Need do." Garbage had been quiet, at least for her, as the faeries flew high above us. That was changing now as the entrance was within sight. War sticks were up and waving around again.

Bunky and the gargoyle buzzed down close. "Are they wearing war feathers?" They both flew high again after their quick pass, but I'd seen something stuck all over their sides.

"Yes. Is good." Leaf flew down close and patted my hair. There was a slight pull, as she must have pulled her hand back with an extra hair or two. "See? Flyers have feathers."

I reached up and felt a mass of something that felt like feathers and tree sap in my hair. No wonder some of my hair had stuck to her hand. I couldn't pull it free, at least not without losing a chunk of hair. "But I don't fly on my own." One more tug at the feathers and I gave up. They weren't moving.

"Not yet," Leaf said, then tumbled in the air as Garbage slammed into her.

"Now time to get back." Garbage growled after subduing Leaf, then turned toward the exit. It was odd seeing a desert on the other side of a tree-filled glen, but definitely not the oddest thing I'd ever seen.

Lorcan held out one hand for Garbage to land on and

she did with a grace I was surprised to see. "Now, my powerful little friend, you can find the knights, can't you? You will lead us to them?"

She slowly nodded her head. "We do."

I was shocked. I'd figured the only reason the faeries had come to find us had been that they couldn't find Flarinen and Kelm on their own. That they had actually obeyed a command and came to get us, even when they were so mad, was startling.

"How can they…" I let my comment die as Garbage slowly pulled out two strands of hair from her tiny black bag. One short and red, the other long and blond.

"We no trust." She reverently placed the hairs down on Lorcan's open hand. "You use now, we no need." She flew up to join the others without even a mention of wanting a sweet for her work. This new Garbage was impressive and scary at the same time.

"So they used those hairs to find where they are?" Covey patted her own hair. Actually, if they could do that with anyone we'd never lose track of each other.

Lorcan studied both hairs, then put one hand over the other and softly spoke a few words. "Somewhat, they are regaining their tracking abilities. But I think in this case there was some faery saliva involved—and the level of Garbage's anger might have bumped up her abilities some." He removed the hand that was covering the hairs and two small golden arrows hovered there. "Excellent work, ladies. Between you and these we should have no trouble finding them."

The two tiny arrows hovered over his hand and flickered slightly. "That is an excellent trick, but they won't last long," Nasif said as he took the lead to take us through the entrance.

I felt a strange tingle as I crossed and saw my friends react as well.

"One more safety item. Getting out would be extremely

dangerous for anyone without our approval." Dueble said proudly. "If someone makes it inside, we want to make sure we can deal with them before they leave."

Lorcan and his arrows, along with a few of the faeries, took the lead. They kept an eye on the arrows as we detoured to the house to get our things ready and wait the short time until night fell. It had been a short consensus, but it was determined we'd be less noticeable trooping around in the dark, instead of daylight. I seriously doubted anyone in Null would notice, but it did give more time to pack supplies.

The horses and wagons had been in a stable on the side of the house. Alric readied them but kept the horses in light tack.

"I'm not sure that we can come back for them when we leave. Travel would be much easier with wagons, but I don't know that we want to leave them wherever Nivinal is. I've set a spell, if we're not back in twelve hours, the horses will be able to get out. I've told them to find Rue. He's a good soul, even if he was mixed up with Mackil." He rubbed the nose of one of the horses.

I'd forgotten about Mackil's assistant. He'd seemed nice enough and the horses should help him get out of Null.

Once we'd finished, we all stood together while Lorcan held up the arrows. I'd figured Nivinal was probably near the edge of town. He and Reginald might not have started there, but after their partnership fell apart, being on the edge was safer. But why were they both still here if Nivinal had the relics? Reginald would be trying to get them back, but Nivinal could have continued on to the Spheres.

"Do we know where the basilisk is?" I asked, as we started moving closer to the town center than I'd expected. Since the faeries and the arrows agreed, I wasn't one to argue.

"Not fully, but I think you're thinking what I'm pondering," Nasif said. "Why else would Nivinal stay here once the geas was broken? You would be a good trinket for him to grab, and he will come for you again, I fear." He looked to my cheek where the manticore was hidden. "But there has to be more than that. They came here for a reason."

"Avoiding coming here was impossible for us." Alric dropped in alongside us. "Whatever that entrapment spell was, it was incredibly powerful."

Nasif took a short bow. "I'm glad you found it as such. It didn't work as I'd intended, and I had nothing to do with the geas around Null. I created the trap to keep the curious from the Spheres. There are too many things, energies and the like, that can't be explained. It was supposed to simply send the adventurers a few hundred miles away. I had armies of knights, fighting syclarions, rampaging minotaurs, and the like." He beamed as if someone had complimented him on his newest handicraft. "Which did you hit?"

Alric raised his eyebrow, and then shook his head. "The syclarions. Taryn finally beat them, but we all were dumped over here anyway."

"Oh, Flarinen and Kelm had seen an army before that; it was before we'd gotten into the plains, and none of the rest of us saw it." I'd almost forgot about that.

Nasif's smile dropped. "That's not good. I lost control of the spell years ago, but there shouldn't have been any escaping of the images. They should only block the path from the plains."

"They shouldn't be sending everyone to Null, either," Dueble said, then clapped Nasif on the shoulder. "He's gotten stronger over the decades, but still not as much control as would be liked. Not to mention, I think Null, as it previously was, messed with the transport spell."

Nasif didn't take offense at Dueble's words and even nodded. "True. I am disturbed to hear the images are moving out of their areas though. Maybe when we have fixed this little relic issue Lorcan and I can try to join forces to shut them down."

A thought struck me. "You didn't happen to also create some weird flying purple flower creatures that knock people out, did you?" We'd never seen them again after the one time, but I'd feel better if they were part of Nasif's defenses.

He shook his head. "Not mine. How large were they? Did they attack at night or in the day?"

"About the size of the back of your hand, and they hit at night," Padraig said. "I fear they might have been gloughstrikes." He'd not mentioned what he thought they had been to us, just that he wanted to research them. We hadn't really had much time after their attack, but clearly he'd found time to discover something.

"Gloughstrikes?" Dueble stumbled over a rock in the road. "Surely they aren't anything more than myths?"

"I don't know. These creatures came in the middle of the night and would have taken us all if not for Taryn. The faeries helped us recover, but I fear that's what they were." Padraig said, but his voice dropped as a drunk stumbled past us. "And there was a time fracture in the rock wall next to us the next morning."

I happened to be watching Nasif, so I saw all the color drain from his face. No one had mentioned a connection between the weird nighttime flying things and the odd crack in the walls that closed up on its own.

"Crap, a time fracture? So this time stuff is spreading outward?" I was not okay with time things going around. There had been time waves surrounding Null, until Alric and I supposedly fixed them by going back in time. Now we were finding out there had been time problems before we even got near anything time messed up? I was quickly falling into the, 'let me go back home and get drunk' idea. That I had no idea which way Beccia was, how far away it was, or how I would get there were problems I was willing to overlook.

In theory. I looked at the people around me, and thought

of the others I cared about. All of whom were giving up their normal lives to stop whatever was happening with the relics. I'd become a magic user, was in love with an elf, and had a weird manticore relic inside me—I shouldn't be too weirded out by time fluctuations.

Then I looked at Nasif who was paler than any living being I'd ever seen.

"You know about them." I didn't ask a question, but Nasif nodded anyway.

"The time cracks mean events are advancing far faster than we thought. Than we predicted. Those were most likely gloughstrikes; they flock to hard time slices. The ones that force their way into the past. Or future." He shook his head. "There's no way to know which ones those were, but it is not a good sign."

"But that is," Alric said. Ahead of us was a distillery, one that looked like it might have been one of the first buildings in Null, and closed down before I was born. Both arrows were pointing at it and vibrating so hard that the hairs inside each one bounced.

"He's hiding here in public? Where anyone can find him?" I had to admit, while I wanted to get the relics back, and find a way to destroy him, I really didn't feel up to facing Nivinal at this time. "And how are we treating Flarinen and Kelm? Captured prisoners? Or willful participants?"

The faeries had been quiet up until now. "We take." Garbage and her band started forward. Subtleties were often lost on the faeries. All they cared about was that Flarinen and Kelm had tricked them when they were supposed to be watching them. Notions like against their will meant nothing.

"No!" Lorcan had been looking at something on the side of the building but his yell was enough to stop the faeries in mid-flight. "It's a trap. Nivinal knew we'd find our men one way or another."

He said a few nasty sounding words, causing all three of

the other strong magic users to cringe. A mark appeared on the side of the wall—the mark of the Dark.

"You need to warn us when you're going to use that language, my old friend," Nasif said as he shook his head. "That's going to be bouncing around in my skull for a few days." Both Padraig and Alric looked to be in the same state.

"So how come I didn't react like the rest of you?" I seemed to be the only one not affected. Dueble and Covey didn't show any reactions, but neither were magic users.

"It might have something to do with your odd magic," Alric said. "Or your tag-along friend. You didn't feel anything when he said those words?"

I shook my head. "They sounded like rusted metal grating, but nothing else."

"I'm afraid we can't deal with this now." Padraig pointed to the sigil on the side of the building as it started to glow. "We've triggered something."

Even the faeries flew back as the rest of us moved into the street. The sigil glowed red, then died down. I waited a few minutes for whatever the big thing was that was going to destroy us. Nothing happened.

Alric muttered a few words that I first thought was swearing but then realized was a spell. The difference between his words and Lorcan's earlier ones were painfully clear. The red letters reappeared.

"So any magic will trigger it, yet what else was it supposed to do? Our men are in there and whether they went of their own volition or because of that emerald dragon, we need to get them out." Alric had loosened his sword and didn't look happy.

CHAPTER THIRTY FOUR

"NO TALK!" GARBAGE CHARGED FORWARD with her war stick waving and a fleet of crazed faeries behind her. I'd never seen any of them go through a solid object that quickly. They were gone before I could even yell at them.

"We can't let them go in alone." Yes, I knew they were damn close to being indestructible, and I certainly wasn't. But I couldn't take a chance on them actually being hurt.

Bunky and the gargoyle flew around us bleating and gronking furiously. They couldn't follow their little friends unless we opened the door.

"I can't sense anything on the other side," Padraig said. "Not even the faeries." He shook his head and dropped his hand toward his sword.

"There could be anything on the other side." Lorcan was starting to walk to the side of the building. He was looking up, clearly for another way in.

I wasn't waiting that long. "Come get me if I don't come back out." I didn't give anyone a chance to stop me as I ran for the door. My sword wasn't out, although it was still along for the ride. Instead I held one hand out, trying to mimic both Padraig and Lorcan to focus my push spell.

Apparently anger, and in my case fear, focused more than just the faeries abilities to go through solid objects. I blew both doors off the building and a good swath of wall on either side before I even got near it.

The inside was one huge room with the upper floors reduced to nothing but a ledge that circled the main area. The faeries had already started tormenting Flarinen and Kelm, both of whom were hanging upside down from the top rafter. However, neither of them seemed to notice, as they were both swinging to reach the emerald dragon, also hanging from the ceiling.

"Seriously?" I looked around at the trap. Such as it was. This looked far more like something Reginald would come up with rather than Nivinal.

Bunky and the gargoyle flew over my head and circled the faeries. They both were more concerned with protecting the girls than tormenting the knights.

Neither knight had their armor on, and both were covered in scratches. None of them looked deep and I figured they'd done it to each other.

I hadn't been subtle about getting inside, and my friends were right behind me.

The knights kept fighting each other, the faeries kept poking them, and nothing happened beyond that.

"Shouldn't there have been—" My words were cut off as a small shape tore out from behind the refuse of the interior of the building and slammed me into the ground.

The rakasa before me wasn't the one I'd fought before, but he was fast and agile. He got a bite in, but barely scratched my arm before I rolled free. I got both my knife and my sword out and sliced his head off.

Didn't help as much as I'd hoped, as a dozen more swarmed out from the hiding spaces they'd been in. Yes, Null was too rocky for their regular mode of underground travel but that didn't stop them from being excellent at sneak attacks.

Both Alric and Padraig had their swords out as more rakasa flooded the room. We might have been wrong about who had control of the emerald dragon and who created the trap.

Dueble screamed and ran forward with his sword out. "I wasn't expecting them to be so vile." His strikes weren't as clean or effective as Padraig and Alric's, but he managed to kill the one that was closest to him.

Unfortunately, there weren't that many near him or any of the others because they were all closing in on me.

Covey was closest to me and started ripping the rakasa apart with her bare hands. Lorcan and Nasif were fighting to get to the knights who were still fighting with each other, and Dueble had gotten closer to Alric and Padraig. He was fighting, but the other two were far better fighters.

I sliced through two rakasa who'd gotten too close, but didn't kill either one. They were holding back, trying to damage me but not kill me. That wasn't as reassuring as it could be. We'd thought the rakasa had only been working with Nivinal and that might have been a serious error on our part. We'd also thought the rakasa wanted the emerald dragon as a religious relic of their past. By the way they kept looking where I knew the manticore's mark was hidden on my cheek, that was wrong too.

I'd forgotten something else too.

"Girls?" I couldn't look away from the rakasa closing in on me, but I heard the faeries yelling at the knights over my head.

"What? You say we yell..." Garbage's voice dropped as she finally noticed the swarming rakasa. The faeries could be a bit single-minded at times.

A much louder round of faery war cries descended upon the room as all twenty-three dove down to meet the rakasa. An interesting note: their yells themselves caused the rakasa nearest me to flinch and grab their ears.

"Yell louder! Sing if you have to." I was able to slice through another rakasa but the second one stumbled close enough to grab me.

I pulled back but it was hanging on. Bunky bleated from above then he and the gargoyle slammed into the rakasa with enough force to dislodge him. Bunky emitted a bolt of light and the gargoyle pushed the rakasa into it. The rakasa ended up a pile of burnt ash.

I'd seen the mass of chimera constructs attack the rakasa in the battle of the enclave, but I hadn't seen what they did up close. Having ashes of what was once a rakasa scattered on me was a little too close.

The rakasa were being slowed down by the faery yelling and singing, but it wasn't stopping them.

Alric was fighting toward the center of the room, I assumed to help Nasif and Lorcan. Both of them were fighting to get to the knights, but it was slow going. Alric started cutting a path.

"Garbage, take some faeries and help Alric. Use your sticks." I wasn't sure why they hadn't used them yet; they were still just waving them about. They did seem to be more focused on the yelling at this point.

I didn't know if she'd heard me over the din, but she and five faeries broke off and flew above Alric. They kept yelling but were also whirling their war blades. Then they dove as a single unit and struck a rakasa. It froze, and then shattered. Interesting. When they'd done that to other creatures they usually turned to ash. Maybe they didn't want to step on Bunky's skill set.

A bleating pulled my attention back to my own fight. A group of rakasa had managed to get a net and had thrown it on Bunky. The gargoyle was buzzing around but Bunky was so distressed he wasn't charging. Or maybe he had a limit. There were three piles of ash around me.

The rakasa nearest us were focusing on Bunky, but I was boxed in away from the door so they hadn't forgotten me. They were going for a bonus grab by bringing in Bunky as well.

"Help him," I yelled to the faeries around me. They obeyed and took off. Leaving me facing two annoyed rakasa. They also had a net and I had a feeling it was for me.

I held my sword and knife ready. Both the rakasa were fighting the effects of the faeries' yells, but I'd dispersed the faeries too well helping the others and none were near me. They charged and I raised my sword—and it vanished. I swore as my empty hand swung out and I quickly jabbed out to force back the attacking rakasa with my knife. I got in a good strike, but I wasn't as proficient with the knife as I'd like. Orenda had left before we'd gotten far in my knife training. I was able to force back the first rakasa but the second kept moving forward.

A number of things all happened simultaneously. The faeries freed Bunky, the rakasa managed to get the net over me, and Lorcan cut the rope holding Flarinen and Kelm in the air. He also cut the line holding the emerald dragon in the air.

Every rakasa in the building, including the two trying to get a net on me, ran forward as the emerald dragon fell.

Nasif was there first. He'd put on some sort of gloves and grabbed the emerald dragon a foot before it hit the ground. He finished the roll he started and then threw the relic to Padraig. He also had the odd gloves on and the second he caught the dragon he dropped it into one of the faeries' bags.

The bags must not only protect the handler from the effects of the relic, but also cut off its influence on those previously affected by it. All of the rakasa still standing stopped, shook their heads, and then turned toward me.

I'd gotten free of the net, but my sword hadn't reappeared. Bunky was now free and he and the gargoyle tried to save the day as they led the faeries in a massive dive at the rakasas coming for me. They weren't going to make it.

Three rakasa hit me and dragged me to the ground before Bunky and his flight of faeries could get to me. They did get there before any more could attack.

The three who'd landed on me were trying to subdue, not kill, so that was a plus. I heard Alric yelling and one of the rakasa on me suddenly learned to fly. I don't think it was something it would repeat though, as the flying lesson came from Alric throwing it, and a number of faeries followed it and stabbed it with their war sticks. Pieces of rakasa rained down upon Nasif and Padraig at the far end of the room.

The remaining two rakasa and I fought as I tried to stab them with my knife at the same time they were trying to get a net on me. I fought harder when I realized there were tiny spell balls on the edges of the net. Rakasa for the most part weren't magic users. They clearly were working with one—and I knew whom.

Alric dislodged another rakasa. He was fighting on numerous fronts as most of the remaining ones focused on trying to get to me and he was trying to stop them. I managed to stab the rakasa closest to me, and not throw up as its blood poured over my hand.

My strike and my willpower were useless. In his last action, the dying rakasa got the net secured and he crushed one of the spell balls in his hand.

CHAPTER THIRTY FIVE

THE BUILDING I WAS IN vanished, only to be replaced by the inside of a small cell. Actually, it was a cage. I was fine sitting, but I wouldn't be able to do more than crouch inside of it. The netting was gone, or had turned into the cage. Smaller versions of the spell balls that had been anchoring the net lined the edges of the cage.

There was a blanket or cloth over the cage, not heavy enough to make it too dark so that I couldn't see, but enough to block me from seeing beyond the cage. I had my knife but my sword had abandoned me. That my fear had finally come true—aka my sword vanishing in mid-fight—hadn't proven as horrific as I'd imagined it. Of course, I'd imagined me dying because of it and that hadn't happened. Yet.

I poked my knife into the fabric covering the cage; the space was wide enough for me to get almost all of the blade out. I couldn't really dislodge the fabric, or stab through it, but my attempts did get most of the rakasa blood off of it.

I'd been in there for about five minutes before I heard any sounds. I would have thought that anyone who'd sent a bunch of rakasa after me with spelled nets would have been a bit more attentive as to when I arrived.

Sharp booted steps came to my cage. "You have done well and will be rewarded. Go and join the others."

It took me a moment to adjust. I'd really been expecting Nivinal, but that voice belonged to Mackil. Rather, it belonged to Reginald who was now inhabiting Mackil's former body.

The fabric was whipped off the cage with a flourish. Or what would have been a flourish if the person doing the whipping off had been a bit taller.

Mackil stood before me. It was interesting that even though the body hadn't changed, he looked so different than he had before. Like when Reginald had taken over Lorcan's body, the change to the inside reflected on the outside. Mackil before had been crusty and tough. A sneaky thief and con man, but solid.

The person before me managed to look petulant and weak. Already the muscular bulk of the dwarf was starting to turn to flab. He scowled at me.

"Now, I am trying to figure out why Nivinal wanted you so badly." He slowly walked around my cage. "He wouldn't tell me, you see. Must not have trusted me." The laugh that followed would have sent Mackil into hiding with shame. It was more of a wheezing giggle.

"But I managed to get you away from him anyway," he said. "He won't be happy that his great plan to capture you was thwarted. No, no, no. And I left a calling card so he would know it was me who had swayed some of his rakasa and stolen his prize." He peered in closely. One thing stayed the same, Reginald was a madman no matter what body he was in. "Now why don't you tell me what is so important about you that the great Nivinal would work so hard to get you?"

"I have no idea. You probably grabbed the wrong person." As I spoke I called up the push spell. Or tried to. One moment I was setting up the spell in my head, the next I was screaming in pain and had dropped to a fetal position.

"Forgot to mention this is a spell cage. It bounces spells back at the person inside. I am trying to build one large enough and strong enough to hold Nivinal, but the bastard has more secrets than even I knew, and this is the largest cage I could create so far."

I whimpered in answer. It felt like my eyes were bleeding from the inside.

Reginald stomped around the cage again, each step shattering part of my skull.

"Yes, well. I suppose this is my fault. Had I told you about the spelled cage you probably wouldn't have tried your spell," he finally said. "Or perhaps you would have anyway. You don't appear to be the brightest of girls. Nor the most powerful." He stopped in front of me and I forced open my eyes. "But you did manage to help stop us in the enclave. Now, I know Siabiane and Padraig were involved, both serious magic users. Yet I do feel you helped some. Which might be why he wants you so bad."

I looked at him with bleary eyes. Neither my brain nor my eyes felt like they were bleeding anymore, but I wasn't in the mood to play guessing games. I knew why Nivinal wanted me—the damn manticore.

"I have no idea." I grunted out through clenched teeth.

Reginald shook his head. "Now, I know that is a lie. And not even a good one." He spread one hand over the cage. His grin was terrifying and disgusting at the same time. The chill that passed through me wasn't only from his grin though. He'd adjusted the cage's spell.

"Let's try that again. What is he looking for?"

He leaned closer to the cage. I had my knife but I couldn't have gotten in any sort of fatal shot through the cage.

"I don't—" I screamed as a thousand pins stabbed me in the head.

"See? If you don't tell me the truth, the cage attacks you. Try again. Why does Nivinal want you?"

"I know where the sapphire manticore is," I gasped out. It was the truth so the cage was satisfied.

Reginald's face lit up. "The manticore? It was lost in the elven ruins centuries ago. Yes, Nivinal would want you for that information. You must show me where it is."

"It's not visible. I cannot show you what I can't see." I ground my jaw tight after I spoke. It was the truth but I didn't know how touchy the spell would be since I was dancing around the truth.

"Then you will tell me how to get to it." He shook the cage and I noticed the spell balls were loose. Two bounced off at his rough handling.

"I don't know how to get it." That answer didn't worry me. It was the absolute truth.

"Then who does? Tell me now or I will destroy you in this cage." He was really losing his temper and three more balls came off. There were only a few left.

"No one knows how to get it. It is hidden from all."

"You know where it is!"

"Yes." I would have liked to lie but that spell packed a punch. I couldn't count on the spell being weakened enough by lack of spell balls to not shatter my head if it went off.

"You will show me! Now!" That temper of his was never going to do him any good, but it helped me. He was so busy shaking the cage and yelling at me that he didn't notice when the last spell balls fell off. I noticed, however.

The cage weakened once the spells were freed from it. I waited until Reginald had taken a step back, most likely to kick the cage, and then I kicked it first, with both legs. He got caught as the cage piece flew at him, and I rolled out after it with my knife up.

"Want to try that again?" I did the most impressive knife moves that Orenda had shown me. Most of her knife work was using smaller throwing knives. Even if this had been that type of knife I wouldn't want to lose my only weapon. I thought about trying to call up a spell, but my head was still too tender.

Reginald narrowed his eyes. I thought for a moment he was going to charge me, but instead he spun and ran into the next room. Yelling.

I knew there had been at least one rakasa who had come through his little net trick with me; he'd been talking to it earlier. Most likely the yelling was directed at however many more he had lurking around.

I ran the other way. I was in yet another warehouse, but, unlike the prior one, this one looked like it had started out as an actual warehouse. I rounded the corner and ran right into a rakasa. Not having a choice, I took advantage of his surprise at seeing me and I stabbed him with my knife, getting more than a few tears in my arm from his claws as I did so.

I kicked out at him then kept running. There was a door, a simple door with no guards. I sprinted for it as I heard yelling and running feet behind me. If I could make it outside I would have a better chance to hide until I figured out where I was. I took a chance and glanced back.

Reginald was behind about eight rakasa, none of whom stopped or even slowed down to help the one I'd stabbed.

I hit the door hard, trying to get out, and ran into another group of hooded attackers.

"Taryn! It's me!" I was so caught up in fighting to get free, that I almost stabbed Alric.

He grabbed my arms and held them still. "I've got you."

That was as much of a reunion as we got as the rakasa hit us. Covey handed me her sword and we took care of them quickly. Reginald had vanished and none of the rakasa we fought were of the same fighting caliber as any we'd seen before. Reginald must have recruited the cast-offs from Nivinal.

"How did you find me?" I asked as Alric pulled his sword from the last rakasa. I really got a good look at the ones we'd been fighting; these were all far unhealthier looking than the others we'd seen.

"We do!" Garbage yelled. The faeries had stayed back and I'd not seen them, but they swarmed down now.

Lorcan held up another tiny glowing arrow. "Your friend

Leaf took a few hairs with her when she gave you your war feathers." He nodded toward the clump of feathers and tree sap on my head. "Once you vanished, we were able to put down most of the rakasa. Some did run away however. We used your hair to find you."

I looked around. The building we were in was on the same block as the one we'd found Flarinen and Kelm in. Who were not around us, I noticed.

"Where are the knights? And thank you all for coming to get me," I said. "Reginald escaped though. And he's now aware that I know where the manticore is and that's why Nivinal is looking for me. That trap with Flarinen and Kelm was to catch me." Reginald's trick to have a spelled net transport me and turn into a cage was dang impressive. Considering that he'd only moved me two stores down, it lost a little of the magic.

"We have them tied up for now," Padraig said but I noticed he gave Alric a sideways glance. "Rather, we re-tied them up. They are both acting odd even though the influence of the dragon has been removed. Bunky and the gargoyle are sitting on them down that alley."

"We help!" Crusty came flying over and landed on the side of my head. "I sit on them too."

A mostly sober Crusty wasn't any less goofy than a drunk one really and she started swinging back and forth on my hair.

Alric finally grabbed her and removed her. "It's hard to try and talk to you with her doing that."

Crusty seemed perfectly happy to stay in Alric's hand, even hanging on when he tried to shake her free.

"There was more than trying to grab you going on though. Again, Nivinal wasn't there and sent his rakasa henchmen to deal with us." Alric spoke as we walked over to the alley. Covey and Dueble trailed behind us, and the other three had gone back into the warehouse I'd been in. If there was any magic residue in there from Reginald, those three would find it.

Without the street glows, it was dark as we went down the alley, but there was no way I'd miss Flarinen and Kelm. Actually, I couldn't have missed their guards. Bunky sat on Flarinen's chest and the gargoyle mimicked the position on Kelm's. Both knights were securely tied. Kelm looked resigned; Flarinen looked ready to start ripping heads off.

"We're fine now, I told you. We didn't have control over our actions." Flarinen didn't sound remorseful at all.

"He's right," Kelm said softly. He'd shown some backbone when Flarinen was moping about as the tortured soul, but now that the captain was stepping back into the arrogant bastard we knew and hated, Kelm was falling back into the shadows.

"Really?" Alric stepped up to within kicking distance of Flarinen. "You want to tell Taryn what you said when she vanished?"

Flarinen quickly looked up at me, and then looked away. "I wasn't recovered. I wasn't myself."

"I'll refresh your memory. You said, 'Good riddance, now I can do what I need to do.'" Alric walked around Flarinen and bent down to untie Kelm. "Kelm on the other hand tried to tackle you when you tried to run out of the building."

"I didn't mean anything…I wasn't myself. That dragon is horrible." Flarinen nodded to me in apology, which was more than I'd expected, so I nodded back. "The rakasa took it again, right?"

That answered a few questions. Neither knight had seen what had been done with the greed-causing relic, and the faery bag it was in was still secure. And that we couldn't let either one of them know we had it. I had no idea how long it would take for the dragon's hold to die off, and I doubt anyone else did either.

Covey looked down at Flarinen. "Yup. And it's a good thing for you two. I would have killed you had you grabbed it again. Actually, had Padraig not held me back, I would have killed you when you made your comment about Taryn." She wasn't kidding, and the look on both of the knights' faces showed they knew it.

Kelm rubbed his wrists where they'd been tied. "I can tell you, we had no choice. The pull of that thing was too strong—none of you could have held back from answering it." Kelm stood next to Flarinen. There were bruises along his jaw and cheekbone, but considering the way I'd seen the two of them swinging at each other in their attempts to get the dragon, I figured those were from Flarinen, not the rakasa.

"Who captured you? The rakasa?" I wasn't feeling charitable to Flarinen; he could be an ass with or without dangerous relics messing with his head. However, they might have noticed something. I knew I wasn't certain who had been setting the trap. I directed my question to Kelm, however.

"A large hooded man," Kelm said. "He seemed bigger than Nivinal, or at least what I'd seen of him when he was in the enclave."

Alric scowled and hauled Flarinen to his feet. "Did he say anything?"

"No, sadly he didn't have to. He had that relic in the middle of the floor. He waved at it, we both ran, and the next thing I knew we were swinging in the air trying to get to it."

"Aren't you going to untie me?" A closer look at Flarinen's face showed that Kelm had gotten some good strikes in as well.

Lorcan and the rest had joined us. None of them looked happy, so I assumed there hadn't been anything to find in the warehouse. "Not yet, my lad." Lorcan was more sympathetic than the rest of us, but he didn't back down. "You were the most exposed and the fact that Nivinal was able to manipulate you so strongly cannot be taken lightly." He turned to Kelm. "I heard what you said, and while it might not have been Nivinal, I think we can assume it was. We didn't find much in my brother's lair, but he had a collection of things and notes about Nivinal. He wasn't who any of us thought, even Reginald—per his journal that was why he left Nivinal; to save everyone from what he was becoming." He rolled his eyes at the idea of Reginald saving anyone except himself.

There was evidence that the person the elves had known as the inquisitor was not the real Nivinal, which pretty much meant he'd been hiding his true self with them for more than a thousand years. But I agreed with Lorcan about his brother. Reginald wouldn't have cared who Nivinal was if being with him gave him power. Something must have changed in that dynamic for Reginald to try and go solo.

"Can hurt it now?" Garbage and the rest of the faeries had been silently hovering overhead, along with the constructs. She flew down now and flapped her wings right in Flarinen's face. The way his hands were tied he couldn't move out of their way without falling over.

We could try explaining to Garbage about the spell of the dragon relic, and how he'd not been acting like himself. But looking at her face, I knew she didn't care. Flarinen had befriended them and then betrayed them—payment had to be made.

I looked around the street we were now walking onto. Null during the day was far less active than nighttime. Our changing things about the city hadn't changed that. More people were prowling around, heading for pubs, shops, or other less socially accepted places. Being out here, with a handcuffed Flarinen being berated by the faeries, wasn't a good idea.

"We need to get out of here first. Once we're on the road I want you all to make Flarinen your priority. Punch him, sing to him, tell him the history of ale, I don't care."

Garbage glared at Flarinen long enough to make him look away. She finally nodded. "Agreed. It ours." I'd noticed the faeries could and usually did identify gender. But when someone made them mad they often became genderless.

Flarinen's eyes flew open and I saw Leaf fly around him. She'd been coming from his backside and appeared to have a piece of fabric in her mouth. "It ours." She grinned then flew up to the others.

"That thing bit me!" If Flarinen was looking for sympathy he wasn't getting it from any of us. Kelm had moved ahead with Covey so he didn't even notice his captain's distress.

Flarinen continued to mutter but kept it to himself as we made our way back to the house. Lorcan had created a small mage ball for light and was furiously going over the pages of his brother's notes and journal as he walked.

"This isn't good. Not good at all." Lorcan flipped between a pair of pages and started swearing. "And blast my brother for being such a sloppy pig. He actually might have made some valuable observations but I'm missing at least three pages of notes."

"Any idea what Nivinal is up to, or is it standard world domination?" Padraig had been speaking softly to Bunky, in some language I didn't recognize but sounded vaguely elvish. But he stopped at Lorcan's words.

"It appears that while the Spheres were their destination, they did intend on getting caught in Null—as we expected. Nivinal created the trap to fall back in time, but Taryn and Alric weren't the intended victims. He'd planned on trapping Reginald back there for some reason that is lost in the missing pages." He looked up. "Of course, my brother is a self-centered narcissist so he might have been over stating his worth or threat to Nivinal for his own ego."

Lorcan shuffled through the pages again, waving the mage glow closer as something became difficult to read. "Damn it. We have to get to the Spheres immediately;

Nivinal might have already made his way there. He could have left days ago."

"But we've seen him," Kelm said.

"We've seen his projections. I think Nivinal might have taken a page from Glorinal—the chimera appears to be inside him. He was dangerous before, he is even more so now."

Everyone was silent on the way back, only the sound of Lorcan shuffling through pages and softly swearing was heard.

I looked up. "Where are the faeries? And Bunky and the gargoyle?" I hadn't noticed when they faded off, but at some point the girls had gotten bored of antagonizing Flarinen.

Alric looked around as well. "They need to get back here if we're going to get out soon." He rubbed his arms. "Did it get colder?"

I hadn't noticed at first, but now that he mentioned it, he was right. The temperature was dropping rapidly.

"I think there's more than that," Padraig pointed toward the center of town. A whirling vortex of light was forming, reaching higher and higher. It started blue-white but was now turning orange and red on the edges.

"What is it? Could Reginald be doing something?" I asked. I picked up my pace, the temperature was becoming unbearable.

"Untie me and I will find out," Flarinen said.

None of us even acknowledged him.

The house was locked up and we grabbed our things and got the horses ready. I kept trying to call the faeries but none of them had shown up yet. Nor had the constructs, but aside from the faeries I had no way of mentally reaching them.

"I think we need to see what that is," Padraig said. Nasif and Lorcan nodded in agreement, Covey and Alric shook their heads. Dueble and I both shrugged to each other.

"That desert is going to get hot by mid-day, my people are adapted for it, the rest of you certainly aren't." Covey secured one more pack on the top of the wagon. We were using both wagons and the horses seemed ready to go after their rest.

"We need to get out of here. I can't explain why. But we do," Alric said as he took the driver's seat for the large wagon. I'm sure I wasn't the only one disturbed by that. Alric was straightforward—he didn't have undefined inclinations. His being unable to define why he was feeling weird about something was enough to pull me into the 'let's get the hell out of here' camp.

Padraig silently climbed atop the smaller wagon. Nasif rode with Lorcan, while Dueble joined us. We finally untied Flarinen so he could get his armor on and mount his horse, but Alric took away his weapons and tethered his horse to the back of the smaller wagon. Kelm watched with wide eyes but didn't say anything.

The vortex over the center of Null was mostly reds and yellows now. The fact that people weren't running out from that area made me feel a little better. Not a lot, but it was enough to let me tell myself leaving was a better idea. The faeries not responding bothered me, but they could catch up with us. I was really doing a lot of self-counseling right now.

Lorcan watched it for a few moments before he finally got in the wagon. I understood his pensiveness. We were in the middle of a lot of strange things, but we couldn't go hounding after all of them.

I was the last one in the wagon when a frantic gronking filled the air.

CHAPTER THIRTY SIX

I DROPPED OFF THE STEP INTO the wagon as Bunky and the gargoyle flew into the torchlight. Both were extremely agitated and kept flying around all of us. Bunky stopped in front of me and gronked a few times, but I had never been able to understand him. Alric came over and held up his hand.

Bunky switched to him and repeated his gronks, a bit louder this time.

"Damn it, we have to go get them." Alric grabbed his sword and cape. "The faeries are trapped in the bar—and they've been drinking heavily."

I grabbed the sword Covey had lent me. "What happened? And how did it happen so soon? They couldn't have left us more than a half hour ago."

He shrugged. "I can't get that out of him, I'm honestly not sure if he knows. The faeries flew to the pub and started drinking hard. He and the gargoyle were watching over them, but within minutes two men caged the faeries. Bunky tried to free them but one of the men was a magic user and kept the constructs at bay."

"Reginald?" Padraig was also arming himself.

"Not from what it sounds like," Alric said. "We shouldn't all go, though. Padraig and I can get them back and meet you on the edge of town." He pointed out into the dark. I knew there was a road out of town over there, but only because I'd seen it in the daylight. It was completely dark away from the lights of the town.

"I'm going as well. Those miscreants are my problem—no one locks them up except me." I had my knife, Covey's sword, and my heavy cloak that I'd pulled out of my pack. The temperature had stopped dropping but it hadn't gone up yet either.

"If she's going, I'm going," Covey hadn't added any more clothing, nor weapons, but she flexed her fingers.

"I don't think we want too many people to go," Nasif said as he watched the sky over the center of town. The reds were heavier now. "If that is any sort of a magic buildup, and I think we have to assume it is, we might have a hard time getting the wagons out of here if things go bad."

"Agreed. Padraig, myself, and Taryn." I knew from the slight pause that Alric didn't want me to go, but we'd have to deal with that issue later.

The others sorted themselves out and Covey backed down. She'd drive our wagon, and Nasif would drive Lorcan's.

Kelm and Flarinen hadn't said a thing. In Kelm's case, I figured it was because he was used to taking orders. Flarinen appeared to be pouting. I had too much going on to deal with the emotional issues of an annoying elven knight, so I ignored him.

The wagons got off with orders to keep riding toward the Spheres, a good four-day ride, if we didn't show up at the meeting place within an hour.

We made our way towards the center of town but didn't see a lot of people on the street. Far different from less than an hour ago. The few we did see where heading toward the pub. Of course, the pub appeared to be directly under the swirling vertex. On a plus side the closer we got to it the warmer the air became.

The pub must have held almost every citizen of Null, and all of them were watching a group of thugs poking a large cage.

I was sure Alric and Padraig had an actual plan, but once I saw the cage on the bar, and my faeries inside, I pretty much lost it. My push spell was up and running in a second, shoving the closest jackasses back from the cage. I had to temper it since I didn't want to hurt the faeries.

I shook my head at that thought. Faeries were damage proof. I tried to send another spell but a stabbing in my head told me I hadn't fully recovered from Reginald's little spelled cage.

Which was fine. I waved my borrowed sword in the air and ran toward the bar. I knew that wasn't the best fighting stance, but I didn't care. Alric and Padraig had dropped whatever plan they might have had and followed me in fighting.

I'd damaged the cage more than I'd realized with my spell and the faeries kicked it open. All of them seemed fine albeit soggy. There was alcohol all over the bar. It didn't look or smell like ale, and I'd never seen the girls drink the hard stuff. From the smell, they had been drinking it, bathing in it, and soaking the bar with it. Or someone else had.

I'd also never seen the girls use their war sticks to start a fire.

Twenty-three sticks were out, and all of them appeared to be on fire. They actually looked to be the same color as the vortex I knew was above us. I had a bad feeling those twenty-three were behind it, and the results weren't going to be good.

Fire and a bar covered in hard alcohol. I'd been so focused on my anger at what was done to the faeries it took me a moment to have those two thoughts latch to each other.

"No!" I was about a foot away from the faeries when I yelled. All of them looked at me. Then tipped their war sticks onto the bar.

I expected a fire, not the rumbling lightning crack that sliced through half the bar. And the roof. The vortex had gone purple, but all of the energy was now coming down through the faeries' war sticks.

"We have to run, now!" Alric yelled in my ear.

A whirlwind was building inside the bar with my faeries inside of it.

"Not without them!" I yelled back. "Bunky! Get them out of here!" The wind from the vortex stole my voice. The faeries were radiating anger and the bar was going up in flames.

"Girls! Now!"

Garbage finally looked up and nodded.

"We go now." She yelled as she, the constructs, and the rest of the faeries flew out of the bar.

Another crack of red lightening shot through the hole in the roof and blew out the back of the bar.

Everyone was now running out, so we did as well. The difference was most of the population only ran out of the bar, and then stood in the street to watch the destruction.

I started to as well; it was strangely transfixing. But Alric grabbed my arm and pulled me. "I've never seen anything like that vortex spell. It appears that the faeries created it, but they have no control over it. We might not get out of town in time."

"We're out of the bar though," I said. The faeries and their construct escorts were out of sight. I'd sent an image of the wagons to them, but wasn't sure if they'd received it or not.

"The bar isn't the only thing under attack." Padraig ran alongside us and looked ready to grab my other arm if I didn't run faster. I wasn't short, but both had much longer legs than me. I picked up speed.

Alric was partially right—we didn't get out of town fast enough. At least not by our feet. The explosion of the entire block the pub had been on threw us past the last few buildings.

The landing wasn't as hard as it should have been but Alric had been muttering spells as we got picked up, so maybe he had slowed our descent. I scrambled to my feet and looked back.

A wall of fire and flying debris rushed toward us as well as panicked people trying to outrun it. Alric and Padraig stood up and both held out their hands. Green fire crackled from Padraig's hand and a soothing blue came from Alric's.

A moment later the explosion rushed over us.

The blue from Alric had been a shield; it was close, barely coming an inch over Padraig's head. But it held.

The effects of Padraig's spell were all around us as well—the explosion froze. Everything, debris, flame, people were locked in a light green film. I wasn't sure how much further the explosion would have gone, but it looked plenty strong in its frozen state.

Alric closed his fist and the shield vanished. Padraig pushed on a piece of the green frozen spell, and the frozen, green explosion crumbled. We worked our way out a bit at a time.

People who had survived the initial blast were running out from the frozen green mass, but the entire town was destroyed.

Once I got past the frozen explosion I turned back and shook my head. "The faeries caused all of that?" I knew they could be destructive, but this was on an entirely new level. Yes, the bastards who'd been tormenting them should be punished, but to take out an entire town? That seemed a bit much even for the mercurial Garbage Blossom.

Alric stomped a large piece of frozen explosion into dust and joined me. The view was impressive. Aside from the frozen explosion, nothing was left standing. "I don't know. Whatever caused that vortex above the pub seemed to be feeding into them. But if they had that much power, I have a hard time believing whoever caged them could hold them against their will."

"We need to get moving," Padraig said. As Alric and I

had been transfixed by the frozen mass of debris, Padraig had been shifting the broken pieces through his hand. "My spell isn't going to hold. There's another force pushing at it, trying to release the power behind the explosion."

He started running and Alric and I were right behind him. We'd gotten to the furthest buildings outside of town when a second explosion knocked us all off our feet. I got up as quickly as I could and was in time to see the entire town of Null implode on itself.

Aside from a few more aftershocks as the ground adjusted to the change, nothing came our way.

"Do either of you have the slightest idea what happened?" I looked from one to the other. "And be honest."

"Not at all," Padraig said. "I've never seen anything of the like. My spell should have dissolved the force of the explosion completely, yet all it did was slow it down."

"I've no idea." Alric shook his head at the damage behind us. "As for the faeries involvement, I think we need to find out from them what they did. Too bad Siabiane isn't with us; she's more of the faery talker."

I opened my mouth to debate that; the girls were mine as much as they were anyone's. But I held back in agreement. Even after all these years, fully understanding them was a painful and often useless endeavor. I also wished Siabiane was with us but not only for the faeries. The level of magic being used was getting higher and more complicated. The more serious magic users we had the better.

We started walking toward the road and our friends. I was grateful to be with two sharp-eyed elves; with the light from the explosion gone, I had no idea where we were going.

Silence filled the air as those people who could get away had fled, and the rest had been sucked into the giant hole in the ground that was once Null.

I heard the faeries before I saw them. Normally they were quiet in flight; their chattering was what gave them away, not their wings. This time they weren't chattering, but they were flying so fast I heard a buzzing sound as they approached. In fact, the swarm flew past us then doubled back.

"Is bad. Not all go boom," Garbage said to Alric.

"Did you cause the boom back there?" I asked. Garbage stayed near Alric but Crusty came toward me.

"That little boom. Big boom not us. But bad here." She looked soggy and smelled as if a vat of hundred proof alcohol had been dumped on her.

She also looked exhausted. They all did. I opened my cloak. "Do you want to ride inside? We'll catch up to the others soon and all of you can ride in the wagon."

Crusty gratefully flew into my cloak and nestled into a pocket. Garbage turned to me with a frown.

"Gone. Wagon people gone." She also looked like she was about to drop out of the sky. I couldn't fit twenty-three faeries in my cloak, but maybe between the three of us we could. None of them looked like they could stay in the air much longer. Bunky and the gargoyle seemed fine, but I was afraid to put the faeries on their backs—they'd probably fall off in their condition.

Padraig took off his cloak and held it out. "I really don't need this, maybe they could ride in it?"

I took it and knotted the ends to make a pouch. I didn't even say anything but all of the faeries except Garbage and Crusty dove into it. Crusty was snoring in my pocket, and Garbage settled on my hand.

"Sweetie, what happened to our friends?"

Garbage was fading fast. "They go. Bad take them all. Sleep now."

CHAPTER THIRTY SEVEN

I WANTED TO ASK MORE QUESTIONS, and from Alric and Padraig's faces they did as well. But Garbage tumbled over before she got near the pouch I'd made. Alric caught her and gently put her in with the others.

"Bad could mean anything or anyone," I said, as I tied the corners of the pouch together and worked it over my shoulder like a baby sling. Seeing the faeries being tormented like that had torn something inside of me. They were as much my friends as the rest of the people I travelled with, and for all of their trouble making they were innocent in a fashion. If the idiots behind the attack on the faeries hadn't blown up with the town, and I ever found them, they might regret surviving. I forced myself not to think about what might be happening to the rest of our people. Garbage could be wrong. I'd only believe her when we got to where the meet was.

"I think we can guess who, however." Alric had no trouble in the dark and led us down the road. "Nivinal might have also been behind what happened to the faeries."

"Agreed and that would be why he set up the faeries—he was counting on Taryn going into town." Padraig's look was mostly lost in the darkness, but I was sure I was missing something. "The plan being once your body was no longer intact, he could get the manticore. We have to assume the manticore, like all of the relics, is indestructible."

I had to start jogging since Alric was setting a fast pace,

but I shot a quick look at Padraig. "The manticore isn't intact inside me. I think I would know if a lump that big was physically inside my body. It dispersed, or something, when it decided to jump in me." I hadn't thought of it before, not really. That thing was inside me, but not intact—I knew it somehow. I also knew I didn't want to think about it too much or I'd run screaming into the night.

"When the body it inhabits is gone, it will reconstruct." Padraig sounded far too sure to be speculating on this, and Alric was staying out of it and silently leading the way.

"You've read something." I kept walking faster. Alric was picking up the pace again. I shook my finger at Padraig as we walked. "This isn't speculation, you've found out something about the manticore." I refrained from adding that it was something they knew I didn't want to hear.

"Now, it's not a verified source." Alric didn't look back, but he did slow down a bit. "I asked them not to tell you until we were certain."

I wanted to stop and yell at both of them. "What is it you know, Padraig?" I was going to have to have a long talk with Alric. With everything that was going on, our romance was going to die before it got started. I think I saw Alric's shoulder twitch, but he stayed silent.

"Alric is correct; the book I found the note in is obscure and not properly sourced."

I tilted my head at him, and he resumed talking.

"Now, that being taken into consideration, I do not want you to view what I'm about to say as the absolute truth. When we found Nasif I was hoping to ask him for his view on things."

"Stalling now." I wasn't sure I wanted to hear it, but I needed to know.

"Yes, I am," Padraig said. "Fine. It appears that the manticore works within a living being, such as yourself. It can only come out when the person is dead."

Alric stopped this time.

"So he doesn't want me, he wants me dead?" This wasn't good. To be honest, I hadn't been sure how he was going to get the manticore out of me anyway—so dead wasn't that much of a shock.

I jumped and bit back a scream as my sword appeared in my hand. "Would you stop doing that? And what were you thinking, leaving in the middle of a fight?" I didn't care that both Alric and Padraig were looking at me with concern. The sword rattled when I yelled at it. They might think these swords weren't alive—but I was beginning to doubt it. At least in the case of the one that had latched on to me.

The sword didn't vanish. I'd put Covey's sword in the only scabbard I'd had even though it didn't fit properly. I switched the swords out and Alric took Covey's sword.

"Now, back to me being dead, and you two not wanting me to know someone wanted me that way?"

Alric adjusted Covey's sword—his had now vanished—and resumed walking. "How were we supposed to tell you? And we're not even sure that's how it works."

"The thing absorbed itself into my body, and it's believed it was inside the person who caused the destruction of the Ancients, right? And whoever caused the death of the Ancients is dead now, right?"

Even in the dark I was close enough to both to see them nod. "The being who destroyed the Ancients is thought to have been destroyed when they were. That is from a more substantial source, so most likely true."

I rubbed the cold spot on my cheek. If the only way to get rid of this was death, it and I were stuck together. Hopefully for a very long time.

"Okay. I'm not happy, but I do need to know these things." I grabbed Alric's shoulder and turned him toward me. "You can't hide things from me."

He smiled and kissed me. "I know." He nodded to

Padraig. "He told me the same thing."

He slipped his arm around me and the three of us kept walking. Bunky and the gargoyle had been flying a little ahead of us, buzzing back every few minutes to make sure we were okay.

We must have gotten closer to the spot the wagons had been waiting at when Bunky gronked and blocked our path. A soft whinny in the shrubs a few feet back led us to the horse and the wagons. Intact and unmolested. Even all of the arcane books and whatnot were inside—only our friends were missing. Bunky and the gargoyle must have been as tired as I felt—even constructs needed a rest, and neither had had one for a long time. Both flew over to the larger wagon, landed on top, and did their version of sleeping.

"You seriously think Nivinal would do this? Leave us the wagons?" I rubbed the nose of the horse that pulled our wagon. He didn't seem disturbed at all. No violence had taken place when our friends vanished.

"He might have thought we'd been killed in the town?" Padraig didn't even sound as if he believed it.

Alric studied the ground around the wagons and horses carefully, sifting the dirt, looking for what clues only he knew. I couldn't see a foot in front of my face and he was tracking people by dirt. He finally looked up. "I agree with Taryn. Nivinal is a lot of things, but stupid isn't one of them or he never would have survived as he has. Therefore, he didn't take the others."

I rubbed my face and folded to the ground. I wasn't sure I could handle yet another random person out to get us. Or me. Nivinal might not be the only one who knew about the manticore, and how to get it out of me.

Alric dropped to my side immediately. "Are you hurt?" He turned me to face him and looked for any visible injuries.

"See? That right there? I sit down and immediately the

thoughts go to someone attacking us. I'm not sure I can do this anymore." I was whining and I didn't care. "I want my old life back." Relics, murdering mages, time travel…I was done.

He resettled himself so he was mirroring the way I sat and took my hands. "I know you do. You and Covey didn't ask for this. For Padraig and me, it's part of who we are. The more we find out about the relic and what happened to the Ancients, the more I know we can't let anyone else have it. We have to get the pieces, and destroy them. Or at least one." He touched the side of my face. "One other than yours."

His face was sincere. He wouldn't think any less of me if I walked away from this entire thing right now. I leaned over our crossed legs and kissed him.

And got kicked in my gut. Yet another brief romantic interlude ruined by faery feet.

I pulled away from Alric and reached into the pouch I'd made for the faeries. A few were stirring, most noticeably Garbage. I thought I recognized those tiny feet of destruction. They'd been out for less than an hour, so I was surprised any of them were up.

Even more surprising was that Garbage was kicking her friends awake.

"We no sleep. Up. Do. Now." She stomped on the rest of them until one by one they woke up. "Need bath." She flew out of the pouch and landed on Alric's knee. "Bath."

I'd never specifically seen them bathe. They usually took off and did their business elsewhere, although back in Beccia they did have a large bowl I kept filled with water in the toy castle they lived in. None of them had ever asked for a bath beyond demanding it be refilled daily.

Padraig had been checking the contents of both wagons, and got a lantern lit on the large one, but quickly came out with a water pouch and bucket. "I think we can help our valiant little friends." He poured the water into the bucket, and then sat it down next to us.

"They no move, dump in." Garbage ran and jumped into the bucket—overalls, flower petal hat, and all.

I looked into the pouch. A few of the faeries were upright, but mostly they were simply flopping around on each other. I wasn't going to argue with Garbage on this—not to mention all of them smelled awful. Padraig might want to leave this cloak behind. I emptied the pouch into the bucket.

Padraig watched the faeries for a moment, and then turned to us. "Nothing is taken, not even a single scroll. Except for our friends. Is there a reason you two are both on the ground?"

I looked at Alric and shook my head. There was no way I could leave them. Not to mention they were my best defense against Nivinal killing me for the relic. I knew it was more than that. I couldn't remember my parents very well. But a feeling of sadness, not related to their deaths, hit me when I thought of them. I'd never really had much of a family. I looked at the two elves and the faeries' water free-for-all. I had a family now and I wasn't leaving them.

"Absolutely no reason. I was tired for a moment and Alric was helping me up." Close enough, I was really tired.

Alric rose and held out a hand to help me up.

"Are there any clues as to who took them?" Alric nodded to where the horses were tied up, even Kelm and Flarinen's horses had their saddles and tack removed and sat to the side. They'd even been left with food and water. "Someone was extremely considerate."

Padraig held out a small piece of paper with extremely tiny writing on it. Covey was the only one I knew who could write that small.

"I've had some trouble with your friend's writing, but according to her, Nasif took them all."

I grabbed the paper, but it was too dark to read even with the lantern. I could see the scribbles, but not enough to make out the words. Magic had kicked back at me in the pub, but maybe it had been long enough now to have completely shaken off whatever Reginald's little cage had done to me. I slowed down my thoughts and envisioned a mage glow. I wasn't terribly adept at the little balls of light, mine usually ending up huge and unable to fly, but I wanted to see if I could do it this time.

It felt like it took forever but a small glow appeared over my head. With a bit of nudging I got it over the paper. Yup. Definitely Covey. She didn't seem distressed, but not happy either.

Nasif is making us leave you and the wagons behind. He wanted the faeries too. No one is hurt, but he suggests you don't follow us. Won't say where, but he keeps muttering about the Spheres. No choice—must leave.

There was more of a tone of annoyance to the note than fear. I was glad he hadn't been able to get the faeries. It was good for us to know he wanted them though. "Why would Nasif take them? *How* could Nasif take them? Two fully trained knights, a serious magic user, and Covey?"

I handed Alric the note in case I missed something. He read it quickly, didn't even need my mage glow, then handed it back. "Nasif must have gotten the upper hand on Lorcan and used a spell on them before they could react. Dueble isn't mentioned, but I doubt after all these years he would go against Nasif."

"But we were all going to the Spheres anyway. Why would he kidnap them?" Things kept getting weirder. More dangerous, I understood. I wasn't happy but things had been getting more dangerous pretty much since I first met Alric. Weirdness was starting to get annoying though.

The faeries flew out of the bucket and all hovered in the air. A moment later twenty-three tiny soaking faeries shook like dogs. "Damn it!" I'd been the closest and got most of the water. "Don't do that." I wiped off the wet spots. The faeries didn't even look my way.

"Is good. We go that way." Garbage pointed across the desert. And not in the vague direction I understood the Spheres to be.

Alric and Padraig hadn't answered my questions, had managed to dodge most of the soggy faeries, and were now hooking up the horses and the wagons. The knights' saddles were going in Lorcan's wagon and the extra horses were each tied behind a wagon.

"But don't we need to go that way?" I pointed toward the general direction of the Spheres.

"No. Spheres that way. No go." Leaf flew by me and nodded sagely.

"That's where we need to go. To the Spheres." I looked to the two elves for help, but they were busy finishing the horses. "Where is it you think we need to go?" The faeries couldn't force us to go their direction, but if we went a way they didn't like they could make the trip miserable.

"To find lizard chicken." Crusty had to join in. She was dripping a lot and looked like she was going to shake at any moment. I pushed her away.

"Lizard chicken? Have either of you the slightest clue as to what that means?"

Both looked up from finishing with the horses. "Lizard chicken? I have no idea." Alric sat Covey's sword on the driver's bench for the larger wagon.

"Is the thing. Big, kill thing. Like this." Garbage reached over and punched my cheek.

Right where the manticore was.

"The basilisk?" I'd never heard of them being called lizard chickens before. Then again until recently I hadn't heard of them at all. Not to mention, the relic was supposed to be at the Spheres.

"Is true. That way. Far that way." Now Dingle Bottom and Penqow were coming up, repeating it.

I narrowed my eyes and looked as close as I dared at the damp faeries. They flew like them, sounded like them, and up until this new obsession with sending us the opposite direction than we needed to go, acted like them. But right now, I didn't think they were them.

"Padraig?" I asked, as I kept my eyes on the faeries as they hovered in front of me. "Is it possible that Nasif found a way to take over the faeries? A spell that made them do what he wanted?" That all of them were hovering there looking at me was proving my point. And freaking me out.

I heard the crunching of gravel behind me and felt Alric at my side. Padraig stepped around me and got closer to the faeries.

"No, at least no spell I've ever heard of could take over beings and make them do their bidding on that level. Even if any similar spells were modified, holding on to twenty-three faery brains would not be easy. Actually, I think even holding one of those minds would tax the most powerful magic user." He dropped his voice and raised one hand slowly to the lowest hovering faery. "However, sending copies, while extremely difficult, would not be beyond the range of a mage like Lorcan. I think we can all agree Nasif appears to at least be Lorcan's equal." As he said the last word, he grabbed the lowest faery and uttered a spell word.

The faery's eyes went wide and it vanished. The spell was broken and within moments all of the faeries popped out of existence.

I waved in the air where they had been. "How can they have been fake? They got water on me."

Padraig looked into the bucket. "That was a clever spell. The water transference was part of it. Why, I don't know, unless it was simply to verify the faeries were real. This is fascinating."

Alric clasped his friend on the shoulder. "Rather, it would be if the person who did it hadn't kidnapped all of our friends, including the faeries. He must have managed to grab them when they first fled Null."

I was looking where the faeries had been. Or rather where their spelled copies had been. "But why? Why do any of this?"

Alric nodded to the wagons. "Had we listened to the faeries, we'd have rode hard in the opposite direction. Taking us further from the Spheres. It sounds simplistic, but the Nasif we knew was a scatterbrained academic—I think he still is. I can't say why he doesn't want us there, but I don't believe he meant harm to anyone. Including the faeries."

"I agree. He doesn't want us there, or he doesn't want Taryn there."

Damn it. If Nasif hadn't turned bad in the last thousand years or so, then him *not* wanting me somewhere involved with the relics might be a great reason for not being there. But good guy or bad guy, he'd crossed a line by kidnapping my friends and setting up a spell of duplicate faeries. I was going wherever he and they were.

"I don't care. He should have waited and talked to all of us. Not done whatever it was he did to the faeries. We're going to those Spheres." I marched to the larger wagon and started to climb inside. I paused, wrapped my hands in a cloak, and grabbed Bunky and the gargoyle—still in their construct sleep mode on top of the wagon—and brought them into the wagon with me. Riding with Alric was my first idea, but the two elves could go for far longer without sleep than I could. I could sleep while they drove. And I needed sleep. I had a sinking feeling things were going to get crazy again once we reached the Spheres.

I'd finished getting the two constructs secured on one of the benches; Bunky gave a little twitch like a sleeping cat that had partially woken up, as I adjusted them. Aside from that, both were completely out. Alric came to the open door of the wagon.

"We *will* find them. And whatever the reason behind it, I will protect you from whatever is at the Spheres."

"Thank you," I said, then kissed him. "Try and keep the bumps down as well, we'll be sleeping in here."

"If you two are ready, we should move. Nasif wouldn't have left these just to help us go the wrong direction faster. He didn't need this type of transportation."

CHAPTER THIRTY EIGHT

ALRIC QUICKLY GOT OUR WAGON moving after that comment from Padraig. It hadn't dawned on me, but obviously, taking everyone and everything would have been easier than carefully leaving things behind. Unless Nasif had another mode of transportation.

He was a serious academic who'd been, more or less, in hiding mode for hundreds of years—who knew what he'd come up with during that time. The larger concern was why he did it.

Even only knowing him for a few days, I doubted he'd gone evil. The Nasif I knew in the past had been willing to risk his life to get Alric and me out and back to our correct time. There was some reason behind what he did now, something that wasn't evil—hopefully—but might not be in our best interests. Covey's note had indicated two things: she didn't have a choice and wasn't happy about the situation. That was good enough for me. He didn't take all of my friends to keep me from following—in fact, taking them guaranteed I would.

He and Dueble could have taken off on their own and gotten there before us. Heck, if he knew where the basilisk was, why hadn't they gotten it before? Something in the last few hours had changed everything for Nasif and, by association, Dueble.

The wagon jolted to one side, but then corrected.

"Sorry." Alric's voice was faint, but at least we weren't

under attack.

I tried sorting through Nasif's actions a few more times, but they narrowed down to some recent information changing his plans—or rather, giving him new ones. In addition, I didn't really know him. There could be anything and everything in his mind justifying his actions. Rabid academics could be a dangerous lot. Covey once commented about selling half her family for some scrolls she really needed. I wasn't completely sure she'd been joking, even to this day.

If Nasif was on an academic search, anything he had to do in obtaining his goal was worth it in his mind.

The wagon had settled down into a soft rocking roll, and thoughts of anything were replaced by sleep.

I dreamed I was in a cavern, working on the biggest find ever. An intact elven courthouse. The walls and ornate decorations were clear through the dirt; I needed to dig down to them. The dirt finally opened before me and I tumbled inside. Within moments, a spectral judge appeared. An elf, but wearing my face. Around me thousands of other ghosts filled the space: elves, humans, dryads, syclarions, trellians, chatalings, and more. All of them shouting at me. It was my fault, whatever had killed them and left them here—it was my fault. They pressed closer and closer. Yelling and pushing them back did nothing—they kept coming.

A bright light stabbed through the dark and I fought to get to it.

"Taryn? Wake up," Alric said. There was enough concern in his voice that he might have been shaking me for a while.

"I had a dream...it was so real." Shaking my head did nothing to dispel the lingering images. The coldness in the eyes that had surrounded me was terrifying.

"Are you going to be okay? Do you need to talk about

it?"

Covey had told me that in her studies, she'd found that some elves believed dreams were powerful and showed us where we were in life. Alric wasn't one of those elves. For him to ask if I needed to talk about it was strictly a sign of how he felt about me—not because he thought the dream meant anything.

"I'm going to be okay. It was really disturbing, but it's fading now." Looking over his shoulder, I saw they'd set up a small camp. "So we've stopped for the day?" Judging by the sky, we'd ridden through the night and a good portion of the next day.

"We're within walking distance of the Spheres." He helped me up and I noticed both Bunky and the gargoyle were gone. "Nasif created a spell to travel here and we found it pulling back to its place of destination a few hours into our trip."

"So he made a spell and sent them all here? How'd we get in it if it was closing?"

Padraig stuck his head into the wagon. "Because someone has more guts than education and figured we could chance it." The scowl he threw at Alric was tempered by friendship, but he shook his head at him. "Those spells aren't used anymore because they are extremely dangerous. Not only to the people conducting them, but also to anyone who gets caught in the receding tail. Depending on how long the trip is they can take days to dissipate."

"And you thought we should jump in it?" I was half-glad I'd been asleep when it happened. The echoes of my dream made me wonder which would have been worse though.

We stepped out of the wagon. Padraig had gone to the other side of the small camp and was putting together three packs.

"It was a calculated risk," Alric said with a pointed look at his friend's back. "I recognized what it was as we started following it. Whatever his reasons for taking them, Nasif and the others would have been four days ahead of us if we hadn't. There's no way to know what could have happened to them in that time."

"I'm not going to say anything more about it, except that next time you decide to do something bone-headedly stupid give me more warning. I almost couldn't catch you." Padraig handed each of us a pack. "We have to hike in from here; the ground around the Spheres is too sensitive for horses and wagons."

"Have you been out here before?" I knew few people had made the trip and came back to tell the tale, but obviously some did or there wouldn't be any big academic books on it hanging around. I would have thought mention might have been made if Padraig was one of those lucky folks.

"No, sadly. I was setting up an expedition for it when I was attacked, before our battle with the Dark. But I did a lot of study on them. The Spheres themselves are massive, but part of the spell, or spells, that destroyed the Ancients, weakened the ground around them. The sand is unstable."

I slipped the pack on my back. Bunky and the gargoyle were waiting for us at the edge of the small clearing that made up our camp. We were clearly still in the desert, but there were a fair number of waist-high shrubs. They would at least provide a windbreak for our camp. There were also some boulders, but the ground around them wasn't friendly and was covered in small, sharp rocks. The horses were picketed and had food and water nearby. In case we didn't come back, was my guess for the large size of both.

"So, in this research, do they say why the Ancients made these things?" We'd come around one of the boulders. The desert spread out before us. At the far end a purple haze showed where the other mountain range was—the one closest to Beccia. Between it and us were the massive Spheres.

In open spaces like these and with nothing else around, it was difficult to determine true size. They were huge. Six round boulders almost crowding each other in a semi-circle. The only large gap was a large pile of small stones. If the rumors and myths were true, that was the seventh Sphere—the one that had shattered when the Ancients were destroyed.

Padraig led the way through the sand. A hard trail lurked under the shifting sands but it wasn't easy to see. There were tales of travelers who had been swallowed by these shifting sands in an instant. Alric stayed behind me, and although neither of them said it, I had a feeling they were both protecting me from whatever Nasif didn't want me there for.

"It is believed that they were a focus for power and were in use long before whatever calamity befell the Ancients. Remember, this entire desert was a green and thriving land. The gapen trees grew easily three times the size of the ones around today. Beautiful towns filled the land and they were at peace with everyone."

"Except the syclarions," Alric said, but he kept his voice low. He was in his element now, slinking about, looking for someone doing something bad. Although his real element would be as the one doing something wrong.

"That does appear to be true, although there were scholars who debate that. It would keep with what you mentioned before; that a thousand years ago the syclarions had rumors of the Ancients somehow weakening their entire race." He froze and I barely stopped in time. Alric, of course, had no problem stopping without hitting me even though he was right on my heel.

Padraig looked at something off the hard path and low to the ground. It took me a moment to realize what he was looking at, I believe in part because I couldn't wrap my head around it. In the deep sand to the right, a chunk of hand-shaped rock stuck out. It was only seeing the rock fingers, and at least three more hands near the first that made me realize those had once been people.

"I need you both to keep your heads down and eyes averted as we slowly start making our way back." Padraig's voice was its usual calm self, except for the tiny bit of tension I'd heard. "There are more on the other side, so try not to look in either direction."

"What is it?" My bigger issue was why did I want to know? There was something bad out here, something that killed by turning presumably innocent people into stone. We needed to retreat to fight another day.

"The basilisk. The rumors appear to be correct—this relic is alive. Or probably not alive in our sense, but like the constructs. And doesn't like people coming this way."

I glanced at the hands sticking out of the sand. My heart dropped to my feet. "Are these Covey and the others?"

We slowly stepped backwards. Alric led the way since he was now first, but he stopped and put his hand on my back. "I don't think so, and neither does Padraig."

Padraig's few seconds of silence told me I wasn't the only one thinking it. But lying was the better side of not having your travelling companion do something stupid. If I truly thought everyone else was gone, we all knew stupid actions on my part would be following.

"I agree with Alric. Those people have been here a long time to sink that deep into the sand. Even though the ground isn't terribly sturdy here, they wouldn't have gone that deep this soon."

He sounded like he was convincing himself, but I was willing to go along for the ride.

The sound of scrabbling on rock-covered sand almost caused me to look up, but I didn't. It seemed to be coming from all around us, but if it was the basilisk relic, then there was only one. Unless this wasn't the relic and instead there were real basilisks turning people to stone. Neither option was good.

"I think it is following us." Granted, we were walking backwards with our heads down at weird angles, so we weren't making great time. Keeping up with us wouldn't be hard for a drunken, one-legged satyr, let alone whatever was actually stalking us.

"I know, but hopefully when we get—" Padraig's voice was cut off as I saw him stumble. My reaction was automatic. I turned, saw a nasty-looking creature staring at Padraig—who was a moment away from looking up—and I dropped a shield around us. It wasn't a conscious thought, just a reaction—like you'd jump out of the way of a runaway horse. The coldness from the manticore inside of me flared as the shield formed around us—but it was a welcome chill.

The shield flashed blue as the creature's gaze hit it—but couldn't break through.

Padraig caught himself and Alric and I pulled him back onto the trail. He stared at the basilisk, and then turned back to us.

"How is this happening? We should all be stone statues at this point."

"The magic of Taryn." Alric's voice echoed Padraig's terror though—at least a little.

"They're both relics, right? Came from the same person, and used in the same weapon. I guess they know each other, or the manticore's shield really is too strong for even the basilisk's gaze." I allowed myself a look at the creature. It was about the size of Bunky and looked like someone had mashed a chicken and an extremely ugly legged-snake together. I now understood the faeries calling it a lizard chicken. A stab of pain hit me at that thought; those hadn't been the real faeries, and I had no idea where the real ones were.

The creature blinked slowly and tipped its head. It appeared to be confused about why we weren't stone now.

"I'm glad my weird internal roommate was able to hold

this off—but that thing is still staring at us and I'm afraid if we move I can't keep the shield up."

"You two keep moving, as the shield falls I'll place myself to block you both. Get back to the camp and run." Padraig pulled back his shoulders and took a deep breath. A dramatic tragic hero in the making.

"Nope," I said. "I'm not leaving people behind. We have to figure out a way to—" My words were cut off as Bunky and the gargoyle swooped in low over the basilisk.

The creature shifted its gaze to both of them. And nothing happened. Since constructs weren't flesh, I guessed it couldn't change them to stone either. If it weren't a matter of life or death for all of us, I'd feel sorry for it.

Bunky and the gargoyle made another pass and this time the basilisk crouched and let out a shrill cry. The gargoyle opened its mouth to impossibly large proportions, and swallowed the basilisk.

All three of us stared in silence. The gargoyle did a victory lap, then it and Bunky flew over to us.

"How did that happen? Where did the basilisk go?" The gargoyle was larger than it had been, but not by much. Certainly not by enough for the one to fit inside the other.

Alric held out his hand and Bunky flew near. "How is this possible, my friend?"

Bunky made a few noises at the gargoyle, who gronked back. Alric nodded.

"He ate it."

"We saw that," I said. I really wished I could understand Bunky like Alric and Padraig could. "How did he do it? And is that it? We're safe now from the relic weapon because the basilisk has been destroyed?" I wasn't going to complain if that was the case. Heading back to the Shimmering Dewdrop and my normal life sounded wonderful.

Padraig was petting the gargoyle and crooning to it. "He didn't destroy it, he swallowed it. The basilisk is functioning, but it can't do any harm to our friend here. So, while we're safe from the basilisk for now, if someone else gets the gargoyle and can get the basilisk out, there is still a danger from the relic weapon."

I walked over and petted the gargoyle as well. He might be a metal construct, but, like Bunky, he liked being petted. "Siabiane designed him to swallow things?" That was odd, but he'd seemed quite content with swallowing the basilisk.

"Constructs were all designed with functions," Alric said. "Bunky seems to hold memories, but we don't know whose. Most likely the thousands of years buried in the ground jumbled them a bit." Bunky buzzed over and head butted him. This time, Alric let him.

"Siabiane probably designed the gargoyle to carry things for her. This was a happy off-shoot of that."

I watched both constructs. To say I was happy they saved us was an understatement, but I wasn't sure how I felt about the gargoyle carrying around that deadly basilisk. I shook my head. There wasn't anything I could do about it. We had no place else to put the thing. Maybe when this was done the elves could create a cage or something for it. For now, we simply had to make sure no one startled the gargoyle.

Neither one seemed the least concerned about anything, but Bunky was trying to get us moving toward the Spheres. He'd fly ahead a bit, and then circle back and try nudging from behind. Padraig followed his lead and we made our way past the stone hands.

I wanted to see the Spheres; they were legend after all, and few people could claim they had seen them. But I wasn't sure if this was the wisest idea right now. "So, if Nasif wasn't looking for the basilisk, then why did they come out here? And which way did they go if they didn't become statues?"

"I'd guess they tried to come this way first. It's the most direct route," Padraig said as he studied the arms we passed.

The field of hands was a lot larger than I'd thought. "Somehow Nasif or Lorcan was able to hold off the basilisk long enough for them to escape. And they went another route."

"Aside from the Spheres being where Nivinal and Reginald were going, do we have a clue as to what's here?" I waved a hand toward the distant boulders in question. "Aside from seeing them, that is."

"Not at all. Nasif was into the relics, but taking our people has to be about something more than just the basilisk." Alric had been dropping behind us. He quickly caught up as we passed a grouping of large standing stones. He dropped his voice. "Keep going. I think there is someone following us." With that he ducked behind the stones.

Alric was a great tracker and spy, but how he thought he could hide in the desert—even behind rocks—was beyond me. Not to mention it would be clear to anyone watching us that there were only two of us on the trail now.

We'd been walking for at least fifteen minutes, with Bunky and the gargoyle buzzing by occasionally to check on our progress. The Spheres seemed as far away as when we started.

If this was going to take as long as I feared, I had a feeling I was going to be missing the wagon soon. A crash, punctuated by yells and the sound of a scuffle came from behind us.

"No, stop, you'll ruin everything!" The voice, even muffled as it was in Alric's cloak, was familiar. Dueble. "He said she mustn't come in—you all have to go back immediately." The form in the cloak thrashed around, but Alric had a strong hold on him.

Padraig and I walked back to the two of them.

"Do you need help?" Padraig didn't move closer, nor did he sound like he really believed that Alric needed assistance.

"Did you bring any rope?" Alric jerked forward as Dueble tried to break free. He wasn't successful.

Padraig swung his pack around and immediately brought out a neatly coiled bit of rope. "I did. I think it might have even been Dueble's so that's fitting."

Padraig and Alric removed the cloak and tied Dueble up. Bunky flew down and buzzed menacingly into Dueble's face. No one messed with his faeries, and Bunky had been as fooled by the fakes as we were. He was not happy.

"You can tell us what Nasif is up to, or we can let Bunky and the gargoyle get it from you," Alric said as he leaned forward into Dueble's face. Bunky buzzed even lower.

"Nothing bad! Please keep it away." Dueble looked ready to cry—not an attractive look for a syclarion. "We have to keep her away from the Spheres. Nasif wasn't exactly sure until recently, but he knew there was a bad thing engaged around the Spheres. He wasn't sure who or what was going to trigger it. But then when we saw you again, we knew…well, not exactly…but then Reginald grabbed you and you have the manticore, so it obviously was you."

Scaring Dueble was going to lead to more babbling and he was already hurting my head. I slapped on my best smile and crouched down to be face to face with him as he sat on the ground. "I'm not going to do anything to the Spheres, Dueble. They've survived for thousands of years; I seriously doubt I *could* do anything to them."

"No, you don't understand. It's not what you could do to them; it's what they could do to you. Oh, this is all wrong. Nasif knew there was something different about you—well, he guessed, but over the years he might have found hints and clues." He looked to each one of us as if we were supposed to understand him. "Nasif knows something will happen. He didn't want you here until he knew what." Dueble leaned forward. "He thinks you'll get turned to stone by the basilisk, but we haven't seen the creature yet."

I looked to the other two with a shrug. That at least told us Nasif hadn't taken our friends down this main path. "We're fine on that." The gargoyle flew past us. "I have it on good authority that the basilisk won't be going after anyone for a while."

"That was the only reason?" Padraig nudged Dueble when he started retreating into his own thoughts. He came back with a start.

"What? Well, no. That was one of the reasons, but the other was that Taryn gives off a deep time disturbance. Nasif believes it happened when you went back in time." He tilted his head toward Alric. "He wasn't sure why you, nor either of us have it though. It could be Taryn's human nature—they are weaker, you know."

He grinned at me to take the sting out. There was no sting to take out. I knew most species were far hardier than my human ancestors.

"Well, I'm here now. The basilisk didn't get me, and I want my friends back. Where are Nasif and my friends?"

Dueble pulled back as if he was afraid that I, of all people, would hit him. "They got captured. Nasif worked the travel spell perfectly. They are almost impossible to control, you realize. But he did his first one without a hitch. However, when we arrived we ran directly into a problem. Nasif saw them coming and threw me out of the spell tunnel right before it closed. It took me a while to find them, but by then it was too late."

I wasn't sure if I was going to choke the answers out of him or Alric was.

"Too late for what? Who came after them?" Padraig stepped in, but even his patience was fading.

"Nivinal and Reginald. They're back together. They grabbed Nasif and your friends as they came out of the spell tunnel. They're their prisoners now." He looked to me. "Even your little faeries."

CHAPTER THIRTY NINE

"WE HAVE TO GET THEM," I said. I wasn't too worried when Nasif had my friends. I was annoyed and pissed. Betrayed that someone I thought of as a friend had broken that trust. But not afraid. That they were all with Nivinal and Reginald struck me with terror.

"We can't rush in, not with Nivinal being involved," Padraig said. "And Reginald has shown to be far craftier than we gave him credit for. I do wonder why Nivinal is working with him again?"

Alric untied Dueble.

"I think it might have to do with a spell cast on him. Reginald was doing a lot of bowing in Nivinal's direction," Dueble said. He slowly got to his feet as if unsure that Alric wouldn't tackle him again.

The question was if Nivinal was coming here because he knew the basilisk was here, for something about the Spheres, or something completely different. I had a bad feeling he was covering a number of agendas in one location.

"Where does he have them?" Padraig asked. He recoiled the rope and put it in his pack.

Dueble kept watching Bunky and the gargoyle. He might not be tied any more but the two constructs were making it clear that he wasn't going anywhere without us. "They went to the Spheres—right in the middle of them. But she can't go."

He looked ready to cry again. I wasn't ready to forgive him or Nasif. If they hadn't grabbed my friends and used that traveling spell thing we wouldn't be in this mess.

"Why is Nivinal focused on the Spheres and not the basilisk? He's obsessed with getting the relic weapon back together." This change of plans couldn't be good for anyone.

"Maybe he wants to take you." Alric spoke before Padraig did. "He's tried to get you a few times, and seems to know more about you than even you do. Perhaps Nasif knew something would happen to you at the Spheres and it was that Nivinal would kidnap you."

I'd thought he was going to say Nivinal was going to try to kill me. Nasif and Dueble were seriously upset about me being near the Spheres and death would be serious. Yet, Nivinal could have killed me a number of times, both in the enclave and after. He didn't really try. I felt more as if I was one of the relics he was gathering. Obviously, if Padraig's research into the manticore were accurate, Nivinal would need to kill me eventually. But he had some reason for wanting me alive as well.

I ignored the flash of cold in my check that reminded me I sort of was one of the relics.

"I don't think we can ignore that he could be after Taryn as well as the relics," Padraig said. "The scroll said the basilisk was here, but not where. He might not realize it was terrorizing people on the trails. So, he wants Taryn, the manticore, and the basilisk, none of which we are going to give him."

"But we can't leave our friends behind." There was no way that was going to happen, but part of me pointed out that if I and the gargoyle, with its belly full of basilisk, left, we'd be increasing the chances of success. There was also no way to know if my leaving might make it easier for Nivinal to grab me. We needed our friends back, and I felt it was safer if we all stuck together to do it. I folded my arms to prepare for the objections.

Padraig and Alric both looked concerned, but neither said anything. Dueble started babbling and grabbing my arms.

"You can't. It will destroy you. Nasif wouldn't say that directly, but he was scared for you. You and I can leave this place."

"Can you protect her against Nivinal if this is a trap to get us to separate? He doesn't know what's happened to the basilisk, but he wants the manticore." Padraig removed Dueble's hands from my arms. "You don't have to go with us, but he does have Nasif as well."

Dueble gave me one more sad look, and then nodded as if he was coming to terms. "I'm coming along. I can fight and they aren't going to be allowed to hurt any of our friends." He looked up. "I lost my sword in the spell tunnel; do any of you have an extra?"

Alric handed over Covey's sword to Dueble. An instant later his own spirit sword reappeared and he sheathed it. "No sheath for that one, but I have a feeling we'll be needing them soon anyway."

Bunky and the gargoyle dove by again, but this time in a less menacing manner. Dueble gave them a quick smile and didn't flinch.

So, two elves, two constructs, one syclarion, and me. Up against Nivinal. Even ignoring Reginald, since he might also be a prisoner, we were screwed.

Padraig resumed leading us toward the Spheres, and Alric dropped to the back to take the last position. I went back with him. "How can we tell if it's the real Nivinal or another of his images? I've only seen the real him once that I know of, in the throne room of the palace in the enclave—but I couldn't tell the difference between him then and the image versions I've seen. Do we have a better chance if it's only his image?"

"I wouldn't count on it," Alric answered. Padraig and

Dueble were carrying on their own conversation a bit ahead of us. "He's shown a lot of power even through his image. I've never seen anyone who can make himself work through his image like that. Siabiane has her ghosting bit, but she's extremely limited in what she can do."

"That doesn't make me feel better. He also has the rakasa." I'd managed to forget about them until now. Now their tiny teeth-filled mouths were all I could think of.

"The ground under this sand is too hard. Nasif believes the rakasa couldn't get through." Dueble kept to the center of the path, however.

Padraig kept his eye on the trail ahead of him, but he responded. "We should watch for them. The ground here, off the trail, is far looser than it is supposed to be. The areas under the sand have gone through some recent transformations."

I moved closer to the center of the trail as well. There was nothing more to say, we were going to a fight that we might not win but had to do anyway. I watched Bunky and the gargoyle fly a bit ahead, then come back and complete their circle again. I turned to Alric. "Is there any way we could use the basilisk against Nivinal—without damaging any of us or our friends?"

Alric watched the constructs as they faded to small specks above us. "I can't think of a way. Maybe if things get really dire we stand behind the gargoyle and tell him to spit it out."

"You have the basilisk?" Dueble picked up on that quickly. "Where is it?" He wasn't paying enough attention, which wasn't a bad thing.

"Sort of. It's secure, you don't need anything more than that," Alric said.

The rest of the way we stayed silent, but we never heard the attackers until they hit us.

The first wave was familiar to three of us. The purple floating creatures who'd attacked us in the canyon. Dueble didn't realize what they were and was raising a hand to pet one when Alric tackled him.

"Gloughstrikes! Don't let them touch you, they are deadly." Padraig yelled. We weren't sure what exactly happened after they knocked out everyone. None of them had a problem after the faeries had woken them up. But we didn't have the faeries with us right now.

There were at least thirty of the creatures coming for us, there was no way we could avoid all of them.

Padraig muttered a spell at them, but instead of anything happening to them the spell came back at him and burnt one of the shrubs behind him off the trail. "Don't use magic against them, they're shielded."

The creatures weren't moving fast, but there were enough of them that they didn't need to. We were surrounded.

"So Nivinal is behind these things?" One came too close and I smacked it with the flat of my blade. Bunky and the gargoyle were trying to push off as many as they could but Bunky's defensive lightning did nothing to the things. At least it didn't bounce back like the spell did.

More appeared and continued surrounding us. Then some of them started growing larger.

I batted three more out of the air. They tumbled a few feet away, but then slowly came back again. There were now five of the things bulging into something larger, but they seemed to be fighting it. Maybe a spell was working? They looked almost like they were slowly exploding. Very slowly. A quick look told me neither Alric nor Padraig had cast a spell, as they were busy swinging at the ones attacking them. Likewise for Dueble.

The exploding ones weren't exploding, but changing form. The former purple blobs grew a pair of long legs, arms, a head…and giant wings? The five turned into what looked like a combination of an elf and a giant faery.

"Male faeries." I swung my sword faster as the speed of the gloughstrikes increased. Many of them were turning to go after the male faeries who looked a bit confused and unfinished. Garbage had said the one who'd found me back in Null shouldn't have been on this plane, and judging by the vague confusion on the faces of the faeries in front of me—these five shouldn't be here either.

I screamed as the gloughstrikes landed on each one of them. And stopped screaming when the male faeries grabbed them, smashed them between their hands, and ate them. I rubbed my eyes with my free hand. Nope. That's what they were doing.

The gloughstrikes turned their focus on the five faeries, but they mostly were becoming food for them. The looks on the faery faces were akin to a giant lizard who was snacking on bugs. Satisfaction, but not a lot of intelligence. It was far more disturbing when the creatures doing the mindless killing and eating looked like the elves standing next to you.

"What are they?" Dueble was swatting at the purple things but spread his horrified glances between them and the male faeries.

"The purple things are gloughstrikes, according to Padraig. Those five are male faeries. Garbage says they're not supposed to be here—or she did say that when I ran into one before. I have no idea how they came to be here."

By now the faeries had severely reduced the gloughstrikes and no more were appearing. Whatever had called them to attack us couldn't motivate more of them to come to their deaths.

Finally all of the creatures were gone, and the faeries were looking at us in confusion. Then the closest one pointed at me. "You." His voice was rusty, as if it hadn't been used in a long time, or ever. He nodded, the other four nodded, and they vanished.

Five lifeless gloughstrikes tumbled to the ground where the faeries had been.

"What happened?" Alric had his sword out and poked at

the lifeless purple gloughstrikes with it.

Garbage had said the male faeries weren't finished. That something had happened long ago to send them out of this plane and into another. She really didn't like them. After they'd somehow managed to take over and modify the bodies of some of the gloughstrikes—then destroy the rest—I had to say I didn't agree with her. Except I really didn't like the way they'd gotten rid of them, nor the mindless look in their eyes as they did it. But I would definitely tell her about this. Once we got her and the others back.

"These ones are dead, and I don't see any more around." Padraig had crouched down to the closest body, which now looked like a dried flower. He didn't touch it with his hand, but like Alric, tapped it with his sword. He also didn't go off the trail. He took the potential threat of a rakasa attack seriously.

"I haven't had time to find out a lot about the gloughstrikes. They were little more than myths back when they were written about. They paralyze their victims and then drain the life from them over a matter of weeks." He got back to his feet. "They also were called into being by a powerful mage and always worked under the control of one. They're possibly even more mindless than those faeries who ate them."

"Those were faeries?" Dueble shuddered. "I like your little ones much better. Those were wrong. Unfinished."

It was interesting that he used the same words Garbage had. "So Nivinal is the one behind the gloughstrikes? Even the ones we saw before?" We'd believed Nivinal and Reginald were operating under the assumption that no one was following them. And maybe they were. But they'd left a nice trap for anyone who came down after them through the canyons.

"I'd have to guess he is." Padraig started searching his pack. Only because I'd been around my own crazed academic for over fifteen years did I know what he was looking for.

Our friends were captured, we'd been attacked, and he was looking for something to hold one of the gloughstrike bodies so he could study it after this was all over.

I was about to suggest we deal with that later, when a movement to my left caught my eye. Small, white, six legs...it was the minkie. Except for the fact that I could see the dirt and rocks covering the ground through him. It was looking right at me, and when I reached to tap on Alric's arm to get his attention, it slowly shook its head.

Then it used an upper arm to motion me to follow it.

CHAPTER FORTY

I WAS GOING TO SAY SOMETHING to the others anyway, but I had a bad feeling I was the only one seeing it. It might not even really be a minkie. Since the girls had never agreed to having actually had one visit, who knew what it was. Its eyes were bright blue as it grinned.

It was a minkie, or a spirit of one, and only I could see it. And I was going to follow it.

"I think we should go that way," I said as I started walking toward my ghost minkie, or crazed hallucination. It was a few feet to the left of the trail we were following. As I looked closer I saw there was a second trail. One that passed far closer to the Spheres than the one we were on. "Look." I pointed to the thin line of the trail through the sand. It was even wider than the one we were on. And there was no way I could have seen it from where we'd been without a ghost minkie, something that I couldn't explain, helping.

Hopefully no one would ask.

"I don't know," Alric said slowly. Then he walked over to where the two trails met. "This one is solid, and less of a curve." He turned to me and tilted his head. "How did you see it?"

I shrugged. "Just the way the sand drifted. I thought I saw more of the gloughstrikes over there." The minkie nodded then motioned to follow. It was only a few feet from us, but since the other three were now looking at the trail it was on, and no one reacted as if they saw it, I figured I was on my own with this.

"Good spotting. We'll make a tracker of you yet." Alric smiled and led the way on the new trail.

This did seem faster, and was more direct. After one false side trail, which the minkie shook its head sharply at, we made very good time.

To find the Spheres looming before us. Massive. Overwhelming. And empty. Rather the area around them was empty. They looked even more solid and rock-like the closer I got.

We'd slowed down as we approached the black semi-circle of the Spheres. They were more clumped together. The missing one was to the front. But we were hard to miss and anyone watching for us should have been visible as well.

Even with the current situation, and a high probability of death lurking before us, I couldn't help but be awed by the Spheres. They were plainer than the scrolls had claimed. The ground around them was the same dull gray and brown as the entire area. The Spheres, on the other hand, were amazing. A good section of each was sunk into the ground but they loomed over us and were perfectly round.

Their full usage was lost to time, but the scrolls said this was a place of immense power in the time of the Ancients. The place where the relic weapon had been forged. There was debate if it had been used here or in their city under the elven ruins of Beccia.

I couldn't help myself—I reached out to touch one.

And landed flat on my ass as too many images to count flooded my head. I looked up expecting that Bunky had touched me, but he and the gargoyle were staying high in the air to look for our people.

Great. Amazing things of the past and I couldn't touch them. Probably the best way to torture a digger.

Alric helped me to my feet. He started to speak, but a

scream came from in front of the stones. We all ran around the stone closest to us.

A wavering shield, looking like the surface of water, only vertical instead of horizontal, hung before us. It wavered more, then exploded as two forms came tumbling through it. As it vanished, our friends appeared.

The two that were fighting, and had shattered the shield, were Lorcan and Mackil—rather Reginald in Mackil's former body. Both of them had a collar around their necks and I noticed neither was using magic. Nasif and Covey stood to the side, watching the fight but not looking at us—they also had collars on their necks. The faeries were in a cage and were yelling at the two fighters.

The minkie had vanished, which was unfortunate because maybe it could have done something. I still wasn't sure what exactly the creature was, nor what it might be able to do. But at this point any help would have been good. At first I didn't see Nivinal, then Flarinen, Kelm, and he appeared to step out of thin air. Flarinen and Kelm both held their swords ready and looked to be escorting Nivinal, and they were also wearing the collars.

Whatever the collars on their necks were gave Nivinal some control. Not complete control. I didn't think Nivinal looked happy about his shield shattering.

Reginald was swearing like mad, and I realized that it didn't sound like him—it sounded like Mackil.

"I'm me! Yer bastard brother is under control, stop attacking me."

"That's not me," Mackil's ghost appeared next to me. He was so faint that I was surprised he was still on this plane of existence.

Reginald's ploy worked as Lorcan pulled back for a moment.

"It's not Mackil, it's Reginald!" I couldn't help myself.

In fact, it might not have been all me. Mackil's ghost brushed closer. "Thank you. Kill that bastard for me, okay?"

A breeze went through me and he was gone.

Nivinal didn't look surprised at our appearance; he already knew we were there. We weren't supposed to know they were there—Reginald's fight destroyed whatever sneaky plan Nivinal had for us. Covey and Nasif looked up and shook their heads as if waking up, but whatever else those collars did, they didn't allow them to move.

Lorcan heeded my yell and went after Reginald anew.

Nivinal nodded to Flarinen and Kelm and both of them moved toward us. Nasif and Covey didn't move. The faeries yelled from their cage.

Lorcan plowed into Reginald, slamming him into one of the Spheres. Reginald recovered and pulled a knife out of his waistband. Why he hadn't before, I had no idea. Then I saw the look on Nivinal's face. Most likely the knife hadn't been there before.

Nivinal had expected us, he'd set this trap to bring us, so why wasn't anything happening? Aside from Dueble standing an inch away from me at all times, and Padraig and Alric trying to fight off Flarinen and Kelm without actually hurting them.

I watched Nivinal. The breaking of his hiding shield when Reginald and Lorcan fell through it caused some other problems for him as well. He wasn't making any moves towards any of us but watched the interactions with an annoyed glare. Nasif and Covey hadn't moved though, so he still had too much control over my friends.

The faeries were jumping around in their cage and even from this distance they looked pissed. They'd been spelled and captured a lot lately, and I knew that wasn't sitting well with Garbage.

Nivinal hadn't looked at Dueble or I, but he obviously knew we were there. He was trying to get his original plan back on track.

I didn't have a lot of options. "Garbage! That man behind you is who put you all in a cage—twice. He thinks you've lost and that male faeries will have to come save us." Not a great taunt, but all I could think of at the moment. Making them mad might get them out of the cage.

Nivinal looked up at my yelling, but he was concentrating on something else. At first I thought it was Reginald and Lorcan, then I realized he was intently focusing on the Sphere behind them. He gave me a sneer, then went back to what he was doing.

The cage holding the faeries rocked, but they couldn't tip it or kick it open. Bunky bleated, and he and the gargoyle dove down before I could say anything. They each grabbed part of the cage—Bunky in his mouth, the gargoyle in his talons—and rose up with it. Nasif tried to grab it but only when Nivinal turned to him. Nasif's actions were slow, and I swear I saw him wink. Those collars could be losing power.

The faeries yelling had changed and they were now encouraging Bunky and the gargoyle to go higher. Which they did.

I should have realized what their plan was, but I naively thought Bunky would bring the cage to me and I could try and get them out. Bunky and the faeries had a more direct approach. I could barely see them in the sky above us when I noticed the cage was dropping fast. Directly toward one of the Spheres.

I yelled, but there was nothing I could do as the cage plummeted. It hit the Sphere furthest from the fighting, and shattered.

The burst of flying color that came from behind the Sphere was a welcome sight. Bunky and the gargoyle flew low over our heads, gronking and bleating. The faeries dove in as well and began harassing Reginald.

Nivinal was focusing on the Sphere he'd been staring at, but I wasn't sure why. It looked the same as the others, but something about it was important to him. Which meant we needed him not to be able to do whatever he was doing.

Alric and Padraig were trying to disarm Kelm and Flarinen without hurting them. Kelm's responses seemed a bit sluggish against Padraig, but Flarinen seemed to enjoy going after Alric far too much for it to have been simply the spell.

Lorcan and Reginald were fighting as well, the knife had been knocked out of Reginald's hand, but Lorcan couldn't reach it. I noticed that while Lorcan had one of Nivinal's collars on, it seemed to be hanging on by a scrap.

The faeries were dive-bombing Reginald, but whereas Lorcan hadn't shown signs of being able to use magic, Reginald was creating some sort of shield.

It was up to me to block Nivinal and whatever he was doing.

Sand. There was a lot of sand around us and that could work. I twisted my push spell and rose the sand around Nivinal's Sphere into a sand curtain. Even I was surprised when it stayed hanging there. Almost immediately, Nivinal swore and spun in my direction.

I stared him down then yelled out, "Girls, grab Lorcan's collar!" If the faeries could destroy the thing, then at least Lorcan had a chance. Which might be more than Dueble and I were going to have, judging by Nivinal's glare.

I thought he'd start throwing spells, but he didn't. Not directly. The ground between him and the sand-blocked Sphere roiled as if it was alive. Moments later, rakasa started swarming from under the sand. Unlike their usual underground activities, they weren't coming out from a tunnel, but under the sand.

Garbage and Leaf were almost to Lorcan and his collar when the rakasa came out. Unfortunately, Bunky and the gargoyle were watching the faeries and flew too low; three rakasa jumped on Bunky and pulled him to the ground. Unlike my faeries, Bunky could be destroyed. I'd seen others of his kind ripped apart. Before the faeries or I could try to help, the gargoyle dove low and screeched at the rakasa.

I don't know whether the gargoyle planned on using the basilisk as a weapon, or had forgotten it had it. The screech didn't do much, but the glare of the basilisk from its open mouth managed to turn the three rakasa who were pounding on Bunky to stone. Bunky shattered their arms and rose to freedom, but the basilisk fell out of the gargoyle's mouth.

"Don't look near the Sphere! The basilisk is free." Everyone dropped their eyes, even as they fought—except the rakasa. There were about twenty and seemed focused on grabbing the basilisk as it scrabbled around the sand. It wasn't long before they were all stone. The gargoyle swallowed it again, and both it and Bunky flew higher.

The faeries were all gathering around the Sphere Nivinal had been staring at and appeared to be trying to help block it. Nivinal was a serious magic user and yet hadn't moved from that spot. Then I realized that sand or not, projected image or not, he'd built up a serious spell and was about to let it loose.

My faeries were in the way. Most things couldn't hurt them. But a strong enough spell could. Or send them to a different time.

I didn't even think, just ran forward toward the Sphere. My plan was to get a spell between his spell and the girls, and somehow slow down or stop the spell.

That didn't happen.

I'll never know if Nivinal planned what happened next; this whole thing appeared to have been poor planning on his part. The look of surprise on his face as I dove in front of the faeries was real though.

The faeries managed to lift up enough to clear the Sphere—I didn't have that ability. The spell from Nivinal didn't hit me directly, but the glancing shot slammed me backwards into the Sphere.

All of the images from when I'd touched the other one hit me harder than the rock itself against my back. My body felt broken and pulled apart as lives, too many lives, tore through me. And I tore through the Sphere.

At first I thought I was unconscious or dead, there was smoke and shattered rock all around me. I was alive and conscious. The blow of Nivinal's spell had shattered the Sphere.

CHAPTER FORTY ONE

I HAD TO THINK HE WASN'T planning on destroying the Sphere. There was no purpose for doing it. Luckily, the images in my head vanished once I scrambled out of the rubble.

Unfortunately, a moment later I realized I'd been wrong. He had planned to destroy it.

We'd thought the basilisk had done its hunting on the paths leading to the Spheres, but at some point, long ago, it had allowed people to get closer to the Spheres before it attacked. It was long enough ago that no stone arms stuck out and we wouldn't have seen them at all except that they were now coming back to life and crawling out of the sand.

Actually, *life* was too generous. Their white eyes and slack jaws said they were dead, just no longer stone and not happy to be in the sand.

Nivinal was focused on the slowly moving bodies; they were moving at his command. That new spell must have been too much for the spell he had on my friends because all of the collars popped off.

Covey and Nasif charged Nivinal, but he simply faded his image and they ran through him. The bodies were closest to where Lorcan and Reginald fought. I'd thought the bodies were really going too slow to hurt anyone, but that thought was shattered as two darted forward and grabbed Lorcan. Alric had been fighting Flarinen nearby and turned to fight the bodies, but how did someone kill a dead thing? Alric and Padraig were able to get Lorcan away but couldn't stop them. Two more grabbed Reginald and tore him in half before anyone could get to them. Nivinal showed no grief as his former partner died, but he was very focused on controlling the creatures.

I was cut off from my friends as more of the bodies came out of the ground. There would soon be hundreds, all under the control of Nivinal. He wouldn't need the Ancients' weapon to control the world—he could do it with an army of these things.

I was standing near the rubble, knowing my friends couldn't survive and that I couldn't save them. I raised my sword to charge forward anyway when a horrible pain ripped through me. Fog filled the world around me and my body felt as if every single bone was being constantly broken and torn apart. My mouth felt too small for the teeth now growing, my jaw expanded, my back screamed in pain as it felt like a hundred swords ripped from the inside out.

Anger. The pain as my body changed was replaced by anger. The stabbing and grating stopped, and I felt odd. The world around me was smaller and my dropped sword looked too far away, like a child's toy. I screamed as my hand came into view as I reached to grab the sword. My hand was now massive, scaled, and had talons coming from it. It looked as if someone had taken a large lizard's leg and replaced my hand with it.

The fog I'd thought was visible only to me was spreading everywhere but I could still see my friends. The number of stone bodies were growing and my friends were backed against another Sphere.

Fear for my friends battled against the terror of the changes my body was going through. I was a monster, but even as such I wasn't going to let the people I loved be killed.

My horror and fear at what had happened to me vanished a moment later, along with the pain. I ran forward, clawing, biting, and slamming the stone bodies into dust. Swords might not be able to stop them, but massive claws almost as big as the bodies themselves could. When I finished with them, none of them got back up.

My friends were still screaming, but at me now. I tried to speak, to tell them it was okay, but no words came out. The sounds that did emerge were little more than clicks and growls. I backed away from them, they weren't charging me, but all of them, including Alric, had looks of fear and anger. They would come after me. I backed up still more and then the minkie I'd seen before appeared in the air in front of me. The fog around everyone increased. It didn't hurt me at all, but my friends all collapsed as the fog overwhelmed them.

I needed to see if they were okay, but there was no way I could touch them like this. Even through the fog I could make out the movement of their chests—they were alive. I stumbled away from them.

One form was still moving, unaffected by the fog, Nivinal's image was running to the pile of rocks near me. A flash of clear blue caught my eye in the rubble—the manticore. Nivinal looked at me with a sneer as he reached forward for it.

Hate filled my mind and I sent any spell I could think of at him. He was an image so I couldn't destroy him as I had the formerly stone bodies. But I wasn't letting him get the manticore.

Shock replaced the sneer as his image slowly shredded. His hands and feet went first, with his form finally vanishing in the middle. Pain and agony filled his face. Apparently having your image destroyed in that fashion was painful as hell. I really hoped so. I glanced back at my friends, the fog was still covering them but it was thinning now. They all looked to be asleep. I wanted to go to them but pain tore through my body.

I stumbled behind a Sphere. The top of it came to my shoulder now. Then the entire world grew around me and my body twisted and broke. Agony ripped through me as every muscle and joint burned and I collapsed to the ground.

For a few moments I fought just to breathe. When that wasn't a problem anymore, I looked around. My hand looked like mine again, and the Sphere I was collapsed against loomed over me again. The manticore was near me and looked intact. I looked for something to grab it with but it slammed back into me. I rubbed the cold spot on my cheek. It said a lot about what had just happened that reabsorbing the manticore didn't feel odd at all.

My body might have changed back, but I felt whatever I'd changed into still alive inside of me. Horrible and vile. I didn't know what I'd become, but I couldn't let anyone know the truth. How could I be this…thing? What if it happened again? What if I went after one of my friends? Yes, I hadn't hurt them this time, but the massive amount of power that flowed through me was beyond terrifying. The need to destroy had been almost overwhelming. I needed to hide somewhere until this passed. It had to pass.

Another thought hit me; had I actually died at the moment I changed? Something had caused the manticore to let me go—that it went right back in once I became me again didn't matter. It was only supposed to let go when the person was dead.

I heard Alric and the others yelling for me. I was right; whatever the fog was, it only knocked them out. A thought hit me—or I had knocked them out myself. Along with becoming that creature, I'd felt magic—old and deep—burn inside me. It vanished once I'd changed back. I snuck deeper into the fog surrounding us.

The fog ripped at my hair and I pulled back.

"We come." Garbage's voice was soft, as if she knew we

couldn't let the others find us. The fog wasn't yanking my hair, my three faeries were.

"No, sweetie, you can't come. It's too dangerous, I might hurt you."

All three let go of the hair they hung onto and flew in front of me. "Is okay. We know."

They all looked sad, but Crusty was trying to smile. "We help."

"Where are the rest of the faeries?" It looked to only be my original three here.

"Stay with others. Know what do." Garbage sounded proud of her fellow faeries.

There was no way I could get rid of them. No matter where I went, they'd find me. And I believed Garbage when she said they knew what I was—and they still wanted to be with me. Going into hiding would be a lot easier with friends. Maybe they could even tell me what I was turning into and how to stop it.

"Okay, but only you three, right? We have to find a place to hide for a bit." I looked back toward the fog where my friends were calling for me. Alric's voice was taking a frantic tone. "Can you have the other faeries tell Alric I'm okay? They can't let any of them know what happened. But let them know I'm okay, they don't need to worry." I knew they'd worry and probably try to find us. Hiding from a tracker wasn't going to be easy, but I had to do it until I figured out what I'd become.

Garbage rose up and patted my cheek. "They will tell."

A familiar, albeit low sounding gronk came out of the fog.

"They come too. Needed." Leaf flew up to pet Bunky and the gargoyle.

I looked at all five. The odds of me, even when changed into whatever in the hell I'd changed into, being able to actually damage any of them were slim. They were all fairly indestructible. Not completely, but they would fare better than Alric and the rest of them if I changed form again and lost control. At the very least, all of them could fly away.

"Okay, we'll all go together. But you all need to stay hidden; no one can see you, or me."

The faeries landed on me. "Like this?" I couldn't tell, but I had a feeling if anyone looked through the fog right now they would only see Bunky and the gargoyle. Too bad the faeries couldn't keep this hidden trick up when I moved. It would make for a much easier escape if no one could see me.

The fog was slowly lifting around us. Even the way it dissipated wasn't natural. The ground below me was turning green, as millions of tiny blades of grass that hadn't been seen in this area in a few thousand years poked through the dirt and sand. I would have loved to see what things ended up looking like, but I needed to be far away when the fog completely lifted.

The ghostlike minkie that I'd seen before appeared and scurried a few feet ahead. I'd almost pointed him out to the girls, but they got upset before when I did that. I swear the creature nodded his head to the right. It seemed as good as a direction as any, so I followed him.

This world was changing. I was changing. I didn't think either change was for the better.

THE END

DEAR READER,

Thank you for joining Taryn, Alric, and the faeries in the fifth book of the six book series—The Lost Ancients. We all really appreciate when folks come to play in "our" world, and hope you enjoyed it too.

This series will continue with THE DIAMOND SPHINX in winter 2018/2019.

If you're also interested in a little bit of space opera, please check out the first book in The Asarlaí Wars trilogy- WARRIOR WENCH.

For steampunk fans, A CURIOUS INVASION is launchingThe Adventures of Smith and Jones series.

I really appreciate each and every one of you so please keep in touch.You can find me at www.marieandreas.com.

And please feel free to email me directly at Marie@marieandreas.com as well, I love to hear from readers!

If you enjoyed this book (or any book for that matter:) please spread the word! Positive reviews on Amazon, Goodreads, and blogs are like emotional gold to any writer and mean more than you know.

Thank you again, and we all hope to see you back here in THE DIAMOND SPHINX!

About the Author

MARIE IS A FANTASY AND science fiction reader with a serious writing addiction. If she wasn't writing about all of the people in her head, she'd be lurking about coffee shops annoying innocent passer-by with her stories. So really, writing is a way of saving the masses. She lives in Southern California and is currently owned by two very faery-minded cats. And yes, sometimes they race.

When not saving the general populace from coffee shop shenanigans, Marie likes to visit the UK and keeps hoping someone will give her a nice summer home in the Forest of Dean.

More information can be found on her website *www.marieandreas.com*

Made in the USA
San Bernardino, CA
03 May 2018